Through Darkness
To Light

By Andrew M. Ferrell

Published by:
Cloaked Press, LLC
P.O. Box 341
Suring, WI 54174
http://www.cloakedpress.com

Cover Design by:
Steger Productions
https://stegerproduction.wixsite.com/design/

ISBN: 978-0-9991690-7-0

Library of Congress Control Number: 2019952212

For Mason, Emma, and Jackson.

Never give up on your dreams.

Chapter 1

"So, how was the flight?" Uncle Jim asked as they stowed Mike's bags in the trunk of the car. "Didn't have too much turbulence or anything, did it?" Jim smiled at his nephew. He noticed a lot of his sister in his nephew's features. Clearly, Mike received many his physical attributes from his mother's side of the family. Mike's father had been a broad-shouldered man, while Mike possessed a leaner frame.

"Nope," Mike replied, shaking his head for emphasis. "It was a little boring actually. We had clouds most of the way so I couldn't see anything below us. I was looking forward to the view the most since I've never been on an airplane before." Mike kept back the bit about worrying at any minute he was going to be detained about Kevin's death. The last week before he left home had been stressful. Finals, Colleen leaving town, and the suspicion of those who didn't believe Walt was responsible for Kevin's death. Mike knew Walt was innocent, but every time Walt repeated his confession, it became easier to keep quiet. *Maybe he did find Kevin in the bathroom and finished him off. I didn't hit Kevin that hard anyway.* The Darkness inside always laughed at his rationales for not coming forward.

"Maybe another time then," Aunt Jenny said sympathetically as she started to climb into the passenger seat of the car.

Mike climbed in the back and the trio headed out of the parking garage to make their way to the highway. Mike had looked forward to getting away from home for the summer. As he watched the airport disappear behind him, however, he felt homesick. *"I'm even going to miss Connie."*

The drive to Uncle Jim and Aunt Jenny's home started off with everyone talking at once as the trio tried to cover the highlights of the last several years. Aunt Jenny grilled Mike about school and his final grades. When he recounted the story of Prom Night for her, she gasped in all the right places. Him narrowly avoiding getting doused by punch caused her to laugh. Making himself so dizzy he passed out elicited a motherly pat as she reached into the backseat. Mike glossed over the accident and his brief coma. He knew his mother had talked to Uncle Jim about it, but there were details Mike wasn't ready to share with anyone outside of his friend, Darrell.

The anger reared its head with Kevin's memory. Mike gripped the armrest on the door hard enough to cramp his fingers. He attempted to fight off the surge of adrenaline and the desire to hit something. Mike rubbed his hands together when the discomfort was finally enough to chase off the anger. This blinding anger scared him. He gave it a name the last week, calling it his 'Darkness'. The term felt appropriate based on the research he completed on his own, instead of going to the grief counselors at school. He felt sure he wouldn't be able to keep his secret if he was forced to talk to them. The Darkness seemed to find a lot of things funny lately, except during its attempts to take over. *"I hope I'm not losing it,"* Mike pondered in the brief silence after relating his story.

After a moment of quiet, Uncle Jim began speaking, "My regular office clerk had a beautiful little girl just last week, so she's already started her maternity leave. I had hoped she'd be here for your first few days, but we'll make it work. You'll be in charge of phones and paperwork, as well as helping my office manager with whatever she needs." He kept watching Mike with a strange, weighing look in the rear-view mirror the whole ride. *"I hope I'm ready for this,"* Uncle Jim thought to himself.

It struck Mike how much Uncle Jim's look reminded him of his mother ever since he woke up from his coma. *"Maybe the resemblance is because they are siblings,"* Mike wondered, *"or I could be imagining things."* Mike yawned and put the thought away for another time.

With his accident and the stressful end of the year with Kevin's death, Mike reasoned it made sense for everyone to be more concerned for him. Mike felt his Darkness trying to rise again each time he thought about Kevin. Even casual connections to his school's former star quarterback left him shaking in rage. Hearing his aunt ask another question snapped Mike's attention back to the present and away from those painful memories.

Aunt Jenny failed to notice Mike's distraction as she kept asking questions from the front seat. "So what are your hobbies? What do you and your friends do these days? I spend a lot of time volunteering at the high school. My goddaughter and her friends would be perfect to show you around." Her sights were set on distracting him from the heartbreak and trauma of the last month.

Uncle Jim tried to steer the conversation away from girls, but Mike ended up talking about Colleen anyway.

"I really don't understand what happened, Aunt Jenny," Mike confessed after he told the whole story. "I cannot get a hold of her and her phone line is disconnected already. It makes me wonder what I did wrong."

Aunt Jenny expressed her condolences on the whole situation. She reached back to pat her nephew's shoulder again. "I am sure you did nothing wrong, honey. Just put it out of your mind and try to enjoy your summer. This might be your last fun summer. Next year means the real world is going to come knocking." She giggled, trying to lighten the mood.

Mike laughed with her, though for different reasons. He had thought his plans would include Colleen. Now he wasn't sure they would even include his hometown. The 'real world' as Aunt Jenny called it, already clamping down on his life. *"What am I going to do?"* Mike thought discouragingly.

After a little more than a half hour, Mike's eyelids started drooping more. He let out another yawn.

Jim turned to his wife, "Leave him alone a bit, Jenny. He only just got here. You have all summer to tease him about girls. I am sure he's worn out from the flight and time change." He shifted to direct his voice into the backseat before continuing, "Mike, we should be there in another hour or so if you want to grab a quick nap. If you are anything like the rest of the men in our family, you could sleep on the rocks as they rolled down a hill if you're tired enough."

Mike nodded, chuckling, before he settled back in the seat. He closed exhausted eyes and soon drifted off to sleep to the sound of the car's engine humming while they cruised down the highway.

As Mike slipped off to sleep, he thought he heard Aunt Jenny say, "Do you think we distracted him enough? If you weren't staring at him like you expected him to start flying or something it might go a little easier, you know."

As soon as his eyes closed Mike returned to the same dream from the last several weeks. Mike found himself in the woods again, still pondering what he was sure he heard his aunt say as he dozed off. This time in the dream, however, the colors appeared a bit closer to living color, although still a little fuzzy around the edges. Mike started down the path, the improved colors revealed in the shade of the trees caused by the moonlight. A faint but distinct scent of moisture hung in the air, like the feel after a rainstorm, and tickled Mike's nose. The feel of nature calmed him. He sensed the Darkness retreat further into the depths of his subconscious.

The scene changed abruptly and Mike knew for sure he was back at school. The dimmed lights left long shadows in the hallway. Strange sounds echoed down the hall. Following the odd shuffling sound led him to the bathroom near the cafeteria. Mike heard the sound again, like something scraping on the tiled floor. He walked slowly toward the bathroom entrance. "Anyone in there?" Mike called tentatively as he rounded the corner to the bathroom.

The scene before him caused bile to rise in his throat even though it's the hundredth time he's seen this dream. Kevin lays on the floor, just as Mike left him after their confrontation at school. Mike saw the shattered tiles where he bashed Kevin against the wall. Plaster dust and shards of tile decorated the shoulders and head of his classmate. Kevin tried to stand but kept slipping in the pool of blood forming around him from his head wound. He looked up after a moment, his eyes glazed over in death. "Why?" asked Kevin. The dream vanished in a blindingly bright light.

Awakened by the crunch of gravel and a car door shutting, Mike's disorientation was complete at first. Sure that the dream ended, Mike instinctively reached for his glasses where they normally rested on his bedside table. He realized quickly there was no table or bed. It all flooded back when Uncle Jim pulled open the trunk and grabbed one of the suitcases. Mike climbed out of the car and took the other before he turned to follow his uncle into the long, one level home. Groggily, Mike thought, *"Fitting for a lumber company owner to have a log cabin house."* The suitcases quickly stowed in the spare bedroom, Mike collapsed on the bed with a mumbled "Goodnight" before drifting back to sleep. The nightmare of discovering Kevin in the bathroom at school alternated with the dream of the wooded path with the bonfire. He jerked awake several times, panting and his heart racing. Each time, Kevin's body asked a single question, "Why?" Mike feared the answers his mind produced. "It's not my fault," he told himself again and again. The Darkness laughed in the recesses of his mind.

Sitting upright, Leonard Mauston smiled to himself. *"The boy is finally here. Years of planning about to come to fruition. This time there will be no half measures or failed attempts. The Keller boy will belong to the Council, and specifically to me. All I have to do is trust my impetuous offspring to handle things properly."* Damien's fitness for the task concerned the older man. He would much rather handle things himself. He was pulled from his musings by a knock on his study door. Knowing this would come, he opened the door with a flip of his hand, leaving his son standing there about to knock a second time. "Come in son," he said calmly.

"Father, I felt his power become stronger about an hour ago until just now. It winked out near the Johnson property," Damien spoke softly, being very careful in the presence of his powerful father. He remembered a recent visit which ended poorly. Damien strived to work on the faults his father feels he suffers from. The faults he finds with his father continued unabated. Damien quickly stuffed those dangerous thoughts as deep as he could. He hoped his father never catches wind of them.

"Yes, the arrival of Mr. Johnson's nephew," the old man stated. "As we discussed, he is your final task. It falls to you to turn him to our ways. The Council will not interfere in any way with this. If you fail them, and more importantly fail me, I suspect your punishment will be most severe. He has no working knowledge of his powers and they seem to be growing with every passing day. If I know his uncle, he will paint it as completely noble and serving of some greater good. But, like you, he is a teenager. He will have a teenager's desires and way of thinking. I think what you can show him will grab his interest and cause him to turn away from his Uncle's stricter guidance. Do not approach until after his birthday next week. He must come into his powers before he can be actively recruited. Tradition and Council law accepts no other option. Until then you have free access to observe and plan."

"I think I can handle him, Father," Damien said. A smile lit up his face for the first time about this mysterious task the High Council had put before him. A mere outsider stood in his way of earning a place as a full member and breaking away from his father's shadow. His dream was to sit alongside his father, earning a seat of his own. Damien did not want to just take over for his father by default when the older man grew too old to hold the seat himself. Damien's dream was not often granted. Unless his father took on an apprentice later in life, it would leave Damien wielding two votes instead of one when his father did retire. These votes would then be split off amongst children or branches of a family line in subsequent generations. Damien would also be free to elevate a trusted underling. "I will not fail you in this."

"Your success or failure is obscured in mist son," the old man mused aloud. "I just hope I have done what is necessary to prepare you for this. Now, go. I must report to some of the others."

***

When Damien retreated to his private rooms after his conversation with his father, he found his two closest friends standing around in the small study attached to his bedroom. They often gathered there, but Damien had not expected them tonight, having arrived and made themselves at home while he was talking to his father.

"Derek, Cliff, to what do I owe the pleasure guys?" Damien said calmly, shutting the door behind him. Derek, while tolerated as the son of a Council member, carried little favor in the Mauston household since his assault of a girl that nearly exposed their world. The older Mauston fixed the situation to conceal the crime and the involvement of the Council out of respect for the friendship between their two families.

Damien's nobler attitude still twitched in irritation at the slap on the wrist Derek received. Damien only continued to tolerate Derek because their fathers remained close associates.

"We were just talking and decided to visit," piped up Clifford in his small voice. Clifford Van Doornick, the Third, was from the most prestigious family of the three friends, his father being the most senior member of the Council. The Van Doornick line had ruled the Council for over two hundred years. This generation signaled a weakening in the bloodline, however. Though Cliff's eyes always shined with admiration for the talents of his friends, he was often considered little more than a lackey by those looking from the outside.

"Did you feel what arrived in our little world tonight?" Derek Gohr ran over the end of his chubby friend's comment. He glared at Cliff, who he considered barely better than a "normal", his favorite term for non-gifted people. It was a term often used amongst their kind, but still not considered polite. Derek had wasted no time getting close to Damien. From practically in his friend's face, he continued, "Do you think it was the kid our fathers have been talking about?"

Taking a moment to grab a soda from the mini fridge the housekeeper kept stocked, Damien plopped himself into a leather armchair and waved his friends to seats before he spoke, "I know it was. Mr. Johnson, a name we all know, has asked his nephew to come visit. The Council has decreed my family gets a chance to turn this generation, to bring them into the fold. Specifically, that I get to." Damien tried to place as much emphasis as possible on his status in the situation.

Derek fooled no one by playing ignorant. One trick he never learned was to hide emotions well, and his mind sent out signals like a bullhorn. Damien was well aware Derek's game here was to insert himself into the task and gain some status himself.

"So what are we going to do about this little upstart"? Derek asked, using his gift to summon a soda of his own as he dropped into a chair across from his friend. Technically, Damien ranked higher than Derek on two counts, one he was a few months older, and two, the Mauston Family stood higher than Derek's own. In Derek's mind, however, he ruled as the leader of their little band.

"There is no 'we' in this," Damien replied calmly, having taken the time to open his soda. He sipped it, letting the silence drag out. "This is my task, and I am seeking no outside assistants nor do I think I need them." *"Especially your lack of regard for others,"* Damien added to himself.

"We are all friends here. We should be a team," Cliff chimed in, clearly seeing a confrontation coming between his two friends and wanting to play his part quickly. He was tasked to be the negotiator and peacemaker, as Derek put it. "Why shouldn't the three of us handle this Council problem together? We are the next generation after all. The Council will clearly be ours eventually."

"Cliffy here makes sense Damien, you should hear him out," Derek said, hoping his calculated retreat and manipulation of the trio's weakest link would work. When his father had told him to insert himself into this task and see to it Damien failed, Derek was thrilled. To do so in a way which would benefit their family would even be better. Derek and his father both saw the writing on the wall and hoped to secure control and power directly. Failing that, they pursued holding sway over Cliff when, or if, he took his father's place atop their hierarchy.

"I appreciate you two offering to help," Damien replied dryly, nearly imitating his father's lecturing tone. "However, this is up to me to handle and it is very delicate. His family has a tradition of not discussing their gifts until one reaches the age of maturity. So even if he can tap into the raw power you felt, his control is less than what we were doing when we were in kindergarten. He will not understand what has been happening to him and when he is told, there will be confusion and distrust. This will take subtlety and guile, sadly talents you lack Derek. No offense intended my friend. We all have our weaknesses."

"You are a fool, Damien," Derek blurted our heatedly, standing and waving his hands in front of him. His inability to hold his temper in the wake of disappointment raged forward. "You mark my words, you shut me out on this and you will regret it." He vanished from the room, his soda left on the table next to the chair he abruptly vacated.

Shaking his head sadly, Cliff stood up as if to go as well. He turned to his seated friend, "You know he has a violent temper, D. Why do you insist on provoking him? We only want to be involved. This is exciting stuff. How often is there a new family brought in which isn't simply a branch of an existing one?" After waiting a moment in silence, Cliff sat back down at a wave from Damien.

"I appreciate your candor, Clifford," Damien began. "You have always been a good friend and our fathers serve as two of the three highest members of our Council. Derek is bad for our kind. He has the worst sort of attitude regarding those not of our ilk and has delusions of rising above his betters. Be careful if you keep as close an association with him as in the past. We aren't kids anymore where our parents will rush to clean up our messes and make it all better. We have to make our own way now if we want to be taken seriously as adults."

Clifford thought over Damien's words. For his part, Damien sipped his soda and watched as the wheels turned in his naïve friend's mind. Finally, sighing, Clifford stood. "I know you make sense. Derek has some faults, but you two have been my best friends my whole life. I can't abandon either of you lightly. I will be careful though. Thanks, D." Without another word, Clifford disappeared back home, concentrating fully because teleportation was close to the limits of his power. Because of this, he failed to see the frown crease Damien's face.

Chapter 2

Mike's dream began as it had for weeks, though sharper now than even in the car. He walked through the wooded area towards the fire in the distance on a slightly worn path. First instincts, again, tried to tell him it was a forest fire. The smell of moisture in the air flooded his senses. The damp earth squished beneath his feet. Mike recalled a thunderstorm and seeing lots of lightning.

A tall figure moved around the fire, appearing faint and shadowy, as unfamiliar as the woods Mike found himself walking in. Something nagged at Mike's mind the closer he got to the fire.

When Mike reached the edge of the clearing, the figure stopped pacing and stood, facing the flames. A pile of cut and split logs burned neatly in the center of a clearing. Slightly relieved no emergency existed, Mike stepped into the clearing. The figure seemed unaware of Mike's presence. A twig snapped loudly under his foot and Mike froze. His heart raced being this close. Mike's stomach knotted up, fearing the figure could be the Darkness again. Even up close, details were difficult to make out. The shadowy figure started to turn around, as a voice, soft and definitely feminine, intruded on Mike's mind.

Aunt Jenny called from down the hall. "Mike, it's time for breakfast. I am sure you're starving, all you young men usually are." She giggled as she went back to the kitchen.

Aunt Jenny reminded Mike a bit then of his mom, she often made similar comments when she dished up the nightly family dinners. While he wasn't exactly a stick, like Connie was, Mike never seemed to gain weight either. His too lean frame often concerned his mother.

"Be right there," Mike called groggily, this time finding his glasses on a small stand next to the bed with a clock reading just after six AM.

With no memory of taking them off, Aunt Jenny had probably came into the room to check on him during the course of the night. His shoes sat next to the bed, neatly, not as if kicked off. A little embarrassed, Mike rubbed the sleep from his eyes and headed towards the hallway. The smells of breakfast started to reach his nose as he exited his room. His aunt and uncle were both already seated at the table.

"It would be alright if you wanted to take a couple days to enjoy your summer vacation. I know things went pretty quickly and I wouldn't want you to feel too overwhelmed. I would then have to deal with your mother," Uncle Jim said before sipping from his hot coffee cup. The morning breakfast topic of conversation revolved around everyone's plans for the week.

"We will have so much fun." Aunt Jenny let out a cheer. "We can get you all unpacked and maybe take a little drive to show you around town. Maybe introduce you to a few of the young people I have volunteered with at the high school. Do you like blondes or brunettes? I know just the girl who can help you get adjusted to the area. Laurie and her friends are a great group of young people." Aunt Jenny positively shook with excitement at the possibility of playing matchmaker for her nephew.

Mike could see she had put a lot of thought into his visit. "I feel pretty good Uncle Jim," Mike replied before taking a drink from his glass of orange juice. While loving the smell of coffee, it was not his morning beverage of choice. "And while I appreciate the offer Aunt Jenny, I think I would rather just get started on the job before I worry about making friends. I'm not sure I would be good company at first, anyway. I have had a rough week and can only take so much right now. Besides, Uncle Jim is down a person at the office and that's why I'm here." Mike tried to let his Aunt down easy, but from her expression, he saw she was disappointed.

"I think your Aunt was looking forward to not being alone in the house for a day." Uncle Jim laughed, earning himself a slap on the shoulder from his wife. He feigned injury so she did it again, which caused him to roar in laughter. When he managed to catch his breath, he continued, "But if you feel up to it, we will have to leave in about forty-five minutes or so to make it on time. At least, on time for me."

"I really wish you would consider staying home a day or two," Aunt Jenny spoke softly, a mischievous twinkle in her eyes. "I do get bored sitting around the house all by myself and I have made it my mission to see to it that you have some fun. Teenagers need to have fun during their summer break. Once you grow up and get jobs and all there isn't as much time for fun."

"Thank you, Aunt Jenny," Mike said after swallowing the last bite of his breakfast toast. She had fixed a magnificent spread of eggs, bacon, sausage, toast and even some hash browns. Mike devoured enough food for three people while the two adults did most of the earlier talking. "Rain-check? And if I don't make it through today successfully, I promise I will take a few days off." She nodded in acceptance. Mike stood and took his plate to the sink, "I am going to take a quick shower then if it is alright, Uncle Jim?"

"Sure, sure..." he replied absently, having returned to the morning paper already.

Aunt Jenny started cleaning up the table as Mike exited. Returning to his room for the summer, Mike considered what his Uncle said about the office. It was mostly a casual environment so he grabbed a nicer pair of blue jeans and a long sleeved button down shirt from his suitcase *"I will have to do some unpacking after work,"* Mike thought to himself as he headed to the bathroom. Just over a half hour later, Mike joined his uncle in the truck to head to the office building where the company was headquartered. As they drove, Mike saw more of the scenery.

The images of Kevin in his dreams haunted Mike. He knew he should have told someone about the fight. Each time he had lied to Colleen, it felt like he was stabbing himself in the heart. "*What was I supposed to do? Give up my life because of that jerk?*" Mike tried to shut the voice up, not liking the implications.

"It's really pretty out here," Uncle Jim said, breaking the silence of the first few minutes, noticing Mike's stare out the window. The road ran through thick trees scattered with a few stout houses. "I think it was the land that caught me first. Before your aunt got me," he added with a chuckle. "Be careful or she will have you set up with one of the young women in this town before the summer is over. She's well connected since her family has been here for at least six generations. She also does a lot of volunteer work at the high school and with youth groups since we don't have any children of our own. She has always fancied herself a real matchmaker too; if you failed to notice how she's been hounding you since you arrived. Your mother did clue us into the situation with Colleen, and your aunt's opinion was that you needed a new group of friends with plenty of girls to take your mind off your heartache."

"I appreciate the thought, but I'm not sure I'm ready to go down that road right now, Uncle. Is that why she started right away asking what hair color I liked?" Mike asked, to which Uncle Jim nodded in the affirmative. Not really thinking why, Mike added, "Oh boy, I can just picture her sitting down with a bunch of index cards sorting them out based on different criteria so she can have a ready supply based on my answers." Jim gave his nephew a weighing look again before he laughed. "You aren't telling me she really did that, did she?" Mike asked incredulously once it appeared that Uncle Jim wasn't going to volunteer what he saw as so funny about the statement.

"I'm not sure, to be honest, but I wouldn't put it past her. I am sure, though, her mind sorted it all out and she doesn't need the cards anymore." He grinned. "At least not after the first week that we knew you were coming up here. Besides, I think she has her mind set on getting our goddaughter Laurie to be your chaperone for the summer. Anyway, when we get to the office I will give you a tour, then we have to head out to the current job site for a little, uh, hands-on work experience. You wear a thirteen, right?" he asked slowly, to which Mike nodded. "That is what your mom said, so I took the liberty of picking you up a pair of boots for when you are at a site, or if you want to go hiking near the house. Your aunt and I own about a hundred acres of the old forest area around the house that we have blazed a few trails through. I will have to show you some of the older, well-trodden ones this weekend if you feel up to it."

Mike agreed it might be fun and soon they neared the town. The first part of the morning passed quickly making the rounds. Jim introduced the other office staff which consisted of two people to be: secretary, payroll, and billing. After getting Mike familiar with the system and clocked in on the time card machine, they headed back to the road to go to one of the current job sites. Mike changed out his tennis shoes for the work boots while in the truck.

As Uncle Jim and Mike talked, it became clear the company fared well under Jim's direction. The company originally belonged to Aunt Jenny's father and grandfather before that, but Jim took over when his father-in-law retired. While he ran a company whose premise was to cut down trees, Uncle Jim loved nature and preferred to replace as much of what he removed as possible.

Mike's head started to spin a little as Uncle Jim explained different aspects of the logging business. He watched workers plant some trees brought in from a greenhouse the company owned. The company grew the trees there until ready to be transplanted to one of the lots. Then the trees remained on the lot until ready to be cut for lumber. Then the process started over again. After the batch of trees got planted, Jim drove the duo to a little restaurant in town to grab lunch.

Mike spent the drive back to the office watching the cars around them and focused on the landmarks. Suddenly, a chirping sound erupted in the truck. Uncle Jim grabbed his cell phone from the breast pocket of his denim work shirt. Mike tried not to eavesdrop, but it sounded like something terrible occurred from the yelling on the other end of the line. After a moment Uncle Jim told someone he would be right there and clicked the phone shut, dropping it in the console area of the truck.

"We have a small accident at one of the cutting sites," Uncle Jim said, glancing over in Mike's direction as he shifted the truck into another lane and pressed the gas down hard. "Hope you don't mind getting a little dirty, I think I'm going to need all the hands I can get."

"I'll do what I can," Mike replied, nodding. They barreled down the highway, then down several side roads, before turning off into a wooded area. The truck bounced in the deeper ruts of the slightly muddy dirt road. Up ahead someone waved a hardhat; a small ATV parked just off the road idled loudly. Jim brought the truck to a halt alongside the man on foot and the two exchanged words. He turned to Mike.

"One of the cables broke on a log hauler, it smashed up the equipment a bit, but the worst thing is that it hit the fuel tanks on a truck and spilled diesel everywhere. When we get up ahead, grab a shovel and help us get all the contaminated dirt into wheelbarrows, barrels, and the back of the truck there. It will ruin the soil if we don't get it cleaned up quick. Most of the logs are now moved out of the way so they are ready for cleanup." Mike nodded as the truck pulled ahead.

People ran all over as they got closer to the site. Some carried shovels, others pushed wheelbarrows or dragged barrels away from the main area where the workers parked their vehicles. A large truck still idled nearby, full of equipment. When Uncle Jim stopped, Mike jumped out and ran as fast as he could towards someone trying to carry an armful of shovels and pull a barrel at the same time. Mike took the shovels from him and started following towards the spill. He saw the crew consisted of just over a half-dozen people, including him and his uncle. The guy from the road came by on the ATV and parked alongside a short trailer. He ran inside. Mike asked, "What's going on with that guy?"

"That's my foreman," Uncle Jim replied. "He's going to call the local Department of Natural Resources agent. We have to report any accidents to the DNR and have them come out and test the soil before we can declare it cleaned up. I would rather not lose my license or pay any big fines."

Mike nodded that he understood. He shouldered his remaining shovel and trudged towards the cleared area. After working through most of the afternoon, the crew felt the area ready for testing. The DNR official arrived with his case to take soil samples and a report of the accident. Jim and he appeared old friends by their casual conversation. The man seemed assured that the workers did everything possible to prevent the accident and to clean it up after it happened. Mike leaned on the shovel near some of the other workers as the agent took multiple samples. After the official left, everyone headed home for the day. The results would take hours to come in and the gaping hole in the fuel tank of one of the large trucks required several hours to replace as well.

Sweating, and more than a little muddy, Mike followed some of the workmen back to the main parking area where they stowed the tools in a portable shed. They lined the barrels holding the contaminated soil alongside it. A company that would attempt to clean the soil by extracting the diesel fuel from it, would pick up the barrels. Then the soil could be returned to the ground. Jim tossed Mike an already filthy work towel to clean up. They climbed back in the truck to head home. Jim called Aunt Jenny on the way and they decided to grab pizzas for dinner. Mike was thankful that he could change back to his tennis shoes in the truck, leaving his muddy boots in the truck bed.

Jim pulled into the driveway, parking next to a car Mike didn't recognize. Mike looked to his Uncle, the question clear in his eyes. Jim's mouth formed a hard line before he responded, "I guess we better go see who your Aunt invited over for supper."

As soon as the two males walked in, Mike's arms laden with the pizza boxes, they heard Aunt Jenny calling from the living room, "Come on in here, guys. I have paper plates ready." Stepping around the corner they found the driver of the other car. A young woman about Mike's age, with a blond ponytail to match his aunt's brunette one sat off to the side. *"She's pretty,"* Mike noticed, *"in a typical girl next door sort of way."*

"Oh, Mike, this is Laurie. She was bringing some things over I ordered from her mom. Figured I would introduce you two so you know someone your own age here in town." Laurie stood, not speaking, but gazed from Uncle Jim to Aunt Jenny, then to Mike in rapid succession. Something in Uncle Jim's face clearly distracted the young woman enough to make her not speak. *"This must the goddaughter that Uncle Jim mentioned,"* Mike thought to himself.

Mike followed her gaze to his uncle and discovered the intense stare Jim was directing at his wife. She must have caught the implications of his look because Aunt Jenny glanced from him to Mike nervously, taking in their disheveled look.

"Hi," Mike said feeling a little embarrassed given the state of his clothes, but determined to break the growing tension in the room before it got out of hand. He started by setting the pizzas down on the coffee table. The movement snapped the other three people out of their stares as much as him speaking did. Mike decided against trying to shake

Laurie's hand but pressed on in the only way he saw to defuse the situation, "I would sit down and chat, but I think I ought to take a shower and change. There was a bit of an accident involving some diesel fuel and mud today so I am not really fit for visitors. As you can probably see." Mike forced a laugh. "Perhaps if things aren't so hectic, my aunt can get me in touch with you later in the week and maybe we can talk then?"

Checking the reactions of the adults, Mike's speech seemed to bail out Aunt Jenny as Uncle Jim nodded his agreement. He said goodbye to Laurie and headed for his room. Mike waved and started for the other end of the house.

Laurie's soft, "Goodbye" stopped Mike in his tracks. A sudden and unexplainable pull to go back to her flowed through him like a lightning bolt going off in his chest. He turned and they locked eyes. The similarities between Laurie and Colleen struck him. They both possess the 'girl next door' look so beautiful on Colleen. Mike thought, *"Maybe this is why Aunt Jenny picked her."* Mike struggled to shrug off the feeling while Laurie waved and opened the front door. *"She is kind of pretty, and Aunt Jenny is practically setting me up to hang out with her. That was probably all it was. I am definitely not ready to go down that road again,"* he thought to himself, trying to rationalize his sudden shift in feelings.

The jolt felt oddly familiar, like the feeling Mike got right before he saw a vision of something about to happen. The subtle difference was it came from his chest instead of his brain. Shaking his head as he went down the hall, he tried to refocus his thoughts on a shower. He knew he needed to decide what to do the first time something does happen and he had to explain to Uncle Jim and Aunt Jenny about his visions or stumbling incidents. *"It would be a disaster if they caught something moving around the room."* Mike shuddered.

Mike pondered his situation in a quick shower which helped him to feel a tad more human. Throwing on a pair of fresh jeans and a t-shirt, he returned to the living room where the adults talked in slightly hushed tones. As Mike tried to be quiet and listen, he felt a jolt and could hear them quite clearly, almost as if he was in the same room with them.

"I told you don't harass him about girls," Uncle Jim said. Clearly, Aunt Jenny only slightly escaped the frying pan about her matchmaking endeavors beginning on Mike's first day in the state.

For his part, Mike thought his Aunt could have waited a bit, but if not for the events at the job site today, what would it have hurt? The weird sensation when Laurie spoke the first time puzzled Mike as well. He felt guilty for even thinking it. *What about Colleen? The love of my life who hasn't even emailed me back in over a week. Is it over between the two of us? Is that what she was trying to tell me with her disappearing act?* Mike considered the situation before his aunt's voice pulled him back to the present.

"Well, your sister says he didn't go out hardly at all and almost never with any girls, you know, like on a date, until that Colleen who broke his heart," she continued to plead her case.

Mike couldn't believe his mother would say that, even though it was mostly true. It wasn't that he didn't like girls or anything, but he never really met one that would compare with Colleen. Other than a brief relationship Sophomore year, but that was more just friends hanging out than a real relationship. Emily enjoyed the same games and movies so it was almost like she was just one of the guys. Mike felt the Darkness inside start to rise up in his distraction and he stamped it down to listen when his aunt spoke again.

"Besides, Laurie is a nice girl and she really did stop by this afternoon to drop off that stuff I ordered from her mom. I just kept her over a little longer than she planned so I could see if they might hit it off. He should have some friends his own age here. If we don't get him introduced to young people now, we won't ever get him out. I wonder if I read him wrong, but he didn't seem interested. I thought you said that the men in your family always knew right away or something like that. Like you said it was when you met me."

"I don't disagree with you about him not spending a lot of time with just us, but you could at least give us a warning," Uncle Jim replied. "As for the rest of that, I don't think he has figured out anything about that part of the family and his heritage. My sister said he hasn't asked anything even though she noticed a few things happening. Mike was too young when his grandfather passed away. Besides, we had a diesel spill today and I am sure he wouldn't want to meet someone covered in mud and smelling like a gas tank. Give him a couple days to get settled before you start parading the local single girls in front of him. How do you know he even likes blondes anyway? Maybe it's a brunette like myself and his dad that he fancies."

Mike could almost hear Aunt Jenny's gasp. A vision of her slugging his Uncle in the arm playfully passed across his vision before she spoke, "Well, I thought another blonde might soften things a little, given how his mother said he acted around that Colleen. She was blonde, and a cheerleader to boot. Maybe that's the connection that would count." Their voices quieted as it sounded like Uncle Jim decided to dig into dinner.

Mike couldn't believe the two of them standing around so casually talking about his love life, or lack thereof. He wondered about the part of a family heritage he knew nothing about. Mike felt anger rising again, along with the Darkness, and recoiled from it. The reference to his grandfather confused him. Mike's memories of Grandpa Johnson centered on how he always seemed on the verge of saying something profound, with a knowing grin on his face whenever he visited. Connie

22

and Mike would try to tell him about what they had been up to since the last time they saw him and he would just continue grinning while he nodded as if he already knew what they were going to say. *"Could Grandpa Johnson have been like me?"*

As far as blonde or brunette, Mike couldn't figure a reason to pick one hair color over the other since it can be dyed at any time. Something most of the girls in his school did at some point. Besides, he wasn't sure he was ready to cross that line again so soon. He had only lost Colleen a little over a week ago. If that was what had happened. Not even in the state a full day yet and here they were worried about how he was going to spend his free time. He felt quite sure he could entertain himself for the most part. A good book or two and he would never miss the summer flying by with the hours probably put in at the office.

Why go through all the hassle if he was only going to be around for the summer anyway? At least, he didn't think he would be here beyond the end of summer despite his conversation with Darrell. While a summer romance could be fun, it could also lead to a lot of hurt feelings if Laurie was as important to Aunt Jenny as she said.

Shoving down the strange rise in anger, Mike decided not to let them think he heard. He crept back down the hall and shut the door loudly, stretching and calling out, "Do we have any soda in the house? I could use some caffeine something fierce." Partially true, having not had anything to drink since lunch, Mike was starting to get a little headache right behind the eyes from lack of caffeine in his system. At home, it was nothing to have quite a bit of caffeine, from either soda or a strongly brewed iced tea. Mike hoped it was just that and not a headache brought on by his swirling thoughts and visions. He considered taking one of the leftover prescription pills he had packed just in case.

Aunt Jenny entered the hallway and led the way into the kitchen to show him where to find everything. While alone, Mike whispered to her,

"I'm sure she is nice, Aunt Jenny, but I just don't think tonight was a good time with what happened at work today. By the way, you did pick well, she's very pretty." Mike added with a wink.

"Perhaps another time then," she replied, nodding and patting her nephew's shoulder. They grabbed the glasses and returned to the living room to chat and eat dinner. After the evening bout of prime-time TV programming, everyone retired to bed. Uncle Jim reminded Mike to set the alarm for work in the morning. Mike, though sorely tempted the entire evening to ask one of them what they were talking about earlier, caved in to the fear that admitting he was eavesdropping might upset his relatives. Maybe an opportunity to say something while in the course of work would arise. Mike worried it might upset Uncle Jim enough to send him home, but it seemed important to his uncle to have Mike here this summer.

Mike replayed the conversation in his head, looking for a scenario in which he could ask about it without revealing how he listened in. Still not finding a suitable option after ten, Mike drifted off to sleep. Almost immediately he found himself in the same patch of woods again. The bonfire burned ahead in the distance. Mike set off resolutely towards the clearing, thinking this time he would find out what was going on. As he got closer, the figure seemed to go fuzzy as the scene changed to the bathroom at his high school. Mike saw Kevin trying and failing to rise. The blood pool looked ridiculously large as his dead classmate slipped and fell continuously. When Kevin looked up and asked the same question as before, Mike wanted to scream. Soon a buzzing drew him awake and Mike breathed in relief for the end of his dream. The fire dream frustrated him, while the horror at seeing what Mike felt sure was Kevin's last moments disturbed him. Mike quickly shut the alarm off and started his new weekday routine.

Chapter 3

Nothing exciting like the first day happened the rest of the week. The fire dream only occurred once more, but Mike's legs felt made of lead. Before traveling a step or two the dream ended and he woke up. Unfortunately, the one with Kevin tortured him nightly. Friday night, on the way home from work, Mike finally worked up the nerve to ask his uncle about Monday evening. Mike avoided bringing up the family heritage, merely asking about his Aunt setting him up right away and the worry over him making friends this summer. The incident, or how he would spend his free time, had not been brought up all week. "You and Aunt Jenny aren't still worried about what I'm going to do this summer are you? With work and all I just want to get settled and relax a bit without worrying about any drama. I hope that is ok and that you guys won't fight over it at all."

"So you heard some of that huh?" Uncle Jim asked.

Mike shrugged it off, "I heard something about spending too much time with old folks as I went from the bathroom to the bedroom."

"Your aunt is a card, that is for sure," Jim continued. "I told her to back off you a bit because I figured you would make your own decisions anyway. There are a few places in town that cater to the younger crowd on the weekends. We are also less than an hour from a pretty decent sized mall if that is your cup of tea."

"Sounds like fun, I could use a good book or two," Mike started, figuring if Uncle Jim wasn't going to bring up the other part then he would leave it alone. His uncle gave him that weighing look again as he had on the ride home from the airport and had been giving Mike all week. Having not spent much time around him, Mike began to think it's part of still getting used to a teenager in the house even though it was his uncle's idea for one to be there. "Laurie is very pretty. I'm sure she's a nice girl and we'll get along fine. I just wasn't fit to hang out with someone. I would've felt a little weird if she had stayed after I showered and changed. You know?"

"Certainly," Uncle Jim agreed. "Her mom is an old friend of your aunt's. I think they go all the way back to elementary school or something. Her family has been in this town for generations as well. One of the first to move here I guess. That's hy we were asked to be Laurie's Godparents. From what I know of her, she is a sweet girl. Your aunt spends more time with her than I do."

"Hmm, maybe I should have made a bigger deal about it," Mike said, "for Aunt Jenny's sake. She wasn't too upset was she? That I wasn't more sociable and all."

"No, your aunt understood what was going on with work and all that day. I am sure she called Laurie the next day and explained the whole thing. Probably blamed it on jet lag and a rough day at the office." He laughed.

Mike nodded before joining in laughing at the joke. "I hope Laurie will be ok with my situation. I'm only here for the summer, and besides, I just don't know if I'm ready to go on any sort of a real date or anything. Not with what happened with Colleen." Uncle Jim just smiled in support and soon they arrived at the house. Everyone tried to put the week behind them as the weekend officially began.

At dinner, Aunt Jenny said, "Mike, you can use my car to go to the mall tomorrow if you want." She told Mike how to get there and back.

Uncle Jim saved Mike from having her repeat it by pushing a small box across the edge of the table towards his nephew. The box held a cell phone and directions with a map to and from the mall. "That should make things easier," he added while Mike checked out the phone.

They had programmed both of their cell numbers and the house line into the phone already. Mike noticed the fourth number in it. Aunt Jenny hadn't given up on setting her nephew up, as the entry was labeled "Laurie – Cell". Mike looked at her, grinning. She caught the message in the look and her smile grew wider, lasting all night long. Uncle Jim made it clear that Mike would be able to keep the cell phone when he left, it was his to do with as he wanted.

Something strange happened as they settled into the meal. Mike, about to ask for the salt and pepper, noticed a set right in front of his own plate. They normally sat across the table next to his uncle's plate. Thinking there must be a second set, Mike was confused when Uncle Jim asked for someone to pass him the pepper a minute later. Uncle Jim chuckled at the confused expression on his nephew's face as Mike handed it across to him. "Here you go. I thought just a minute ago that you had a set too," Mike said slowly.

"No," Uncle Jim replied, still chuckling as he sprinkled the pepper on his plate. A wide grin split his face. "This is the only set of salt and pepper shakers we own. They were a wedding gift from your mom if I remember right. Made of a thick crystal or something. That's why they are so heavy. Pretty though," he added, setting it down next to his plate. Mike shrugged off the feeling of having missed something in what just happened, even though Uncle Jim returned to giving him that strange look the rest of the night.

Mike began to think the look his uncle kept giving him was because he expected Mike to have an accident or prevent a disaster. *"Maybe Mom mentioned the events at school. Maybe he's waiting for me to have a breakdown or something. If he still wanted me to come here after all that happened at school, maybe I could tell my uncle about the strange dreams. I have to be safe from getting sent home, right? Or maybe that was part of why Uncle Jim wanted me to come visit. There was that talk about some family legacy and all from the other night to consider."*

While Aunt Jenny busied herself in the kitchen after dinner, Uncle Jim and Mike went onto the back porch. As Mike stood and looked into the darkening forest off the back of their property, he wanted to ask his uncle about the shakers. Mike started having trouble focusing, a little voice in his head repeating, "Not yet". Mike turned toward his uncle and noticed the older man muttering under his breath as he stared off into the woods, his eyes closed. Mike wondered whether he remembered his nephew standing there or not.

Aunt Jenny came out of the house just as Mike opened his mouth to ask Uncle Jim about what happened at dinner. She called to the two, "I just put a pie in the oven to warm and it should be ready shortly."

Having turned to look at her when the sliding glass door opened, Mike looked back to his uncle to find him also staring in her direction. The two males stayed outside gazing quietly into the forest until the timer on the stove beeped, signaling that Aunt Jenny's latest dessert was ready for tasting.

Mike went to bed shortly after dessert, intending to get an early start to the morning and see some of the trails his uncle mentioned. *"It will be nice to take a walk by myself before heading into town,"* he thought to himself. The Darkness laughed. *"You are never alone, Mike. You always have me."* The small envelope his uncle Jim gave him after dessert rested on the nightstand. It contained a couple of day's pay, plus a bonus for the cleanup on Monday his uncle called "hazard pay", in cash. Normal payroll was the following week, but Uncle Jim explained he wanted Mike to have some money in his pocket for the weekend. Mike knew saving from the start should be his priority, but part of him wanted to just go a little crazy with the first real paycheck in his life. It wasn't much, but it was more money than he had had at one time ever before. So, with a smile, Mike shoved down the Darkness and fell sleep. As far as he remembered, having no dreams whatsoever.

***

"James," Sally Keller said from the other end of the phone, "What is the matter? How's he doing?" It was pretty late and she couldn't keep a yawn from catching her at the end of the second question.

"I saw it today, Sis," he replied, careful to keep his voice low so as not to disturb his wife. He worried should his voice carry down the hall towards his nephew's room. "I purposefully kept the salt and pepper shakers on my end of the table all week so that he had to ask for them. Tonight, he moved them to his side without even realizing it. However, he came close to asking me about it later when we were alone."

"You didn't tell him anything, did you?" she started. "No, of course you wouldn't have. You know the so-called 'rules' of this better than I do. Why couldn't my baby have been left out of this nonsense?" A little bit of anger crept around a second yawn. She understood why the calls came so late at night, given the time zone difference, but it didn't stop her from being tired.

"I haven't said anything concrete, but he may have overheard Jenny and I talking about family history," Jim said. "She is dead set on setting him up with her friend's kid, Laurie, our Goddaughter. It seems to be working as a distraction to him. They are about the same age. You would think Jenny was the one with some kind of prophetic power or something the way she seems 'so sure' they will be great together."

"You think he will end up not coming home still don't you?" she asked, disappointment and sadness slipped into her voice. She knew what her brother said recently about it being unlikely that her son would return home from this summer. Like most mothers, she still didn't want to let go. She had a nagging suspicion that his not returning home could also mean something horrible happened to her only son.

The words of their father passed onto her from her brother didn't indicate much, just that Mike might not return to his hometown.

"I don't have the gift for foretelling that our father had," Jim began. Pure luck brought him to the letter written by their father before he died, sealed within the bindings of a certain family book kept secret for generations. The letter intimated Mike would be the one to carry on the family legacy, along with several other things which could be interpreted as dire. Those Jim didn't share with his sister. No sense worrying her over what "might be" or "could happen". The only thing for sure was Mike wouldn't be returning east in the fall. Whether for good or ill relied on the "what could happen" the elder James Johnson had written. Withholding information for the sake of his sister's peace of mind ate at Jim every day.

"Well," she said, once again resigning herself to the realization this was out of her hands. "I have put together all the important paperwork and talked to his school. When he makes that decision, I will send it to you. Until he says he is staying though, I will hold onto it, hopeful that my baby will be coming home."

"I understand, Sis." Jim never had kids so he couldn't truly empathize with his sister's plight, though he felt bad it was tearing her up. "You know Jenny and I will treat him like he was our own. She is happy as a cat with a saucer of milk to have two of us to cook and look out for." He forced a laugh and heard it echoed not quite wholeheartedly on the other end of the line.

"Alright, James," she said after a moment's pause. "You and Jenny take care of my boy. Give her my best. I always did think she would have been a great mother if not for your particular problem." They exchange goodbyes and hang up for the night.

Though not the first call this week, it gave Jim the most bittersweet feelings to make. On the one hand, seeing proof for himself of his nephew's gifts excited him. Telling his sister their father predicted things right so far, pained him. He couldn't imagine how hard it would be for her if she knew the rest of the story. As he stared at the phone on the nightstand, he thought again about what their father wrote. He pulled the letter from a drawer and reread it one more time before turning out the light and going to sleep.

Chapter 4

The utter silence woke Mike. He reached for his glasses as he realized he forgot to set an alarm. The clock read just after nine. By this time on a Saturday, his old neighborhood would have been alive with noise. With his current nearest neighbor almost a mile away; there were no lawns being mowed, kids playing, or driving cars to disturb his slumber.

Mike headed down the hall and found a note tucked under a set of keys on the dining room table. "Mike, Here are the keys to your aunt's car. If you wouldn't mind topping off the gas tank while you are out, there is a twenty under the note. We are going to be gone most of the day so please lock up when you leave. Love, Uncle Jim and Aunt Jenny. P.S. – I had already programmed the house and the mall into your phone's map program for you." Leaving everything on the table, Mike went to his bathroom to shower and change. His stomach grumbled but figured it would hold until he got to the mall and grabbed an early lunch there.

A chirping sound greeted Mike when he exited the shower. He followed the oddly familiar sound to his bedroom where the cell phone his relatives gave him sat plugged into a wall charger. Someone had called while he was in the shower, setting off the annoying chirping sound. Mike grabbed the phone, pushing the button to dial the voicemail. Thankfully this stopped the annoying chirp. As he waited for the message to start, Mike thought, *"I'm going to have to change that to something more tolerable."* It was his phone to do with as he liked, according to his aunt and uncle.

"Hi Mike," began a female voice he didn't recognize at first, except for the same strange jolt he felt when he met her for the first and only time. "This is Laurie. Your aunt told me to give you a call this morning because she thought you might be going to the mall and thought that you might like someone to show you around town. Some friends of mine and I were going to an afternoon matinee at the movie theater which shares the same parking lot. It starts about two, but I am sure you know all about how those previews usually take forever. If you want to go, just give me a call back or not, or whatever." Laurie's message developed a small bout of giggles at this point. *"Why can't girls leave a normal voice mail and then just hang-up when they are done? Although her giggle is a little cute,"* Mike thought to himself, pondering what little he remembered of her from the brief encounter on Monday evening. "Anyways," she continued, snapping him out of his musing, "Maybe I will see you there. Later."

Aunt Jenny had clearly spoken to Laurie after Monday night, if there had been anything to smooth over. After all, Mike had a valid excuse for not being fit for company. Thinking about her giggle again and the blonde ponytail, Mike resolved to try to get to know her this summer. What could it hurt? It could be fun, despite his recent heartache still jabbing him when he thought about Colleen. The pull towards Laurie, and feeling that something important involved her, made him curious as well. A spike of pain in his forehead, signaling one of the visions he had been missing for a couple weeks, struck him as he turned towards the front door. He saw a brief flash and a scene very similar to the one where he had tucked Colleen's hair behind her ear, only this time the blonde standing in his arms was Laurie. Shaking his head to clear his mind, Mike filed it away and checked to make sure he had everything to leave.

Mike tossed the phone in a pocket. After picking up the keys and money, he locked the door and headed for his aunt's car. He made it to the highway easy enough and once sure of his exit, decided to call Laurie back. She answered the phone immediately. "Hey Laurie, it's Mike."

"Oh hey, Mike," she replied cheerfully. "I suppose you got my message. What do you think?" The anticipation in her voice clear.

Mike wasn't sure what Aunt Jenny had told her, but clearly being new in town had its own appeal. *"Or maybe Aunt Jenny talked up her nephew,"* Mike considered briefly.

"Sounds like fun," Mike said, keeping an eye on the road, even through an image of her appearing in his mind. He tried to recall everything about her so it will be easy to recognize her when they meet up. The image in his mind sharpened. He saw her talking on a phone. Mike chalked it up to his imagination filling in the blanks. "I am actually on the highway on my way to the mall now. I slept in longer than I planned so was going to grab lunch there. Any recommendations?"

"Well, they have a pizza place, and of course the usual fast food places have a spot," she began. "They have a great sandwich place though that serves real fresh cut fries, not the processed potato stuff. Some friends of mine and I should be there about twenty of two if you want to meet us over by the theater entrance."

"That'll work," Mike replied. "I'm probably going to just wander around a bit anyway. Got my first paycheck so it's burning a hole in my pocket." She laughed with him and the two teens said their goodbyes. Mike pressed the gas down a little harder to pass someone not quite doing the speed limit. He watched for the mall exit, the radio blaring over the little voice from his GPS on the phone. Luckily, several stations already existed on the presets, so Mike found something worth listening to. What he had learned about Laurie the past week from Aunt Jenny hadn't been much. Laurie was going to be a senior this year like himself, and had turned eighteen about a month ago so she was a little older.

Cruising along while his mind drifted, the ringing of his phone snapped him out of his daydreaming. He turned the radio off and glanced at the ID before answering. "Hi Aunt Jenny."

"Hello, Mike. Your uncle and I were wondering if you were up yet. You were sawing logs when we left. What are your plans for the day? Did you get our note?"

"I'm up. On my way to the mall. I got the note and I will top off the gas tank before I bring the car home. Thank you for letting me use it."

"No problem, sweetie. Don't spend all your money in one place. You will need some spending money for any dates that may pop up." The hint in Aunt Jenny's voice plain to Mike.

"Oh, right. Before I forget, I'm meeting Laurie and some of her friends for a movie. I don't know when it will get out but if we are going to be too late I'll call."

"Sounds great," Aunt Jenny replied , her joy leeched into her voice. "Oh," she said suddenly, "I normally only listen to one station, so feel free to set the other stations to anything you find on the scanner."

Puzzled because of the several stations set when he looked for something to listen to, Mike was about to bring it up when Aunt Jenny abruptly said, "Have fun, I gotta run." The line went dead. Mike shrugged off his minor confusion. *Uncle Jim probably set them at some point when he drove the car and didn't say anything to her.* Mike dismissed the laughter in the deeper recesses of his mind. *Not today Darkness.*

Reaching the mall, Mike searched for a parking spot equal distance between the movie theater and a mall entrance. Figuring this would save him time later, he headed inside to the tune of his grumbling stomach. Considering what Laurie said, Mike quickly spied the sandwich place and ordered. Sitting down at a table fairly close to one of the stands with a map of the mall, he set to enjoy the meal and do a little people watching. The mall bustled with activity and many people passed by. Most seemed too absorbed in their own business to pay any mind to one more person eating in the food court.

After eating, Mike checked the map a little closer, confirming the location of his next stop. The name of the store marked with the "Book" symbol was not a chain he recognized. As the front displays came into view, he realized it wasn't a chain at all but a small independent bookstore. The décor was plain and functional, suiting him just fine. Mike didn't care to have salespeople pushing lattes or cappuccinos on him while just trying to buy a book.

Checking the latest releases, someone walked up to his side. A female voice interrupted his thoughts, "May I help you find anything in particular?"

Mike replied, "Just browsing at the moment," without really even looking up. Finishing up the small paragraph on the back of the paperback he had in hand, he glanced up as the sales clerk walked away. Pushing his glasses up on his nose a bit, Mike mentally groaned in frustration. Having worn glasses for years, he still never developed a fondness for them. Mike tried contacts once, but his eyes dried out so much it wasn't worth the hassle.

The clerk looked to be about his age, maybe younger. She was short and petite, with her dark hair pushed back with one of those hair bands that ran from ear to ear over the top of her head. As Mike watched her walk away to help someone else, she glanced back just once. Mike looked away and went to another section of the store. As he flipped through a few other books, he kept seeing the sales clerk in his peripheral vision as she moved about. Once, when she walked by with someone else, Mike thought he heard her say very softly, "Is he looking at me? I can't tell. I haven't seen him in the store before. I wonder if he's new in town?" When Mike looked her way she was standing with her side towards him so he couldn't get a good look at her lips. She must have noticed Mike watching her closer as she jumped slightly and headed into the back room. As she turned away Mike clearly heard her say, "Oh God, he is looking at me." The odd thing being it didn't sound like a whisper, more like she was talking through a hand clasped over her lips.

Mike shrugged, going to the counter to pay for the few books he had selected. Mike didn't know what to make of the girl running off, but she didn't return. Standing at the register was an older lady with similar hair, but with a little gray streaked through it, ringing up customer purchases. Mike considered asking who the sales girl was, but decided against it when he saw a picture behind the register. From the people in the picture and the caption below it, he could see that this was truly a family owned business and the woman ringing up purchases was the younger woman's mother. Both of them and a stern looking man that must be the patriarch of the family were receiving an award for local businesses in the picture.

Making a note in his mind that the caption said her name was Julie, Mike wished her mother a good day and left with books in tow. The selection in the store was great, and the prices very competitive with what he was used to, which was even better. Stepping out the entryway, he spied a little stand with fliers of an upcoming sale and what was due to be released in the next few weeks. At the bottom was the phone number for the store, so Mike grabbed one and tucked it into the bag with the books. *"I usually spend a lot of time with my nose buried in a book, maybe I will see her the next time I come to the store."* Uncertainty at this thought nagged at his mind, but the Darkness kept silent this time. It wasn't like Mike was checking her out or anything, but it had stoked his ego a little to have been noticed. Subconsciously he was starting to enjoy not being ignored by girls like his life had been up to his brief relationship with Colleen. First, there was Laurie's interest, no doubt encouraged by his Aunt, and now the gal in the bookstore.

Checking the time on his phone, Mike wandered around through a few other stores until it got close to one-thirty. He walked out to the car to drop off the books before heading to the movie theater. The part of the lot Mike parked in had been mostly empty, but now was starting to fill up as the showtimes for the movies began. Mike dropped off the books, but when he began walking towards the front doors of the theater, a car honked repeatedly and parked only two spots away. Not knowing the car, Mike figured he must have drifted too far from the side and they were thinking he would walk in front of them. He kept walking until a door slammed shut and someone yelled his name. The lightning bolt in his chest told him who it was before he even turned around to see Laurie. She had just gotten out of the honking car with two other people. Mike's heart started racing like each time she'd spoken to him before.

The flower print shirt left unbuttoned over her white tank top fanned out like a cape behind as Laurie ran over to Mike. She dragged the other female from the car behind her. The guy walked over after locking the car with the keychain remote. "Mike," Laurie started, "I'm so glad you decided to come. This is my friend Deb, and her boyfriend Chad. Liz and Anne should be joining us if they aren't already inside."

Mike shook Chad's hand, struck immediately that the guy was a jock of some sort. It momentarily brought up bad memories of the last jock he was around, Kevin. Mike felt the Darkness rumble awake. *"Not now, damn it."*

Laurie released Deb's arm and hooked hers with Mike's instead. She started leading the way. The sudden jolt from their skin making contact sent the Darkness deeper into his subconscious and surprised Mike. He stumbled a step before being able to catch up to walk alongside Laurie. She glanced at him and released his arm quickly. "Sorry," she said before giggling.

Mike felt the strange pull again as he reached to take back her arm. "No big deal," Mike replied, smiling as charmingly as possible and hooking her arm in his again. Thinking he should act on his assumptions and attempt to make friends with the group he found himself thrust into, he looked back at Chad, "So, what sports you play?" The Darkness raged to end Chad because of his resemblance to Kevin, but Mike shoved it down forcefully.

"Basketball and soccer mostly," Chad replied. "You?"

"At least it isn't football," Mike thought while laughing. He responded, "No sports here. I shoot hoops with the guys, but nothing on a league or school team. I'm not quite star potential honestly. I did bowl in a league once, but I didn't bring my bowling ball with me from home. Not sure that counts as a sport though." Mike chuckled.

Chad nodded, laughing along, and the four teens exchanged basics as they waited in line for tickets and snacks. Chad and Deb, going out for almost two years now, would be Seniors this year as well. The violent tendency towards Chad became easier to suppress the longer the four teens talked. Mike decided Chad and Kevin shared very little in common. Laurie's arm in his sent the rumbling Darkness to the depths of his subconscious. Mike split a combo with Laurie for the soda. Anne and Liz waited in the lobby beyond the snack bar. Laurie introduced Mike as her "New friend from out of town", while never releasing his arm.

The first show of the day let out as the teens approached. The sweeping crew swooped in to clean up. The girls left Chad and Mike in the hallway, loaded down with sodas, boxes of candy, and buckets of popcorn as the four of them headed to the bathroom. The two guys shared a look of amusement with a few other people lining up to get into the theater.

As the girls passed out of earshot, Mike heard one of the girls say, "What a cutie. Laurie's already all over him. What's up with that..." before it trailed off. Mike strained to hear a reply, but only some giggling drifted back. Mike looked at Chad, "Which one was that?"

He stared at the girls' retreating backs a moment, "Giggling? All of them I think, although Laurie didn't look like she was enjoying the joke as much as the other three. Must have been on her."

"Oh, I thought I heard one of them say something before they started giggling, but then they were out of range," Mike replied, shrugging. Mike realized as the two chatted that Chad had been friends with Laurie and Deb for most of their lives. Mike felt Chad sizing him up to see what intentions Mike had with Laurie, especially because of her hanging onto his arm since they met up. "I am glad my Aunt Jenny introduced me to Laurie so I could meet the rest of you guys. I might have gone crazy with just my family to spend time with this summer," Mike started, testing to see if his judgement of Chad was right again.

"That's right. You're Mrs. Johnson's nephew," Chad said, brightening at the mention of Aunt Jenny. "Laurie mentioned it, but it must have slipped my mind with your last name not being the same. Your Aunt is like an Aunt to most of us around here. So what made you want to come out here instead of spending the summer at home?"

"My uncle said he had a job opening, and I thought why not," Mike replied, glad that some of Chad's suspicions seem laid to rest. "Say, my Aunt sort of put me and Laurie together since she is friends with Laurie's mom, but, Laurie isn't seeing anyone, is she? I wouldn't want to end up with some crazy boyfriend wanting to tear my head off because I was seen with his girl, you know?"

Chad laughed before turning serious, "No, Laurie hasn't dated anyone that I know of in at least a year or two. She has been focusing on her job and school. Deb could tell ya if she has any crushes, but she's the closest thing to a sister I have so I would think Laurie would have mentioned it to me if she did."

"That's cool," Mike replied quickly. "I wouldn't want to cause any problems since I'm just here for the summer and all anyway. I'm just glad to have some people to hang out with." Chad nodded as they settled back to wait for the girls to reappear. A couple of the other people waiting in line headed in when the cleaning crew finished.

***

"So, Laurie," Anne began as soon as they entered the bathroom, "Who's the new boy toy?"

"He is not a boy toy, Anne," Laurie snapped back. *"I wish Liz wouldn't insist on including her. She drives me crazy."* "He is Mr. and Mrs. Johnson's nephew from out east. She asked if I would show him around and introduce him to some people so he didn't have to 'hang out with the old fogies all the time' as she put it." *"I wish this had just been a double date, but Liz and Anne were already invited. Mike is everything my Godmother said he was."*

"So does showing him around and introducing him to people include hanging on him like a cheap hussy?" Anne replied, laughing and throwing a wadded up paper towel in Laurie's direction. *"She still doesn't like being around me. I wish she would get over that, it was almost three years ago and she doesn't know half the story."*

"I am not hanging all over him like a cheap hussy. I just want him to feel welcome and all. It's not like I jumped him and offered myself to him in the first few minutes like you do to greet any male you lay eyes on." The jab a bit harsh and exaggerated, but it made Laurie feel better. *"That should teach her to keep her mouth shut. Maybe her legs, too."*

"Well if I can pry your arm off him long enough, I might do just that," Anne stated matter-of-factly, clicking her makeup case closed for emphasis and heading for the door. Laurie beat her there, barely, and

41

the quartet trekked back to the two guys waiting in line. *"I wish I could make her understand."* She smiles at the glare from her friend Liz. *"I'll be nice when Laurie does."* Soon they were within earshot of the guys and could hear them talking about bowling or some other such "guy" nonsense.

***

As they waited for the girls to get back, Chad told Mike about the bowling alley on the other side of town with summer leagues starting soon. Mike expressed interest as they watched the girls approach. Mike noticed the cutting glares passing between Laurie and Anne. *"I wonder what is going on."* Mike reached toward Laurie, but in her distraction, she didn't take his arm like before.

The pleasant feeling brought on by contact with Laurie faded, causing Mike to reconsider his situation. At first, the strange pull he received from hearing her speak had jumped a notch when Laurie's skin made contact with his. It had then settled into something akin to a hum in his chest, like the purring of a cat. The analogy his head jumped to being the strangest part of the whole thing. Her touch had also kept him from wanting to lash out at Chad for being a jock. The rage kept barely in check scared Mike and brought images of Kevin's dead face from his dreams to the forefront of his mind. The Darkness muttered in the fringes of his mind, freeing itself from its imprisonment.

Mike, puzzled by the sudden shift in Laurie's attitude, filed into the theater with the rest of the group. The sparsely populated theatre boasted a plethora of seats to choose from. The group stood in the entryway. Chad and Deb, just ahead of Laurie and Mike, debated on which of several rows to sit in. Mike almost dropped the drink and popcorn when Laurie grabbed his arm and started pushing him down a row of seats ahead of her. Not sure how far he should go, Mike counted out enough seats for them all before starting to sit down. Apparently, that was the wrong thing to do as Laurie pushed him right to the end of the row and sat down next to him. With a wall on one side and her on the other, Mike watched the rest of the group take their seats. Chad and Deb followed behind Laurie with Liz and Anne bringing up the rear. Anne shot a dark look at Laurie. Mike pondered it but the lights start to dim as the previews got underway. Laurie suddenly took his left hand in a vise-like grip. The hum in his chest reappeared, but almost predatory and possessive instead of content and comfortable.

Mike stared at the screen before a female voice broke his focus. The whispered voice sounded close to his ear, "What nerve that girl has. She doesn't even know him yet she hangs on him like they have been dating for years. Who does she think she is? She had the nerve to have said that to me. I thought we were finally getting past that. Oh no, she gets all worked up because I teased her about hanging all over a guy she just met and she has to throw that in my face again." The rambling continued for several minutes.

About a third of the way into the movie, Mike shifted slightly and used the motion to glance around at the people sitting close enough for him to have heard them whisper. Everyone's gaze was trained intently on the screen except for Anne, whose eyes met Mike's. Her frown and clenched forehead softened into a bright smile when she saw Mike looking her way. The litany Mike heard changed as well, "Oh, maybe he won't be so taken with her as she would like to think. Perhaps I can find time to slip him my number on the way out. If she still thinks that harshly of me, it would just burn his aunt up if I got him to hang out with me this summer."

Mike kept his face devoid of emotion and turned back toward the screen. *"I am definitely imagining something. If she was talking out loud like that, why wasn't anyone else hearing her?"* However, he knew her lips weren't moving. *"What is going on? Was it even her I was hearing? I hadn't really been paying attention to the movie, could part of it have been from there and my overactive imagination?"* His distraction kept him from focusing on the movie at all. He barely remembered the plot when the credits started and the lights came on. Mike failed to notice Laurie snuggled up against him, having slipped his arm up over her head and across her shoulders during the movie.

She held onto Mike's hand all the way out to the front doors, where they all started to part ways. The feeling in Mike's chest when Laurie held his hand settled back into the contented and casual hum, except when she looked at Anne. The spikes and lulls made him even jumpier, as well as confused. Liz and Anne waved goodbye at the theatre entrance. Laurie planned to ride back to Deb's because she left her work clothes there. Mike walked with them towards Chad's car.

At the car, Laurie let go of Mike's hand and threw her arms around him in a hug. "I hope you had a good time, and call me sometime if you want to hang out, ok?" she asked, holding onto him.

Mike replied, "Sure". He hugged her back. The two stared at each other awkwardly a moment, before Mike leaned in and gave Laurie a quick kiss on the cheek. "Thanks for the advice earlier on lunch," Mike continued. She slipped into the car and Chad started the engine. Mike waved to him and Deb, calling out, "We should get together again soon." Laurie's reaction raised his own interest. Chad making it clear Laurie was single caused Mike to consider it might be fun for the summer. As long as it didn't go too far. *"I don't want it to get messy this fall when I go home."* "If I go back home, I guess," Mike corrected himself out loud. The Darkness chuckled, crawling out of the hole in the recesses of Mike's subconscious.

As Mike watched them back out and pull away, he considered again what he was sure he heard in the movie theater. Shaking himself out of his thoughts, Mike headed over to Aunt Jenny's car. Anne crashed into him, almost knocking him over. Liz followed a few car lengths behind her. "Hey Mike, Liz's car won't start. You think you could give us a ride home so her parents can come take a look at it later? Nobody's answering their phone right now that can come get us." she said, grabbing Mike's arm and giving him a pleading look. Locking eyes with her again, Mike felt lost a moment before he realized she expected a response. There was a reaction to her touch and the eye contact similar to what he felt with Laurie, but it bordered much more on the predatory. The Darkness reacted favorably, causing Mike to recoil from Anne a little.

"Sure," Mike started, politely untangling himself from Anne before continuing, "but you will have to give me directions. I barely know my way here and home. This is my first visit to town and all." The darker part of Mike wanted Anne to wrap herself back around him.

"No problem," Anne purred, waving at Liz. "Hurry up slowpoke, before he changes his mind." Mike gently deflected Anne's attempts to hold his hand or arm as he focused on unlocking the car doors.

"No worries. I can't leave you two stranded here. That wouldn't be proper." Mike felt Anne's eyes on him. He knew if he met her gaze he would feel drawn in again. As similar as it felt to his reaction to Laurie, the differences were a little off-putting. He wasn't sure what he thought about the Darkness reacting to Anne either. Something tickled the back of his mind. *"Maybe it's something like what Aunt Jenny had said about the way Uncle Jim knew that she was the one for him. Not that I'm considering marrying anyone anytime soon. Hopefully, this whole family legacy isn't just nonsense in my head. Maybe I really am going crazy."*

"I bet you couldn't," Anne said slowly, looking up into Mike's eyes when he straightened. Anne was a good six inches shorter than Mike and she used it to her advantage to gaze up pleadingly. Mike hadn't noticed before, having been distracted by Laurie, but Anne's low cut top left little to the imagination. He again shoved down the Darkness inside as it reacted to Anne's gaze. "Such a gentleman." Anne brushed up against him as she slipped into the shotgun seat.

Liz whispered her thanks and climbed in the back. Mike didn't need to see Liz's face to feel the exasperation rolling off her.

He climbed into the driver seat and started the car. The radio blared and he reached to turn it down, Anne's hand met his at the dial. For a moment the Darkness took control and Mike's hand locked with Anne's. Liz began giving directions from the back seat on how to get to her house. Her voice snapped Mike back into control and he released Anne's hand. Twenty-five minutes later, the trio pulled into Liz's driveway.

Liz whispered, "Thanks," as she got out of the car. She paused a minute when Anne didn't get out as well.

Mike started to catch on. Anne struck him as a bit of a drama queen. First Laurie and now Liz both seemed annoyed with Anne's antics. Paired with the slight protectiveness Laurie displayed after the movie gave Mike the idea Anne must have said something to upset Laurie when the girls were in the bathroom. Anne however, still wasn't moving as if she was going to get out of the car with Liz.

"Would you mind dropping me off at my house, Mike?" Anne asked, putting her hand on his forearm again like she had a couple times on the ride so far. Each time had elicited the same feeling of being hunted prey, the Darkness humming as it enjoyed her attentions. Mike spent most of the drive with his right arm on the steering wheel to prevent Anne from latching onto him. "I don't live far, and I can tell you how to get to the highway to get back to your Aunt and Uncle's from there."

Mike nodded, and Anne squealed with delight. She jumped out of the car and followed Liz inside, reappearing in mere moments with a light blue backpack and a plastic bag from some store Mike didn't recognize. She put the bags in the back seat before getting back in the front next to him. She slid over until almost sitting on the console in the middle. "Thank you so much. You are my hero today. Liz is moping about her car and would be just horrible company for the rest of the afternoon until one of our parents could get me home." Mike shrugged and shifted the car into reverse, watching for cross traffic.

"He is cute. And so nice. I can't believe she thinks she deserves to monopolize his time just because her mom and his aunt are best friends." This pulled Mike's attention from watching for cross traffic. He recognized Anne's voice, but with the same muted quality as before when he couldn't see her lips moving in the theatre.

Mike looked over at her and asked, "What did you say?"

"What?" Anne replied, her expression and voice protesting innocence to the point of being suspicious. "I didn't say anything. I don't want to distract you while you are driving." She batted her eyes at him.

Mike nodded and, after a car passed by, backed onto the road. *"She had certainly not been worried about my driving on the way to Liz's house. She nearly pulled my arm off the steering wheel several times."*

The next few minutes passed with Anne talking about herself, interjecting directions in between. When she mentioned she was co-captain of the varsity cheer squad, Mike's focus turned more to the road than her. Hearing the word 'cheerleader' set off his memories of Colleen. He only half heard anything Anne said from that point on. Mike did catch how she leaned towards him as much as she could with the seatbelt on. She also kept touching his arm or leg when she was talking. *"She must be trying to spite Laurie by flirting with me."* The Darkness chimed in, "I like it. I vote we see what she's up to." Mike

47

mentally pummeled the Darkness to the depths of his mind, where it laughed at his efforts to ignore the feelings Anne was eliciting. The strange feeling of being drawn toward her never quite faded, but it became easier to manage when he didn't look at her or she wasn't touching him.

Mike hoped her flirting would end as they pulled into the driveway at her house. The Darkness fought Mike's control each time he felt the strange sense of being drawn to Anne intensify. *"She's pretty, but nothing like Laurie."* Anne started to give directions back to the highway, taking the opportunity to remove her seat belt and slide a little closer to Mike. He had already worked out his route, but his nod didn't seem to be enough for her.

"Thank you again so much, Mike," Anne said softly, moving over. She shifted until she actually sat on the console between the seats and grabbed his arm. Before Mike could react, she pulled him as close to her as the seat belt he still wore allowed. She kissed Mike on the cheek, lingering slightly to whisper in his ear, "Would you like to come in for a soda or something? I feel like I owe you for going out of your way. My parents won't be home for hours."

The shock of her action disrupted his battle with the Darkness. Mike felt himself fall into her eyes. His answer was to place a hand on the back of Anne's neck and begin kissing her soundly. Mike's detachment continued as he and Anne continue kissing for several minutes. Their lips pressed firmly together and their hands clutched at each other in the car. When Mike started to kiss up Anne's cheek toward her ear he hears her voice in his head, "I knew I could get him. Laurie is going to be so pissed."

Mike snapped back into control, pulling away abruptly. *"Clearly this is about me being new in town and some jealous war with Laurie. I should have seen this coming, especially the way they had been shooting daggers at each other with their eyes."* He filed the differences between Laurie and Anne away for the time being.

Shock registered on Anne's face and Mike felt a desire to kiss her again build. He wasn't sure why, but he found a part of himself entertained the idea of going along with her offer. A few different enticing scenarios began flashing in his head, which reminded him of the visions he received sometimes. The Darkness smiled in anticipation. Mike reinforced his control as he pulled further away, blinking. The feeling of being drawn to Anne faded the more he focused on Laurie and the electric hum her holding his hand had initiated.

"I appreciate the offer Anne, but I really should be getting home. My aunt and uncle are going to be expecting me home for dinner." Trying to fight down the urge to kiss her felt like trying to walk into a stiff wind. *"I win this round, Darkness."* Mike asserted to himself. The Darkness retreated, lamenting the opportunity given up.

"Oh," Anne replied, pouting. "I understand. Well, I better get going then." She squeezed Mike's hand again, stalling in case he changed his mind. When Mike failed to respond, she pouted again and reached for the door handle. She collected her things from the back seat and walked up to the front door of her house. She dawdled, turning back several times to look in Mike's direction. Mike watched her walk away, warring with the Darkness to follow her and take what is offered, consequences be damned. He pushed those thoughts down. From the steps of her porch, she turned a final time and waved. Mike waved back and started backing out of the drive.

Once back on the road, heading in the direction of home, Mike cranked up the radio and rolled down the window a little for some cool air. *"Something is going on here. Am I losing my mind? Did Anne really say those things? Why does my Darkness react to Anne the way it did when it fled while Laurie held my hand. Not that I need any complications right now. I still don't know what happened to Colleen. Why did Laurie replace Colleen in my vision?"*

Once set in cruise, Mike reached over to change the station and noticed a piece of paper on the passenger seat. He picked it up, glancing at it while he watched the traffic. "Thanks for the ride, call me sometime. Anne" followed by her phone number. The little pink kiss left in the corner caught his eye. Mike puzzled over when she managed to have time to write that while she was sitting in the car. Maybe she did it while she was inside at Liz's and just hadn't found any other way to slip it to him while they were driving to her house.

Mike exited the highway and pulled to the last stoplight before his Aunt and Uncle's road. Catching his reflection in the edge of the rearview mirror, he saw a little pink kiss left there that matched the piece of paper. He also noticed smudged pink on his own lips. Mike chuckled as he wet a couple fingertips to try to wipe it off his cheek while he licked his lips. The pink lip gloss carried a faint strawberry flavor. Though it came off his lips easily enough, the spot on his cheek was being particularly stubborn. When the light changed green, he decided to just wash it off at home. A few minutes later, Mike pulled into the drive, slightly surprised to see Uncle Jim's truck there. They had left a note that they might be gone all day, but obviously not. Mike parked next to the truck. He pocketed the note from Anne, grabbed his new books, and headed up the walk to the porch. Aunt Jenny met him at the front door, the look on her face set Mike back on his heels.

"Oh thank goodness you're alright," she exclaimed, looking him over, her eyes lingering on her nephew's face. Apparently, she saw the slightly smudged lip gloss kiss on his cheek. "Your Uncle and I have been worried half to death. We've been trying to call you for the last half hour. I was about to send your uncle out to look for you."

"I am sorry Aunt Jenny," Mike said, pulling the phone out of his shirt pocket. "I must not have turned it on when I left the movie I saw with Laurie and her friends."

"Well," she began, donning her best 'concerned mom' look. She was quite competent at it given she wasn't a mother herself. Mike figured his mother couldn't do much better. "I suppose we can let it slide this time. But don't you dare scare me like that again mister. Laurie called here a half hour ago when she couldn't get a hold of you on the phone and she thought you would have been back by now. That was when we started to worry that you got lost or were in an accident."

"No, nothing was wrong. The car drives really great." *"Now I've done it. Why didn't I turn on my phone. In my defense, I did have other problems to deal with."* Mike didn't think that revelation would really get him out of the hot seat with Aunt Jenny. It was clear there was some sort of animosity between Anne and Laurie that his Aunt knew about. "Laurie's friend Liz had some car trouble, so I gave her and Anne a ride home. They probably would have asked Laurie, but she rode with Deb and Chad who were already leaving. I was slower leaving since I'd walked Laurie to the car, so they caught me. I'm sorry I worried you, Aunt Jenny." It all came out in a rush, and she didn't change expression much, so she must have recognized all the names.

"That is very nice of you." Aunt Jenny eyes the mark on Mike's cheek and broke into a giggling fit, her stern look faded quickly. "Apparently chivalry is not dead, no matter what I tell your uncle sometimes. It is also apparently still rewarded," she continued, again giggling as they headed into the house.

Once inside the front door, she called out to her husband that everything is alright and detoured into the living room. Mike went to his room to drop off the books and then into the bathroom to wash off the mark on his cheek. A few minutes later he joined her in the living room. *"Might as well apologize to Uncle Jim and get this over with."*

"Aw, he removed his little reward before you got to see it, Jim," Aunt Jenny said as soon as Mike enters the room. He turned a little red, which apparently was what she was going for. "Well, honey, if you look closely you can see where it was, it's a little less red than the rest of his face. More of a pink I would say." By now her giggle fit kept her from being able to heckle her nephew anymore. Mike rolled his eyes as his embarrassment grew.

"So nephew," Uncle Jim started, grinning widely, "and just who was the young lady who got her mark on you already? I would have thought that you would have waited a little before letting yourself get roped in. You have to play hard to get with the girls around here, or you might end up stuck here like I did." He looked to his wife. She punched his arm, not liking the implications of his statement. "Not that I am complaining, mind you," he added quickly, rubbing his arm in mock pain and winking. "Just that you are too young for that sort of thing." He dodged a second jab from his wife.

"Actually, it was Anne," Mike replied. From the look on Aunt Jenny's face when Mike said the name, she was more than a little disappointed. "She gave me a kiss on the cheek only, as a thank you for the ride home. Don't worry, I am not tied down yet, I escaped with only a temporary brand from my first battle with Aunt Jenny's girls." Mike tried to make it sound like he had only taken a flesh wound in some major battle, and the acting job came off poorly. *"No Oscar this year. I don't like lying to them, but clearly Aunt Jenny doesn't like Anne. I don't want to cause any problems."* Lying to his Aunt and Uncle hurt, but even Mike wasn't ready to face what had happened to him during that brief moment when the Darkness took over.

"Well, tell us all about what you did today," Aunt Jenny pressed on, pushing Mike for details. Mike told them about the drive there and what he saw in the stores. He kept back the several instances where he thought he heard things because he was not sure what he really heard. When Mike failed to remember much about the movie, Aunt Jenny started in on him again about the girls, especially Laurie.

Mike fended her off, saying, "I don't want to spoil the movie for you." *"I'm certainly not telling them I was hearing Anne's voice in my head, or about the feelings her and Laurie sparked. I need to sort it out first."* Aunt Jenny seemed disappointed in the lack of juicy details, but Uncle Jim kept giving Mike the same look as if he was weighing the words against some internal scale. Mike worried his Uncle was going to call his bluff at any minute.

It never happened, much to Mike's relief. After a little more teasing from his Aunt, the trio settled into what had become routine. Aunt Jenny cooked another delicious dinner, and they watched some television together. Mike turned in early, thankful to get away from Aunt Jenny and her questions. She seemed intent on asking what Mike thought and bringing up Laurie every possible chance she could get.

Mike sat on his bed, staring at his phone. He put it on its charger and promptly fell asleep. His dreams became more of a mix after the day's events. The dream about the woods, and Kevin's dying question, swirled with scenes involving dates with Laurie or private moments with Anne. It was clear two different halves of himself reacted to the girls. Mike's darker half seemed more than willing to court both girls and be damned the consequences. He woke up several times that night with his heart racing.

***

"Something is going on, honey," Jim said to his wife that evening in the quiet of their room. "He was holding back something. I could see it in his eyes." He finished putting back on a pair of hiking boots and stood up from the bed.

"I could see it too," she replied, preparing for bed even as her husband appeared to be getting ready to go out. "I kept hoping he would bring it up and confirm everything himself so that we could talk to him. The radio stations, the salt and pepper shakers from the other night, and whatever happened today. It is only a matter of time before he is going to open up to us. Then what do we do?"

"We can't tell him anything," Jim stated, patiently. He had been over this in his mind several times, but after today he wavered. Only a few more days and things would be settled one way or the other. Would he be strong enough to guide his nephew? He wondered again for the thousandth time. The words of his father's letter burned in the back of his mind. There was potential for disaster if he failed to teach his nephew properly. His father had said something about a darkness that Mike would have to fight, though he wasn't clear who or what that darkness was. Jim hoped his nephew would not be noticed by the Council until he was ready.

"Maybe we can keep stalling him," his wife began again when he paused. She had been told some of what to expect, but even she was against all the secrecy that had existed for as long as anyone in the family had recorded. There were too many tales of misfortune and woe when the 'rules' were not followed, but she held that the alternatives had to be worse if something were to happen without the knowledge passed on. "Do you think it would be alright if maybe I told him? Since I am not a blood relative?" she asked suddenly, following her husband out of the room towards the back door. He was going to meditate in the woods. "The best place to think" he had always told her.

Her husband turned and looked at her, considering her words. The same thought had crossed his mind, but while the book was explicit about withholding the knowledge until the eighteenth year was reached, it didn't explain much about the why's and how's of the whole ordeal. Finally shaking his head, he replied softly, "No, we better not risk it. If what my father wrote is true, things are going to be different after Michael's generation. I don't know if that is good or bad, but until I see it, I cannot stomach the thought of anything happening to you or him by playing with the traditions." He pitched his voice low, trying to make sure they wouldn't wake their nephew down the hall. He kissed his wife gently when she nodded acceptance of his decision. He then slipped out the back door as quickly and quietly as he could. Jenny returned to their bedroom.

***

Sometime in the early hours that Sunday morning, Mike laid awake, staring at the ceiling, thinking about everything that had happened during the previous day. *"Am I going crazy? Am I hearing things? Thoughts? I can't let the Darkness get ahold again if I'm around Anne. No telling what I might do. It was almost like the fight with Kevin outside of Tony's. I wasn't in control then. This wasn't 'anger' though. This was... possession. Like the Darkness was claiming Anne as his. Or mine? How far would it have gone?"* The teenage male in Mike took a moment to consider Anne's charms. Guilt over his still fresh feelings for Colleen slammed back into place and Mike shook his head.

A sound he knew wasn't in his head snapped him back to the present. The sliding glass door that led to the back deck quietly clicked shut. Then Mike heard Uncle Jim's voice, answering something that Aunt Jenny must have asked that he didn't hear.

"It is settled," Uncle Jim said. "Neither of us are going to tell him anything. I know things have been happening for him. Those radio stations, he thought I may have set them, but he must have done it without realizing it. That alone is a staggering display of his potential. He didn't even have to scan the stations to get what he wanted. It just happened subconsciously. Not to mention the salt and pepper shakers the other night at dinner. Even you saw that happen. I think I confused him enough that he didn't ask, but I cannot put him off much longer. I think something happened today that may have confused him even more. He was definitely holding back something. My sister said his mind is like a steel trap when it comes to just about anything he sees or reads. He wouldn't have forgotten details about the movie and made up that excuse unless something else was going on. But we cannot tell him."

"I know dear," Aunt Jenny's voice carried down the hall. "We have to wait until his birthday you said. If you tell him anything for sure before then, you said it could have consequences. Make him a target or something because of the gifts."

Mike waited, hoping to hear what came next, but they must have moved off to the other end of the house towards their bedroom. He wondered why and how they seemed to know so much about what he was going through. Mike drove himself in circles with one thought taking dominance, *"Only a few days until my birthday, then I guess they will have to tell me."* He laid there for a few more minutes fighting down the anger within before a fitful sleep finally claimed him. His last thought was how he needed to get the Darkness under control or he was going to end up doing something he'd regret.

Chapter 5

Mike planned a calm Sunday, reading on the back porch. Burying himself in his book, he tried to forget what he overheard. His aunt and uncle left for town before he woke up. A note on the table next to his Aunt's car keys read, "We had some things to do in town. Feel free to borrow the car if you decide to go somewhere, just leave us a note or leave your phone on if you do. Sorry for scaring you yesterday. Not used to having a teenager in the house. Love, Aunt Jenny." Mike had no plans except to read so, after fixing a glass of tea, he tossed his phone into a pocket. With the ringer on vibrate he took a seat on the long bench swing on the back porch. The morning breeze carried a hint of chill and raised goosebumps on his arms under the long sleeve shirt he wore. He sipped the tea. *"It's not Mom's, but it's pretty good."*

His mind drifted to the odd occurrences of the last few months. Drawing from the books he had read, he tried to put labels on everything he experienced. First, the premonitions, which were the only way he could describe the visions, began with the near miss of the surely fatal car crash during the school year. Could he also be moving things with his mind, and perhaps he heard the thoughts of those around him. That would explain the salt and pepper shakers the other night. Also, the things he heard in the mall and from Anne at the movie. Part of him agreed with the Darkness, who was relishing these thoughts. *"What geek didn't fantasize about having psychic powers?"* However, the dire warning in his Uncle's admonition to Aunt Jenny worried him. Mike fought to put it away from his mind and focus on the book.

When his phone vibrated, he almost dropped the book. Checking the display, he saw Laurie's cell, and it was approaching noon. "Hello," Mike croaked out, quickly taking a sip of the tea to wet his dry throat.

Mike could feel the midday sun finally starting to win the day through the light t-shirt he had thrown on.

"Hey Mike," Laurie said. Mike could tell something was wrong from her tone. "I just wanted to call and see what you were up to today." She was guarded, not nearly as friendly and giggly as she had been yesterday. He thought about his kiss with Anne.

"Nothing much really," Mike replied, "just enjoying my book and the cool breeze on my aunt and uncle's back porch. They took off before I got up so I am just hanging out. I'm glad you called because I wanted to say, I had fun yesterday at the movie. We really should get together next weekend, maybe just you, me, Chad and Deb if that works for everyone else." Mike hoped by intentionally not listing Anne it might defuse the situation a little. Thoughts of Anne recalled the strange sensation he felt when the two locked eyes; which was so different from the reaction to Laurie. The loss of control felt different than his previous experiences with the Darkness.

Mike wondered how long after he dropped her off did Anne take to call Laurie and say something about the two of them. Mike recognized the kind of game Anne would play. He had seen it before when his friends had been targets. *"Truth be told,"* Mike thought to himself, *"I am not interested in anything serious because I might be going back east at the end of summer. Friends to spend my off hours with would be nice though, and the bowling alley Chad had mentioned sounded like fun."* Even knowing he could be going home in the fall, Mike still felt drawn to spending time with Laurie. The Darkness wanted to see how far Anne would go, spinning his mind in circles.

"That sounds great," she said, brightening a little. "I have Friday night off if you want to go out that night. I can talk to Deb and Chad and see what they are up to."

"Fantastic," Mike said, enthusiastic despite his swirling thoughts. Mike decided to come at the problem from a different angle. "By the way, did you hear from Liz to see if her car is alright? I gave her and Anne a ride home yesterday after you left, apparently something was wrong with it and they couldn't get it to start? I'd ask her myself, but no way to reach her. I could give her a ride back out there. I'm not doing anything today."

"Oh, yeah. It was flooded, so it's fine now. Anne mentioned that you gave them a ride home. How very gentlemanly of you. Liz told me that if I talked to you to tell you thank you and apologize for her attitude." The elephant in the room still wasn't dancing.

"I'm glad everything's ok with her car. What else did Anne say? I noticed something going on between you two at the movie. Not sure if I know for sure the problem, but I don't want to be the cause of any problems between you and your friends."

"Well, Anne and I used to be good friends, but we aren't that close anymore." Laurie trailed off.

"She kissed me and invited me in for a soda as a thank you for the ride," Mike said, oversimplifying the situation. "I turned her down. I had fun hanging out yesterday, but I felt like I needed to go. Turns out I had forgotten to turn on my phone after the movie. My aunt and uncle were worried about me because I was so late getting back. I knew that there was something I'd forgotten."

"It's a good idea you did go home right away." She brightened up considerably. "You shouldn't worry your aunt like that. She is a wonderful woman." Laurie teased, giggling again like she had on the voicemail the day before. "She talked non-stop the last couple weeks of school about how exciting it would be to have you come visit and how she thought we should meet."

"I'm glad we did. Don't forget to give me a call later in the week and we can figure out what to do on Friday night, ok?" *"What am I going to do the next time I see Anne?"* Mike pondered.

"Sure. I should probably get going now anyway. I have choir practice this afternoon and then have to work tonight. Talk to you soon, Mike."

Mike repeated the sentiment, hanging up the phone. As he delved back into the book he found his focus wandering. He kept seeing Laurie's face, and hearing her voice. Not like he was replaying their phone conversation. It was more like the litany of thoughts from the movie he realized later sounded like Anne. "I knew he would see through that tramp. She won't fool him. He's too smart for her. It was fun meeting him, would be nice if we get to spend more time together this summer. Mrs. Johnson talked incessantly about how smart he was. She said he might not be going home by September if he ended up liking it out here. She said it would be great if we hit it off, and so far I think so too." This repeated a few times before being interrupted by the crunch of gravel from out front of the house. Mike shook his head as if to clear it from what he thought he was hearing. *"Things are definitely getting weirder by the day. Maybe I should call Darrell. He should be able to help me make sense of things. Can I tell Darrell everything else without telling him the truth about Kevin?"* Mike shuddered at the thought of the conversation.

The shutting of the truck doors signaled the arrival of his relatives. *"Did I hear what I thought? Does Aunt Jenny want me to stay? Is it because of Prom? Mom could have said something about it and maybe that's why Aunt Jenny is pushing me to make friends so hard. She's planning on pitching the idea of me staying as well."* Mike got up, considering how much convincing he will need to stay. A brief bout of sadness at leaving his sister and mother behind made him regret considering staying.

Mike dropped his book on the kitchen table as he saw Uncle Jim coming in the front door, his arms laden with plastic bags. As Aunt Jenny put them away inside, Mike and Uncle Jim made a couple trips in and out. They soon had everything in the kitchen on the counters and table.

"Did you have a good morning?" Aunt Jenny asked, putting canned goods into a cupboard. "Laurie called this morning before she went to church. Was she able to get hold of you?" She stopped for Mike's response, watching his reaction. Mike wondered just how much Laurie said and if the Anne situation was going to cause problems at home. Mike was certain he knew which side his aunt fell on.

"I just spent the morning reading on the back porch," Mike replied, trying to be as casual about it as possible. "She called back. We hung up just a little bit before you two got home. She said something about choir practice and then working tonight. We're thinking about going out on Friday night with Deb and Chad, but no idea what we are doing yet or if the two of them are free. Do you think that would be alright with you and Uncle Jim?"

"That should be fine," Aunt Jenny said, smiling. "I'm glad you two hit it off. Her mother and I have been friends since we were little girls and I just knew that you two would get along."

"Uncle Jim said something about you two going way back." Mike handed cans over to her from a bag on the table. "She is really sweet, Aunt Jenny. I'm glad you introduced us. I think we will get along well this summer. Who knows, maybe she will want me to stick around when summer is over. That might not be too bad." Aunt Jenny dropped the can she was holding, but quickly caught it after it hit the countertop once. Mike laughed and they continued working for another minute in silence.

"So, have you thought about what you want for your birthday dinner on Wednesday?" she asked next, barely able to suppress her enthusiastic smile.

It told Mike all he needed to know about Aunt Jenny's feelings. Not having any children of her own, this summer must have really appealed to her. Mike knew he would have to be careful with this decision because it would probably hurt his mother deeply. Thinking about Laurie, it occurred to him he had had no visions of the future in some time, and certainly nothing dire about spending time with Laurie, like had happened with Colleen. The only case being the brief flash reminiscent of his previous vision, except Colleen was replaced with Laurie.

Thinking of his first real love dampened his mood a little. He puzzled over the almost tangible responses to both Laurie and Anne when he never felt quite the same about Colleen. It wasn't because he didn't love Colleen, of that Mike is sure. What he wondered is what the difference between his feelings for Colleen and his recent introductions to Anne and Laurie really meant. Every time Mike considered confronting his aunt and uncle about what was happening to him, in light of the conversations he had overheard, something stopped him. The warning to Aunt Jenny paralyzed his tongue.

"Not really, but maybe we can go out?" Mike replied to her question after his silence went on too long. "That way you don't have to cook anything and Uncle Jim and I won't have to do dishes."

"That sounds like a splendid plan," Uncle Jim said, joining the conversation from the living room where he had turned on an afternoon baseball game. "There is a great steakhouse in town. You do like steak, don't you?"

"Of course." Mike chuckled at the odd question. "Who in our family doesn't? Does this place have a good loaded baked potato to go with it?"

"That they do, and you might even meet a cute waitress." He laughed, but then fell silent. His team came up to bat and he put all of his focus on the screen. Mike refilled his glass of tea and grabbed an apple from the counter before heading in to watch the game with him. Mike brought along the book just in case the game ended up being less than riveting.

Before long both uncle and nephew were yelling at the umpire, the batter, the pitcher, the coaches, and whoever else they felt wasn't doing the proper job on the field. When the game finally ended, Uncle Jim was pleased his team won by two runs.

During the last few innings, Aunt Jenny provided burgers, hotdogs, and fries. "Ballpark food" she called it. Everyone shared a laugh when Uncle Jim asked for a bag of peanuts to go with it.

Mike's trip into the kitchen to get a refill of tea was interrupted when Uncle Jim called out, "Would you bring me one of those beers from the bottom of the fridge? You can have one if you like, I won't tell your mother." After a moment, "Ouch Jenny, that one hurt," he continued as she gave him a punch in the arm. Mike didn't take the beer himself but grabbed one for Uncle Jim before returning to watch the second game. One of the teams was in the same division as Uncle Jim's favorite team, so all three of them spent the next several hours rooting against the rivals. Despite the constant yelling at the umpire to tell him he was blind, the game ended in a victory for the wrong team. After a Sunday night TV movie, everyone turned in for the night. Tomorrow started another work week.

***

A slightly timid knock brought the old man from his reading with a start. He must have been very close to nodding off as he reviewed the

63

ancient tome on his lap. Mentally marking the page in his mind, he closed and placed it on the table next to him before waving the door open with his hand. As he suspected, his son stood on the other side. No members of the staff would dare knock on his door unless it was life or death. They would normally be so worried about it that he would know they were coming before they knocked anyway. Not so with his progeny. "What brings you here tonight, Damien?" the old man asked softly.

"Mr. Johnson's nephew," Damien began, to which his father nodded, knowing that his son had been watching his target for a week in preparation for however he was going to approach him. "He seems to know nothing at all. I was only able to briefly scan his mind when he was out from under that infernal shield for work and Saturday when he was away from his uncle, but it seems like he is oblivious of his abilities even if he has been using them somewhat sporadically. Mr. Johnson is also doing his best to shield his nephew as well. I do not think he has caught on to my spying, but only because he is very limited in his capabilities."

"That secrecy is the way of their family," Leonard Mauston confirmed, glad the fact had not been lost on his son. It was what the older man hoped would allow a chance of success in this plan. Letting a boy go recruiting for the High Council seemed like insanity without the target's lack of knowledge taken into account. Even if that boy doing the recruiting was his own. "That is why the Council feels that it would be best if someone his own age approached him. You could relate to him better than any of us could. We would approach as a teacher, or mentor, where you can approach as a friend. A young man just coming into his powers with the type of family he has, would go to a friend before he would approach a teacher outside of his uncle. You will have to be very careful regarding his upbringing. Surely you must turn him against the restrictions of his family, but push too hard too fast and you may end up sealing him away from us. You must also remember that you and your abilities cannot cross the shield. So you will have to draw him out and away from his family."

"Yes, Father." Damien smiled. "I have a few ideas on that, but of course I will have to wait to approach him away from his uncle the first time. I think it will confuse him to be confronted with a peer who can wield the powers he is just coming into. In that moment of confusion I will be able to plant the seeds of doubt that will have us best friends before summer's end." Damien appeared pleased with his plan, as simple as it really came out to be. The High Council had already considered the same process, the elder Mauston thought to himself. Leonard merely nodded and his young progeny departed the room with steps lightened in the wake of his father's apparent approval.

Chapter 6

With only two days left until his birthday, Mike spent all day replaying the conversation overheard the night before between his aunt and uncle. His head hurt trying to process what the two of them said. He was not totally mollified by the assurance that it would all sort itself out on his birthday. *"What is happening to me,"* he thought as he worked through a stack of invoices his uncle asked him to file on Monday afternoon. Mike felt himself getting angry several times as he thought about how everyone was sneaking around and not talking to him. The only thing that kept him from confronting them was the fear that perhaps he was going crazy and that they would lock him away.

Halfway through the afternoon, his mind made a jump his distraction kept him from making sooner. "If Uncle Jim knows so much, what if he is like me?," Mike asked aloud to the filing cabinet. "What if he can hear things that no one says out loud? Or can predict the future as well?" The possibilities spinning in Mike's head pulled his focus and the filing took much longer than it should have. His uncle didn't comment on the drive home, but he seemed tenser than the previous week. Uncle Jim's near silence extended the rest of the night.

Mike's thoughts pushed sleep away for a long time. When he finally succumbed, he found himself right back on the same forest path he had walked many times over the last month and a half. This time, Mike ran toward the clearing ahead, hoping the dream wouldn't take him away too soon. The shadowy, moonlit trees passed by on either side, sometimes close enough to force Mike to shift slightly to one side or the other of the path to avoid colliding with the edge of one. Mike almost tripped several times on roots that crisscrossed the path. He managed to keep his feet and get to the clearing without taking a tumble.

As he stepped into the clearing Mike went straight for the shadowy figure. The figure appeared translucent as Mike crept into the clearing, trying to avoid making any noise. The dancing light of the bonfire flames shifted and twisted along its shape. Mike reached out, and grabbed the arm of the figure, intent on finding out exactly who or what haunted this dream. When it spun around, Mike found himself face to face with his uncle. In shock Mike stepped backward, tripping over his own feet. His arms pinwheeled uselessly as he crashed to the ground. His head exploded in pain before everything fell into darkness.

Mike sat bolt upright in bed to the sound of the alarm buzzing. Based on the time it had just gone off, coinciding exactly with his crash in the dream. Turning it off, he grabbed his glasses and laid in bed a minute. Heart racing and head pounding, Mike lightly touched the back of his head. His fingers came away with a small spot of tacky, nearly dried blood. *"Clearly the dream ended long before the alarm, right?"*

Mike jumped out of bed, shocked to see a small spot of red on his pillow, barely the size of a dime. He immediately flipped the pillow over and made the bed in an attempt to give Aunt Jenny no cause to come into the room today. He also checked to be sure there were no dirty clothes on the floor. Grabbing clothes for work, he went for the shower. Someone stirred in the kitchen but Mike wanted a shower before facing anyone.

"It had to be my imagination. Why else would Uncle Jim be in my dream?" He tried to put it out of mind as the hot water washed away the blood. He stared downward, the water hitting the back of his head. Shock rolled through him when he spotted a leaf stuck in the shower drain. Shutting down the shower he retrieved the leaf and flushed it down the toilet. How he managed to bring the leaf out of his dream he didn't want to contemplate.

***

"Well, he can definitely dream walk," Jim said to his wife as they dressed for the day. "Or, if he can't, my imagination is getting the better of me. It was so vivid."

"Well," Jenny started, looking at herself in the mirror over their dresser, "You two just be careful on your little jaunts into dreams. I remember some pretty real bruises and marks you came back with from time to time before you got control of it. And even after you did."

"Most certainly honey," he replied. "I am so excited for him though. Able to dream walk is at least one ability I know enough about to help him for sure. I was worried what it might be that I had to teach and that they might be something from the book that I have no ability with." She patted his arm as they exited the room together towards the kitchen.

As she started to get breakfast ready and he retrieved the morning paper, they heard their nephew slip into the shower on his end of the house. Jim quietly tiptoed down the hall and looked in the room Mike had just vacated. Everything sat neat and orderly, but given Jim witnessed his nephew's fall, he walked over to the bed to see if any physical signs show. Flipping the pillow over, he found his confirmation in the mark left by a wound to the back of his nephew's head. He quickly replaced it as it was and returned to the kitchen.

***

Showered and dressed, Mike came out to breakfast. His uncle continued his recent silence all through breakfast and the ride to work. Several times Mike wanted to ask, but something about Uncle Jim's expression held him at bay. As the day wore on their interactions were strictly formal and businesslike. *"It had to be my imagination seeing Uncle Jim in my dream."*

By lunch Mike was sure Uncle Jim knew at least some of what was going on, and was fighting desperately with his conscience not to say anything. The discussion Mike overheard regarding some warning about telling him anything replayed in his mind. *"Well, in less than twenty four hours it will all be over,"* Mike guessed. The weather outside turned progressively worse as the sky darkened and clouds rapidly rolled in around lunch time. The overcast sky quickly threatened rain. Around the time everyone started to return to work, the heavens let loose with a heavy thunderstorm. Mike stood looking out the small window in the file storage room, staring at the lightning. The patter of rain on the building brought to mind the smells and dampness he felt in his dream the last few times.

Suddenly the dream came roaring back, clearer and sharper than ever. Mike could see the dancing flames of the bonfire in the clearing ahead and can almost feel the heat from them even at the distance he was. In his head he knew he was in the filing room, briefly wondering if he fainted and hit his head again like at school. Instead of being daylight, the dream began as it always did with moonlight and darkness. The shadowy figure was gone, at least as far as Mike could tell from his current position. Mike started toward the fire again as always, before stopping and looking around. A split-second decision caused Mike to turn away from the clearing and follow the trail at his feet away from the flames. As it wound through the woods Mike soon spotted a different sort of light up ahead. The red and orange dance of the bonfire was replaced by a steady yellow glow. The light hung several feet above the ground.

As Mike closed the distance to the light, he could make out the shape of the side of a house. *"Is that my aunt and uncle's?"* Mike pressed on, seeking an answer he already knew. The light came from one of the windows belonging to his aunt and uncle's bedroom. Looking around Mike tried to determine exactly where the trail exited the forest. He turned and retraced his steps back into the woods. As the bonfire came into view, Mike woke up to a particularly loud thunderclap that rattled the office building. Having not fallen at all, he found himself leaning against one of the metal cabinets; it and the wall having held him up through his daydream. The dream hadn't occurred during the day in weeks, but his decision to backtrack instead of going straight for the fire felt right. Confident he could find the trail from the back of the house if he had to, Mike shook off the remnants of the vision. Knowing that the trail led to his uncle's house seemed to cement for Mike that his uncle could more than clear up the situation Mike was in. Quickly finishing the stack of vendor slips that he had to file, Mike went to look for his uncle.

Between the heavy rain and the lightning strikes, the day for the work sites ended early and everyone began to trudge home. Uncle Jim called it a day and everyone in the office headed home as well.

After being almost ignored the whole day, Mike wanted to confront his uncle on the ride home. Deciding to be a little more circumspect, he asked, "Uncle Jim, is everything alright? You seem a little upset today. This doesn't have anything to do with this weekend, does it? I will remember to turn my phone on next time."

Uncle Jim shook his head and smiled for the first time all day. "I was a lot less worried than your Aunt. I figured you would call if you were in trouble," Uncle Jim confessed.

Mike's mind swirled, considering his uncle's words and recent conversations. His thoughts interrupted when his uncle spoke again.

"So, you and Laurie got along well Saturday?" Uncle Jim asked a moment later, changing the direction of conversation rather blatantly. He seemed genuinely interested in what Mike had to say however, waiting intently for a response.

Mike figured if his uncle was going to put it behind them, then Mike would for now as well. The overheard promise of revelation on his birthday rang in the back of Mike's mind. Tomorrow would be the day that settled everything one way or the other. "Yeah. She's very nice and we're still planning to go out on Friday night with a couple friends of hers. I am glad that Aunt Jenny introduced me to her."

"She's a sweet girl," his uncle mused aloud, pausing before continuing in a much sterner tone. "I am sure I don't have to say it, but you behave like a gentleman befitting your upbringing, young man." He then laughed at the tone of voice he had adopted for his brief lecture.

"Of course, Uncle Jim." Mike chuckled at his uncle's attempt at playing the stern father figure. "Mom would fly out here and kill me otherwise. Then you would have her to deal with." Thinking about his mother, Mike remembered the broken promise to her regarding Colleen. The memories of Colleen spiraled up to take over Mike's mind until his uncle's voice cut through.

"Well, I love my sister very much, but let's just avoid that scenario if we can." Jim laughed again. "I don't think I would want to face her and my wife whenever I stepped a toenail out of line. One is bad enough."

"Good thing Aunt Jenny can't hear you say that." The mood lightened a little. "She would probably get something stronger than her hand to hit you with for that one." His uncle nodded and put his attention back to the rain covered roads for a few miles. They were coming up on a set of flashing lights so he switched lanes and slowed down. They watched an officer assisting someone who hydroplaned off the road.

The ride home failed to improve at all and Uncle Jim drove slower than normal. The two eventually made it home safe and sound. On the count of three they both dove from the truck and ran into the house. The short ten or twenty feet still allowed the rain enough time to drop a good bit of water on their heads. Both came into the house looking a bit like shaggy wet dogs. Aunt Jenny was prepared because she showed up with two towels she just pulled from the dryer. The warmth took the chill from the rainwater soaking their clothes.

"You two look like cats caught in the bathtub," she joked after she handed over the towels. She watched her husband and nephew like a mother hen as they tried to dry off before the cold rain set them to shivering too badly.

"Not that bad for us, Aunt Jenny. We just had the trip from the truck to the porch," Mike replied, wrapping the towel around his head and shoulders, where the dampness was worst. He didn't realize at first just how cold the rain could be, despite the summer temperatures. Even with the warm towel, he shivered. "At least the drive home was dry, since Uncle Jim parked in the garage next to the office building."

She took on a very motherly tone for someone with no children of her own. "Those Canadian rainstorms they send down here are like ice water when they hit. You go get changed and warmed up before the chill sets in your chest and you get sick. That goes for you too," she finished as she gave her husband a shove towards their hallway.

Like dutiful children they both went straight to change into drier clothes. When they returned from their respective rooms, Aunt Jenny was busy in the kitchen preparing something. Though too early to tell what she was making, it would probably be as delicious as always. Not wanting to get in her way, Uncle Jim motioned to the living room where he and Mike caught an afternoon rerun while keeping out of sight. At several points they heard Aunt Jenny mumble something about umbrellas and fool men not knowing anything.

"Your aunt means well." Uncle Jim laughed softly. "She's been happier this last week than I have seen her in a long time having a third here to cook for. Now she gets to fuss over both of us, instead of just me."

Mike laughed with him. "That's good to know." They settled into the shows until it was time for supper. Conversation remained light during dinner. Mike, unable to read his uncle's mood, just left things alone.

"I called and made a reservation for about six at the restaurant," Aunt Jenny said later while the three were seated around the dining room table. "You two think you can manage to be home and ready to go by quarter after five?"

"Shouldn't be an issue," Uncle Jim replied between mouthfuls. "Can't think of anything that would keep us. Can you?" He then looked to his nephew.

"No," Mike commented slowly, as if thinking over a busy schedule in his mind. "I think six will work just perfectly Aunt Jenny. Excellent choice."

"Did you manage to get our favorite booth?" Uncle Jim asked, giving his nephew a mischievous look as he posed the question to his wife. Uncle Jim transitioned back to his normal self.

"Yes. I did." She broke into a wide smile. "You will really like this place, Mike." The conversation drifted off a little as everyone dug into the meal before them. Afterwards everyone retired to the living room for the usual evening television. His aunt and uncle headed to bed before ten, but since Mike didn't feel that drowsy, he sat up reading for a bit. Sometime around eleven, Mike closed the book and turned out the reading light. Tomorrow was another work day and he couldn't stay up all night. Sleep comes swiftly.

Chapter 7

Minutes later, Mike awoke to the sound of the sliding glass door rolling open. He waited to hear any conversation. After a moment it closed and the house fell silent. Fearing someone may be inside or that his uncle had gone outside to investigate something, Mike slowly got out of bed. He slipped on a long sleeve shirt and jeans. He sat down softly on the bed to put on his socks and shoes before heading into the hall. A gut feeling told him to be fully dressed for whatever he found outside of his room. The Darkness stirred in the depths of Mike's mind, anticipating violence of some sort.

Mike crept down the hall, watching for movement or lights from the far end of the house. All Mike could think about was focusing on remaining silent and unheard by anyone lurking in the shadows. A check of the readout on the microwave reveals the time was not quite one in the morning. *"Happy Birthday to me, I guess."* Mike reached the sliding doors that led to the back porch.

Mike grabbed the handle and paused, waiting a full minute. Hearing no other sound but his shallow breathing, he mentally prayed for the door to be as quiet as possible. He began opening it slowly. When it slid quickly and silently all the way open, Mike nearly fell forward onto the back porch. Catching himself on the doorframe, he took a steadying breath. Mike carefully closed the door, making sure it didn't slam shut.

Mike froze on the back deck, waiting for his eyes to adjust further to the moonlight. The moon was nearly full and lit up the back yard area well enough. From the porch he could tell there was a light on in the corner window, similar to the one from his afternoon daydream. Mike followed it with his eyes to the edge of the woods, where it barely lit a break in the trees he failed to notice the last week.

Treading softly to the steps that lead down to the ground, Mike headed in the direction of the path. Using the light as a guide, he soon found himself in the forest, following a small footpath fairly well used and with obvious recent activity. There were a few boot prints in the soft earth made since the rain today. They were large, and given their proximity to the house, Mike hoped they belonged to his uncle. Mike gave a relieved sigh when he didn't see any other tracks.

Walking for what must have been almost twenty minutes, Mike began to see a flickering light ahead in the woods. In the trees around him, he noted familiar shapes from the dream. The stark pale moonlight bathed the forest as he started for the clearing lying ahead. The closer Mike got, the more he sees a shadow move in front of the flames. *"No chance I am sneaking up on whoever that is,"* Mike told himself with a shrug. The Darkness laughed in the background. In Mike's moment of confusion, It stole control. Mike became a passenger as his body crept through the forest, silent as a stalking wolf.

There, next to the fire, stood his relative. Uncle Jim wore one of his flannel shirts, facing towards the flames, a long stick in his hand. He poked at the fire. The wet ground must have made building the fire a difficult chore. *"What is he doing out here?"*

The Darkness forced Mike to stalk resolutely towards his uncle. Uncle Jim seemed oblivious to the presence of his nephew. Mike stepped on a twig, the sound comparable to a gunshot in his ears. Uncle Jim never budged except to poke at a log in the fire threatening to fall over and roll away, as its neighbors underneath were consumed by the flames. Soon, Mike stood right behind him. Mike wrestled with the Darkness as it raised a clenched fist as if to strike Uncle Jim. Instead, Mike reached out and grabbed his uncle's arm. Uncle Jim startled, spun around and raised the stick he held into a defensive position like a swordsman.

Wild eyed, Jim stared at his nephew a moment before speaking. "Mike." He took a breath before continuing, "You just about gave me a heart attack. How on earth did you get out here?"

"I have been walking to this clearing for over two months in my dreams, although I never knew why," Mike replied, his voice more calm and assured sounding than he felt. The Darkness still held the lion's share of Mike's functions, but looking his uncle in the eyes began to turn the tide. Mike's heart raced, the answers to everything would, hopefully, soon be revealed.

"You were dream-walking that far back? And to this very clearing?" Jim looked at him questioningly. Mike shrugged and nodded, not really knowing if his uncle meant what it sounded like he meant. "Then you really were here the other night when I thought I saw you. You disappeared so quickly I wasn't sure if it was my imagination getting the better of me or not. The blood stain on your pillow made me think for sure it really was you. I bet you have a lot of questions. First, I have to apologize for the secrecy. I promise it was necessary."

"That would be helpful, Uncle. I really don't understand how I knew about this clearing before I even got to this state, much less had seen your house," Mike snapped, the Darkness put more attitude into the response. With Mike's focus diverted from trying to sneak up to the clearing, all the sounds of the woods at night rushed back as if a bubble encasing him popped. Mike puzzled about this development until Uncle Jim moved away from the fire, lowering the stick he still held.

Mike followed his elder over to a large log on the far side of the fire and sat down. After a minute, it became apparent Uncle Jim was struggling to find the words for where to begin. Mike wondered how his uncle knew about the stain on the pillow.

The Darkness piped up from his subconscious, *"He was spying on you. Lovely how much trust he has in you. Do you think he knows what you did? What you are capable of?"* Mike had read enough fiction novels to have an idea the implications of what "dream-walking" meant. He wondered briefly if he should tell his uncle about the leaf that he had brought back as well.

"Shut up." Mike made an effort to wrench complete control back from the Darkness. Impatient now, Mike turned to his uncle, "Why don't we start with this family heritage I don't know anything about?" His voice heated instead of cold and emotionless like before. He breathed deep, awaiting some sort of reprimand for the forceful tone. Mike didn't want to upset his uncle but he had been driving himself crazy the last few months. To have his uncle referring to the event so casually made Mike angry and the Darkness rose to the bait.

Uncle Jim's crestfallen expression calmed the edge of Mike's sudden rage. "So, you heard that part too, I guess," Jim replied softly, looking at his nephew. *"It would make sense he had really heard it all,"* Jim thought to himself. "Ok. Well, our family, the men in the family that is, have almost always been gifted with abilities and senses that are far beyond those of the average person. Everything is not great news however, we're also cursed by these gifts."

"Wait. Cursed?" Mike interrupted. This business of 'gifts' would certainly explain all the weird things that had happened over the last couple months. Dream walking, the déjà-vu incidents at school, and the hearing of thoughts lately must be these gifts Uncle Jim meant. *"Did that mean he could hear my thoughts all along?"* Mike worried internally. He stared at his uncle, awaiting clarification on the curses as well. Mike's first thoughts became filled with the stories of those who claimed to be cursed by disturbing some Egyptian tomb. Strange wounds, lingering diseases and suffering, before death finally came to claim the offender.

"Yes, but I haven't experienced anything horrific like some of the stories your grandfather told me when I was your age," Jim continued. "I think he was just trying to scare me though. It has been blamed on a freak mutation in my genes, but I can't have children. Your grandfather said that it has happened before, and then everything just passes to the next male in the family, usually through any sisters or brothers that the first born male has."

"Ok." Mike tried to piece things together. "So, this is happening to me, why? Because Mom is your only sibling, so it passed to me? Where did this come from? Why couldn't anyone have told me this the past few months so I didn't think I was going crazy."

"That is a little harder to explain," Jim began thoughtfully, searching for where to begin. "I'm going to tell this as quickly as possible. The story goes that the men in our family were the shamans of a tribe in Europe, back in the days before there were the countries they have now. Throughout the centuries, they used their abilities to help their clan survive and prosper, but never becoming tyrants over their neighbors. Eventually, as the tribes of Europe were assimilated or destroyed by one empire or the other, we went into hiding. Our family hid its gifts from those in charge of these great armies, for fear they would be used improperly. Things were much simpler when you were a respected shaman of a small tribe. Once larger military powers with rulers got involved, there was always a danger of unintended consequences across a much larger scale. The abilities also seemed to wax and wane, sometimes becoming so minimal that it seemed that they were dormant for a generation or two." He paused, watching his nephew's reaction to the story thus far.

"Then it became necessary to hide from the Roman Catholic Church because it would have persecuted them as witches and heretics, as well as the fears of the Inquisition in Spain. Eventually our family fled to the Americas, but before you ask, we settled in the South, not in Salem. We weren't involved in that little debacle even though not all of our ancestors were as noble in the use of their gifts as others had been in the past. At times it became necessary to use them in order to survive in the world."

"So no one really knows where this came from then?" Mike asked, starting to line up the immense span of history his uncle condensed into such a short narrative. To hear so casually that he was descended from a tribal shaman, possibly a witch doctor or wizard of sorts, seemed to be right out of a fantasy tale. "And what do you mean by using them to survive? What did they do?"

"Well," Jim paused a few breaths. "The gifts are always changing. Apparently you can dream walk like I can. You also can move things, although you probably didn't realize it when you did it. Some of the other gifts that have shown up from time to time are a little direct in what they can do to other people. Even to the point of controlling them."

"The salt and pepper shakers," Mike interrupted again in his excitement. "I knew they were next to you, but I have no idea how they got over next to me that night at dinner. There were times before when I thought something like that was going on. Do you think my trips out to this clearing are somehow because of your dream-walking?"

"Yes. Those are both manifestations of your gift. Although it is usually more erratic and unpredictable before your eighteenth birthday, which is when you are able to more actively control it. I have to caution you though with the dream walking. What happens in your dreams can hurt you in the real world, as I am sure you are aware of by now."

"I did sort of figure that out, although I didn't know why it happened." Mike rubbed the back of his head, remembering the wound from the other night. "Can things be brought back from a dream?"

"I have only ever brought back scrapes and bruises. There are stories of our ancestors being able to bring food or medicines back from the dream world in order to help themselves or others. Why do you ask?"

"The night I fell, I brought a leaf back. It was stuck in my hair. The dream started out almost black and white, but it got stronger and clearer as time went on. Especially the last week. Is that because of being near your dream walking?"

"It's possible your gift was reaching out to mine. I often come out here physically and just sit with nature. If I cannot for some reason, I usually am out here in my dreams. That night you startled me, I was trying to figure out if there was anything I could do to help you understand, how to tell you what is happening. Dream walking, and a small amount of moving things around with telekinesis, is just about all I have as gifts. But since I am the only member of the family able to, it falls to me to help you through this adjustment."

Mike relayed the strange things that happened at school in the weeks leading up to the accident: the test tube in Chemistry class, the chalkboard, knowing things before the teacher could say them.

Uncle Jim smiled. "Perhaps you have a bit of the foretelling that your grandfather had. He always knew before your mother and I did anything that we were going to get in trouble for it. He often would stop us on our way out the door and warn us before we even knew ourselves where we were going. Not that we listened all the time. From the conversations I had with your mother, it certainly seemed like your gifts were leaning in that direction."

"So how do I control it?" While Mike certainly wouldn't mind avoiding trouble, the visions had thus far proved unpredictable, so they were not very helpful for basing any long-term plans on. For the moment, Mike shelved the revelation that his mother knew all along what was wrong with him.

"Well, that I can help with," his uncle replied, reaching into his shirt pocket and taking out a small object, a chain dangled from his fist. He pressed it into his nephew's hand, a small metal disk with a swirling pattern on it. The metal felt cool and the Darkness inside Mike reacted violently. The ensuing internal struggle for control caused Mike to drop the necklace.

Uncle Jim leaned down and picked up the pendant. He hung it around Mike's neck before continuing, "This was your grandfather's. He gave it to me to give to you, should you manifest the gifts. He wanted badly to be around to see you grow up, but sometimes the flesh is weaker than the spirit. He said that there used to be many of these pendants in our family. Over the centuries, it appears they were lost and we only have two. Yours and mine. I was told that at one point there was someone who knew how to make things with some raw materials and their will. Sadly, no one seems to remember how in a very long time." Jim checked his watch, "It is almost your exact birthday."

Mike eyed the necklace, not sure what his uncle meant. A flash brought to mind his mother telling Mike he was born very early in the morning. Mike recalled her saying that he was going to be an early riser because apparently he couldn't wait until morning to be born. "So what does this do?" Mike ran a finger across the pattern stamped into the metal. It felt familiar to him but at the moment he couldn't place why.

"It will help you to control your powers after they fully manifest," his uncle replied. "When mine first came to me, I got a little vertigo because your senses get much sharper. It is something very different to find that you can see much better than even a person with supposed 'perfect vision'. I had never worn glasses, but it was a big adjustment for me nonetheless. You probably won't need your glasses, and I am sure it will be a bigger change for you. I'm sure you remember the story of me falling off that tractor and getting my leg run over by the trailer. That was when my gifts actually kicked in." He laughed slightly as Mike reached up and took his glasses off. He looked at them with the world more than a foot away from his face going blurry like it always did when he took them off.

Mike wondered what life would be like without them, given his uncle's example. As he sat there staring at the glasses, his uncle watched, clearly amused. Suddenly, Mike felt the necklace go cold even through the shirt he was wearing. Immediately, the ground and his glasses came into sharp focus and sprung towards his face. Flinching back, Mike reacted instinctively to the errant thought that he was falling forward and ended up crashing backwards off the log when he tried to correct his motion.

Before Mike could even attempt to catch himself, a sensation like floating took him just an inch or two from the ground. Then he noticed the slight pressure on his back and legs as if someone held him in a cradling position. Mike looked to his uncle whose his brow was wrinkled up and his eyes squinted. Soon Mike was sat upright on the log again and the invisible hands of air let go. Uncle Jim took several deep breaths before grinning at his nephew.

"It is much easier to move inanimate objects than it is to move people, at least for me. Your grandfather was capable of picking both of us up into the air several feet, but he could tell me nothing of dream walking. That particular talent I had to learn from my grandfather, as well as by experimenting on my own. You can do both of the things I can do, so at least I can help you to learn to control those abilities. However, you must understand that using your gifts will drain you physically. Those headaches you had been getting were from your powers waking up. A headache will seem like a walk in the park if you overdo it now that you are eighteen. Do too much too soon, and you may find yourself unable to even move. Push it beyond that, and you could end your own life. This is of the utmost importance. Do not push blindly beyond the boundaries I set. Certainly be careful of doing anything when we are not together for me to help guide you. Most importantly is to do nothing without that pendant on, and if possible, touching your skin. It will help immensely."

"The headaches were because of this? And you are saying that I could kill myself by using these gifts? That sounds just lovely," Mike replied a bit too flippantly. Mike could feel a bit of the anger and darkness rising within. The Darkness chimed in, softly and as if from behind a closed door, *"He has no idea what you are capable of. Get rid of that silly pendant and let me show you your powers."* Mike shook his head, finding it easier to silence the Darkness at the moment. *"The warning is only to protect me. Uncle Jim has lived with his for his entire life."*

"You should be fine as long as you have the pendant on. It should pull you back from overextending yourself. As you gain in knowledge and experience in the use of your gifts, it will become second nature to protect yourself," Uncle Jim continued. "I know this is a lot to absorb at one time, but it is imperative I explain things so that no harm comes to you. Your mother would probably kill me if something did. Which reminds me, I talked to her a couple times this past week. She hasn't been very excited about you continuing the family legacy." He paused as if to say something more, but fell silent.

"She hasn't mentioned anything to me when I talked to her." Mike's anger rose again over all the secrecy. He could feel the Darkness reaching out to take control. "Someone could have warned me what was happening. I thought I was going crazy with this dream and odd things moving when I didn't remember moving them physically. Not to mention the fortune telling, or rather, doom foretelling."

"If we had," Uncle Jim started, "you would not have been protected like you were and now by that talisman. If you have assured knowledge of your abilities before your eighteenth birthday, they can overwhelm you for some reason. Even if you suspect what is going on, as long as a member of your family doesn't directly tell you, then for some reason you are shielded from causing any real harm to yourself or others. That's why it has manifested as your little excursions here into the woods, then the moving of the shakers on the table. I suspect that the radio stations in your aunt's car are also a manifestation of your powers acting without you even realizing it. Not all generations of our family were so lucky to know this and some very nasty things have happened to unfortunate young men. Believe me, I was angry with your grandfather when he finally told me what was going on. At least you weren't on a farm tractor when your powers fully awakened and were sitting in a hospital with a broken leg when you were finally told."

Mike pondered his uncle's words. Something he said scared Mike, the part about being overwhelmed by his powers. *"Is that the anger and darkness that took over when I fought Kevin?"* Mike wondered to himself. *"Should I tell him that I have been fighting it off already? What about what I did to Kevin at school? They closed the case, but what if someone talks."* Thinking about Kevin gave fuel to the Darkness inside, and Mike tried to stamp it down. He found doing so easier, the pendant around his neck went cold again.

"So I can do this dream walking stuff, and I can move things with my mind?" Mike asked, wrapping his mind around the fact that his inheritance in life was some sort of psychic powers. "What about telepathy? Or clairvoyance? Can I really predict the future too, or is it going to be as erratic as the stuff that's happened to me?"

"It is possible." Uncle Jim appeared to turn inward. After a minute, he said, "The only thing I learned to do outside of the dream-walking and moving objects was to build a shield in my mind. It's supposed to keep others from breaking into your mind, but it helps when working with your powers as well. It is sort of a meditation to help you focus. The shielding of thoughts is actually just a mental focus, it has nothing to do with our gifts. It is something that anyone could do with the right attitude and enough discipline or focus. It just is infinitely easier for those of us gifted like we are."

"Well, something else is going on." The talk of thoughts had brought it to mind for Mike. "Just since Saturday really. Or at least, I never noticed it before then. When I was at the mall and again at the movies, I thought I heard someone's thoughts. It happened again Sunday after I hung up the phone with Laurie."

"Were you the subject of their thoughts?" his uncle asked, to which Mike nodded. "That would probably explain why you heard them then. I was told that it is very hard to penetrate the mind of another person. However, it is much easier if you or someone close to you is the subject of the thoughts and the thoughts are particularly strong. While I sometimes catch an errant thought or two, I have no real talent in that area. Be careful though, as you may not hear things you really wanted to know. While your aunt and I were dating I did discover that I could hear her planning things. It ruined a lot of surprises so things were much smoother after she learned to block me from accidently hearing her. Thankfully your grandfather was able to explain it to us both and help in teaching her."

"Well, it turned out to be beneficial I think," Mike said, relieved somewhat that this too was something that was normal in his family. "It looked like there was something going on between Anne and Laurie because of Aunt Jenny pairing me up with Laurie. Anne seemed jealous and intent on getting back at Laurie by flirting with me." Uncle Jim laughed heartily at the tale of being stuck in some weird game of tug-of-war between the two girls. Mike kept back the difference in reactions he experienced. He wasn't ready to discuss the Darkness with his uncle, or Its strange reaction to the girls.

"Women," Uncle Jim began. "If that is your biggest problem, then you will be a lucky young man. So, it would seem that you have inherited a bit more than I did. I don't think I can say that I envy you. Before I forget, this is of the utmost importance. The easiest way to explain it will be to use something you are familiar with. Whatever you do in life and with your gifts will come back to you. If you abuse them or use them to control other people, you may find that you do not like the life that you end up creating for yourself, or what is drawn to you by using your gifts that way. That is, unless you delight in the misery of others, but I doubt that is the case."

"So do unto others and such." Mike recalled how many times his mother used the clichéd "Golden Rule" to teach his sister and him how she wished for them to behave. It was her cautioning that made him naturally against the games of the heart that people often played in high school with each other. It was also probably why Mike had never really gotten close to anyone other than Colleen, which had proved to be a torment all its own. Caution taken too far become isolation. *What am I going to bring on when I get my due for my part in Kevin's death?* Mike considered darkly.

"Exactly. You were always a sharp boy growing up, and certainly became an intelligent young man. I am sure you will figure out how to not get yourself into much trouble. If you have any doubts or questions then I will answer what I can. I know that this sounds kind of silly, but unless there is something your grandfather never told me, you are on your own for the most part once I give you the pendant and show you the few things I can. Most of us have to make our way in the world from that point with whatever life brings before us."

At this point, Mike noticed he still held his old pair of glasses. They weren't necessary now, so he folded them up and hung them from the collar of his shirt like he had seen people do with a pair of sunglasses. "Is it possible that my gifts may have reacted to someone else?" Mike paused a moment, and his uncle waited for some bit of clarification. "I mean, to feel some sort of pull towards a person when they speak or touch you?"

"Well," Jim mused, thinking to himself he had an idea of where this was coming from. "If you mean something other than the natural reaction a young man has to a pretty girl paying attention to him, then yes. It is possible. Your grandfather said he knew the moment he met your grandmother that she was the one for him, because it felt so natural from the moment they met. It was a blind date that mutual friends had set them up on. However, he said it may have been something tied to his ability to foretell the future. He had seen your grandmother in visions long before they had been introduced. It was his description of meeting your grandmother that made it easy for me when I met your Aunt Jenny. I didn't have as strong a feeling about her initially that your grandfather says he did, but I knew that she would be accepting of the abilities in our family. It was difficult when we realized that we could not have any children of our own because the gifts caused my sterility. But, what exactly happened to make you ask about that?"

"I had this feeling of being drawn towards Laurie from the moment she spoke that evening when we got home," Mike said, feeling a little strange talking about this with his uncle. He made a snap decision to just lay it all out there and see what his elder had to say. "It just seemed like a good idea to spend time with her, even though it seemed odd that Aunt Jenny was so insistent. In spite of that odd feeling, I didn't have any problem or rejection of the idea. It felt like a current running from her hand to mine when we were together at the movies. Anytime she looked at Anne though, it was like the voltage got cranked up. Then in the car when I took Anne home, it felt like I was being pulled towards Anne any time she got close to me." Mike stopped himself from telling his uncle about the Darkness.

"I don't know about feeling pulled. The other part sounds a little like what your grandfather described," he began, "And a little like how I felt when I met your Aunt. I took it as a sign she would be accepting of the truth. I didn't feel as anxious about telling her or worry over her rejecting me because of the kind of life I would be opening her up to."

"Maybe it means that Anne wouldn't accept it but Laurie would," Mike commented, partly to himself as he turned to face the flames in the clearing. They sat there for a couple minutes, silently processing the change in not only their relationship but Mike's life. Facing his uncle again, Mike asked cautiously, "So, what do I do now? And you mentioned something about Salem. Do you mean those witch trials we studied in school? Are there others like us?" Mike had almost forgotten about that part of his Uncle's narration.

"That, nephew, is unfortunately true. There are others out there, and they may approach you now that you are fully within your powers. I would be careful. As to what to do now, it is entirely up to you. You have to choose how to use your gifts and live your life. One thing I am sure of, this will be a summer you will never forget." They were both soon laughing at how ridiculous the second cliché of the night sounded when said out loud. "That is part of why I caution you about the use of your powers. It may draw others to you who recognize your gifts. Not all of them will be friendly."

They watched the flames in silence. After a few moments of being lost in his own thoughts, Uncle Jim stood up slowly, stretching. Mike jumped to his feet as well.

"Why don't you grab that bucket over there and help me put this fire out so we can go grab a little sleep before work in the morning." Mike started to walk over and his uncle put a hand on his arm. "No, see if you can move the bucket to yourself. Just visualize in your mind what you want, then concentrate to make it reality."

Mike concentrated on the bucket. He pictured it appearing at his feet, thinking first of the salt and pepper shakers and how they must have moved because he was thinking about them. Suddenly, the bucket sat at his feet, not even a ripple in the water. Mike stared at it a moment, surprised almost to the point of backing away. He felt a subtle change in the pendant, not like a warning, but more like it was augmenting and helping him through what he wanted to accomplish. Mike thought again about everything he had read about the paranormal. *"Perhaps this won't be so difficult as long as I don't end up as some sort of science experiment. Uncle Jim gets to lead a normal life, why can't I?"* Mike wondered to himself. The Darkness whispered, *"Normal is so boring. Let me show you extraordinary."*

Uncle Jim started clapping, snapping Mike from his thoughts. "Now put the fire out, but don't use the water." Mike looked at him, puzzled, but began to catch on a bit. He focused on the fire, picturing just a pile of blackened logs, the flames extinguished. After a moment, the flames subsided and disappeared, leaving a pile of ashes and half burned wood. The talisman around his neck reacted again, acting as a focus and helper in what its bearer was trying to accomplish.

"Excellent, excellent," Uncle Jim kept repeating as he poked at the pile of wood, checking for any smoldering coals. He found nothing that could possibly serve as an ignition source should they leave the fire at that moment. The coals of the fire appeared as cold as a day old campsite. "That is just fantastic, nephew. You have the hang of it already, I think."

"I have read a lot of paranormal books," Mike replied, inwardly glowing from the compliment. "I am a bit of a science fiction geek, so maybe that helped." Mike hoped that was the case, but the pendant seemed to be as helpful as his uncle indicated, although, not in the way Mike imagined when it was explained. Suddenly Mike thought of his grandfather, his smile and calloused hands resting on his shoulders as they awaited a turn at a carnival ride when he was seven. Mike had been scared, but his grandfather told him everything would be alright, and his younger self became filled with confidence. Mike began to feel like that again.

"Probably, but you seem to have quite a bit of raw talent. What you did is a part of telekinesis, but you aren't really moving an object, you are moving air molecules. Your grandfather thought it was a great way to make me think outside the supposed limits on my ability I had put on myself. My preconceived notions of what it meant to have that ability. It took me weeks to actually put out a fire without having to poor water or dirt on it. Once, I got so frustrated I actually made the fire worse and almost burned down the barn where your grandfather was helping me practice. Thankfully he was there and able to stop it before it did any real damage. He said that sometimes, it is not necessary to directly move something, but just to affect the air around it. Like when you fell backwards. To be honest I couldn't lift you with my power. I just made the air thicker underneath you to the point that it lifted you up. It was much easier to compress the air into a small space. I cannot really explain why, but it has always been easier that way for me."

"So, how am I supposed to know if I am pushing my limits?" What his uncle described with the compressed air sounded like what he must have done with the car accident. He wasn't quite ready to share that in case it meant trouble for his friend who he had already inadvertently involved in this. Mike knew he would have to get ahold of Darrell and reinforce his friend's secrecy pledge. He would also have to be more careful in the future. *"Perhaps the pendant would simply shut me off when I went too far. While this would be helpful if I was on the ground and safe, but what if I happened to be in the air, or in danger of something falling on me."* Mike recalled Uncle Jim getting lifted into the air and shuddered inside at the potential fall that would result if he were to fly himself too far off the ground.

"The pendant around your neck should go cold as ice if you are nearing the limits of what your body can handle. If it starts to get hot, then you are in dangerous territory," he explained. "After some practice, you won't need that warning or its protection. You will learn your own limits, and the signals your body will send you when you are using your powers. Do you feel anything at all right now?"

"Not really," Mike said quickly, reaching up to hold the necklace in a hand. Mike didn't mention it felt like the necklace was guiding him. He needed time to process. The pendant was cool, but just a normal metallic cool. Mike felt prompted that it was made of real silver and probably worth a fair amount of money. "Nothing out of the ordinary for a large piece of silver." Uncle Jim raised an eyebrow in his nephew's direction before shrugging and turning towards the house.

"Where had that last part come from? And, why would I have volunteered that," Mike's mind started to swirl with thoughts again.

Mike looked around a moment and noticed his uncle still held the stick in his hand he had been poking the fire with. Focusing on the stick, Mike began mentally pulling it away and causing it to fly up above their heads, thinking about how he had moved the bucket and changing the tactic slightly. Jim whipped back to face his nephew, then looked up at the stick in the forest canopy. Still clasping the talisman in his left fist, Mike spun the stick in the air, causing it to dance and twirl. While he knew it wasn't necessary, Mike felt compelled to actually direct the motions with his outstretched right hand. Jim kept looking back and forth from the stick to his nephew, watching the hand motions and how the stick mimicked them immediately as it floated above the clearing.

As there was no change in the feel of the metal, Mike decided to try something else. He began to mentally pick up the half burned logs from the pile and sent those up to dance with the stick snatched from his uncle. Now the motions became a little more confusing as he tried to switch from stick to log to stick without losing control of any of them. Mike noticed the objects reacting to his thoughts much faster than his hand motions. Soon nothing was left in the pile but ash and a few smaller pieces of wood. His uncle stared wide eyed at the display. Mike thought of the movie he had watched as a kid where Mickey, as a wizard, made a veritable symphony of a castle cleaning itself. Smiling to himself, and really working up to what he was doing, Mike began humming the tune from the movie in his head as he worked.

Every so often a piece of the burned wood would break loose, or some ash would start to fall as the logs and the stick collided, rebounding against each other. Mike, not wanting to get covered with the ash, tried to come up with a solution. Thinking of it like the force field Darrell joked had protected him from the worst of the car crash made it seem easy. Mike, unsure how he came up with it, kept using examples from what he had read or seen. The pendant seemed to coach him in the right way to enact his will into reality as he went along. Tying it into the theory of Uncle Jim's compressed air method, Mike formed a thick shell of compressed air around the two of them and most of the clearing. Mike spared a glance at his uncle's face, whose mouth hung open in amazement at all the separate objects his nephew was controlling. The barrier Mike put up was not lost on the older man either and he studied it almost as much as his nephew over the next few minutes. Even seeing the strength and purpose of what had been erected, Jim couldn't help but flinch as one of the logs bounced off it before returning to its aerial acrobatics.

"How are you doing?" he asked, still staring at the complicated loops and curls Mike sent the wood through. Having noticed the log bounce off the 'shield' he grew more concerned and anxious the longer his nephew's little display went on.

"I honestly don't feel any change in this thing. Maybe I just am not feeling it because I haven't done this before," Mike replied, still clutching the talisman. The multiple objects got easier to handle the longer he continued. He compared it to the story of a conductor directing his first orchestra, the stage fright beginning to melt as he really got into it. The coaching and guidance from the pendant gradually backed off and he is again reminded of his grandfather at the carnival. When they got to the front of the line, and sufficiently buoyed by the older man's faith, Mike stepped up the final steps alone. Last thing he remembered was his grandfather's hand giving a final gentle shove as he moved back to let the next person head up the stairs behind his grandson.

Jim continued to stare from his nephew to the flying debris above their heads. Finally, after several more minutes, Mike shifted everything, the ash blanketing the barrier above them included, into a compact pile by inverting his bubble shield of air and sent it to the ground off to the side. Once done, Mike released his death grip on the necklace and looked to his uncle. The last act had brought back the feel of someone guiding him in how to release the energy that had been coursing through his body, leaving him slightly drained, but still excited about what he had done.

"Well, just be careful nephew. We should head back to the house. I think we can grab another few hours of sleep before we have to get ready for work." He led the way back through the woods. Just before the duo reached the house again, he turned to Mike in the moonlit darkness, "Happy birthday, nephew."

Mike grinned wearily in response, starting to come off the adrenaline rush he had felt in the forest. They crept slowly and quietly into the house and to their respective beds. Mike thought he might never fall asleep, but almost as if he had willed it, sleep came as soon as his eyes were closed. Thankfully it was a dreamless sleep, finally comforted by the thought that the events of the last couple months were not something he had to fear outright. They were a natural part of who he was. Just what that would entail for the rest of his life, Mike still wasn't sure.

***

The old man snapped awake and gazed south out of the window in his study. He had fallen asleep again in his oversized armchair. He paused, reaching out to feel the power being expended from the Johnson's land. "Excellent," he said softly, smiling to himself, "the boy has awakened to his powers." As Mike really built into his orchestra of burned logs, the man's smile became a grim mask of concern at the amount of energy he detected. Shaking his head, he once again reconsidered setting his son on this task. Untrained, this boy was doing better maintaining multiple tasks that would have been troublesome for any new apprentice during the first six months to a year of their training.

The old man wondered whether or not the subject of his study was even aware of his potential, or the excess of power being used in such simple tricks. James Johnson never had near this potential or power, and thought himself safe behind his little shield when it was really the indulgence of the Council that allowed his façade to continue. Leonard pondered this until a knock at the door interrupted him. With a casual and unnecessary flick of his wrist he jerked it open without rising from his chair, revealing his son, frozen in the act of about to knock a second time.

"Father," Damien began, clearly excited about something. "I can feel something happening. It feels like it is coming from the Johnson place. You don't think Mr. Johnson is trying to go against his bargain with the Council do you?"

"You would be partially right son," the old man said, reflecting again on recent decisions regarding his son. "The boy, his nephew, has awakened to his powers and is having a bit of fun I suspect. The task of turning him is yours. No member of the Council will interfere to help or hinder from this moment on. Now, go to your preparations. I have things of my own to attend to." Damien bowed from the doorway and walked away.

The old man, sighing, flicked the door closed with a casual thought. Turning back to the south, he waited as the energy being used subsided abruptly and winked out. Shaking his head at himself, he returned to the book he had been perusing before he fell asleep. If only he could be sure that direct intervention by his own hand would not spell disaster. As it was, no one with the gift of foretelling had been able to determine what would occur when Damien and Mike met.

Chapter 8

The alarm blared way too soon. Without thinking, Mike reached for his glasses as he shut the buzzing off. Grabbing them before opening an eye, Mike slipped the glasses over his ears like countless mornings before. Finally opening his eyes, everything blurred out of focus. Taking the glasses off quickly, everything cleared to the way it should be. Remembering the events of just a few hours ago, Mike set the glasses on the table again. He stared at them for a moment. "I guess I really won't need these anymore," Mike said softly to himself, jumping out of bed to get ready for work.

"Morning Mike, Happy Birthday," his uncle called, echoed by Aunt Jenny from the kitchen. He looked almost as sleepy as Mike felt due to their outing earlier in the morning. Mike joined them in the kitchen after taking a shower to try and wake up. The hot water, while nice, only made him want to go back to sleep instead of get motivated to face the day.

Fussing over something in the kitchen Mike was sure he heard his aunt mutter, "Fool men, up gallivanting half the night when they should have been sleeping."

"Sorry, Aunt Jenny," Mike began, before having to pause to stifle a long yawn. "Some caffeine and I should be as good as new," Mike finished, noticing the big mug in front of his uncle. Normally not a coffee drinker, this morning it smelled like a good idea. Mike perused the small collection of flavored creamers, hoping enough of one will make the coffee tolerable.

"What are you sorry for dear?" she asked, turning to her nephew, looking puzzled.

"You were just talking about us gallivanting off in the night when we should've been sleeping," Mike replied, grabbing a mug from the cabinet and moving to pour a cup of coffee from the pot near the stove. He added a little sugar and liberal amounts of the liquid creamer to the mug until the coffee changed to a light brown color.

"I," she started, but paused for too long. Mike noticed how quiet the kitchen became. She and her husband shared a look before both eyed their nephew. "I didn't say that out loud, but I was certainly thinking it." Her eyes widened a little with realization. "So I can give up any hope of surprising you with anything this summer now, huh?"

"I don't know about that, honey," Jim chimed in. "It seems to be pretty erratic what he does and doesn't hear. Right, Mike?" Jim started laughing and had to put down his coffee mug before he spilled it.

"Definitely," Mike answered quickly. "I need to figure out how to find out which is someone talking and which is thoughts until I get better control over it. I didn't mean to hear anything you didn't want me to, Aunt Jenny."

"It is quite alright dear," she said, smiling at him as she took the fruit she cut up over to the table. "Just caught me a little off guard is all. Your Uncle told me after we got serious that he had trained himself not to listen so that we would actually have to communicate. Sometimes I wonder when he gives me that look like he is up to no good whether he was completely serious or not about the lessons he gave me on shielding my thoughts. It would appear I am going to have to focus and remember everything he taught me now with two of you in the house."

Mike joined them at the table with his cup of coffee in hand. The hot liquid burned a bit going down, but the vanilla taste from the flavored creamer made it palatable. He felt the caffeine jolt hit and was wide awake before time to head to the office. Before leaving the house,

Uncle Jim cautioned it would be best to tell people at the office Mike was wearing contacts if they ask about his glasses.

"Aside from your mom and Jenny, no one else knows about my gifts," Uncle Jim continued. "I think it best to keep it that way about yours as well."

Mike agreed wholeheartedly and failed to stop himself from reaching up to adjust a pair of glasses he didn't wear any longer. *"This will take some getting used to, that is for sure,"* Mike thought to himself. *"I wonder if I have to count Darrell in on the ones knowing about my powers. He certainly knows enough already."*

Mike's new and improved vision became the least of his worries, however. Patting the pendant where it pressed against his skin under his shirt, Mike remembered how it had seemed to help guide him. Hopefully its assistance continued to work as effectively in the future. *"Or you could listen to me instead of that piece of metal,"* the Darkness chimed from deep within Mike's mind. Mike stamped hard on the voice, quieting it.

Just before lunch, Mike felt his cell phone vibrated in his pocket. Glancing at the number, he saw it was home. "Hi Mom," he answered it while he continued to sort the stack of papers on his desk.

"Happy Birthday, sweetheart." Sally's mind rolled in turmoil. Her brother had relayed his breaking the news to Mike earlier that morning. She hoped giving Mike a few hours to process before she called would help him to not be upset with her. "How is your day so far?" The loaded question hung there on the line.

"Just a second, Mom," Mike said, putting his hand over the phone. "Hey Vicky, I am going to take this out in the hallway, it's my mom. I promise I will make it quick."

"Take your time birthday, boy," Vicky replied, chuckling as she punched more numbers into the computer.

Mike slipped out into the hallway where there was little chance of being overheard, "Back. And today has been interesting. Uncle Jim and I had a nice talk this morning really early, then I went back to bed. I guess we have a lot to discuss, huh?"

"I'm sorry it had to be like this honey, but your Uncle knows best with this situation you are in," Sally rushed, trying to keep her worry and fear out of her voice. "I wish your grandfather were here, not that I don't trust my brother to help you, but our father was such a wise man."

"Uncle Jim gave me Grandpa's necklace," Mike stated casually, the thought prompting him to touch the metal through his shirt like he had done often today. Almost to assure himself it was there and he wasn't dreaming. Mike heard his mother sigh, "Look Mom, I'm not upset with you at all for not telling me what was going on. I know Uncle Jim said there are reasons, and I guess I'm ok with having not known before. This way I don't have to face any consequences today."

"I'm worried about you." Sally sniffled, unable to hold back the start of tears. "Your birthday is supposed to be fun and a rite of passage now that you are eighteen, but all this is just more hassle and trouble coming your way."

"Hey, don't worry, Mom. I think this will be just fine. At least now everything makes more sense. Don't be too upset. How is Connie doing in her practices?" Mike made a stab at changing the subject. As much as he wanted to ask his mother about growing up with Uncle Jim's abilities, he doesn't want to press her now when she seemed so upset over Mike's own gifts. All the questioning looks started to make sense. She, and Uncle Jim upon his arrival in Washington, had been waiting for something to happen.

"She is doing well." Sally smiled, thinking about the look on Connie's face when she was accepted to the squad. "She's passed her conditioning for the team and seems to be settling into the group of girls quite well. To hear her tell it, she is going to be running the popular clique since some of the other girls are graduating after this year. She almost is now with Colleen and Kevin gone. She seems very happy." Then she winced, realizing she had brought up two topics she had wanted to avoid since his arrival in Washington.

"Tell her I said congratulations," Mike said, covering the small twinge he felt at Colleen's name. *"Doesn't help that I am the cause of at least one of those,"* Mike thought before continuing. "You haven't heard from Colleen have you? Or has Connie mentioned any of the girls talking about her?"

"No sweetie. I'm sorry," Sally spoke softly. Sally knew that Mike hadn't heard anything back from his attempt to contact her. Her attempts to track down the Nicholson family had met with more dead ends than she thought natural. "I hate to say it honey, because you know how much I adore Colleen, but you might be best to focus on your future. It is obvious she isn't going to be playing a part in it anymore and I'm sorry for you. I know that must hurt."

Wiping away a tear from his cheek, Mike pushed his emotions down inside and found an almost scary calmness waiting for him, in that moment he thought he saw Colleen and her dad in a strange room with a large desk. Shaking his head to clear the image, he replied, "I know, Mom. I've a lot on my plate right now, don't I? I better get back to work, though. Love you, Mom." His mother returned the sentiment and he headed back into the office.

Work passed quickly with only a couple references made about Mike's lack of glasses. Vicky, the middle aged woman who helped with the payroll said he looked better without them anyway, and commented on the resemblance to his uncle. "One would almost mistake you two for father and son if they didn't know better," she remarked before going back to the stack of forms on her desk.

Similar comments were made by several of the other workers who were in and out during the day when they saw the both of them together. Mike had begun to get the hang of things after a week and a half and was mostly being left to his own supervision. As afternoon crept by, Mike could tell Uncle Jim was watching the clock closely. Finally he came out of his office after a lengthy phone call and said he and Mike would be calling it a day since it was Mike's birthday. Vicky called out a last "Happy Birthday" and promised to lock up when she finished with the final invoices from the afternoon mail delivery. The two started home to get ready for dinner out at the steakhouse. As Mike stared at the passing scenery, he resolved to make himself let go of Colleen. He also decided to call Laurie after dinner so they can firm up their plans to meet up. He knew he needed to give Darrell a call too.

***

Aunt Jenny met them at the door, barking orders and hurrying them along to get ready. Though they were earlier than planned, she acted as if it was nearing six o'clock already. About a half hour later all three were heading back out the door and it was not quite five-fifteen. Mike offered to sit in the small backseat of the truck but Aunt Jenny took one long look at him and said, "Nonsense, Mike, you are much too tall to be stuffed back there." Uncle Jim claimed they would all fit in the front and had Aunt Jenny sit in the middle where the console folded up into the seat anyway to make a bench seat. The drive was short and they stood outside the restaurant with more than fifteen minutes to spare.

"Table for three, under Johnson," Uncle Jim stated when they stepped through the door and the hostess looked up expectantly.

"Of course Mr. Johnson, your booth is right this way," she said cheerfully and led the way, menus in hand. It was obvious the couple frequented the restaurant often as several of the servers turned and waved. Or maybe it was because most of them looked to be teenagers and probably knew Aunt Jenny. When they got to the table, the hostess set out the menus. "Your server will be right with you." She retreated back to the front stand.

Aunt Jenny excused herself to go to the ladies room, so the two men slid into the corner booth and Mike began to peruse the menu, knowing already that there would be a steak of some sort, he just didn't know what he wanted with it. Uncle Jim made a comment about women and their bathroom trips. "Not like we didn't just leave the house and all." He laughed and Mike joined in. "If she hadn't been so worried about us, she would have remembered herself I think," he continued after a moment. When she returned, they were both laughing again and she frowned at them.

"Men," she said, giving them a dark look. "Can't take you two out in public it would appear. I guess I'll have to separate you both. Mike honey, hop up and let me sit between you and your uncle. That way I can reach either of you if you misbehave."

Exchanging another look with his uncle, they both chuckled as Mike started to get up. Just as he moved out of his aunt's way, he collided with someone walking towards the table from the other direction. Mike never saw the person coming, but as he spun around to apologize, he came face to face with Laurie. The same feeling of being drawn towards her was stronger this time. It felt like an electric current traveling up from Mike's hand where he had caught hold of Laurie's arm to prevent her from falling.

Mike's first thought was Aunt Jenny tipping her off to them being here so that she could show up. Then he noticed the blouse she wore had the restaurant's name imprinted on it, and she had one of those waist pouches with pockets for straws and napkins. In her hand she held a pad for taking orders and Mike suddenly recalled the comment Uncle Jim made about cute waitresses. It clicked with the remarks

Laurie had made about working at a restaurant and Mike quickly swallowed the jibe he was going to make to his aunt about her matchmaking. Reluctantly releasing Laurie's arm, Mike apologized, knowing his face was more than a little red.

"No problem," Laurie replied, a little breathless from the near tumble. "I'm sure I don't have to introduce myself then," she continued, giggling slightly. "I will be your server tonight. Mr. and Mrs. Johnson, I suppose you will be having your usual drinks and Mike what would you like?" Mike noticed how quickly she got back to business while lingering closer to his side of the booth. The electric pulse subsided with their contact broken, but it seemed to hang around, crackling like a good static charge. Ordering a cola, Mike listened as she went over the specials for his uncle. Since everyone was pretty much ready to order, she waited a moment for Mike to decide on sides to go with the steak and then left to get the drinks and place their order with the cook staff.

Jim laughed after Laurie departed. "See, I told you, you might meet a cute waitress. Smooth move with nearly knocking her over but saving her at the last minute. Romeo could learn a thing or two from you on that one."

Mike felt his face turning even redder, but with a scolding exclamation of his name Aunt Jenny slugged her husband in the shoulder and Mike started laughing. Uncle Jim laughed along. Laurie returned with the drinks.

"Oh Mike," she said after handing out straws, "Deb said she and Chad were thinking of going bowling and to the under twenty-one club on Friday if we wanted to join them. Chad said something about seeing how good you really were at the lanes."

"That sounds great," Mike replied, slowly unwrapping the straw and putting it in the drink in order to have something else to occupy his focus. Mike feared making eye contact because of the strange electric sensation from earlier. If it really meant she would be ok with his, 'gifts', then that was wonderful, but would he really have reason to tell her? And did the sudden upswing in the reaction to her have anything to do with the awakening of the rest of his powers that his Uncle said happened this morning?

"Did you get contacts?" she asked, but then another of her tables waved to her and she left with a hurried, "I'll be back shortly." As she walked away Mike glanced over at her and caught what else he had been trying to avoid; a stray thought, *"That was a silly thing to ask him."* It was Laurie's voice, but now he noticed a distinct echo to the tone that wouldn't have existed had she said the words out loud. Maybe this was how he could tell what was said and not without having to see the person's lips. Mike made a mental note to ask his uncle about it when they are alone.

Mike frowned and muttered to himself as he took a sip of the cold cola. His aunt and uncle gave him a look, clearly expecting some clarification to his sudden darkening of mood. "I was trying not to hear anything other than her spoken words, but it didn't work," Mike whispered softly by way of explanation. They both nodded and things lightened up from there after Aunt Jenny patted her nephew's arm reassuringly.

Uncle Jim whispered, "You can't expect to master everything in less than a day. Don't be so hard on yourself."

During the course of the meal, Laurie and Mike were able to exchange a few words and finalized plans for Friday night. Aunt Jenny assured them both Mike would have use of the car. Her only requirement was to be home by midnight. Since the club usually emptied by eleven, according to Laurie, he would have plenty of time to drop her off at home and be home before midnight.

After dinner, as the trio prepared to leave, Laurie came over to say "Happy Birthday" again and, after a moment's hesitation, gave Mike a quick hug before going off to one of her other tables. Aunt Jenny patted her nephew on the shoulder again as she stepped past and Uncle Jim started chuckling. Leaving a generous tip for their "favorite waitress" he clapped Mike on the back and steered him towards the exit. Mike froze because, in the moment of the hug, a familiar spike in his head came back to him. He saw himself and Laurie kissing with a porch light turning on, startling them. It had to be the first vision since waking up from the accident. To Mike, the pressure in his head was a clear indication of the 'vision' being authentic. Now he wasn't so sure about the replacement of Colleen with Laurie in the other flash being his imagination.

As they piled back into the truck outside the restaurant, Mike's phone vibrated. Not recognizing the number, Mike put the phone back in his pocket. *"Probably a wrong number anyway,"* Mike thought. A minute down the road it vibrated again, the "Voicemail" light flashing. Aunt Jenny gave him an odd look when he replaced it in a pocket and didn't answer it. "Probably a wrong number, I didn't recognize it when it went off before," Mike replied to her questioning gaze. At this she shrugged and they rode home mostly in silence, the radio the only sound providing competition for the engine and other cars.

***

Having observed what he could of Mike and the Johnsons when they went out for dinner, Damien was pleased to note the lack of confidence that Mike had shown. Unlike his friend Derek, Damien held no delusions those with power should be ruling openly, there were too many ways they are vulnerable to people who would be scared or envious of their gifts. In Damien's opinion it was too much hassle to rule openly. He would rather be left mostly alone. Damien shook off his

105

musing and turned his focus towards his plan. Since it appeared Mike was going to be away from his Aunt and Uncle on Friday night, it provided a perfect way to insert himself into his peer's life.

Unknown to Damien, Mike had another observer during his evening out. Derek had cloaked himself in shadows and watched the newcomer as well. Derek recognized Laurie as one of the girls he had briefly toyed with when he went to public school, "To show him how the other side lived" as his father had put it. *"What a colossal waste of time that turned out to be,"* Derek mused as he felt Damien shift away from the area. Derek had counted on the 'potential' of his target to keep Damien from noticing that someone else was around. In this he was right. Muttering to himself, Derek shifted himself home, "I can't wait to see Damien fall flat on his face. I'm going to make sure of it."

***

When the three of them arrived home Mike went to his room to grab a book and read a little before bed. The shortened sleep from the night before started to catch up and he yawned as he emptied his pockets of wallet and cellphone. Glancing at the phone again Mike decided he couldn't leave it in voicemail indefinitely. He unlocked the phone and pushed the button to retrieve messages. "Hi, Mike?" came a voice, hesitant, but familiar. "This is Anne. I got your number through Laurie. I told her I wanted to wish you a happy birthday when I heard it was today, so, Happy Birthday," she broke out a little into the song before dissolving into a fit of giggles. "I was curious if you might like to get together sometime this weekend. Maybe see a movie or just hang out. I know you said you were visiting and working for your uncle this summer so thought you could use a tour guide until you got used to the area. I know some great walking trails and most of the stores around here too. Well, this is my cell phone so give me a call or a text message sometime if you want. Happy Birthday again," she finished, breaking into a fit of giggles again before the line went dead.

Pressing the button to delete the message Mike flipped to the recent calls. Saving the number with the tag of "Anne – Cell", Mike put the phone on the charger. Definitely not in the mood to deal with her tonight, Mike knew he would have to at some point. Of that he was sure. The more he thought about Laurie, the more drawn to the idea of seeing where things would go he became. The vision of the two of them kissing having brought up unexpected feelings a little bittersweet, given the recent thrashing his heart had taken from Colleen. Colleen still hadn't responded to his email and he had taken it as a sign that she was moving on with her life already. Pursuing something with Laurie left little room for entertaining Anne's interest, whether it was genuine or just some game she was playing. *Or did it?* Mike was surprised at himself over the thought.

Sighing to himself, Mike settled back to read, only glancing at the clock every now and then to make sure it wasn't too late. Playing a little with his powers, Mike had the book floating in the air, turning the pages without physically touching them. This got easier the more he practiced and soon the book was locked in place, instead of it dipping slightly when his focus shifted to the story of the book, instead of holding it in the air. The necklace felt cool against his skin, showing no signs of strain like his uncle had described. Mike hoped the practice would also help him to fall asleep and not dream tonight. The rest would be very nice after the tumultuous day he had had.

The book was still floating there when his aunt came by to say goodnight and she paused midway through the word. His concentration broken by her arrival, the book fell to the bed and Mike looked back at her a little sheepishly. She merely smiled and finished saying "Goodnight", before heading off toward the other end of the house.

Mike gathered up the book and quickly flipped through it to find where he had been. Placing the sales receipt in the page as a bookmark Mike briefly thought of the sales clerk who seemed so odd. Knowing now he was hearing her thoughts didn't make him feel much better about it than it had at the time. Even unintentionally hearing it made him think it was a violation of some sort, even if he was the subject of the thoughts.

His cellphone did a little dance on the bedside table as it lit up and vibrated, alerting Mike to an incoming text message. He was happy to see the message is from Laurie, not Anne as he feared. "Hope your day was special, was nice to see you again. Can't wait until Friday. Sleep well" Mike quickly sent back, "Nice to see you again as well. Was a pleasant surprise. I can't wait either. Sounds like fun. Sweet Dreams." He set the phone on silent and put it back on the charger. Laying the book next to it where his glasses would have gone like every night before, Mike turned off the light and prepared to go to sleep. He had no idea what the rest of this summer would hold, but so far it was looking like it was going to be very interesting, to say the least.

***

"Hey James, how is he doing? Really?" Sally asked as soon as her brother answered. She knew they should be home by now and she was worried to hear his take on how her baby boy was doing. Her conversation with Mike earlier in the day had only been slightly encouraging.

"He's handling it well, I think," Jim replied to his sister. They had had a long conversation earlier in the day while he was at the office where he explained about Mike's display that morning. Even though he knew it was breaking his sister's heart, Jim couldn't help the excitement in his voice when he had recounted the show he had witnessed. "Has he brought up that gal he was seeing when you two talk? He isn't saying much, but it looks like he has a date with Laurie Friday night."

"Colleen," Sally confirmed. "He asked about her today because I slipped and brought her up. Your niece seems to be taking over the lead with the popular kids because Colleen has moved away. Do you think this Laurie will hurt my boy?"

"No," Jim assured his sister. "Laurie is one of the best and her mother is childhood friends with Jenny. In fact, Jenny is Laurie's godmother, remember?"

"That's good," Sally said, smiling for the first time. "I hope he has fun this summer. I miss having him home. Well, I'm going to bed, James. Let me know if there is anything you or my boy needs. Give Jenny my best." Jim said his goodbye and they hung up.

Chapter 9

Friday afternoon Mike helped Vicky finish cutting the payroll checks and handing them out to those who didn't use direct deposit. He stifled a yawn and Vicky giggled at him.

"I'm gonna grab a soda from the fridge, want anything?" Mike turned to the older woman.

"A bottle of water, please," Vicky replied.

Mike nodded and shuffled off, yawning again. *"If only Uncle Jim hadn't kept asking me to demonstrate my telekinesis last night, I might have gotten more sleep."* He thought about the praise his uncle kept giving him. *"It is fun, though."* They were supposed to start working on dream walking once Mike had a grip on his other powers. Uncle Jim told him, "Your other gifts will work while dreaming so it's good to have a grasp of your limits." Mike tried to catch a second wind as he returned to work, beverages in hand.

About four in the afternoon, his uncle came out of his office. "Time to get going if we're going to make it to the bank before it closes." He had direct deposit, but knew Mike would need to cash what was left of the check and open an account.

A half hour later, Mike walked out of the bank with a shiny new ATM card and a starter book of checks. With his direct deposit setup, his debit card would arrive in a week to ten days, but the generic ATM card would give him access to cash. Keeping a little cash for bowling and sodas at the club, Mike suddenly felt more awake than he had all day.

The thought of his date with Laurie buoyed his spirits, giving him a boost in energy.

While his uncle drove, Mike checked his phone to find several text messages waiting. Between tiredness and work, he hadn't bothered to look at the phone all day. Several were from Anne, wondering if Mike got her message Wednesday and what he thought. Mike told his uncle about Anne's offer.

When he finished laughing , Uncle Jim replied, "You're still a free man, but I'd be careful if it seems like there is some sort of competition brewing between Laurie and Anne. Just be upfront with both of them and you should be fine." The other message from Laurie just said to let her know when he was on the way, and that they could grab a pizza at the bowling alley if he wanted. While Uncle Jim weaved his way through traffic to get home, Mike sent a reply, "Call when I'm on the way." As they pulled into the driveway, Mike received a reply consisting of a smiley face. Glancing from his phone to his uncle, Mike said, "You know, I really think I'm going to like spending time with Laurie. For some reason it just feels like a good idea." Uncle Jim smiled, but his eyes hid something, at least in Mike's view. *"Course, Anne seems like she could be fun too,"* Mike thought.

Mike raced to get ready, quickly returning to the dining room. Aunt Jenny handed him a small key ring with three keys on it. "Those are a set for you to keep while you are here. Door, ignition, and a house key. Don't be too late now, and have fun," she said with a giggle before turning back to watching the movie she had rented during the day.

Smiling a little broader, Mike headed outside as Uncle Jim echoed his wife's sentiment, but he added, "Don't do anything I wouldn't do," before he broke into a fit of laughter.

"Hey Laurie," Mike said when she picked up, having dialed her number as soon as he got in the car. "Ready to go? You will have to talk me through how to get to your place."

"Hey, Mike." She giggled and Mike's breath caught as she continued, "No problem. I can tell you how to get here from your aunt and uncle's place." The conversation drifted casually while she gave Mike directions.

In no time Mike pulled into her driveway and Laurie waved enthusiastically from the porch. Mike parked, killing the engine. He steeled himself, mentally preparing himself for meeting her parents. Laurie had warned Mike he would have to before they let him drive away with their only daughter. *"Would think having Aunt Jenny in my corner would be enough, but apparently not. Maybe that's why Laurie's mom wants to meet me,"* Mike pondered, mounting the front steps.

Laurie's father stood inside the house, looking stern, when Laurie led a nervous Mike through the door. A broad shouldered man standing as tall as Mike, Mr. Sterling reminded Mike of his own father. The older man extended his hand and Mike shook it firmly, like his father always said a man should. Nodding his approval, he told the pair to, "Have fun." He retired to a show left on in the living room.

Mrs. Sterling, however, turned out to be a different story. She wanted to know Mike's life story before she would consent to let the two teens go anywhere. Her concern presented as more curiosity about her best friend's nephew than any real interrogation, much to Mike's relief. Finally, Laurie put her foot down to keep them from spending the entire night in.

Back in the car, Laurie started giving directions to the bowling alley where they were meeting Deb and Chad. Knowing it would be awkward,

Mike decided to get it out of the way. "So, did you give Anne my number?"

"She asked about you, and I said that I knew you were coming into the restaurant with your aunt and uncle for your birthday dinner. She said she wanted to wish you happy birthday. She probably would have called your aunt anyway if I hadn't given it to her. So, I gave in and gave her your cell number," Laurie rambled. Mike glanced her direction, noting the pained look on Laurie's face. She continued, haltingly, "I... figured I would leave it up to you... if you... wanted to talk to her other than that. You aren't mad, are you?"

"She left a message, asking if I needed a tour guide to show me around. I figure I have one of those already," Mike replied, placing a hand lightly on Laurie's leg.

Speaking of Anne woke up the Darkness. *"What would it hurt to see what Anne's offering?"* It retreated when Laurie laid her hand on top of Mike's.

"Why does Laurie scare the Darkness into hiding? Besides, Its attraction to Anne makes the hair on the back of my neck stand up even thinking about it. I certainly don't plan on giving it leverage."

The large bowling alley boasted more lanes than Mike had ever seen in one place. Every single lane had people standing around. To save time, Laurie called Deb's phone so the two couples could locate each other in the crowd. They all grabbed shoes from the counter and changed while Mike selected a house ball to use. He owned a sixteen pound ball back home, a gift from his mom the Christmas he joined a teen league with some friends from school. Mike perused the offerings and found a deep green one with finger holes deep enough not to be too uncomfortable. The finger holes were drilled further into his own ball because of his long fingers.

Mike hefted the ball, noticing a dark haired guy standing nearby, not seemingly interested in the choosing of a ball himself. The guy looked away when their eyes met. Shrugging his puzzlement off, Mike shouldered the ball and turned to walk past the guy to join his group. The creepy feeling he got when the guy was already gone was quickly forgotten when he reached Laurie's waiting smile at the lane.

After a couple games, Mike knew something was up. Strikes were coming easily, and most of the time, Mike knew when he threw the ball whether it was good or not. He could feel a connection to the ball, the lane, and the pins as it left his hand, knowing he hit the mark. When he broke two fifty in the third game, Chad conceded defeat. Mike knew he was subconsciously using his powers to guide the ball, which made him feel a bit like he cheated. *"But so what, you have to use what you got,"* the Darkness whispered. Mike shoved down the voice.

Mike's skin prickled. He glanced a few lanes over and the guy from the ball rack looked away as their gazes met again. Laurie's voice brought him back to the group, "Let's go dancing."

With everyone in agreement, Mike excused himself to go to the bathroom. The dark haired guy entered right behind and walked to a urinal two down from Mike's.

"Impressive games you played there, friend, ever think of joining a team?" he asked.

"Kinda odd to make small talk with a total stranger in a public restroom, but I don't need the hassle of a scene." "Not really," Mike replied casually. "I just play for fun, although tonight luck was with me, probably the best games I've ever bowled." Mike chuckled to lighten the weirdness, but something about this guy started to bother him. The prickly feeling on his skin stepped up a notch. The Darkness reached for control as red bled into Mike's vision.

"Well, if you change your mind, I could use another for a team I'm putting together. Maybe that cute gal of yours could be team cheerleader." The guy grinned and Mike read malicious intent in the guy's eyes.

A sudden surge of anger sparked a contest of wills with the Darkness. Mike focused on Laurie but the possible threat to her only fueled his anger. Suddenly, the symbol from his pendant flashed in his mind. As the spiral spun, the red began sliding towards pink before disappearing altogether.

"Thanks for the offer," Mike said, finishing his business and heading to the sink to wash his hands. "I think if I join a league, it will be with my friends."

"Look, we both know something funny was going on out there. Don't deny it." The teen stood right behind Mike. Something tickled along Mike's skin, similar to the sensation he felt when he had moved objects, but not coming from him, just in the vicinity. The pendant around his neck spiked cold briefly before returning to normal. That made Mike more nervous than possibly getting into a fist fight with some stranger in the bathroom of a bowling alley. "I felt something of it when you entered. You have the talent," the other teen continued.

"Back off, man." Mike struggled to maintain control as the Darkness raged to tear the guy apart, bringing to mind his last confrontation in a bathroom. The memory of Kevin's death sobered him slightly. *"He knows. Destroy him!"* shouted the Darkness from its weakening cage. Mike moved to leave and the other teen followed. Mike turned around, putting his back towards the exit. "I don't have a problem with you. I don't want to join your bowling team. For your sake, I would back off now, buddy."

"Bowling team?" He stepped toward Mike. Mike noticed a weird shadow move in front of the guy's face. "This isn't about your meager bowling skills but I was trying to be discreet. We shall chat again soon. I think we will become great friends, someday." The way he said the last words didn't make it clear whether he's made a threat or a promise.

Mike stood dumbfounded as the guy dissolved into smoke and disappeared. He rubbed his eyes. When the bathroom door hit him in the back of the head, Mike stumbled forward, catching himself on a sink.

"Sorry about that, Mike," Chad said as he entered, reaching out a hand to help steady his new friend. "The girls were getting a little worried you were taking so long so I said I would check on you. You alright? You are as pale as a sheet."

"I'll be fine," Mike replied after a moment and put a hand to his face. It came away covered in sweat. "Must have just been the heat, I felt a little dizzy for a second before I got hit with the door. Is it always this warm in here? You would think they would have air conditioning as many people as were out there." The blow to the head granted Mike control, but he feared what he might have done had he lost his hold on the Darkness again.

"Yeah, I think it is on the blink." Chad gave Mike an odd look.

Mike grabbed a towel and wiped his face, trying to steady himself mentally after what he experienced. "I will go let the girls know you will be out in a minute." Chad turned to go back through the door.

"I'm ready, but tell me something," Mike started, tossing the paper towel in the trash and clapping Chad on the shoulder, "Are you and Laurie as close as you said last week?"

"She's like a sister," Chad replied, his tone betraying his confusion regarding the subject change. "Why do you ask?"

"Well, just curious about her is all." Mike grinned, trying to get Chad to let go of the condition he had found Mike in. "I know how girls stick together, so I can't really ask Deb or Liz about her likes and dislikes, you know? I was hoping you might be able to help me out if I needed to get a little info. You know, guy to guy."

"Sure." Chad relaxed, taking Mike's question as sincere interest. "Probably wait until the girls are out of ear shot and I'll answer what I can." The two left the bathroom and rejoined the girls.

Mike tried to put away the encounter with the strange guy for the moment. He would have time to ask his uncle about it later. Seeing Laurie banished all other thoughts from his head and brought a smile to his face. Chad and Mike were both grinning by the time they reached the girls. Their dates both raised an eyebrow, giving the guys the, "What were you two up to?" look that females are so famous for.

"Are you alright, Mike?" Laurie asked softly, grabbing hold of his hand and looking up into his eyes. *"I don't know why I feel like this. Like this is perfect. I wonder if he feels the same?"*

"Just fantastic now," Mike replied, slipping an arm around her and pulling her towards him in a sideways hug. "I think I got overheated. Blasted air conditioning is broken, I think." She accepted the response and snuggled into Mike as the couples walked to their cars. Nothing was official, but as the night went Mike felt himself wanting to get to know her better. *"I'm sure she's interested. I wasn't doing all the flirting. Maybe Aunt Jenny is right."*

Mike followed Chad's car over to the club and they found parking spaces next to each other. The rest of the evening Laurie kept dragging him onto the dance floor, leaving Mike little time to question Chad. In the crowd of people, Mike felt sure he saw the dark haired guy from the bowling alley.

Laurie picked up on his distracted look and asked, "Everything alright?"

Mike pulled her close, trying to reassure her. "I'm great, just a lot of people. Not a big fan of crowds is all."

"Do you want to leave?" Laurie bit her lip nervously.

"Not yet." Mike smiled at the angel in his arms. Before long, the clock pushed eleven. Mike's obvious interest in Laurie was drawing him into the new circle of friends.

While he drove Laurie home, she held Mike's hand. They didn't talk. Mike tried to enjoy the soft feel of her hands wrapped around his one but his mind kept replaying the brief conversation with the guy from the bowling alley. *"I know I saw him at the club. How did he pull that disappearing trick? Hopefully Uncle Jim will have some answers. He did say that sometimes things happened to the men in our line possessing these powers."* Mike began to wonder if seeing people was going to be his curse. There was the guy he had seen around school a few times, and the vision of the old man in the chair to consider. When they arrived at her house, Laurie moved to get out of the car, snapping Mike from his thoughts.

"Let me walk you to the door," Mike said quickly, laying his hand on her knee to restrain her from getting out of the car. She smiled warmly and Mike got out of the car. As he opened her door he extended a hand to her. She took it eagerly and glided out of her seat. They stood face to face.

"This is very gentlemanly of you, Mike," she said breathlessly, holding his hand as they started toward her front door. "I had a nice time, but you seem distracted. Are you sure everything's alright?"

"Yes, I think maybe the pizza or the heat in the bowling alley didn't sit well with me," Mike replied, giving her hand a soft squeeze. "I had a great time though and we should do something again soon. I would really like to see you again."

Her smile brightened at the offer of further outings. "That would be wonderful. Well, thank you for walking me to my door," she said as they climbed the steps of her porch. The only light came from the single bulb next to the door and the two teens stood there staring at each other for a few moments before either moved. Mike pulled Laurie closer, intending to hug her. She looks up into his eyes before closing hers. Wrapping her in his arms Mike tilted his head down and kissed her softly on the lips.

"Thank you for the wonderful evening," Mike said as the moment passed and they separated. A light flickered on inside the house. Their standing on the porch had alerted someone. "I guess I better let you get inside. I should get the car back before midnight." Laurie nodded and whispered a good night before using her key to unlock the front door. She paused just before closing the door to give another small wave and smile. As Mike watched the door close, he realized how difficult it could be leaving Laurie in the fall. *"If I go back home."* Mike considered the implications of the thought as he backed out of Laurie's drive.

"Was that truly even an option?" Mike wondered. He wasn't sure his mother would approve at all. Especially if the reason centered on a girl he had just met. Mike checked the mirrors and shifted into drive. A final glance in the rear view mirror delivered a shock, as the dark haired teenager from earlier lounged in the backseat.

"Aww, wasn't that a pleasant goodnight," the guy said calmly from the backseat. He didn't appear as ruffled by suddenly appearing where he shouldn't be as Mike was by his arrival. "I can see why you would be attracted to her but why should young men of our means settle for just one little blonde when we can have them all?" Mike wasn't entirely sure it was a question or a statement of fact, but the guy seemed to be expecting a response.

"Who are you and how the hell did you get in my car?" Mike tried to focus on him and the road at the same time. *"I'm sure I locked the door at the club. I don't think he was there the whole time. Who is this guy?"* Mike felt the Darkness creeping up to try and seize control. *"Destroy him now,"* It raged again.

"Oh, forgive me," the other teen began, making a short bow of his head as if in apology. "I forgot to introduce myself before, didn't I? My name is Derek, and you are Mike." His chuckle echoed in the relative closeness of the car and Mike could feel the little hairs on the back of his neck stand up again. "As for how I got in the car, don't you think that is a little silly to ask? Go ahead and think, you can do better than that. We are both much smarter than to ask such inane questions."

"Derek, I am going to give you to the count of ten to tell me what the hell is going on or I'm going to pull this car over and throw you out of it," Mike threatened, hoping he sounded more sure of himself than he truly felt. *"I did take that karate class a few years ago."* Perhaps his gift would help him like during the fight with Kevin outside the restaurant. Mike wasn't sure he wanted to face another death at his own hands, but he didn't feel like the world would miss Derek either.

"Idle threats do not become you." Derek grinned, which darkened his countenance even more. "I merely wanted to continue our chat, and since you would be alone for a bit on the drive home, I thought this would work nicely. By the way, you will want to make the next right to get to your uncle's place."

Mike quickly shifted lanes, noticing almost too late that Derek was right and he was about to miss his turn. *"He doesn't know who he's taunting,"* the Darkness spoke up calmly. *"We should teach him a lesson."* For once, Mike wanted to agree with the voice in his head. "It's not an idle threat. If it takes beating it out of you on the side of the road to find out what's going on, then I guess I'm going to do just that." Mike wondered if getting angry would spark his gift to help in a fight, and the prospect of beating Derek to a pulp with his fists made the Darkness purr in contentment. Mike stopped himself from pulling over to the side of the road as the Darkness surged forward.

"Well, that is a little harder to explain," Derek replied softly. "I am sure your uncle mentioned that your family is not alone in its... gifts. Or did he make you believe you were special and unique?"

"He said there are others, but why are you sitting in the backseat talking to me about it?" Mike asked, knowing he would wake Uncle Jim up as soon as he got home. He did mention that they might look Mike up but not that they might disappear in puffs of smoke. Mike's anger took on a harder edge as he wondered if he could move fast enough to catch a person able to disappear and reappear at will.

"Would you prefer I rode shotgun so that you can more easily watch the road?" Derek laughed and suddenly sat in the passenger seat so recently vacated by Laurie. Mike felt and thought he saw something happen when Derek moved, reminding him of the feeling of the energy when Mike practiced his telekinesis. "Yes, this is much nicer. I can see the road so much better from up here as well." Derek ran a finger along the arm rest and then placed it to his nose, sniffing lightly. "Ah, how she lingers even though she is gone. She really is a pretty little thing. So, shall we discuss what two young men of our capabilities can do with the rest of the night that is stretched out before us?"

Mike wasn't quite sure he fully understood what Derek meant but Mike did know he didn't like the look on the guy's face whenever he brought Laurie up. "You will leave her out of this. She knows nothing of any gifts, for which I am assuming you have some talent I don't possess since you can bounce about as if made of air."

"Ah, how little you know of your potential friend," Derek said, flashing a smile. "Don't miss your turn up here, you are almost home." At that moment another figure, not quite as dark of hair but still lanky appeared in the backseat and reached up, grasping Derek's neck.

"You've made a fatal mistake, my friend. When my father finds out what you've done, interfering in my business," the newcomer raged, trying to claw at Derek, who panicked and vanished from the car with an almost audible pop. The newcomer in the backseat looked over at Mike and grinned weakly. "Look, sorry about this. My name is Damien. I was tasked with contacting you on behalf of the Council. I don't have time to explain much now, because I will have to leave you shortly. Your uncle can explain why when you wake him up. I'm sure you two will have much to talk about tonight. Rest assured we'll talk again soon." Damien's worried expression faded as did his form. Mike found himself alone in the car again. Hammering down on the gas pedal, Mike sped the rest of the way home. His heart raced as fast as the wheels of the car.

***

"Father," Damien called as he pushed open the door to his father's study a few moments later. The old man frowned at the interruption. Part of him was anxious enough to hear of progress to forgive the rudeness of his offspring's barging in. He held to the promise not to get involved, which he felt extended to abstaining from actively watching the process as it unfolds.

"Yes, Damien," he said, marking his place in the book with a piece of blood red ribbon and closing the tome.

"Derek Gohr interfered," Damien raged. "I'm going to kill the asshole if I can get my hands on him. He may have undone any chance I had of working my way into Mike's good graces." His father started from his seat, knowing that this betrayal could cause his impulsive son to lose focus. The old man waved for the younger to continue as he paced the room. "I managed to introduce myself to him, but Derek may have caused some harm. He did something to block me and by the time I caught up and got through his wards, they were almost to the Johnson's property. I could only get a glimpse out of either mind of what happened, but it appears he is trying to plant seeds for distrust of Mr. Johnson. Apparently Mr. Johnson didn't elaborate much on the rest of us. Mike was surprised by Derek's appearance. I could almost feel the rage rolling off Mike and it appears to be because Derek brought up the girl Mike was spending time with tonight."

"So you believe this will turn him against you as well?" the old man began. He had to admit, the unexpected revelation that Johnson had not informed his nephew of the presence of the Council and others like them could work to their favor, if he continued to bungle things. Making Mike doubt the older generation could also work, as it may drive the young Mr. Keller towards Damien for friendship for the sake of how close in age they were. Derek's attempt to use the boy's anger to turn him may or may not backfire, but it certainly complicated Damien's attempts to manipulate the Keller boy.

"Not entirely," Damien replied, nearly breathless to continue his tale, "but Derek has made threats and brought our world crashing into Mike in a way I wouldn't have liked. I was hoping to be more subtle and befriend him before revealing my powers. Now I will have to approach him differently, and try to keep Derek out of the picture."

Nodding slightly, the old man agreed the Gohr boy's interference made things more complicated. "The important thing is to make sure that some sort of bargain is struck with young Michael Keller. Unlike his uncle, this time the terms will be more to the liking of the Council. The last two generations of failure have cost us decades of scheming with no return for the investment. Our standing has already suffered a blow. Another failure would be inexcusable. I will speak with Derek's father and see to it that he does not interfere further." That was about the only thing he could do, try to enforce the Council's wishes that Damien be left to his plans.

"Please don't say anything, Father. I think I can use this to my advantage. If Derek's actions cause Mike to panic, perhaps I can turn that. A little good cop/bad cop scenario."

The older Mauston nodded, seeing a wisdom in his son he hadn't before. A burst of pride for his offspring surged through the old man's heart. Sensing the audience was at an end, Damien bowed to his father. The younger man left quickly, trying to decide if befriending his target would work in light of Derek's actions. Damien only had friends who grew up spoiled with their powers, which grated on his nerves. Mike's lack of foreknowledge of the world Damien grew up in was appealing, like having a cousin from the country come to visit and seeing your own world in a whole new light. With that revelation came further insights, and Damien knew he could not follow completely in the paths of his ancestors. Michael Keller might be his ticket to breaking free from his family's traditions.

***

A few minutes later Mike came through the front door like a clap of thunder, already calling for his uncle. *"I don't care if Aunt Jenny wakes up. She's aware of the family heritage anyway."* It took a moment for his uncle to respond, as he entered from the hall into the kitchen still fastening his bathrobe over a pair of gym shorts.

"What on earth is going on, Mike?" Jim asked, rubbing the sleep from his eyes as he stopped in front of his nephew. Something about Mike's expression gave him a clue. He pointed to one of the chairs at the table. He went into the main kitchen area. Mike started to speak, but Uncle Jim waved him off and set about preparing a kettle to boil. He then pulled a small box of teabags from a corner in one of the higher cabinets. While the water heated, he grabbed two large mugs before turning back to Mike. "I am guessing something happened tonight that you have never experienced before, and it had nothing to do with your date." He stated it so matter-of-factly Mike could tell Uncle Jim was reading his face like a book, provided his uncle wasn't picking up any stray thoughts. Mike nodded and Jim continued to stare. "I suspected something like this might happen when I saw what you did with the fire logs your first night. I just hoped we would have some time to prepare you for what was potentially out there. That you might not be spotted before you were ready."

Instead of being a relief that his uncle had some sort of knowledge to impart, his somewhat cryptic statements so far just pushed Mike further into anxiousness and fear. Uncle and nephew stared at each other for a few minutes until the kettle started to whistle. Jim poured its contents into the two mugs. Grabbing two teabags from the cabinet he set them down on the table. Mike started to say something, but the older man again raised his hand to signal Mike should be silent for now. Jim retrieved a little jar of honey and two spoons before sitting across from his nephew. He silently put the tea bags into the mugs to steep. Then he sighed, looking Mike in the eyes again. Mike saw the heavy weight behind those eyes, as his uncle again struggling to find the words to express the thoughts in his head.

"Uncle," Mike began, and this time Uncle Jim didn't wave him off. "Tonight I met two people who seem to possess some sort of gifts as well. The first said he could sense me when I entered the bowling alley. He confronted me in the restroom, but then disappeared as if made of smoke before anyone else entered the room. Later he showed up in the car on my drive home." Once Jim let Mike start, he rambled headlong, and while he backtracked some, Mike finally got out the entire story, including the second arrival. His throat felt raw. Once Mike wound down, Uncle Jim pushed one of the mugs over, taking the teabag out. Mike took a small sip and his face scrunched at the bitter taste. Jim handed his nephew the small jar of honey and Mike added a couple spoonfuls to the tea, stirring slowly.

"As I said, I was afraid this would happen," Jim said, ignoring the mug in front of himself. "Drink that, it will help you to sleep after I tell you this." He paused while Mike took a tentative sip of the tea, the honey making it more palatable. "I mentioned there are others in the world possessing gifts similar to our family. After all, it would be fairly arrogant to think we were the only ones to have them. Most of them are fairly good folk just trying to live their life, but others are true evils in the world. Some of these like to use their gifts maliciously to dominate others. They usually get their rewards in the end, but they can still be trouble for a while. A rather large organization of them call themselves the Council. They are old money businessmen for the most part, running their little worlds. Remember when I told you to be careful how you use your gifts?"

"Yes, because it could come back to haunt me later," Mike replied, feeling the edge of his fear and panic begin to dull as the tea started to fill him with a warmth akin to a mother's embrace. Mike glanced at the mug to realize he drained it already. Uncle Jim stirred a couple spoons of honey into the mug in front of him and pushed it towards his nephew. Mike took mug and tried to sip more slowly as his uncle began talking again.

"Exactly," Jim said softly, his eyes bearing the same calculating look he wore whenever looking at Mike. "Some not only disregard this simple lesson, but shove the bad results off on innocent people. Our family has a long legacy of being protectors, of standing against those who would abuse their gifts and harm others. For that, we are often targets. I have taken precautions around my home to protect myself and those I care about. I think that is why your visitors weren't able to stay with you all the way here. I would venture a guess that he wasn't truly there anyway. He was merely projecting himself to your presence, similar to your dream walking, but done while conscious."

"Like astral projection?" Mike's mind seized upon something familiar. "I have read about that in my paranormal books." Mike couldn't believe he didn't piece it together himself, but he was a little put off by both Derek and Damien's appearances and disappearances to think too clearly. Besides, up until recently, telepathy, telekinesis, and astral projection had all been subjects that only existed truly in science fiction and fantasy novels as far as Mike was concerned. Anyone claiming those powers was quickly debunked as a fraud.

"Similar, but it may have been much stronger than just that." Uncle Jim nodded l, satisfied Mike understood the concept. "Whoever this Derek is, I would be careful if he should show himself, projection or not. Keep your pendant on at all times as that should help to shield you from any direct attacks he may make against you. This Damien sounds a little more level headed."

"But Uncle, why would he want to attack me? I don't even know him. I'm no threat to him I'm aware of. I barely have control of my powers as it is. Besides, dream walking and telekinesis seem to be poor weapons. He acted more interested in getting me upset or doubtful of you. He said that the two of us could do anything we wanted. That we were not bound by anything because of our powers. He also made some comments about Laurie that angered me a little. I think I like her and I wouldn't want her dragged into some sort of battle. I was nearly ready to pull the car over and beat the crap out of him." *"I wanted to hurt him. Really wanted it."*

"Remember though, nephew. That may not be all you can do. You can hear some thoughts, and may possess other talents that you aren't aware of yet. I think we may have to step up your education on our family line, given the circumstances. Your potential alone may be what makes this Derek more hostile than makes sense. He may also be unbalanced a little by his gifts. It has happened in our own line so why not others. Usually that Council takes care of their problem children. They prefer not to let on to others that they exist. And don't worry about

Laurie. She's probably safe from any harm. I know she doesn't possess any talents and that is usually all that attracts these people. He was just using it to get a rise out of you." Jim stood and returned to the same high cabinet where he retrieved the teabags earlier.

Mike took another sip of the tea, warmth and security filling him again. He watched his uncle pull down a large book from the shelf. Jim placed it next to his nephew's mug. Mike noticed the same swirling disk upon the cover they both wore around their necks. Jim opened it slowly to reveal heavy paper pages, some quite yellowed and fragile looking. Most of these were sealed in plastic to protect them from any further ravages of time. Each page held a listing of people like a family tree. One in each row was underlined in bold black ink. After turning several pages, Mike spotted a couple rows with no name underlined. Passing a dozen pages or so, the pages began to be newer. On the page his uncle stopped Mike could see the listings for his grandfather, his uncle, and himself. Amongst them were his aunt, mother and sister. All three of the male's names were written in that same black ink and were underlined. The mark under Mike's name looked fresh.

"Our family tree? What's the purpose of this?" Mike asked, not sure he wanted to know. *"While this is exciting, could I be dreaming all of it? I'm so tired all of a sudden."* As his eyelids started to droop, Mike crushed a yawn behind the back of his hand.

"This is the book of our family. No need to be scared of it. It records any knowledge our family wanted to pass on so that it wouldn't be lost. It began in Europe then was brought to the United States with our ancestors when they came seeking a new and better life. It not only records those who had the gifts manifest, but information about using them, or tapping into the powers of the world around us. Such as that tea you are drinking." For emphasis, Jim pointed at the mug, forgotten next to the book. "The herbs in it will help you to sleep, but are quite harmless unless in very large or concentrated doses. I showed you this because within the pages of this book are the details of every gift shared by our family in remembered history, and what was observed in others. I hope it will be of some help in finding out what your visitor meant by not knowing your potential."

"Potential." Mike let a chuckle escape. *"I hope this is a dream. I'll wake up, and it'll be months ago, none of this will have happened. No Kevin, no mysterious enemies. And no Colleen."*

"Do you really want me gone?" the Darkness piped up from his subconscious.

"Every gift ever shown is chronicled in this book. Some of them our family seemed glad to be rid of, for the temptation to use them for dark purposes were too great. Although I always thought some of them would be useful for good as well."

"What do you mean?" Mike asked, the curious part itching to turn the page into the rest of the book. He felt the Darkness reacting as well.

"Well, your first visitor, called himself Derek, right?" Mike nodded. "Derek talked about not settling for one person when you can have them all. Well, that's exactly what some of our kind are capable of. They're able to tame not only beasts, but people as well. Bending these persons to their will and forcing them to perform only the actions the gifted one wishes. While useful against evil people, the temptation to use it for other purposes is obvious I hope."

"Yeah, I can see both sides." Mike became less excited about the prospects of other gifts in his future, while the Darkness practically salivated in the corner of his mind. *"If I had that kind of power, would I be able to stop myself from lashing out the next time Derek appeared and talked about Laurie? Would I have been able to reprogram Kevin?"* Mike shuddered inside at the implications. Controlling others was a dangerous trail of thought.

"But could be oh so much fun. We could patch up Laurie and Anne and have them both," the Darkness spoke, gaining a little more confidence. Mike struggled to shove down the voice.

"I can see I have given you enough to think about for tonight. Get some rest and I'll see you in the morning." Uncle Jim floated the mugs and honey over to the kitchen sink. The book he carefully closed by hand and placed it back in its spot on the high cabinet shelf. "I will help you in the morning to know how to protect yourself in case either of your visitors shows his face again when I'm not around."

Mike nodded and forced himself to his feet. "Uncle, what if it isn't me he comes after first?" Mike spoke slowly, his mind dull from the tea.

"Don't worry about that for now, nephew," Jim replied after a moment. Seeming to catch the train of thought, he continued, "I think these two will wish to test the waters with you first. See if there is anything to be gained by actions against Laurie. Unless he thinks he can get an edge by it, he will most likely leave her alone. Now, please, try to get some sleep. We will talk in the morning." He turned down the hall opposite towards his room.

Groggily, Mike headed for his bedroom. He barely made it before sleep overtook him and he passed out fully clothed on top of the blankets.

Chapter 10

Sometime mid-morning, Mike awoke to a heated discussion from the direction of the kitchen. He rolled over on one side to listen better and strained to catch every word. Without warning the voices sounded as if they were in the same room, each word carried clearly to his ear.

"What on earth were you thinking, giving Mike that tea?" Aunt Jenny berated her husband. From the tone of her voice she'd asked this question before. "You know what it does. You told me yourself that it's only to be used to confirm if someone has the gifts at all, not as an accelerant of developing abilities. I remember when you gave me that bitter concoction. I wish I had developed telekinesis just so I could have flung the mug at you harder."

"But honey," Uncle Jim pleaded. "He was visited by someone apparently far more advanced than he is at this point. What he described scared the hell out of me. I had to do something that would allow him to reach his potential faster so that he can combat whatever Derek and Damien are plotting. You don't know how difficult this can be. I nearly lost myself and you once. I won't let my nephew run the same risk with his life, if I can help him. At least I had a few years to prepare before they found and approached me. My father had been able to hide my abilities long enough to meet you. They were onto Mike within days. I wonder if they've been watching me. I can't believe I was so stupid, letting that damned Council get a look at him. Sally is going to fly out here and kill me herself."

"I know you're worried, but, isn't there another way?" Jenny begged. "Isn't there some other protection you could have tried to help him. What if it didn't work? What if something went wrong?"

"He will be fine. I could tell right away he was going to be alright. I knew either way he would need rest, so I put a little extra of something different in the tea to make him sleep. That is all I told him it was. I hope he'll forgive me if he ever learns the truth," Uncle Jim whispered the last part.

Mike felt his anger rise up white and hot over the deception. *"Wasn't I capable of being told these things? Why was there still a need for all this secrecy?"* Mike thought to himself as he laid in bed.

Mike knew he had to confront his uncle and rose slowly. Without thinking he shielded himself in silence like the night in the woods. The absolute silence made every small action of his own deafening. He heard his own heartbeat quicken. With footsteps sounding as loud as gunshots in his head, he left the room, entering the hall to the kitchen. *"I need to see their faces. They are my aunt and uncle, not some monsters who drugged me."* His anger still burned white, the Darkness strangely silent.

When Mike stepped into the light of the kitchen from the darkened hallway, Uncle Jim was facing the other way. Aunt Jenny noticed right away, the look in her eyes alerting her husband to Mike's presence. He quickly turned around, forcing a smile as he approached Mike.

"Nephew," he began, "you're awake. Good. Did you sleep well?"

"Very well," Mike replied, much calmer than he felt as he released his cloak of silence. The conversation from last night played in his head, his anxiousness crept back. "I don't know if I can do this, Uncle Jim. I just don't."

"I know it's difficult." He placed a hand on Mike's shoulder. "Unfortunately there isn't much that can be done about it. You were born into this family. But I promise you, I'll do anything I can to help you through any trial that presents itself."

"By drugging me?" Mike's anger lashed out.

"I'm very sorry for doing that to you. I hope, in time, you will consider forgiving me." Uncle Jim's crestfallen expression took the edge off Mike's anger.

"Ok. Then let's get started, shall we." Mike stated resolutely, sitting down at the table. Once seated he looked up at the cabinet Uncle Jim had placed the book in some hours before. Mike envisioned the cabinet opening and the book floating towards him. While the cabinet opened, no book appeared. Puzzled, Mike turned to his uncle, who watched intently.

"The book is warded," Jim said after a moment, retrieving it by hand and coming to sit across from his nephew at the table. "No powers can touch it. The knowledge contained within would be dangerous in the hands of anyone wishing to do harm to us or others. Therefore you cannot even summon the book to you." He set the book down between them. Mike recalled how his uncle had moved everything from the table with his powers, but had put the book away by hand. At first Mike thought this was out of some habit or reverence for the information the book contained, but now Mike knew it was because Uncle Jim couldn't have moved it if he wanted to. *"I bet we could move it,"* the Darkness whispered. *"Another time,"* Mike replied before pushing down the voice.

"So where do I start?" Mike asked, carefully turning the older pages at the front in order to reach the page where his name was written. Uncle Jim turned the book a few more pages and they began going over the entries from some of their ancestors regarding the powers and how to use them.

They spent most of the morning pouring over writing almost faded from view, trying to glean from its pages something to help Mike. The thoughts of the tea and the Council Uncle Jim mentioned was pushed to the back of Mike's mind in the wake of the flood of information in front of him. Some of the stories he read about his ancestors seemed far fetched. There were vague references to lost talents, as well as several references to a foretelling that these talents would return one day.

Aunt Jenny prepared a small brunch and they ate while reading and talking. Before long, Aunt Jenny put sandwiches next to the duo and they looked up to find it was well past lunchtime. Mike had covered everything in the book about dream-walking and telekinesis. They were treated as fairly common gifts though readily apparent no one in their line had shown control and power such as Mike had the first night in several hundred years, if ever.

Several pages were devoted to a Council of Elders, or simply, The Council. It chronicled their attempts to rise to power a couple thousand years ago. The group of men with powers joined together to take over the political structures in several regions. Their coupes failed miserably as they were overwhelmed by the masses arrayed against them. This failure changed their tactics to ruling quietly, from alleys and back rooms behind the public faces of power. The writer said they knew of other families who stood outside this Council. Most were either brought in or eliminated if they showed any thought of acting against the Council's interests. It all reminded Mike of stories relating to the Mafia families in New York and Italy.

Uncle Jim became excited as he showed Mike an entry made by one of their oldest ancestors in Europe. The original, having been copied several times in order to keep it fresh, fell later and later in the book. It spoke of one of their line who would "possess talents unequaled by anyone in remembered history, but that his actions could destroy our line. If he fell into darkness, then we would all be doomed. He would be the prize of prizes for those of evil will, but he could also be the ultimate bane of wickedness." It sounded a bit archaic, but had been written centuries ago and translated multiple times.

"You honestly don't think this is talking about me, do you Uncle?" Mike asked, already knowing the answer by the gleam Uncle Jim had in his eyes. *"You know it's talking about us, Mikey,"* the Darkness rose up. Mike nearly missed Uncle Jim's response in his shock at the Darkness calling him by name.

"I have never heard of such mastery as you showed that first time. Simultaneously shielding us as you controlled all those separate objects," he said in a rush, drawing Mike's attention to the present. "Nephew, this is incredible. Your grandfather had said he thought you would be something special." Uncle Jim added mentally, *"Finally, justice for what they have done to our family."*

"But I don't have any idea what I am doing." Mike pushed the book away. His uncle held it firmly before them and turned another page, pointing to another passage telling much the same thing as the first about one possessing great powers and bringing back all the lost talents.

"Mike," he started, "this is your destiny. I can be here as much as you need to help guide you, but you are in uncharted territory as far as any of our family in recorded history is concerned. Part of me wishes I could take this burden from you, but if you are this one...."

"I think I get it," Mike cut him off. The situation like something from the books he enjoyed reading. "I'm going to have to go it alone at some point. I'm going to have to prove that I can handle the responsibility of these gifts."

Uncle Jim nodded before closing the book, putting it in front of his nephew.

Mike picked it up and stared at the circular design on the front cover. Mike suddenly knew where he recognized the design from, but he didn't know what to do. Putting the book down he looked across at his uncle for a full minute. "I need to get some air and clear my head. Do you mind if I borrow the car and go for a drive?"

"Sure, but be careful," Uncle Jim replied. "Trust your instincts to defend you should you come across your visitors again. It is clear at least one of them is acting on orders from their Council. Which one and what their purpose is this time, I can't say." Mike nodded and went to his room to get some clothes, his mind replaying everything the book contained about the Council and what its aims were. They sounded like an 'old money' club who was intent on holding onto their influence and power to give themselves a life of luxury. Mike couldn't think of a reason to have anything to do with them. *"Maybe it was a recruitment drive trying to add to their ranks?"* Mike thought, which seemed logical to him.

True to form the Darkness added, *"I wonder if they know who they are messing with."*

He showered and dressed in an almost trancelike state. Outward Mike held it together, while inside his mind was a swirling maelstrom from the events of the week. Pieces were now in place that made some sense of what had happened, but he still didn't think he quite believed it all. Mike grabbed his keys and wallet from his room. He almost walked out of his room without his cellphone. As he spun in the doorway to go back and get it, it sailed through the air to his open hand. Placing it in a pocket, Mike headed out to the front room. He waved to his aunt and uncle, who let him go without further word.

Soon Mike sat behind the wheel and aimed the car towards the highway. He didn't know where to go, but he knew he had to go be around other people for a while, people who didn't have destinies and family heritages that included vanquishing evil with powers out of a fantasy novel. It was only when he was on the road that he remembered hearing the thought from his uncle regarding justice for their family. *"I'll have to ask him about that later."* Part of Mike grew angry at the idea of being used. His anger warred with curiosity over what was done to their family. *"Was Uncle Jim referring to something in the book that they had glossed over? Or did this have to do with the strange car accident that took Mike's father and grandfather?"* The thought of the Council being involved in those deaths turned his blood cold.

***

Mike soon lost himself at the mall with the bustling Saturday afternoon crowd. He wandered aimlessly for a while, before buying a soda and sitting down in the food court to people watch. Mike pulled his phone from his pocket to find a couple new messages since last night. When he saw they were from Anne, he almost put the phone away without reading them. Damien chose that moment to sit down across the table from him. Mike started to get up and leave, but Damien smiled at Mike before speaking.

"Now now Mike," he said softly, his grin showing his perfect teeth. "Just relax. You wouldn't want a scene in front of all these people now would you? I can tell you talked to your uncle, and perhaps his words are clouding your judgment. I just want to talk. We can have a little chat, can't we? Then you can get back to your messages. I know Derek said some things last night that probably need explaining. I hope to clear the air. He was acting on his own for his own ends. Though I can only guess what they completely were."

"What do you want with me, Damien?" Mike asked, relaxing only enough to sit comfortably on the plastic chair. "I don't think we have anything to discuss except for you walking away and never bothering me again. I want nothing to do with whatever is going on here. I want nothing to do with your Council either, if that's why you're here."

"Please listen. I'm not here to threaten or turn you against your uncle like Derek was trying to do last night. I think I can offer you something that your uncle cannot in all of this," Damien continued, unperturbed by Mike's stance. "I can offer you friendship. A compatriot of sorts. I agree partly with what Derek said; why should either of us be bound by the rules of our families and this society. We're above such petty matters. We could see the world, experience all that life has to offer and still be home in time for supper if we chose. I don't approve of the methods that he, or some others use, in their dealings. I don't approve entirely of my father's lifestyle, but we are all born into our families and just have to make the best of what we're given."

Not expecting Damien's response, Mike's shocked by the lack of world domination in the whole scenario. Damien recognized the flash of uncertainty and pounced on that moment like a wild animal. "Let me prove to you my willingness to be friends and comrades in arms," Damien said, leaning in conspiratorially. "Let's say you forgot your wallet at home and wanted a soda. It would be pretty awkward, even for us, to have to try and come up with the money after we had already ordered. Come with me a moment." Damien stood quickly and Mike followed him, somewhat numbly as he processed this turn of events. *"He's more normal than I anticipated,"* Mike considered.

Damien led Mike over to one of the counters manned by a single cashier. The other employees were occupied in the back or had gone on break from the look of it. The three of them were alone as even other patrons of the mall seemed to have gravitated to other options at that moment.

"Hi, how may I help you two today?" asked the young woman behind the counter. She was probably in her early twenties, her brown hair pulled back and held out of the way by her cap displaying the logo of the company.

"Two large colas please," Damien said, smiling before his tone changed to something less casual and more commanding, "And no need to ring them up for a couple nice guys like us, is there?" Mike watched as the young woman's eyes glazed over a moment and she quickly served them up two large sodas. Damien handed one to Mike, who was dumbstruck. Damien nodded and thanked the cashier for her assistance before leading Mike over to the table again. As Mike sat down, he pushed the soda towards the middle of the table, while Damien casually enjoyed a drink from his.

"That was stealing," Mike stated heatedly. "If what you offer is breaking the law at every turn, then I'm even more not interested in what you have to say. Is this how you intend to be, what did you say, compatriots? I don't intend to go on a crime spree with you."

"Calm yourself, Mike." Damien put his cup down. "What I said was, Let's pretend you forgot your wallet and had not realized it until you ordered. Would be kind of awkward to pop home to pick it up at that moment, wouldn't it? There is nothing to stop you from returning another day, and doing the exact same thing, but having her ring up four sodas, only give you two, and then you have paid back into society. Besides, for what they charge you should be getting two free for every one you buy. The markup is ridiculous." He took another sip of the soda.

"It's still stealing," Mike repeated, but some of his conviction was lost. He had always thought that markups were too high anyway, but not being a businessman he never sat down to figure out the overhead that seemed to justify it. He just remembered a few simple formulas from his Economics class. And if one returned the next day, or later with your wallet and did take care of it, what was the difference between it and the tabs that Tony's used to allow his friends to run on a Friday night?

Damien could see Mike wavering. "Now," he said, pulling some cash from his pocket, "Shall we go take care of the tab we ran up back there?" Damien went back to the counter. Mike didn't follow this time, but stared from the cup to Damien. When Damien returned, he tucked a receipt in his pocket and then patted it. "All better now. No harm and no foul. By the way, she thought you were kind of cute and didn't buy that you were only eighteen. However, she found me better looking and gave me her number. I told her it was for the best anyway because I knew you were seeing someone. Wouldn't want any messy conflicts with the blonde you were with, would you?"

The comment about Laurie spiked Mike's anger. Seeing no threat in Damien's words, Mike was able to let it go this time. Uncle Jim knew Laurie wasn't gifted and would be below notice unless it got a reaction out of Mike. Instead, Mike turned to Damien, seeing him in a slightly different light. *"Perhaps it would be nice to have someone my age to talk to about my gifts,"* Mike thought to himself. Since Damien already knew much more about everything, what could it hurt to talk to him about it. "No harm, no foul is right, Damien," Mike finally said, conceding to see how things went. "So, how did you do that to her? And is there any permanent damage or something?"

"Not the least bit of damage to her. Something as minor as a couple of sodas wouldn't even be noticed in the inventory check to be honest. We could probably have ordered a full meal and it wouldn't have been noticed. Now, go walking away from a jewelry store or with some high priced electronics and you might get noticed. Not like you can walk into a bank and convince them to hand you all the money in the safe. There are too many factors and witnesses, both human and electronic for that kind of thing." Mike began to feel a little more ok with Damien's act of petty theft. *"What harm was there in a couple sodas? Or even a burger and fries every now and then, as long as one didn't stray into anything of large value or importance?"* His upbringing slammed into place and he quickly pushed down the rebellious desire to test this lifestyle.

"So, you didn't answer, how did you do that?" Mike pressed, keen to understand this ability Damien had. He recalled references and what his uncle said about controlling people, but since it was considered one of the 'lost talents', there was no instruction guide. If Mike really was the one to bring back these abilities thought long gone, then he would really need a teacher who had them, or at least knew more than his family. And, Mike figured, if he knew how Damien and his kind could do these things, he would be better prepared to spot and correct what they did. That is, if they came after him like the book said they had previous generations and other families.

"It is simple really," Damien stated into the ensuing silence. "The problem for you will be that you will be trying to run before you crawl at this point. First, we need to broaden your perspective on life and your abilities. Can you hear thoughts?" When Mike nodded half-heartedly, Damien continued, "Well, that is the first step to being able to tap into someone's mind and do what I just did. You have to be able to trace those thoughts to their source inside the person's mind. Once there, you can simply tell them to ignore you, or to accept commands. Or hell man, you can tell them to haul off and beat the shit out of someone or something if you felt so inclined." Damien laughed.

Mike turned somber a moment, thinking about last night in the car when he wanted to pull over and beat Derek. "Remember, I had nothing to do with that anger, Mike," Damien stated quickly, having picked up the thought. Mike grasped a slight whisper of energy and quickly chased it until he slammed into a wall of some sort. Damien looked shocked, then pleased as he laughed and applauded. "Well done, Mike. You are a quick study. What you felt was my mental shield. I honestly didn't think you would catch on to me listening to your thoughts so quickly, much less be able to trace it back to my mind. That is the danger in touching someone's mind. If they have the talent, they can then touch yours if you're not careful. I think that was how my former friend Derek was attempting to get a reaction from you."

Mike closed his eyes to concentrate, latching onto the wall he felt with his mind, testing how the energy flowed and reacted to his inspection. "So," he began after a moment, "If I learn to do something like you have done, then my thoughts would be protected from others like us? I could protect myself from this Derek. You say he was your friend, huh? Well, do you have to concentrate all the time to keep it maintained? Or just reinforce it when you feel an intrusion?" Uncle Jim mentioned shielding one's mind wasn't totally tied to the gift, but what Mike felt about Damien's mind definitely seemed stronger.

"That," Damien warmed to the topic, "Is entirely up to you, Mike. Personally, I keep my wall up all the time. I've been practicing since I was old enough to talk and understand what my father said. Now it is second nature. Sure, I'm alerted when someone tries to enter my mind, like you have been attempting to without really knowing how you are doing it. That can aid me in reinforcing my defenses, or to counter attack, like this." Damien stopped talking abruptly and Mike felt like his mind had been backhanded. It was so real he actually reached up and touched his cheek and lip, but felt no residual pain.

"That was incredible." Mike stared, wide eyed, Damien's relationship to Derek momentarily forgotten in the excitement over learning something new. "That is absolutely amazing, Damien." Mike began to construct his own wall and when he felt ready to put it up fully he again grasped the tendril of energy that he was beginning to recognize as Damien attempting to keep a crack open in the defenses. By copying what he had felt from Damien, Mike quickly slapped back at the tendril of power. Mike lost all control over his wall though when Damien fell from the chair to the floor. Mike stood up, but was reassured when Damien started laughing hysterically. They drew some attention from passerby, so Mike began laughing too as if Damien had somehow fallen out of the chair on his own accord.

"Now, that was incredible," Damien said, picking himself up off the floor and righting his chair before sitting down again. "You're a natural, man. It took me a few years to even be able to sense my father's presence, much less attack him back. You picked it up in minutes. Even he would have to be impressed with that and trust me, my father is not impressed easily. He can be a real old fart at times." Damien laughed again. "You might want to try to put that wall back in place because even I cannot keep up with the stream of thoughts rolling off you now."

Mike grinned sheepishly and started focusing. As much as their initial encounter had put him on edge, Mike found himself liking Damien. *"Perhaps Uncle Jim is just being overprotective,"* Mike thought as he slid his own wall into place, knowing he had kicked Damien out of his mind.

Damien smiled at the last thought he got before he was shut out of Mike's mind. While dangerous to not be able to manipulate Mike that way, the thoughts he had seen confirmed he had touched the right chords to gain Mike's trust. Now he just had to ingratiate himself a little further and then it would be much easier to handle his target. Soon enough he could see himself presenting Mike to the Council. *"Perhaps we will be presenting those old has-beens with their walking papers."* He quickly locked the thought away as far as possible into the depths of his mind. It could get him killed. The Council did not take kindly to insurgents, though it had been remade several times in its history by uprisings of all kinds. "I hate to cut our little lesson short, but I have some things I have to attend to. I hope we will get to talk again soon, friend." Damien extended his hand to Mike.

"Sounds like a plan," Mike replied, shaking the other teen's hand. Mike really thought this was going to be a good friendship, but knowing how his uncle would react, he decided to keep it to himself for now. Recalling Damien's words, Mike thought to himself, *"No harm and no foul."* Damien disappeared into the crowd further into the mall, but Mike caught the whisper of energy meaning Damien had done his disappearing act again. *"If only I can see it up close again, I might be able to work it out for myself."*

Contemplating the events of the last minutes Mike came to a sudden realization: *Damien had talked about using his powers since he was much younger.* That was why he seemed so sure. He had had the benefit of growing up with the abilities he was born into. Why was Mike limited to finding out the last week while the first non-family gifted person he meets has had years of experience? It didn't seem fair at all. *"Why do we do this to ourselves?"*

"Because your family has a long tradition of being pretentious, asshole, do-gooders," the Darkness chimed in. *"We can do so much better than that."*

"Maybe," Mike found himself replying. The Darkness laughed as it faded back to its corner it usually hid in.

Mike grabbed his soda and took a long sip. While throwing it away, he remembered the messages on his phone. Pulling it from his pocket, Mike pushed the button to retrieve the text messages. The messages all came from Anne and indicated that she would be at the mall around three if Mike wanted to hangout. Checking the time, his phone showed about a quarter after three. Mike replied that he was in the food court if she wanted to swing by.

"Should I be spending time with her?" Mike questioned himself while he waited for Anne to arrive.

The Darkness chuckled as it came out of hiding. *"Why not? A pretty girl wants a piece of you. Give it to her."*

"Seriously? That's the best advice you've got? Just go for it? What about Laurie?" Mike waited for a reply. *"And now I'm talking to myself."*

"Are you? Am I a part of you? If so, then you want to do the things I suggest, don't you?" Mike felt the Darkness waiting for his response.

Mike was saved by Anne's appearance in the food court. She waved with the hand holding her phone before sliding it into a pocket. As she walked over, Mike appraised her again in her denim shorts and skin-tight T-shirt. The shirt boasted an obscene amount of glitter with the word "Princess" written in cursive across her chest. *"She's certainly not leaving much to the imagination,"* Mike and the Darkness shared the same thought.

"Hey Mike." She stepped close and threw her arms around him in a big hug, planting a kiss on Mike's cheek. "Happy belated birthday. Did you get my messages? Well, you must have. I thought at first Laurie gave me a wrong number on purpose because you never responded or called me back."

"I did. Thank you. It's been a busy week," Mike replied, looking down into her eyes. He noted he was still holding her but didn't see any reason to let go.

"I'm so happy to see you." She snuggled close, pressing against him. Mike suddenly pulled her closer, giving in to the Darkness's desire to see how far Anne would go. She paused, looking up at him with a puzzled expression, before smiling and holding on just as tight. "So, what would you like to do this evening? I'm free all night."

Mike gazed into her eyes, trying to catch her thoughts. It doesn't take long for him to find the thread to follow back to her mind, exactly as with Damien.

"This feels nice," Mike picked up Anne's thoughts, *"I bet Laurie tried to convince him I am some evil bitch or something. Now I have him to myself for an afternoon. We will see what Miss Goody-Goody thinks of that when I get through with him."*

"Forgive me for not returning your calls," Mike said, interrupting the train of thought. "It has been a weird couple of days, and I did have plans last night."

"Oh, all's forgiven Mike," Anne practically purred. "I'm glad you're here. So you don't have any plans this afternoon? Maybe all evening?"

Mike locked eyes with her, attempting to access her mind like Damien had with the cashier. Something pushed back at him. Secure in the wall Damien had taught him how to make, Mike tried again only to feel the same resistance. *"Maybe I need more practice. I'll see where she takes this and try later."*

"Not really. As long as I let my aunt and uncle know when to expect me, I should be free for awhile." Damien's comment swirled in Mike's mind. Mike isn't surprised when the Darkness rejoined the conversation, *"Let's have some fun."* Mike smiled at the thought.

"Wonderful!" Anne's exclamation snapped Mike's focus back to her in his arms. "I've gotta do a little clothes shopping. Will you help me pick out some new summer outfits?" Her arms tightened around him making it clear she wasn't expecting or going to accept a refusal. Looking into her eyes brought back the same odd feeling from the car last week, but stronger this time. Mike tested his mental wall, firming it into place. *"It is going to take more than an hour to master that trick,"* he thought to himself.

Anne latched herself to his arm, laying her head on Mike's shoulder as they fell into step with each other. "By the way, love the no glasses look. You should wear contacts more often."

Mike smiled but didn't respond. Playing along with her game, he squeezed her hand. *"If she wants to put on a fashion show, I'm just going to enjoy it and see what happens."* Damien's confident swagger and cavalier attitude with the cashier started to take root within Mike, and he kept Anne close as they threaded their way through the shoppers at the mall to get to the first destination on her list.

***

Damien watched from the shadows as Mike headed off arm and arm with Anne. Something about her seemed familiar and he quickly delved into her mind once he detected Mike backing off. He didn't know what Mike's intentions were with poking in her mind, but if there was someone other than Laurie he should be worried about, Damien felt he should do some research into this Anne girl. After a few moments of probing, Damien paled slightly when he detected his father's presence in Anne's mind. He quickly realized the presence as residual, his father wasn't actively searching the girl's mind. Probing deeper he figured out why Anne looked familiar. Derek had played with her mind a few years before, risking exposure and criminal charges if something wasn't done. As a favor, Damien's father modified Anne's mind, arranging it so she wouldn't go to the police about what Derek had convinced her to do. Damien smiled to himself, *"I'm sure this information will be useful. If Mike discovers Anne's secret, hopefully it won't turn him against me. Now to find Derek and give him a piece of my mind."*

Damien's search for his childhood friend only brought frustration. Every time he got close, Derek would disappear. Knowing this game could go on for a long time, Damien finally relented and returned to his own study. *"At least if Derek's dodging me, he won't have time to try anything to interfere with Mike."* Damien hastily wrote a note for his father regarding his progress before continuing the hunt for his childhood friend.

Chapter 11

As Anne flit from rack to rack, she took every opportunity to cuddle up against Mike while asking his opinion on her choices. After a half hour she ended up with a couple short skirts and some tops to go with them. Mike could almost feel the Darkness drooling over the combinations and he took a moment to check the corners of his mouth. *"This will be fun,"* he and the Darkness thought simultaneously as Anne led him toward the fitting rooms. She directed him to a seat across from the changing room, placing her bag next to him.

He picked at the glitter on his shirt while she tried on a couple outfit combinations. After she settled on one, she threw open the door. She performed a little runway model walk toward him, turning around slowly after a couple steps. *"I could get used to this,"* Mike thought as he admired the way her outfit clung to her curves.

When she returned to the little booth, she called out, "What do you think?"

"I like that one," he offered in response. "Need any help in there?"

"No, silly." Her giggle carried as clearly as her thoughts, *"I'm definitely keeping this one then. I bet the red top would be even better."*

Mike grinned before calling out, "Did you try on the red shirt yet?"

"That's next."

"Ok, I'm going to just call my uncle and let him know I'll be home later. Be right back."

Mike walked closer to the entrance to make the call, " Hey Uncle Jim, I ran into Anne at the mall. We're going to get something to eat and see a movie if that's alright?"

Uncle Jim was surprised at first but replied, "Have fun, and be home before midnight."

Mike hung up, all smiles as he returned to the fitting rooms. He took his seat as Anne asked, "Mike, is that you?"

"Yeah. We're good for the evening. I just gotta be home by midnight. Let's see the red top."

There is a shuffling sound before the door opened a crack. Anne's thought bounced in Mike's head, *"I sure hope he's alone."* When she stepped out, Mike's jaw dropped. The silky red shirt she had chosen fit near perfect, with just enough movement to accent her body. The hem line stopped on the lower half of her hip, leaving about an inch of her black underwear showing. Below the lace of her panties was bare skin down her tanned legs to her sock covered feet.

In his shock, the Darkness seized the opening, forcing Mike to his feet. He met Anne halfway out of the door and guided her back into the little room, pressing his lips to hers. One hand wrapped around her as the other shut the door, turning the lock firmly.

When the kiss broke, Anne whispered breathlessly, "What are you doing? We're going to get in serious trouble." Her protest was spoiled by the intensity of her gaze locked onto Mike's.

He felt a tickle at his mental wall but shoved it away. "We'll be fine. Besides, I don't hear a real complaint there." His body pulled her close with both arms as he wrestled for control with the Darkness. Minutes pass in the next round of kissing. As hands began exploring each other's body, there was a knock at the door.

"Everything ok in there, Miss?" The saleswoman's voice like ice water down their backs.

"Everything was fine," Mike replied without thinking.

They both heard the startled gasp from the clerk. "I'm going to have to call security. You're not supposed to be in there."

Anne paled and pulled back as much as the tiny room allowed. Mike, starting to regain control but not wanting to spoil what's happening, put a finger to her lips before reaching out with his mind to the unseen saleswoman. *"No you won't."* He found no resistance as he took control of the clerk's mind. *"Just give us a few minutes and we'll be ready to make our purchases. Once we're gone, forget about this whole thing."*

"Alright then. I'll be at the register when you're ready to check out," she replied before the teens heard her walk away, her shoes made scuffing noises on the carpet.

Anne opened her mouth to speak, but Mike covered it with his own. This time, when they broke to breathe, Mike said, "As long as you buy the red one I don't care about the rest." Before she could respond he slipped out the door into the hall.

Stunned, Anne changed back into her jean shorts and shirt. She gathered up the clothes. Taking a deep breath, Mike heard her final thought before she opened the door. *"I can't believe that happened, but I want more."*

Mike grinned like the Cheshire cat as he put an arm around her. The two headed to the register where the saleswoman waited. Once they place the items on the counter, she asked, "Did everything fit to your liking?"

"Great," Anne replied, suppressing a giggle while counting out bills to pay for the clothes.

Mike took the bag, adding it to the other he carried. "What's next?" He wrapped his arm around Anne, his hand rested on her hip.

As they left the store, she asked, "Do you swim, Mike?"

"I know how, but haven't been this summer with working and all," Mike replied, the thought of her trying on bikinis caused him to check for drool again.

"Oh. Well, you should come over sometime. My parents put in a pool a few years ago. We usually have a few parties throughout the year since it's heated in the winter. Summer is even better," she said as she led Mike into a store specializing in swimwear and lingerie.

"Sounds like fun." Mike tried to avoid notice as they entered the store. Being anywhere near these kinds of places always made him a little self-conscious, like he was some sort of pervert. He prayed silently for her to hurry up and find something so they could get out of there. Mike puzzled over the reaction in the last store. The Darkness piped up, *"You can't blame me for all of it. You wanted her too. Clearly she is up for it."*

Mentally he replied, *"Guilty, but not the point. I think I like Laurie. Messing around with Anne would kill any chance with Laurie. Unless..."*

"Now you're thinking like me." The Darkness laughed as it retreated back into its hiding spot in the depths of Mike's mind.

Anne squealed in excitement, breaking his train of thought. She pulled him towards the fitting rooms. She pushed Mike into a chair across from a vacant room and quickly disappeared inside. A couple of the other rooms were occupied and Mike prayed again, this time that none of them would come out with him sitting there. *"Why did I agree to this?"* Mike thought to himself. Feeling self conscious, he arranged the shopping bags next to him to make it obvious he was there with someone in case anyone should happen to come by.

Anne took so long two of the other fitting room doors opened and people came out of them. A slightly older woman exited one and saw Mike sitting there. She eyed him oddly before noticing the bags and the occupied room right across. She smiled and walked away towards the checkout lane. Mike heard her thoughts clearly, *"Poor guy looks so uncomfortable. His girlfriend must be making him go shopping with her."* Mike chuckled to himself once the woman passed out of earshot.

A moment later, Anne's voice tentatively asked as she opened the door slightly, "Is there anyone else there with you, Mike?"

Sensing what he may see, Mike leapt to his feet and approached the fitting room. He pushed the door the rest of the way open, revealing Anne's latest outfit. It was a shiny blue bikini leaving very little to the imagination.

Anne stared intently up into his eyes. *"What is he thinking?"*

Mike answered her thought by slipping into the tiny room and pulling her into his arms. The Darkness crowed in triumph as Mike pressed his lips against Anne's. Her body molded to his and their hands began exploring again.

"I don't know what's come over me. I don't do this stuff. But I don't want to stop." Anne's thoughts intruded on Mike's concentration.

Breaking the kiss a moment, he whispered, "Don't think, just do." He clicked the door lock before giving in to the Darkness and the feel of her in his arms.

Too short of a time later they were interrupted by a familiar knock and a different voice asking, "Everything alright in there, Miss?"

This time it was Anne who reacted first. "I'm fine. Leave me alone. I wish you'd forget I'm in here." She groaned in frustration and Mike watched as smoky gray wisps traveled from Anne through the door.

He looked down, Anne's top is askew and he has one hand slipped into the back of her bikini bottom. *"We need to get out of here."*

"Why?" The Darkness asked. *"You know she's not going anywhere. Take her, then take the blonde. We can convince them both it's alright."*

Unbidden, Colleen jumped to his mind and Mike saw the night of his fight with Kevin outside Tony's. This time, when Colleen looked up at him, it's not in gratitude for his support, but disappointment. He pulled away from Anne.

"What's wrong?" Anne attempted to pull him back, but settled for pressing herself against him.

The momentary vision passed, leaving Mike uneasy about the changing room. "Let's get out of here. I'll make sure the coast is clear." He disentangled himself from her again and slipped out of the door. Thankfully there was no one outside for him to have to brainwash.

"That's one way to look at it. I like it. Let's use it on the girls and have some fun," the Darkness said before erupting in laughter.

"Maybe." Mike considered the possibilities. *"I could have them both."*

"That's right. Anyone we want is ours for the taking." The Darkness nudged from the depths of Mike's mind.

When Anne exited the changing room, Mike gathered up the bags. Hand in hand they headed for the register, Anne clutched the small strips of blue fabric she recently tried on. "After I pay for this, we should go put those in my car. This is turning out to be a better shopping trip than I anticipated." She snuggled against Mike's side, his arm sliding around her.

"Mmhmm," Mike agreed. After adding another bag to his collection, Anne guided the way out into the parking lot near her car.

When they reached her car she unlocked the door and turned to take the bags. When their eyes meet, Mike gave in to desire again. The bags hit the ground as the teens locked together, the previous interruptions heightening passion. A honking car broke them apart again.

Anne looked up at Mike. Breathlessly she whispered, "My parents aren't home."

Mike smiled . "I'll grab my aunt's car and follow you." He squeezed her as they kissed again. They reluctantly separated to their respective cars.

Fifteen minutes later Mike pulled into Anne's driveway behind her. The Darkness spouted advice the entire way and ratcheted up Mike's desire. He met her at her car and pressed her against it, his lips against hers. When they stop to breathe, he whispered in her ear, "Inside, now."

The two made a break for the porch, continuously touching each other all the way to Anne's room. Once behind her closed door, the fire stunted by the previous interruptions flared to full bloom. They tore at each other's clothes only to fall onto Anne's bed with socks still on and underwear hanging around their ankles. As they shifted and melded their bodies together, Mike's phone went off.

The two jumped apart and he began frantically searching their discarded clothes to find the device. Just as it went to voicemail, he found it. The Caller ID read, "Laurie-Cell".

"Deal with her later. You've got something to finish here," The Darkness spoke up, pulling Mike's gaze to Anne's nude form as she lay casually on her bed.

Mike's indecision froze him momentarily, and Anne slid to her feet in front of him. She pressed against him, one hand reached up to pull his lips down to hers, the other took his phone and dropped it in the pile of clothes. Any resistance shattered and the two returned to her bed.

"I'm going to enjoy this," Anne's thoughts intruded on Mike's concentration as he was kissing down her chest.

He pushed back into her mind, willing her to stop thinking and just act. His hands and lips continue to explore her body as she pulled at the back of his head. He kissed the inside of her thighs as Anne breathed heavily, trying to pull him into her, when a door closing downstairs stopped them.

"Anne honey, who's car is in the driveway?" a woman's voice called out.

Frustration poured out of Mike as he groaned and pulled away. "I'm done with this," he growled, embracing the same anger which usually allowed the Darkness to take over. Anne moved as well, as if to respond. "Stay there and wait for me," he compelled her with his power, before stalking to the door. He opened it slightly, reaching out with his gift to who he assumed was Anne's mother. Widening his awareness, he found her alone. *"Go out to dinner, see a movie, something, but don't come home until later and forget you saw another car here."*

The woman called out again, "I'm going to try that new italian place so you're on your own for dinner. Don't make a mess. I'll leave you some money for pizza on the counter."

When he heard the door close again and a car start up outside, he turned back to Anne, satisfied. "Now, where were we?" he asked as he approached her.

"What did you do? My mom never would have left like that without coming up here, but I didn't hear you say anything to her."

"Don't worry about it. She's gone and we can pick up where we left off," he leaned down to kiss her, but Anne pulled away.

"Maybe we should cool it. Things are happening too fast."

"So," Mike sat on the bed next to her, turning her face up to his. He pushed into her mind, finding a measure of resistance. *"Forget about your mom coming home. We came from the mall to finish this in private. That's all."* As he pushed to bring her back to what they were doing, Anne went rigid.

Her eyes locked onto his. "No. I want you to leave. Now."

Before he realized what he was doing, he was fully dressed and halfway across the lawn to the car. He turned back towards the house to see Anne closing the door. Confused he climbed behind the wheel, and drove back to the mall.

Chapter 12

Mike wandered the mall, confused about his encounter with Anne. *"What the hell happened to me?"*

"You let her get away is what happened," the Darkness piped up. *"You should have left me in charge. We would still be enjoying what she was offering until you messed up."*

"I don't think that's what happened. Did me messing with her mind backfire?"

No response was forthcoming from the Darkness. Mike found himself standing outside the bookstore he had browsed the week before. Shrugging off his thoughts, he stepped into the store, taking a deep sniff of the smell of books, both older and new that washed over him. He heard a giggle from the register off to the side and turned to see the girl from last week. *"At least now I know she was thinking and not speaking out loud. What was her name? Julie."*

"Really, the bookworm when you left the cheerleader behind? What's wrong with you?" the Darkness barked from its hiding spot.

"Shutup," Mike growled at it before smiling at the clerk. "What's so funny?"

"You," she replied, giggling again. "Who walks into a bookstore and sniffs like that?"

"I love the smell of books." Mike laughed. "Cliche I know, but there is something about the smell of a new book. It's calming."

"I guess I'm immune to it, having grown up with them around all the time. Can I help you find anything today? Or did you just come in to smell the books?" She rested her elbows on the counter and leaned on her arms where it pressed against her stomach. Her brown ponytail swished to the side.

"Just browsing, I guess. Running the show alone today?" Mike stepped closer eyeing the way the counter pressing into her middle pulled her shirt tight. *"Maybe I should practice this brainwashing a bit more."*

"For now. My parents wanted to go out to eat and it's usually slower around here until after dinner time anyway. I don't mind it. I get to catch up on my own reading." She pointed to a worn paperback next to the register.

"That's good," Mike said, approaching until the counter was all that separated them. As he reached into her mind he saw her eyes glaze over. *"I'd like the newest science fiction release I saw the flier for last week, but you will just give it to me, Julie."*

Julie brightened, "Our Science fiction section is over here. We just got in this great new book I think you'll like." She grabbed a copy from the shelf. "Here you go." She handed it to him. "Do you want it in a bag or do you want to just carry it?"

"I'll take it like this. Thank you."

"No problem." Julie waved as he exited the store. She returned to the counter as if nothing strange happened at all.

Outside the store, Mike stared at the book. *"That was easy enough. Why didn't it work with Anne?"* His stomach rumbled. *"Something to ponder over some food. And another practice run with my powers."* He headed to the food court.

After carefully selecting a vendor with a short line, Mike ordered his food, compelling the cashier to not charge him. As he sat down at a table, he looked around to find someone else to practice on. He spotted a group of girls a few tables over, laughing and talking. He focused, trying to hear their conversation as he slowly munched his sandwich and fries.

"You know Katie, Tom is going to love that shirt you bought. I doubt you'll even get to watch the movie," the blonde said to her redhead friend.

"That was the point, Emily," Katie said as she leaned away from the table to run her hands down the shirt. Mike watched how the cut was so low the top of her bra showed when she pulled the hem at her hips.

The third girl caught Mike staring and turned to her friends, "You have a creeper, Katie."

Mike averted his gaze, but still caught their conversation.

"He's not bad looking," Emily said. "If you don't go talk to him, Katie, I will."

"She has Tom, why would she?" the third girl asked.

"Tom can be boring sometimes, Mindy," Katie replied. "And besides, I'm going to college out East in the fall. I can't take boring Tom with me."

"Good. Then Tom and I won't have to sneak around anymore once she leaves. She doesn't deserve him." Mike caught the thought, tracing it back to the one named Mindy.

Mike chuckled as the three continued to discuss whether Katie should talk to Mike or not. *"Now or never."* Mike reached out to touch the girls' minds. First Katie, then Emily, then Mindy. He watched all three of them freeze. *"Katie, come have a seat over here. Let's get to know each other. Your friends can find other things to do for now."*

The girls snapped back to normal when Mike released his hold on their minds. Katie stood up, waving her friends away. She smoothed her shirt; it gripped her body like a glove. She swayed over as her friends left the food court without a backwards glance.

"This seat taken?" She asked, not pointing to the one across from Mike but the one next to him.

"Please, have a seat," Mike replied, standing to pull out the chair for her. "My name's Mike. I'm sorry I was staring at you and your friends. I'm new here and you caught my eye."

"It's alright. My name's Katie. Nice to meet you Mike. What brought you to this corner of the world?"

As soon as Mike sat next to her he placed a hand on her leg. "Staying with my aunt and uncle for the summer. Just trying not to get too bored while I'm here." Mike ran his fingertips along Katie's thigh. "Any ideas to help pass the time?"

"I can think of a few," she replied as she placed her hand on his, moving it to her inner thigh. *"A little forward, but why not. I'm tired of being neglected."*

Mike spotted an average looking guy staring at the two of them. A quick delve into his mind revealed it was her boyfriend, Tom. "What about your boyfriend? Won't he have something to say?"

"Maybe. But I don't care."

As Tom started towards them, Mike moved a chair into his path, causing him to trip. In the wake of his crash the food court fell silent as everyone watched him get up, awkwardly untangling himself from the chair. He glared at those around him, most returned to their food, but a few snickered. His gaze settled on Mike and Katie.

Mike casually put an arm across Katie's shoulders, letting his hand rest on the exposed flesh just below her throat. "This will get interesting, just be quiet and let me handle him."

Katie nodded as her eyes glazed over again when Mike touched her mind.

Tom stood over the pair, taking a deep breath before speaking. "Just what do you think you're doing?"

"Sit down Tom." Mike compelled him to do just that. "What I think and what I know I am doing is that I'm getting to know your soon-to-be ex-girlfriend . And you're not going to do anything about it."

Tom tried to rise, "What did you say to me, asshole? I should..."

Tom cut off as Mike raised a finger on his free hand. The one around Katie traced down across the top of her cleavage. Tom strained to move, his face turning red.

"Should I tell Katie or are you going to put on your big boy panties and fess up?" Mike grinned as he released Tom to speak.

"Fess up? To what? I don't know you. Get your hands off Katie."

Mike shut him up again. "Tsk tsk. Tom, you really shouldn't be screwing around on Katie. Not that she hasn't been considering dumping your sorry ass anyway. But with her friend Mindy? That's just low."

Katie's eyes went wide, her mouth set in a thin line. Mike felt her tense as if she wanted to reach Tom.

"Baby, it's nothing," Tom pleaded when Mike released him. "You were visiting colleges and I got bored and lonely. It means nothing."

"Tom, I think we will come to an understanding here," the Darkness prompted Mike as he took control again. "You're going to give me whatever cash you have to pay for the girls to see a movie and buy snacks. Then, go find Emily and Mindy. You're going to tell them to wait here in the food court for Katie. Then you're going to go home and tomorrow forget all about this, except for Katie and Mindy both breaking up with you."

Tom nodded, his eyes fixed as the red drained from his face.

"You are dismissed, Tom. Be a good boy now."

Tom handed over sixty dollars from his pocket. Mike and the Darkness chuckled as they watched Tom woodenly stand and head off into the mall crowd. Mike turned to Katie, "Shall we continue getting acquainted?"

Her eyes wide, she asked, "How'd you do that? What are you going to do to me?"

"A little trick I've learned. Useful. And I'm not going to do anything you weren't already considering. I haven't so far, have I?"

"No. I guess not," Katie replied. "I can't believe that asshole. And that bitch. Smiling to my face while they're screwing each other."

"Well, I took care of him. And I'll have a talk with Mindy later. Now let's pretend Tom only showed up to confess his crimes and leave you in peace." Mike planted the memory in her mind, making sure she didn't remember how he manipulated them both.

When her eyes cleared, Katie smiled and put her hand on Mike's leg. "Now that I'm a free woman, wanna get out of here and go somewhere we can be alone?"

Mike looked around, spotting the large Family Restroom near the entrance. He guided Katie's attention toward it. "I've got a better idea. You go first. I'll be right behind you."

Giggling, Katie stood and strutted for the bathrooms. She detoured at the last moment, ducking into the larger bathroom.

As Mike made his way toward the restrooms he spotted a mall security guard walking through the food court. Mike compelled a woman nearby to stop the guard and ask directions before he ducked into the restroom with Katie. She waited just inside, fidgeting nervously. Mike locked the door behind him.

"This is so crazy." Katie stepped closer to him. "But kinda hot."

Mike pulled her into his arms as they began to kiss. He pressed her against the counter next to the sink as their hands roamed. Katie reached for his belt. Mike lifted her up onto the counter, slipping forward between her knees.

Some time later, Mike poked his head outside while Katie finished sorting her scarlet hair into some semblance of normalcy. "Coast is clear. You wanna go first. I could go for a movie if you're still interested."

Katie's eyes shined with the afterglow of their exertions. "Definitely." She licked her lips. "A movie sounds great. After I deal with my two-faced friend."

Mike touched her mind. "Let me handle Mindy. Let's just keep this casual and friendly." Katie blinked. "Round up your friends. The movie is on me." Mike grinned, patting Tom's money in his pocket.

Katie pressed up against him, kissing him. "Wait 'til the girls hear about this." She slipped out with a final wink.

Mike waited by the door, reaching out to listen for the reunion of friends. *"This is certainly easier with your help."*

"I know," the satisfaction evident in the Darkness's reply. *"That was fun. Aren't you glad you stopped fighting and started listening to me?"*

"Sure." Mike began to catch Katie's conversation with her friends.

"Hey girls," she said. A chair scraped on the floor as she took a seat. "You're not going to believe this."

"Tom found us. Told us to wait for you here," Emily interrupted.

"He said you two were broken up," Mindy added, her tone carefully neutral.

"Old news," Katie stated. "You know that guy I went to talk to." She began relating some of the details of their liaison in the restroom. Emily and Mindy gasped.

Taking his cue, Mike exited the bathroom, approaching the girls quickly. He stepped up behind Katie and draped his hands onto her shoulders, his fingertips brushed her neck. "Hey. You ladies up for a movie? My treat."

Emily and Mindy both smiled as Katie leaned back into his hands. Her friends' thoughts appraising him anew.

"Maybe I should have talked to him first," Emily lamented.

"Wild. Going to have to try that myself. Tom never would. He's boring," Mindy winked at Mike while Katie was distracted.

Mike returned the wink, his vantage point providing aerial view on all three girls. He felt the Darkness warming up. *"No. Intriguing, and we'll visit that thought later. But no."* The feeling of disappointment warred with anticipation from the depths of Mike's subconscious.

The quartet made their way to the movie theater, Mike walked with a hand in Katie's back pocket while Mindy made eyes at him from the other side of her friend. Once they bought tickets and snacks, they entered the half-light of the auditorium to find seats.

Emily led the way, Katie pointing to the top row, dragging Mike behind. Mindy pinched Mike as they went up the stairs. He gives her a 'Cool it' glare but his heart wasn't in it.

The Darkness chuckled. *"Oh the things she'll do to one up her friend."*

"Kinda figured that one out on my own. Thanks for your input, though," Mike replied sarcastically.

After the movie, Mike and Katie exchanged numbers before she took off in her car.

"Was nice meeting you, Mike," Emily said, fumbling with her purse to find her keys. "Maybe I'll see ya around." She waved and climbed into her car.

Mike checked the time on his phone as he walked back to his car. Knowing Mindy waited nearby, he took his time. As he pulled his key from his pocket, she pressed up against him.

"Hey, lover boy. Where are you running off too?"

Mike grinned before turning and clutching her against him, leaning back against the car. "I know what you're up to. Your game with Katie."

"What do you mean?" She tried to pull back but Mike held tight.

"I'm not her boyfriend. So you don't have to try and 'win' me from her like Tom. I'll take you both whenever I want. Maybe at the same time."

Mindy struggled to pull away. "Who do you think you are? I only do who I want when I want."

"I'm in charge," Mike's voice growled as the Darkness seized control. He pulled her roughly against him before mashing his lips against hers. *"And now you're mine."* The touch on her mind was not subtle or gentle as the Darkness forced submission upon her.

Mike mentally screamed in revulsion as he wrestled for control. *"Not like this. Never like this."* An explosion of white blotted out his vision, a rush of air deafened him. Mike blinked as the sound and light subsided a moment later.

Mindy blinked as well, still pressed against him. "Hey lover boy. Where are you running off to?"

Mike froze. "I'm on my way home," he answered slowly. "Curfew and all."

"Well, if you find time to try that restroom trick again, call me," she kissed him hard as she slipped a piece of paper into his pocket. She gave him a little squeeze before turning and walking away.

Shaken, Mike climbed into his aunt's car. He sat behind the wheel as the engine warmed up. *"What in the hell just happened? Hello? Thoughts?"*

Silence was the only answer he got for the entire drive home. He itched the cold spot on his chest from his necklace. *"When did that happen? Nothing? Some help here would be nice."* The Darkness never responded.

Chapter 13

The next morning Mike awoke to a string of text messages from Anne.

'Hey Mike.'

'U there?'

'We need to talk.'

'Call me?'

'Please?!'

"*Well, she's desperate. Probably regrets missing out yesterday,*" the Darkness commented.

"*Oh. Now you wanna talk? What the hell happened last night? Why did you do that? Mindy was more than willing without forcing it. And then you disappeared.*"

"*Maybe I pushed it too far, but you didn't have to lightning me.*"

"*Lightning you? I did nothing.*"

"*Could've fooled me.*" A moment later, "*So, did you have all three? Or just the redhead?*"

"*Katie yes. Mindy gave me her number. How do you not know? You're in my head and you didn't know this?*" Mike shook himself.

The Darkness gave a mental shrug. "*Things went fuzzy after I tried to mold Mindy to be a bit more pliant.*"

"*Well, we are doing things my way from here on out. Or else. Got it?*"

Mike felt the Darkness nod in agreement. "*Good. I'm starved.*"

"*Happens when you use your powers that much. Among other things.*" The Darkness laughed at his own joke.

Mike headed down the hall where he heard his relatives in the kitchen. As Mike poured a cup of coffee from the pot, Uncle Jim laughed.

"You look like death warmed over. Do I dare ask? And answer quick before your Aunt comes back out here. She's not fond of Anne, you know."

"I ended up meeting someone at the mall and seeing a movie with her and her friends. Anne kinda flaked on me."

"I knew you'd make friends. Are you going to see this new girl again?" Uncle Jim eyed the hallway for his wife's arrival. "What about Laurie?"

Mike shrugged. "I don't know. It was spur of the moment. She seems nice though."

The Darkness chimed in, *"Understatement of the year."*

"True. Should we call Anne or Mindy today?"

"Both?" The Darkness chuckled.

"I want to hear what Anne has to say. I'm still not sure what went wrong yesterday."

Uncle Jim pulled Mike from his thoughts by speaking, "Any plans for today?"

"Not sure. Anne wants to talk about yesterday. And there are the new friends I made. Would it be alright if I borrowed the car again?"

"I don't see why not. Just remember you have work tomorrow. Drive safe."

Aunt Jenny entered the kitchen. "Drive safe? Leaving us again today?"

"Honey, he's a teenager. Let him go have fun without giving him too hard a time," Uncle Jim interrupted his wife.

Aunt Jenny smiled. "Have fun."

After a quick shower, Mike sat behind the wheel. He texted Anne, 'Face to face?'

While he waited for a response, he messaged Mindy. 'Hey. It's Mike. What's up?'

Mindy replied almost immediately, 'Hey lover boy. Was just thinking about you. Free today?'

"We sure are," the Darkness said. It reached for control to text her back.

"I said we are doing things my way. I'd like to talk to Anne first."

"Boring."

Mike replied to Mindy, 'Supposed to meet a friend but if she cancels...'

'Hoping she does.'

Mike put the car in drive and headed toward the mall in hopes Anne would reply before he got there. He put the car in park and checked his phone. The reply from Anne is not what he hoped for, 'I can't. Not today. Can we talk on the phone?'

He dropped a quick reply, 'No. Needs to be face to face.'

He then texted Mindy, 'What are you up to right now?'

Immediately Mindy replied, 'Nothing. Where are you?'

Grinning, Mike took the advice of the Darkness, and replied, 'Waiting for you at the mall.'

'Be there in 20.' Mindy added a kiss face emoji to the message.

Mike found a spot in the food court and waited for Mindy to arrive. As she came through the doors, Mike's jaw dropped when he saw her outfit. Her T-shirt was clearly a size too small as it strained to cover her chest. Her too-short skirt threatened to flash her underwear with every step.

She spotted Mike and bounded over. She sat on his lap. "Hey lover boy."

"Hello to you too," Mike replied, his hand sliding up her inner thigh.

"Mmhmm." Mindy wiggled on Mike's lap.

"Can we hurry this along? She's ready, I'm ready," the Darkness chimed in.

"Why not enjoy this a bit?" Mike replied.

"So little time."

Mike rolled his eyes. "Nice outfit."

"This old thing?" Mindy wiggled against him again. "I just grabbed the first thing in my closet. You like?"

"Definitely." Mike pressed his fingers into her inner thigh. "Shall we?" He cocked his head towards the restroom.

"I thought you'd never ask." Mindy jumped up and headed toward the bathrooms. When she ducked into the family restroom, she was not as subtle as Katie and Mike groaned.

"She's cute," Derek said from Mike's side.

Mike jumped. "Where did you come from?"

"Just checking in. You seem to be enjoying your powers."

"End him," the Darkness tried to take control.

"No. My way." Mike replied. "Can you hurry this up? I'm busy."

"I see that," said Derek. "Our gifts draw them like flies to honey, don't they?"

"What do you mean?"

"It's like a drug. They won't be able to resist you."

The Darkness chimed in, *"Who cares? Mindy is waiting."*

"I know." Then out loud Mike added, "Whatever. If you're done, I'm out of here." Mike started to stand.

Derek grabbed his wrist, "I'm not finished. Have you considered my offer? Join me."

Mike looked down at his wrist before looking up at Derek. "Don't push me." The Darkness raged to be let loose as Mike reached towards Derek's mind, finding the mental wall he expected. He searched for a crack as Derek started laughing.

"What do you think you're doing? Pathetic. You're like a child with a slingshot trying to stop a hurricane."

Fueled by the insult, Mike slammed against Derek's mental shield. A small crack appeared and Derek leapt to his feet, knocking the chair over in his haste.

"Everyone gets lucky once," Derek said as he started to disappear.

Mike tried to study what Derek did but was interrupted by his phone buzzing.

Mindy's text read, 'Coming lover boy?'

Mike glanced around but everyone seemed to be lost in their own activities. He quickly headed for the family restroom.

Damien grabbed his arm halfway there. "Hey buddy. Did Derek come by?"

"Yes. One of you are going to show me how you do that disappearing trick. But later, I have someone waiting for me."

"Laurie? Or Anne?" Damien grinned.

"Neither, now get lost unless you can freeze time to have this conversation."

Damien nodded. "Later then, friend." He disappeared too quickly for Mike to grasp what he did.

Mike slipped into the restroom. As he closed the door, Mindy pressed against him. "What took you so long? I thought you forgot about me."

Mike wrapped his arms around her. "Just had to wait for the coast to clear."

As they kissed, Mike heard her thought, *"This is so hot."*

Mike locked the door with one hand as he slid his other along Mindy's back. She arched into him.

***

Mike waited a few minutes after Mindy exited the restroom. He'd had to get rid of two people who tried to enter while they were together. Luckily Mindy didn't notice.

"This is fun. Who's next?" The Darkness practically salivated at the possibilities.

"Can you think of anything else?"

"Why bother?"

Mike shook his head and left the restroom. He pulled his phone from his pocket to find a message from Laurie, 'Hey Mike. Had a minute before choir practice. Wanted to see how your weekend was going. I had a great time Friday night.'

Mike replied, 'Me too. Let me know when you're free this week.'

Mike's stomach growled. *"Time for some food I guess."*

After he used his powers to get a free sandwich, he found a place to sit and look around. Damien appeared across from him. "Now a good time to talk?"

Mike swallowed the bite he had just taken. "You going to show me how you do that?"

"That's really advanced. You can hurt yourself if you mess up."

"Maybe Derek will teach me. He seems interested in being my friend."

"Derek wants to use you. He thinks you're his ticket to power."

"And you don't?"

"No. I have no desire for the hassles of power. I've seen what it does to my father."

"So what do you want from me?"

"Friends? Most of the other gifted I know are like Derek. So concerned with their powers. When I heard about you, I'd hoped you would be different because you don't come from my world."

"Pathetic. End him and let's call Anne. Or Katie again. Redhead sounds good for dessert," The Darkness chimed in.

"Shut up." Mike took a sip of his soda before responding to Damien. "Your world huh? Look, I'm going home. I've gotta work tomorrow." Mike started to stand, but Damien reached out his hand. "You want to know how to teleport, right?"

Mike nodded, sitting back down. "That's really what it is. Teleportation?"

"It's dangerous. And I'm not saying that to try to get out of teaching you. I've seen people maim or even kill themselves doing it wrong, or before they were ready."

"I don't care. I want to learn."

"Promise you'll do things exactly as I say." Mike nodded. "Ok. It works similar to telekinesis. But instead of moving the object from Point A to Point B through the air, you simply move yourself from one spot to another. Practice on that table sign on the next table. Try to bring it to this table instantly."

Mike concentrated on the display, trying to see it sitting in front of him and Damien instead. In the space of a blink, something happened. The colored insert appeared floating an inch above the table in front of Mike before falling flat. Mike glanced up at Damien.

Damien picked up the insert. "Imagine this is just your insides. You've just left your skin behind in the place you were teleporting from."

Mike stared at the insert, absorbing Damien's warning anew regarding the dangers of teleportation.

"Keep practicing, but not with yourself. Even if you master objects, a live person or animal is harder. Their bodies are in more of a state of movement than inanimate objects."

"I'll be careful."

"Alright. I'll leave you to it. See ya soon."

"Thanks," Mike whispered as Damien disappeared again.

Mike looked around for another empty table to practice with. After an hour of working with the little table displays, he managed to flip one to his table and back perfectly. Mike cheered out loud, drawing the attention of several passerby. He smiled, snatched his phone from the table and headed for the door. *"I can't wait to show Uncle Jim."*

Chapter 14

Mike spent the week working and practicing. His first attempt to show his uncle on Sunday evening ended with him sweeping up salt and pepper because the crystal shakers didn't move. His uncle had laughed with him, but Aunt Jenny handed him a dustpan and broom.

He also made plans with Laurie for Friday night, much to the Darkness's disappointment.

"Why her? Katie and Mindy are much more fun. Maybe we should try that other friend of theirs."

"Because I like Laurie. And we are doing things my way, remember?"

"Yeah yeah. At least we should settle with Anne."

Anne became scarce. She didn't respond to any of Mike's texts or voicemails. By Friday night, Mike had all but given up on her as he prepared for his date with Laurie.

When he knocked on Laurie's front door, he expected her parents to herd him inside again. Instead, Laurie bolted out the door, grabbing him by the hand with a, "Let's go."

The oddity of it pulled the Darkness from its hole it was pouting in. *"What's got her in a hurry?"*

Mike mentally shrugged at it. He opened Laurie's door for her before going around to the driver seat. Once settled in he turned to her, "Parents trust me this time?"

"Mom wanted you to come in, but I didn't want to be late."

"We have plenty of time," Mike replied, glancing at the clock in the dash.

Laurie rolled her eyes at him. "I don't want to share you tonight."

Mike raised an eyebrow. "Share me? Aren't we meeting Deb and Chad?"

Laurie gave him a look painfully reminiscent of Colleen's when she had mischief planned. "Maybe. Maybe not." She winked.

Mike smiled. "Where to, m'lady?"

"The movies."

Mike put the car in reverse and backed out. He pointed it towards the mall as Laurie took his hand. She didn't let go until he had to negotiate the turns to find a parking space.

Once parked, she unbuckled quickly and slid close, pulling Mike in for a kiss.

The Darkness awakened, *"Maybe she won't be so boring."* It reached for control and Laurie's mind.

"Back off," Mike scolded. As the kiss deepened however, the Darkness howled and retreated to the farthest depths of Mike's mind. A sense of calm washed over Mike, with none of the urgency to push things further than a kiss.

They were interrupted by a knock on the window. Chad's voice cut through the moment, "Aren't you supposed to wait until the lights go down in the theater?"

Laurie laughed. "Saves the price of a ticket this way."

As Mike and Laurie climbed out of the car, Deb heckled them, "I didn't know you had become such a cheap date, Laurie."

Conversation stayed light as they headed for the theater doors. They were able to quickly grab seats in the nearly empty theater. When they exited an hour and a half later, none of them had any idea what the movie had been about.

"Next stop. Dancing," Laurie proclaimed when they reached their cars. After they were seated, she leaned toward Mike and the two kissed again. "Let's go."

The club was only slightly crowded so the teens were able to find a table. After an hour, Mike excused himself to go to the bathroom. When he came back out, he heard a voice call his name. He turned around, "Hey, Katie. Fancy meeting you here."

She flipped her red hair back and stepped close, "I was thinking the same thing. Wanna dance? Or maybe just get out of here?"

The last part awakened the Darkness. *"I like that idea. I'm bored."* It reached for control.

"No. We're with Laurie tonight." Mike pushed down the desire to take Katie up on her offer. "I'm here with someone so maybe another time." He tried to step back, but Katie pursued him.

"Oh really? Should I ask her about the mall restroom?"

"Not if you know what's good for you," Mike considered darkly. He reached into her mind, *"You need to go home. Now. Are your friends here?"*

Katie nodded, images of Emily and Mindy flashed through her mind for Mike to pick up. The trio had arrived only a few minutes ago

"Ok. You're going to tell them you changed your mind and want to go home. I'll call you tomorrow or sometime."

Katie's eyes refocused. "I just remembered something so you'll have to wait. Text me tomorrow," she called as she walked away.

As Mike watched her leave, Chad came around the corner. "Who was that?"

"Mistaken identity. She thought I was someone else." Mike read the skepticism in Chad's expression. He reached into Chad's mind to calm the alarm before adding, "I must have one of those faces." He laughed.

Chad chuckled as Mike released his hold. "Maybe you do. The girls want to grab something to eat before everywhere closes."

"Sounds good to me." Mike clapped Chad on the shoulder and the two rejoined their dates.

***

If it weren't for the extra long make out session, the night would have been over early. Eventually Mike and Laurie pulled themselves apart in order to get her home by curfew. Mike pulled into her driveway and put the car in park, the only time his hand left hers. He opened her door and helped her get out. As he shut the door and turned around, Laurie pressed into his arms. Mike looked down, then reached up to brush a lock of her blonde hair behind her ear.

The bolt struck his mind and he was back outside Tony's. He knew Kevin was going to come out of the door any minute, but it's not Colleen in his arms. Laurie smiled up at him. When the bell on the door jingled, Mike looked over to see Derek strut out. Derek is alone, and the anger and rage rolling off of him hit Mike like a furnace blast. The Darkness clawed for control until Laurie's voice broke the vision.

"Mike? You there?" She touched his cheek and he turned to face her, the vision fading to memory for contemplation later. "Where'd you go? You went all rigid on me."

"Sorry." Mike tried to shake it off. "Just an old memory out of nowhere. I'll explain another time."

He wrapped an arm around her and walked her to her door. Laurie finally went inside when the porch light purposely flicked off then on.

Mike settled behind the wheel for the drive home, this time untroubled by the silence of the Darkness.

Chapter 15

The Saturday morning quiet awoke Mike. *"I don't know if I'll ever get used to that."* After he showered and dressed for the day, he entered the kitchen to discover a note from his aunt and uncle. He glanced at it, *"Saturday morning errands. Alright. Guess I'm on my own."*

After a quick cereal breakfast, he grabbed his keys to his aunt's car. He started to text Katie, then canceled the message. *"New day, new adventures."*

He arrived at the mall and spent a couple hours window shopping. After getting his free lunch, he sat in the food court. Focused on eating, Anne startled Mike when she sat down across from him.

"Hey. Sorry I didn't return your messages. I needed time to think."

Mike replied after swallowing his food, "About what?"

"About us." She fidgeted, and Mike's eyes traced her curves under her tight T-shirt.

"There really isn't an us, Anne." He took a drink as she froze from his words. "There almost was something. Two people. Having fun. You put the brakes on, so I found someone else to do."

Anne jerked as if slapped. "I'm happy you and Laurie hit it off."

"We're ok. She's a great kisser and all. So were you."

"I'm not sure what came over me. If you're with Laurie, maybe I should go." Anne started to get up.

"Why? Because I made out with your friend? Wasn't that exactly why you were interested too? Try and 'steal' me from her? I don't belong to either of you. I'll do whatever I want with whoever I want."

"You're right, Mike. I'm jealous that your aunt set you up with Laurie."

"Now that we cleared that up, we can finish what we started last week. Wanna get outta here?"

Before Anne could reply, Mindy's voice cut into their conversation, "Hey lover boy. Why didn't you call? I would have kept you company today."

Anne looked from Mindy to Mike, "What's going on?"

Mike embraced the Darkness who had been lurking in the shadows of his mind. "Sit down, Mindy." He grabbed ahold of both girls' minds. "Mindy, this is Anne. Anne, this is Mindy. Mindy and her friend Katie were willing enough when you weren't." Mike loosened his hold a little but prepared to prevent a scene.

Anne sputtered, "Her and her friend?"

"Not at the same time." Mike chuckled as the Darkness enjoyed the thought. "At least, not yet. Maybe today's the day. I still haven't had Emily yet."

"Do you think Emily will? I've always liked her." Mindy's bold declaration surprised Mike.

"You're both sick. I'm leaving." Anne struggled to stand, realizing she had no control over her body. "What's going on? Why can't I move?"

"Because you don't have my permission." Mike reached into her mind. *"You're going to forget anything except we talked and made plans for later. Nothing about Mindy or any other girls."*

Anne nodded when Mike finally let her go. "I'll see you later, Mike." She stood and waved before turning away.

"What?" Mindy gaped at Anne's abrupt departure.

Mike quickly wiped Anne from Mindy's memory. He slid his chair closer and put a hand on her thigh. "Nice running into you. I was getting bored."

She melted against him. "Katie and Emily won't be here for an hour. Wanna get lost?" She flicked her hair toward the family restroom.

"I've got a better idea." He took her hand, pulling her to her feet.

179

Mike led her to one of the department stores Anne had taken him in before. After scouting for anyone he might have to send packing, he dragged Mindy into one of the changing rooms. They started to kiss, their hands roaming in the confined space.

"Be quiet though," Mike warned as they began undressing each other.

***

When they exited a little while later, Mike scanned the area before opening the door all the way. Mindy slowly followed, ruining the 'act natural' warning Mike had given her. Once in the open he turned to her. "Glad we bumped into each other. But I gotta get going." He gave Mindy one last squeeze before heading off into the mall crowd.

"That was fun." The Darkness sounded satisfied. *"We closing the deal on Anne then?"*

"Maybe. Or we can have some other fun." Mike eyed the clothing display in one of the trendier stores. His jaw dropped when he saw the price tags. *"Are you thinking what I'm thinking?"*

"Maybe." The Darkness chuckled with him as he entered the store. Mike quickly located a salesperson and took hold of their mind.

A half hour later he left in a brand new outfit. His old clothes sat in a bag with another few items he 'bought' for pennies.

His stomach growled. *"My powers really do make me hungry."*

"Just wait until you really use them," the Darkness added.

As Mike enjoyed a second free lunch, Damien plopped down across from him. "You must have mastered the mental tricks. You're mind is locked tight. I didn't know you were out today."

"Damien. If I had your number I could have called you. I think I have the teleporting objects down." To demonstrate, Mike collected several displays from empty tables nearby.

180

Damien nodded. "Impressive. Before you try doing it yourself, let me teleport you."

"You can take someone with you?" Mike's mind churned with possibilities.

"It's a matter of strength and practice. I have no trouble with small groups, but a friend of mine can barely teleport just himself."

"Like my Uncle's telekinesis. He said he could barely lift himself, but my grandfather could lift them both."

"Same concept really. Teleportation might be easier for you if you've experienced it before trying it."

"Let's go then." Mike's anxiousness showing through as he stood up.

Damien stood as well. He reached over and laid a hand on Mike's shoulder. "Now, I just visualize where I want to go and put us there."

In the blink of an eye the pair were in Damien's study. Mike gawked at the luxury furniture around him. The next blink they were back in the mall food court.

"That was incredible," Mike looked around to see if anyone noticed their arrival.

Catching the look, Damien explained, "For the most part mundanes see only what they want to see. We were only gone a few seconds, so to anyone who was watching, they blinked and we were still standing here. Try this in a crowded space or where someone is expecting you and it's a little different."

"Do I have to know the place? Like, do I have to have been there before?"

"Not really. It's certainly easier if the places are familiar. However, if you have the ability to 'see' the place, or a person in it, it helps you to lock on."

"See the place or a person in it." Mike thought it over a moment. "Ok. What's next?"

"Start small. Like from one room to the next in your house."

Mike nodded, looking around the mall. He spotted the family restroom. The door opened and a mom with her little boy stepped out. Mike concentrated and found himself standing inside just as the door finished closing. He quickly tripped the lock, before reaching out towards Damien. *"It worked."*

Damien appeared beside him. "Great job. Everything feel ok? All your parts in the right places?"

Mike patted himself down. "I think so." His pendant felt cold against his chest. His stomach growled loud enough for Damien to hear.

"Ah. The hunger. That will get easier the more you practice and use your powers."

"So it's not just my family with that problem?"

"No. Most of us do at some point. Difference is we train from the moment we can comprehend what's going on."

"Makes sense."

"Go carbo-load like an athlete with a game coming. I've gotta get going." Damien waved as he vanished.

Mike opened the door and walked back into the mall proper, checking out his food options. *"Carbo-load huh? Well, if he says it'll help."* He grabbed two thick crust slices of pizza and a calzone from one stand before ordering a double portion of chili cheese fries from another. He ignored the looks of those nearby when he sat down with his feast.

As he bit into the first slice, he heard a familiar voice. Looking up he saw Aunt Jenny waving. Mike waved as she approached his table. She looked over the tray before she spoke, "Mike. Funny running into you here. Not spoiling your appetite for dinner, are you?"

"No, Aunt Jenny. Just starving." He added in a lower voice, "I've been practicing my gifts a little."

She nodded. "Your uncle used to talk about that. I guess it wears off after awhile. At least it did for him. He's around here somewhere. Said we'd grab a quick lunch before heading home but he wanted to look at something."

"I might be late. I'm meeting Anne later. She wanted to talk about something. I know you don't like her much, but she's been nothing but nice to me."

Aunt Jenny bit her lip. "I just don't want to see you in trouble with some of the girls around here. Especially her. That's why I think you and Laurie are perfect."

"I like Laurie, Aunt Jenny. She's great. But I'm allowed to have friends, right?"

"Yes. I know you'll make the right decisions." Her smile turned to confusion as Katie walked up behind Mike.

Katie wrapped herself around him in a more than friendly way. She started to whisper in Mike's ear, "I was hoping to run into you." Then she noticed Jenny standing there. She stuttered, "Hi Mrs. Johnson. Do you know Mike?"

"Hello Katie. Mike is my nephew. How's Tom?" Ice rolled off Jenny's tongue with her words.

Katie stiffened. "He was cheating on me so we broke up last week. That's when I ran into Mike here at the mall."

Jenny pressed her lips together so hard they turned white. "That's too bad. As I recall you weren't always so faithful either."

"That hurts, Mrs. J." Katie flipped her red hair and turned back to Mike. "Are you free this afternoon? I wanna hang out again."

"Again?" Jenny interrupted. "Just how many girls are you seeing besides Laurie, Mike? I'm disappointed. I thought you two were hitting it off."

Mike threw his hands up defensively. "Wait a minute, Aunt Jenny. I like Laurie and I'm glad you arranged for us to meet. But we aren't a couple or anything. We barely know each other. Is it wrong to make other friends? I thought that's what you and Uncle Jim wanted me to do."

Jenny glared pointedly at Katie. "I don't want you involved with the wrong sort of people. Come on, I've gotta find your uncle. We can talk at home."

"No," Mike thought as he reached for his Aunt's mind. The 'mental wall' she'd built was no match for his abilities. *"You're going to forget you ran into me. You and Uncle Jim will decide to go elsewhere for lunch and I'll call you later to tell you how late I'll be."*

Aunt Jenny blinked and turned around, pulling her phone from her pocket. As she left range Mike heard her telling her husband, "Let's try that Italian place on seventh for lunch instead. Where are you?"

"That was close," the Darkness said.

"I don't like having to lie to her, or use my powers on her. She's family."

"You gotta take care of yourself first. And that means getting what you want. You didn't harm her or anything."

"I still feel bad." Mike tried to put the thought away.

Once his aunt was gone Katie rounded on Mike. "You never told me you were related to Mrs. Johnson."

"Does everyone know my aunt?" Mike slouched down in the chair.

"Anyone who's gone to school with Laurie Sterling does. She's your Aunt's favorite."

"I get it. So what? This just sounds like some sort of sour grapes."

184

"It's clear your aunt has plans for you. It was fun but I'm not going to be dragged around again by another guy. So lose my number, Mike Johnson." Katie started to turn away.

"Sit down," Mike commanded, reaching for her mind. Once Katie was seated he continued, "As far as my aunt goes, I'll decide who I spend my time with. Be it you, or Laurie, or whoever. Am I clear?"

Katie nodded, Mike still controlled her voice.

"Secondly, when you came over and sat down last week, you'd already decided to just hook up and have fun before you left for college. I merely picked a time and place. You weren't complaining then. Were you?"

"No. I liked it. The danger of it all. What if we'd gotten caught. But I don't wanna tangle with your aunt." Her honesty brought out by Mike's touch on her mind surprised him.

"I wonder what the feud between her and my aunt is all about. Thank God she doesn't question the manipulation. I'm tired of modifying memories," Mike thought to himself. To Katie, he said, "I'll handle her. Back to us, I have plans this afternoon. Rain check?"

"I guess." Katie pouted. She reached across the space between them to run her fingertips up his arm. "Sure I can't change your mind?"

"Just take her," the Darkness joined the conversation.

"We had Mindy earlier. If things go sideways with Anne we'll call Katie." Mike's assurances mollified the Darkness for now. *"Maybe,"* Mike added, feeling guilty about messing with his aunt's mind.

The Darkness seized the moment and took control, grabbing Katie's hand as she was getting up. Mike wrestled for control as It used his voice to say, "I can spare a little time if you're done talking." The Darkness reignited the desire in Katie's mind.

Mike fought but ended up a passenger in his own body as the entity within him followed Katie into the family restroom exactly like a week ago.

Chapter 16

When Mike exited the restroom, the Darkness was still in control. Katie was still getting herself together as he walked through the food court, his phone in hand as he texted Anne, 'Where do you want to meet?'

While he waited for a response he ordered another slice of pizza from one of the vendors. After he didn't pay, he strolled through the mall, eating and people watching.

One of the mall security guards approached, "Sir, I'm going to have to ask you to please return to the food court with your food."

Without any hesitation the Darkness reached into the guard's mind as it said, "No thank you. Now run along and look for shoplifters or something, rent-a-cop."

The Darkness taunted Mike. *"I'm having fun. While we wait for Anne should we find someone else to play with?"*

Mike struggled to regain control. *"This is my body. We will do things my way."*

"Tsk tsk, Mike. Every little indulgence brought you closer to me. Betraying your family by messing with your Aunt's mind gave me the leverage I needed. Now, I'm in charge."

Mike continued to fight for control, but he felt his chances dwindling.

His phone vibrated with an incoming message from Anne, 'Main entrance'

'Be right there' The Darkness sent back before turning in that direction.

When Anne came into view, the Darkness started humming to himself. It reached out to Anne's mind, *"We're going to get in my car. You're excited to see me."*

Anne's eyes lit up when she saw Mike. She bounced on her toes and threw her arms around him as soon as she could get close to him. "I'm glad we're finally getting together again. Let's go."

The Darkness wrapped an arm around her, a hand rested on her hip and pulled her tight. "Yes. Let's get out of here." It guided her out to where Mike had parked the car.

After making sure she got in the front passenger seat, It went around and climbed behind the wheel. Instead of turning on the car, the Darkness reached over and pulled Anne towards the console, kissing her hard. As it fed instructions for Anne to comply with Its desires, Mike fought harder.

"This isn't right. Stop it." Mike raged in futility. Nothing he did seemed to get him any closer to regaining control. As things progressed, Mike decided to try something else. He latched onto the power the Darkness was using to control Anne. He followed it into her mind, trying to reach out to her to fight back. Finally, he reached a part of her struggling against the compulsion.

He heard Anne's thoughts, *"Mike. Stop. I don't want to do this. Not like this. Please not like this."*

"Anne, it's not me. I don't know how to explain but it's not me. You have to fight."

"Not again," Anne's thoughts screamed as the Darkness began to pull her clothes off.

A bright light in Anne's mind encompassed Mike. He saw Anne, but she was clearly younger in only the way your teenage years make a year or two yield huge differences. He watched her follow a guy around at a party. The guy seemed familiar and Mike recognized him as Derek when he turned to talk to Anne.

Derek grabbed Anne around the waist, pulling her close. "We're going to have a little fun. You're going to do everything I say." Mike watches as tendrils of smoke curled from Derek to Anne and her eyes glazed over.

Derek led Anne down a hallway to a darkened bedroom. He forced her to start removing her clothes.

Mike could see where things were going. *"No."* He felt rage like he had before his fight with Kevin. The red that usually brought on the Darkness blazed white hot. He dove back to his own mind, shattering into the control he had lost.

The Darkness screamed, *"What do you think you're doing? She's mine. I'm in control."*

Mike saw a swirling disc, reminding him of the one on the pendant around his neck. As it swirled he saw an image of his grandfather. The elder man nodded, his expression grim. Mike heard his grandfather's voice, "You're better than this. You can defeat your Darkness. Just as others have done. As I did. I knew you would have to face this. That's why I gave my pendant to my son to give to you."

A calm spread across Mike's mind, reminding him of times with his grandfather. Mike made one last push and felt the hold the Darkness had on him shatter.

Now back in control Mike pulled away from Anne. As he released her mind he begged, *"I'm so sorry. Please let me explain."*

Anne gazed into his eyes. All traces of the compulsion fled from her and she quickly redid her clothes. "Mike. What happened? What did you do to me? I gotta go." She reached for the car door.

"Wait please," Mike begged aloud. "I know about Derek. About the party."

His words stopped Anne's attempt to leave. She looked over her shoulder at him. "How do you know? Even my parents don't."

"I could see it. In your mind."

"See it? You're joking right? I don't really remember everything. Derek put something in my drink."

"No he didn't. Deep down you know that. You reacted the same way when we were in your room, but I was more in control then. Not like this time."

"You seemed pretty in control when you were attacking me. I'm outta here." She reaches for the door handle again.

"Forgive me," Mike said aloud before he touched her mind. *"Remember that night and how he forced you."* Mike broke the wall built around the shining light of the memory in Anne's mind. He watched, heartbroken for her, while she relived part of her hidden trauma. *"That's enough."* Mike stopped it before the act itself.

Anne's eyes filled with tears as she fell against his chest. When she pulled away again a few minutes later, her cheeks were red and her eyes puffy.

Mike reached into a pocket, wondering if he had a napkin or something from when he bought the soda. They always hand you more than you could possibly need and he hoped some had made it into his pocket. What he found was a handkerchief folded neatly that he didn't remember putting there. Mike quickly handed it to her, but his mind was troubled. It looked just like the handkerchiefs his grandfather always carried. When Mike was little, Grandfather Johnson would always say, "A gentleman must always have a handkerchief. You never know when you might need it."

Anne murmured her thanks and wiped her eyes before blowing her nose loudly. Something about the sound struck her as funny because she giggled, high and strained.

"It's alright," Mike said, trying to sound reassuring. "But he didn't drug you. He... used powers. "

"What do you mean? Powers?" Anne dabbed at the tears still leaking from her eyes.

"Mind control, basically. It sounds crazy but it's true. I can do it too. I may have been using it on you before. Well, a part of me was." Mike reached up and touched the pendant through his shirt. "But that part of me is gone now."

"Gone?"

"You know Dr. Jekyll and Mr. Hyde?" Mike paused until she nodded. "I've destroyed Mr. Hyde. At least, I think so."

"So you're trying to tell me you weren't in control? Something else was?"

"Yes. And I'm so sorry I tried to force you to do anything. That's not how I'd want it to be."

"I wanted you. Just to spite your aunt."

"To spite her? Why? What does she have to do with anything?"

"I'm sorry, Mike. I guess I got a little jealous of Laurie basically being forced upon you by your aunt and uncle. I was afraid that if I wasn't a little more forward I wouldn't get a chance to know you. Your aunt and Laurie's mother are such good friends. Before that party, apparently Laurie was interested in the same guy. She thought I stole him, she doesn't know the truth."

Anne paused and took a deep breath before continuing, "I'd gone out with the guy several times. I didn't know it was him at the time spreading the rumors about me being easy. I thought it was Laurie. Then, he took me to that party out of town. I told my parents I was staying over at a friend's house. While we were there... Well, you know what happened. I thought he'd drugged me because I woke up the next morning with only vague memories." She stopped again, sniffling badly and crying again.

Mike wondered at her confession. *"Even if good came of this, was it worth the invasion of her life? Of her mind?"*

It was several minutes before she was able to continue. Mike sat quietly and let her work through her thoughts.

"Well, then it became clear who was telling people I was easy," Anne continued. "After that, the only guys who would talk to me thought they would get everywhere just because he did. He'd make comments to his buddies who would then make passes at me. He left at the end of that year, and Laurie and I started talking again. I never told anyone about the party. I didn't think anyone would believe me after all the rumors that had gone around school. We stopped talking about it and for the most part, everyone seemed to forget about it. I know Laurie never did, and neither did your aunt it seemed. I've seen her at school, and she still gives me that look. Like I'm some sort of slut. My reputation as a bit of a bitch became secured, even if no one really remembered the why. I didn't try to dissuade them. It was easier than the truth."

Mike was not sure if it was because he liked to believe that most people were honest, or something more of an intuition, but he knew that Anne was being completely truthful. Mike also knew that other than himself, she had really never told anyone the truth about that night. Mike could see where it could have been easier to let people think what they did than explain what had happened, even if she believed it was drugs and not something else. Mike took Anne's hand. She looked up questioningly, Mike could see a measure of fear in her eyes. "It is not your fault, Anne. You shouldn't have been put through that. I shouldn't have let things get carried away between us." Of this Mike was sure, having no respect for anyone who would take advantage of another person that way. Realizing that that was exactly what he had been doing in following the Darkness's advice made Mike start to hate himself more for his actions today with Anne. Mike was going to have to make it up to her. Maybe there was a way to help her get past that pain.

"I've never understood what happened. I still don't."

"It's hard to explain, but there are people with powers. It usually runs in families I guess. My uncle and grandfather had them, so do I. Some people don't use them wisely or justly. I've been using mine to get free stuff by controlling people's minds. I lost control. Seeing the pain in your memory snapped me out of it. I should be thanking you, but that's not enough for making you remember that pain."

She melted against Mike, crying softly into his shoulder. She whispered into his shoulder, "I should hate you, but I don't. I needed to tell someone. Someone who would understand. I didn't think it would be like this."

Mike just patted her softly on her back and let her cry. All Mike could care about was trying to think of a way to help this pretty girl in front of him. It reminded him of the night Colleen had run into his arms outside of Tony's Restaurant. Mike remembered the red in his vision as the beginnings of his Darkness and he stamped it down. He needed to think clearly now, not go into a rage and hit someone.

Finally Anne gained some control of her tears and pulled back into the passenger seat. Mike's shoulder was a little damp from her crying, but he didn't pay it any mind. What really worried him was this misunderstood person in front of him.

"I am really sorry, Mike. This is all ancient history as far as you are concerned," she said, her sniffling calming and her breathing returning to normal. Her cheeks were still flushed and her eyes puffy from crying. "Maybe we can still be friends after this."

"Why wouldn't we?" Mike asked, feigning that he was insulted by the insinuation. "It certainly makes it clear why everyone is acting the way they are. Well, at least enough of it anyway." Mike tried to sound reassuring. He knew he was more interested in Laurie than pursuing anything with Anne, and her admission didn't affect that at all. It just felt more right about Laurie than it did with Anne. That didn't mean that he couldn't be friends with her, or try to help her through what had happened to her. Perhaps if she found a counselor or some sort of support group. There had to be one of those options available.

She looked at Mike deeply for a moment and he was reminded of the calculating look his uncle had been giving him all summer, especially when they discussed their family legacy. Then Mike felt it again, like something touched his mental shield. He watched smoky tendrils reach from Anne towards him. He recognized it as power like his. The expression on his face must have hardened as Anne pulled back from him, fear touched her eyes again.

"What were you doing?" Mike asked, trying to soften his face, but still incredulous over what he felt was occurring. Puzzle pieces in his head started to fall together.

"I... sometimes can tell what people are thinking," she replied softly. "I was trying to read your face and reaction to what I said, but you were a total blank. Then you looked like you were about to hit something. It scared me."

"You have the gift as well?" It suddenly clicked what the feeling had been. It had been similar to what he himself had been trying to do to her. Mike could tell the question raised some sort of alarm with her. Before she could answer, Mike had already started the car and was backing out of the parking spot. His reaction must have shocked her enough that she kept silent, until Mike made the turn onto the highway. His only thought was that he needed to talk to his uncle very quickly. Mike needed to speak to him face to face.

***

Having been monitoring Mike's companion, Damien grew concerned over what Anne had told him, and even more to discover that she was talented as well. *"Was that what had originally pulled Derek to her? Even then had he been trying to gain some sort of status or power on his own?"* The block on the memories his father had placed was gone, shattered by Mike's intrusion into her mind. Something had to be done now. Damien renewed his efforts to track down his old friend.

***

"What do mean the gift? And, where are we going, Mike?" Anne asked, placing a hand on his arm once they were on the highway. "What are you talking about?"

Mike turned to her suddenly, his face locked in concentration. "We are going to my aunt and uncle's. It's like when I knew what you were thinking at the movie, and while you were in the changing room at the store," Mike replied in a rush, turning back to the road. "If you have powers too, my uncle can help." *"Then I'm going to have a talk with Derek."* The rage that normally turned red, blazed a righteous white just under the surface of Mike's consciousness.

He wanted to get there as fast as possible, but he kept trying to hold his speed in check. His every thought focused on getting to Uncle Jim so he could talk to Anne. In Mike's mind he felt that there had to be a reason that Anne was with him when he had snapped the Darkness's control today. Mike wasn't sure how he managed to reach into Anne's mind and see her memory, but helping her tugged at his soul and made overcoming the Darkness easier. He recalled Uncle Jim's thought about Mike bringing justice for their family. *"Are things like this going to fall into my lap, looking for me to solve them somehow?"* Mike wondered.

"Mike, I can't go to your uncle's. Your aunt hates me," she pleaded, squeezing his arm harder. "Why would you want to go there? Please look at me, I want to go home." Mike glanced at her and had to fight the urge to do as she was asking, his speed even dipped slightly before reasserting his plan of action caused the feeling to go away.

"You can do more than hear thoughts, can't you?" Mike asked, she leaned back, processing his response. Part of him started to wonder if she really knew what she was doing and how she was doing it. *"Was it possible that people made it through life not really knowing what was going on? That they were gifted like this?"* he thought to himself. Mike added that to his list of questions to get straight with both his uncle and Damien.

"What do you mean, Mike?" she whispered, clutching his arm even though she had pulled as far away as possible in the confines of the car. Without even trying Mike could hear her mind was a maelstrom of emotions, trying to sort out his reaction to her admission of hearing thoughts. Creeping in the background was the freshly dug up memory of what happened to her during her freshman year. The whole thing bothered Mike. Derek getting off seemingly free angered Mike.

"We will sort that all out as soon as we get there," Mike replied, not even paying attention to the pressure on his arm as he reached over and patted her on the leg. Focused on the thought of talking to his uncle, Mike almost didn't realize when the car gave a sudden lurch and they were heading down the road to the cabin. Mike felt a small coolness trickle over his skin and he knew it had to be the wards Uncle Jim talked about being put around his property. Mike must have somehow moved the car, along with himself and Anne, in an attempt to get there as soon as possible. The wards must have at first tried to resist and that was the lurch the car made. Somehow Mike had forced a way through. Shock threatened to overwhelm him when it struck him he had just teleported two people and a car doing seventy without crashing. *"Take that, Damien."*

"Mike, what just happened?" Anne asked, panic crept into her voice. Mike could no longer ignore the pressure on his arm as her nails were starting to dig in she was gripping so tight. Mike could feel the skin beginning to break and knew she was going to draw blood soon.

"It's alright, Anne," Mike replied. "Just relax. You are going to tear my arm open if you don't let go, though." Mike chuckled and she let go as he turned into the driveway and parked next to Uncle Jim's truck. Anne didn't appear like she was going to move so Mike went around to her side of the car and opened her door. He had to almost pull her out of the car, but after the door was open, she let Mike lead her by the hand to the porch steps. Mike opened the door, calling for his relatives right away.

"In the kitchen, Mike, we didn't expect you home for hours," started Aunt Jenny as she came around the corner from the other room. She spotted Anne and froze. "What is she doing here? I told myself I wasn't going to stop you from associating with anyone you wanted, but I don't care much for some people in this town. I especially don't care for some of them in my home."

"Aunt Jenny," Mike said calmly, cutting off any further argument from her. "I will explain in a moment, but suffice to say there are things you do not know. Where is Uncle Jim? I need to talk to him immediately."

"Well," she started, glancing at Anne, noticing the way she was clinging to Mike's side like a frightened rabbit about to bolt. "He just took off a few minutes ago into the forest. He said he had to check something, but if you showed up you would know where to find him. What is going on, Mike? I don't appreciate being addressed so in my own house. This and her are beyond rudeness and I will not tolerate it." Aunt Jenny's voice took on a very annoyed mother tone during her tirade, but Mike ignored it.

"I am sorry Aunt Jenny, but trust me, this is important," he said, stopping to think a moment. Mike had an idea where Uncle Jim might have gone, and also how to reach him. "You might want to come with us. This is definitely something you need to hear." With that, Mike led the way out the backdoor, having not let go of Anne's hand yet. Thankfully Aunt Jenny followed right after and didn't question Mike when he immediately set off down the trail to the little clearing where Uncle Jim had told him about his heritage the morning of his birthday.

Mike could see Uncle Jim pacing in the clearing before they got close. Mike reached out and tapped him on the shoulder with his gift, feeling the slight resistance from the medallion Uncle Jim wore that was supposed to protect him from any powers. Mike thought it odd at first he was able to reach his uncle, but then remembered how he had been lifted the first night. *"It must be because we are family that the medallions are not as effective against each other's powers,"* Mike concluded to himself. Regardless, Uncle Jim paused and turned to watch the trio approach. The determined look on Mike's face must have registered with him as he crossed his arms and waited patiently for his nephew to reach him. Mike was nearly dragging Anne, and Aunt Jenny was almost jogging to keep up with her nephew's longer strides.

"Uncle, we need to talk," Mike said flatly, Anne was cowering close by Mike's side, watching his aunt intently. From the look in Aunt Jenny's eyes Mike could tell without reading her thoughts what some of them must be. Anne was obviously picking them up as loud and clear as Mike was. "Aunt Jenny, I think something should be explained to you that will change your opinion of Anne here. For one, she can hear your thoughts as clearly as I can."

At this, Aunt Jenny turned very white, then very red. "She can?" she asked hesitantly.

Mike nodded before continuing, "I also need to apologize. You saw me at the mall earlier but I erased it from your memory. My gifts took a turn...." Mike trailed off, unsure how to articulate his experience with his Darkness.

Uncle Jim spoke into the brief silence, "Your grandfather said you would have a battle to face. And your decision would save or doom you, and the rest of our family. I thought he was being dramatic until I felt the power you wielded when you hit the wards around the property. If you'd made the wrong decision, I came here ready to fight you where I was strongest. Though I didn't think I'd win. I'm glad you're still you."

Mike considered his uncle's words, then pulled the pendant from under his shirt. "Grandpa helped me today. Through this."

Uncle Jim smiled. "He must have thought of everything."

Mike took a deep breath. He turned to look down into Anne's fearful eyes, "Anne, you will have to forgive me for breaking the confidence you bestowed on me when you told me your secret today, but it is important to clear up this old business before we go on." Anne looked up into Mike's eyes and nodded silently, resigned that he was going to tell his family what she had just told him. Mike proceeded to relate the tale, slowly and delicately. Before it was over Aunt Jenny had stepped forward and pulled Anne from Mike's side into a big hug, apologizing over and over and saying how sorry she was that Anne had suffered as she had.

While the two women moved over to the side to sit on the log and talk, Mike turned back to his uncle. "I've been talking to Damien. He is very insistent that he has knowledge and power that he could share with me that you can't. I don't know if you will approve, but I trust him. He has shown me an even stronger way to shield myself from him and others. He's shown me how to teleport, though I think even he'll be impressed with how I got here."

Uncle Jim's eyes shined. "I'm proud of you for overcoming your trial. If you trust Damien, then you've got to go with your gut."

"Anne has the gift too, Uncle. I could feel it when she was trying to read my thoughts. I also think she has other powers. She doesn't even know she is doing it, but she can force people to do what she wants them to do. Perhaps she should drink some of that tea you gave me. Perhaps it will help her to defend herself as it has obviously done something for me."

Uncle Jim shook his head slightly, pressing the fingers of one hand to his temple. "I'm glad you're not angry at me over giving you that tea. I kind of knew you would figure it out eventually. Damien's trick would explain why you're such a blank wall. I was sure it was you but all I could tell was a female and some sort of void was approaching. That's why I told your Aunt you would know where to find me. If it wasn't you, well, I had been preparing for far worse. You nearly brought down my wards with that little shift you made bringing the car and you two so close to the house with your powers. I can't believe the power what you did took. Teleporting like that is the most advanced variation on the telekinesis we both share. I could never hope to do something like that."

"I didn't know I could do it. Damien has me starting small with objects. I've never teleported anything bigger than the table displays until today. He said it's dangerous," Mike said in a rush, cutting him off. The look on his uncle's face told Mike he was remembering the passages in their family book that spoke of one with unheard of before powers. Uncle Jim just stared at his nephew a few more moments. Mike suddenly felt the weight of what he had accomplished, and the implications relevant to the passages they had read in the book. Mike nearly dropped to his knees as the revelation fully sank in.

"Nephew, you know what I think," Uncle Jim said softly and putting a hand on Mike's shoulder to steady the younger man. He turned to glance at Anne and Jenny, who were giggling lightly now, apparently healing the rift that had occurred several years ago.

"Uncle," Mike started again, struggling to figure out how to say it. "I almost raped Anne. I was in her mind forcing her. Which means I have that ability as well. I lost control to something inside of me. I've been calling it the Darkness. Because That's how it felt, except when it was a blinding rage. What if it comes back? What if I lose to it again?"

"It's very possible given the challenges you've faced for it to come back," he replied slowly, laying his other hand on his nephew's other shoulder and looking into Mike's eyes intently. "But remember this most important point, Mike, you are still learning to control your powers. You're going to make mistakes and inadvertently cause things to happen. That doesn't mean you are going to head back into darkness, it just means you're human. Anger is nothing to be scared of, if it's anger for the right reasons and at the right people. What bringer of justice doesn't get mad at the villain?" Uncle Jim chuckled lightly, causing his wife to stop whispering with Anne and the two of them looked at Jim and Mike. Uncle Jim turned and smiled at them. They went back to their chatting with a shrug and a look that spoke of the illogical nature of men.

Mike looked up slightly and stared at his uncle a moment. His uncle talking of a 'bringer of justice' struck a little too close to home for Mike. He could also tell his uncle was in part distracted, trying to repair the damage Mike had done to the wards in his attempt to get here. Mike again could see the little strings of power like he had traced to Damien, and to Anne before. This was different though because they were not directed at him, which made them only slightly harder to pick out of the air. As Mike focused on what his uncle was doing, Mike could see them, thin wispy lines like a faint smoke stretching from his uncle outward into the forest. Mike followed them as best he could and came in contact again with the faint cold sensation of what seemed to be a dome surrounding the property.

Figuring out what his uncle was doing was easy with a slight nudge from the necklace he wore, reminding Mike again of his grandfather at the fair those years ago. Mike began copying his uncle as he had copied Damien's instructions, pouring his own energy and will into strengthening the shield Uncle Jim had created and maintained for so many years. Mike kept pushing when suddenly he felt the pendant around his neck where it was touching skin go ice cold. Mike was pushing so hard it changed rapidly to a scalding hot before he could stop himself. He saw the forest around go black and felt a sudden sensation of falling. Just before everything went totally dark, he saw a look of utter surprise and then shock cross Uncle Jim's face. Mike was sure he must have collapsed about that time, the last sound in his ears being Aunt Jenny and Anne calling his name. Then all was a dark silence worse than the coma he had experienced before.

***

Leonard Mauston sat bolt upright in his chair. The changes out at the Johnson place were something he had never anticipated. He still kept an eye on James Johnson, as he had for over a decade. It was part of the bargain struck. If there was anything aggressive from the Johnson property, then the Council would eliminate the threat. He had felt the ward nearly collapse before James began repairing it to what it was. It was times like this when Leonard paid close attention to his target. One toe out of line would give them cause to act.

As he sat there however, he felt the pathetic dome that the elder Johnson maintained change into something far stronger and even sinister. The boy was adding his anger and power to it at an alarming rate without even realizing it. The Council allowed the dome to exist merely to their amusement. It truly offered no protection until now.

They had allowed the Johnson's to live because they needed the next generation to come along. Now that he was here, things were moving along rapidly. Suddenly the power winked out as the dome sealed tighter than ever. Probing it gently, the old man was struck with a mild pain similar to what he had inflicted upon his son for any failure during his studies. Shaking his head, Leonard knew that things had now become far more complicated.

Chapter 17

"Mike, please wake up," came Anne's soft voice. Mike's senses started to creep back to him. First, he could tell he was lying down on something soft. Mike opened his eyes slowly, the light in the room nearly blinding after the darkness he had been in. Mike could see Anne sitting in a chair next to him, his hand pressed against her cheek as she talked to him. When their eyes made contact, she smiled and laid his hand at his side, turning to call for Mike's aunt and uncle. When they arrived Mike could tell how grave the situation must have appeared to them before this.

"What happened? What time is it?" Mike asked groggily, then, as he tried to sit up, the pain began. It felt like every inch of his very bones were on fire. He gasped and collapsed back against his bed. This was sort of how he had felt when he came out of his coma initially. He realized that it truly must have been the gift having protected him from the car before at prom. It had tapped out his limited use of the powers he had before his birthday, and his body needed time to heal. Remembering that the necklace was supposed to protect him, Mike wondered where it was. He couldn't feel it against him, but then, most of what he could feel was pain and soreness.

"Relax, nephew," Uncle Jim said, laying a hand on his Mike's shoulder. Surprisingly, this contact did not create the same pain as trying to move himself had caused. Mike noticed that Anne had again taken hold of his hand. This also did not cause the same blinding pain that had occurred moments before.

"What is happening to me?" Mike asked again, careful not to move any more than he had to. Speaking seemed to be ok, but Mike knew if he moved his head or any other part of his body the pain was likely to return.

"Well, we thought you had killed yourself, or at least put yourself comatose for good. I didn't realize at first what you were doing until I felt the change in the wards I was repairing. You put so much of yourself into it so quickly your body couldn't handle it and collapsed," Uncle Jim replied by way of explanation. "I think the pain is from overextending yourself. Usually I just get tired or a headache from reaching too far, but I have never seen what you did. You have been out for several hours. It's after eleven. If you had stopped breathing at any point, I was going to call an ambulance. I wasn't looking forward to trying to explain what was going on so I'm glad that never happened."

Mike flicked his gaze over to Anne. "I guess I won't be able to take you to get your car now. I'm sorry you'll be late getting home."

"It's alright," she said softly. "Your aunt and I went to get it shortly after your uncle brought you inside. I didn't want to leave. I felt responsible because it was you bringing me here like you did that weakened what your uncle did. He's explained a lot of things to me while you slept."

"We almost couldn't get her to leave, the little dear," Aunt Jenny chimed in, laying a hand on Anne's shoulder in a motherly sort of way. "She planned to sit right here until you woke up. I called her mother and said she might be late, that we were playing board games. I think it shocked her to be hearing from me so much she didn't bother to question it." Aunt Jenny laughed with amusement. Anne seemed to see the humor and laughed with her.

"I appreciate it. And, it's not your fault at all, Anne," Mike said, suddenly aware of how tiring talking was. "I did this to myself by not being careful. I got carried away in trying to help. I am still pretty beat, though, so I think I'll go back to sleep if that's alright with you three.

Anne, you should head home. I'll call you tomorrow when I'm feeling better."

"Ok, Mike," Anne replied, still holding his hand a moment longer. "Get some rest and I hope you feel better in the morning." With that she laid his hand back down on the bed and stood up to leave. Before Mike drifted off again, he could see her give Aunt Jenny a hug and say goodbye. Uncle Jim was the last to leave, pausing at the door before shutting off the light, that calculating look in his eyes again. This time mixed with no small amount of wonder.

***

The intense pain he felt when he brushed against the wards convinced the old man that he would have to take different measures to keep an eye on the Johnson clan in the future. Leonard Mauston couldn't even tell if the boy had killed himself doing what he did, the shield was so solid. He was surprised the most by the offensive additions that struck back at anyone merely touching the shield at all. A way would have to be found to determine if the boy lived or not, and for that he summoned his son. Rules were rules after all, and the Council had ruled that no one else was to interfere in this test.

"What is it, Father?" Damien replied mentally, not appearing in the flesh or even as a projection. The arrogance and attitude from his son was starting to annoy the old man enough that he would have to punish the boy for his insolence. Apparently the little lesson previously had not done the trick well enough.

"Something has happened at the Johnson's. You will watch for anyone leaving and try to determine if the boy still lives, or if he managed to kill himself with his tricks."

"He has to be alive," Damien said, clearly desperate for news himself as Mike's untimely death, not at Damien's hands, would put him even further from his dream of joining his father on the Council. "I will find out if I have to rip someone's mind apart to do it. Ah, it would appear that Anne is leaving now." It was obvious to the old man that Damien had already encountered the strengthened wards, and had set to monitor the roads away from the property instead. The forward thinking of his son made him revise his plan to punish him for the perceived insolence. Damien was obviously already a step ahead and taking his task seriously. "I will get the truth from her and she won't even remember me. Turns out she and the families have history." His father felt Damien extend his powers towards the young woman leaving the Johnson property. The history Damien mentioned was not something that the old man cared to remember. The near exposure to the Council had been very shaming, even if the boy who did the deed was Derek and had only been staying with the Mauston's in order to hone some of his skills with a member of the Council.

***

The next morning Mike lay in bed, too scared to move until nearly nine o'clock. Instead of trying to sit up all at once, he started with just moving a hand. Mike found that the pain was nearly gone, leaving behind a dull ache as if he had over worked himself exercising. As he slowly tested each limb and then started to sit up, Mike found that this aching sensation, while very unpleasant, was just barely tolerable. Soon he was in a sitting position and looked around. The chair Anne had been sitting in, dragged from the dining table, was still there. Mike used it to help pull himself to his feet and then had to wait for the room to stop spinning, clutching the chair for support while his legs got used to holding weight again.

Mike proceeded down the hall and into the bathroom. His shuffling and stumbling must have alerted his aunt as she started down the hall after him. Mike just gave her a weak smile and a nod, then closed the bathroom door. The hot water of the shower seemed to loosen up the

207

stiffness in his joints and muscles. Mike stood there for what felt like only a few minutes but must have been much longer. He heard Aunt Jenny's voice calling from the other side of the bathroom door, "Mike dear, you ok in there? You have been running that shower for over twenty minutes now. I didn't hear any crash but want to make sure you didn't collapse again."

"I'm alright, the hot water just seems to help," Mike called back before again getting lost in the warmth of the water. He heard her say something that sounded like 'OK' and then it was just Mike and the shower again. As the water started to cool down, signaling that he had drained the hot water heater temporarily, Mike turned and shut off the spray. While he could tell that he wasn't back to a hundred percent yet, the soreness was much easier to manage now. Mike wrapped a towel around himself and gathered up his discarded clothes, slipping back down the hall as quickly as he could and into his bedroom. After Mike had redressed he found his cellphone and headed towards the kitchen. The smells wafting down the hall set his mouth to watering. This seemed to be another thing similar to his previous brush with overextending his powers. He was ravenous when he awoke.

"Morning, Aunt Jenny," Mike said weakly, pouring himself into one of the chairs around the table. Mike realized there was one chair still in his room, but as he started to reach towards it with his powers, Mike felt a sharp pain in the front of his skull. Clutching at his temples, he just sat there, Aunt Jenny looking on disapprovingly, but with a touch of concern in her eyes.

"You might as well give up the thought of using those gifts of yours for a few days at least if you ask me. Your uncle says he has never felt raw power like that and you are lucky you didn't kill yourself yesterday. Here, I made some Sunday brunch for you," she said, placing a plate of scrambled eggs, hash browns, bacon, and toast in front of her ailing nephew. She then brought over a large glass of orange juice. "Hopefully some food will help revive you somewhat. Your uncle went off into the woods this morning. Said he wanted to get a really good feel of what you did." She continued muttering about crazy men not caring about what their actions did to worry her while she continued in the kitchen. Mike began eating slowly, but was glad to feel some strength returning with nearly every bite. Bit by bit he was starting to feel more like himself. When he asked for seconds Aunt Jenny brightened considerably and quickly scooped more food onto the plate from the skillet it had been keeping warm in. After a minute she brought a few more slices of toast and a fresh glass of juice, which Mike devoured much quicker than the first. After two more healthy courses of Aunt Jenny's 'Sunday Brunch', Mike felt almost as good as he had when he got up the day before. He also felt very stuffed.

"Thank you, Aunt Jenny," Mike said, feeling much more like himself, except for the sharp pain each time he started to reach towards any of the powers he knew were there. It was a little like trying to not use a limb. Mike stood up slowly and carried his plate, utensils, and glass over to the sink and helped her wash everything up from the meal.

When they were finished, she patted Mike on the shoulder and thanked him for the assistance. "I know this can all be a little overwhelming, but know that your uncle and I are here for you Mike. You can stay as long as you want." Mike just nodded and excused himself. He went onto the back porch to call Anne.

"Hey, Mike," she said when she answered her cell phone. "How are you feeling this morning?"

"Much better than I did last night, but still feel a little like I stuck a penny in a light socket," Mike said, getting the giggle he was trying to elicit from her. Even if he wasn't entertaining the thought of a relationship with her, it didn't mean that he wished her to be depressed.

"Listen, thank you for wanting to stay by my side last night, but it wasn't your fault. I guess I don't know my limits yet, but I seem to have come very close to them yesterday. How do you feel about everything? Still alright with telling me what happened?"

"Yes," Anne replied slowly after a moment. She paused even longer before continuing. Mike could tell she was chewing the words over in her mind. "I called Laurie first thing this morning and told her I needed to talk to her privately. We are going to get together this afternoon before she has choir practice. I need her to know what really happened. Talking with your aunt made me see the friendships I had cost myself by hiding everything from those who were closest to me at the time. Your Aunt Jenny told me that I had nothing to be ashamed of and that it would do no harm to open up to my friends like I did to you. I just hope I am strong enough to tell her everything."

"That's good Anne. I'm sure it will go just fine. Hopefully you two can patch things up," Mike said. "Again, I do appreciate yesterday, but I hope you understand why I am not much interested in anything serious this summer. It would be great to hang out and stuff, but, you see my point right? You know, with everything that's going on?" *Besides, I need to find out why the Darkness was so scared of Laurie from the beginning. Maybe she's the key. And I do enjoy spending time with her.*"

Anne seemed to take a few breaths before responding, "Don't worry about me, Mike. Despite what almost happened, I'm better with this all out in the open now. I'm actually glad that you and Laurie are getting along. She deserves a good guy. Oh, and something your Uncle mentioned, I want you to know that I will keep your secret if you will keep mine. Take care of yourself, Mike. Talk to you again soon, ok?"

Before Mike could say anything, Anne hung up the phone. Between Aunt Jenny's comment about staying as long as he wanted, and Anne throwing it out there about him being a good thing for Laurie, Mike was torn. He felt scared to open up to Laurie, even though he knew it was the right thing to do. He would have to deal with Katie and Mindy as well. He was anxious about his new powers and what might happen to him before summer was over. Maybe he could talk to Damien about it. He had grown up with the gifts and obviously he seemed to do alright in normal society. Maybe it would be manageable. About this time, Uncle Jim came striding out of one of the paths that led into the forest around the house, spotting Mike sitting on the bench. He just waved as he headed towards the porch steps.

"Good to see you up and around, nephew," he said chuckling as he mounted the short flight of stairs to the top of the deck. "You gave us all quite a scare last night. I have to say though, if it weren't for us being blood relatives, I don't think I would be able to pass physically through the shield you put up, much less any sort of powers getting in or out. I have never built anything so strong in my life, and the sheer scale of it! It covers every inch of the property boundary without so much as a single weak point that I can find. It is exactly the same along every inch."

"I am glad that it meets with your approval uncle, but I really had no idea what I was doing," Mike replied, a little embarrassed by the way Uncle Jim was carrying on. "I just started following what you were doing, but with more force and will. I did feel the pendant change, but it was so rapid I didn't know until it was too late to stop. I couldn't find it this morning. Did you or Aunt Jenny take it?" Mike felt odd that he hadn't remembered it before now, after his uncle's warning to never take it off.

"I found it on the ground near where you had collapsed," he replied, pulling it from his shirt pocket, the chain snapped near where it was looped through the pendant. "I can get a new chain for it. That's no big deal."

Mike nodded and took it, rolling it in his palm, "I felt it go ice cold and then to red hot so rapidly. Then it just stopped and I didn't feel it at all. That was when I blacked out."

"I think that is when it must have shattered the chain," Uncle Jim said, watching his nephew closely. "It was able to stop you from killing yourself, but only barely. Next time you might not be so lucky, nephew."

"I know," Mike said as he closed his hand over the pendant. Mike could feel it almost instantly begin to shield again, drawing the remaining aches and pains from his body. Tentatively Mike reached out to touch the wards around the house and land. Instead of the pain he expected to feel, he was greeted with a warm sensation like the hot water in the shower felt. A little shocked at this reaction, Mike withdrew and looked back to his uncle. Uncle Jim seemed to have sensed what happened by the expression on Mike's face or from his thoughts.

"I don't like you being a blank wall, but you might want to consider putting your shield back in place as soon as you are able. You are like an open book with flashing neon signs right now," Uncle Jim laughed and turned to go into the house. "And yes, I do think Laurie would be good for you. Based on what you told me you felt when you two met. At the very least she doesn't seem like the kind that would run screaming the other direction. The other girls will fade away I'm sure. As far as Anne and even Damien, having a friend or two you can trust can make things so much easier during this time."

Chuckling himself, Mike replaced the mental shield, patterning it after what he had learned about the ward he had built around the property coupled with what he had learned from Damien and his Uncle. Then Mike stood slowly and followed his uncle inside.

Things certainly seemed to be getting easier as the morning progressed and Mike recovered more fully. Having the pendant back in his possession seemed to work wonders for his strength. By mid-afternoon Mike was able to move objects again and he practiced as he read over several sections of the family book. Mike found a passage about metal working and fixing the chain turned out to be fairly easy once his strength returned more fully. The metal against his skin seemed to draw all the last remaining bit of soreness from his body as the afternoon turned closer to evening. Mike was startled out of his reading by the ringing of his cell phone where he had placed it on the table. He grabbed it and ducked onto the back porch as he answered it.

"Hey Mike," it was Laurie on the other end of the line instead of Anne, which was who Mike expected when his phone rang. He had answered without checking the display to see who it was. "Before you say anything, I have to tell you about what Anne said to me." Mike just said OK and she continued in a rush, "I am not upset or anything about you two hanging out, and I guess it was a good thing because for some reason she decided to open up a little bit to you, and now I know why she has acted the way she has for the last couple years. I can't believe how mean I was to her and I didn't know how she was hurting because of it. I hope this doesn't change your opinion of me at all. I honestly didn't know what she had been through, she never gave any indication." It was clear Laurie was quite worried about what Mike would think. Anne's last words came back to Mike. He once again considered his options for the summer, knowing that Anne had been right.

"It's quite alright, Laurie," Mike said quickly when she paused, it clear that she was ready for some sort of a response. "I ran into her in the mall, and in the end the story came out. Given that it healed a few old wounds, I am glad that she did." Mike didn't like lying to Laurie, but he wasn't sure that he could tell her about any of the rest of it quite yet.

"I don't think less of you." Mike paused before plunging ahead, "I couldn't think less of you for that."

"Anne also told me that you made it very clear to her that you weren't going to be stuck between her and I. And that, well, that you weren't going to pursue anything serious this summer with anyone because you were going to be going back home anyway when school started," Laurie got out in a rush. Then she paused, clearly catching something in Mike's tone of voice.

"That was what I told her," Mike said matter-of-factly. "I told her you both seem to be great people and I would be happy to be friends with both of you, as well as the rest of the gang. Anne basically called me a fool. I like you, Laurie, and yes, I don't want to lead anyone on since I am only supposed to be here for the summer. But there is nothing to say that something won't change before fall." Mike put just a little bit more hope into his voice, thinking again that maybe he would stay with his aunt and uncle.

"I think I understand," Laurie said softly, but with a little more cheer. "Well, I have to go to choir practice now, so I will talk to you later. I had told Anne I wanted to call you first, but she had said she was supposed to tell you how things went with our get together. I guess that now you know my side, you can call her if you want."

"Thank you for calling me," Mike said, a little of the tiredness of the day creeping into his voice. "I really look forward to spending more time with you and everyone else. I appreciate you understanding the situation." Laurie just gave a quick good bye and hung up. Mike wondered if it was for the best that he told Laurie he might not go home in the fall. A part of him wanted to pursue things with Laurie, but did it make much sense given what he was facing this summer? Was it right to bring her into this world that he had only just discovered? Maybe it wouldn't even matter. Not all high school relationships last the summer.

If he and Laurie were still going good in August, then he would tell her everything. Shaking his head at himself, Mike mentally prepared for the next phone call he had to make. He wasn't really dreading it, it was just that he was starting to get tired again.

Mike dialed Anne's phone so he could get that conversation out of the way. He was fairly sure that he would be asleep very early tonight and he didn't want to miss talking to her. Anne confirmed what Laurie had said and added that they both did a little crying, but that she thought things were going to be alright. The rest of the conversation surprised even Mike though.

"Do you think you could help me with my gift? Or whatever it is your uncle called it," Anne asked hesitantly. "I never really knew what I was doing, but I don't want to hurt anyone, or get hurt." She added quickly.

"I don't know much about what I'm doing myself," Mike admitted. "I would think that would have been obvious with how I nearly killed myself last night. What did you want to know?"

"Well, do you think you can teach me how to shield my thoughts?" Anne asked, nervously. Mike could almost picture her biting her lip, waiting for him to reject her request. When Mike realized that he wasn't just imagining it, he was really seeing her when he closed his eyes, Mike pushed the image away. If it was real time, it could cause some rather embarrassing moments if he thought about someone at the wrong time. The fleeting image that day of the old man in a chair while he was showering came back to Mike, along with a slight remembrance of the pain he had felt.

"Well, I'll try to explain it as easily as possible. It's like seeing yourself wrapped in an impenetrable wall," Mike said, picturing in his head the wall that was again being maintained without really concentrating. "Once it is there, it should stay without you having to actively picture it. At least, I think so, anyway." Mike kept himself on the edge of awareness of Anne, trying to catch whether or not he would feel the wall slide into place. And hoping that somehow by concentrating on her and the wall he might be able to help her achieve the focus she needed to build her own wall around her mind.

"It seems kind of weird," she said slowly, and Mike could tell she was concentrating on the image he had been pushing towards her. Mike could feel it slide between the two of them. Once it was in place, Mike gave it a few mental jabs, like he had learned from Damien. "Oh, I felt that, like someone knocking on a door in my head," Anne exclaimed excitedly. The momentary thrill broke her initial concentration and Mike "fell" headfirst into her thoughts. Given recent events, it didn't surprise Mike that the first images were of what had happened to her those few years ago. He saw her again at the party. Damien had been there too, not just Derek. Seeing Derek's face again brought on Mike's anger. This time he focused on how different it was. He wanted to punish Derek.

Pulling back in shock Mike managed to break the connection right before she put the wall back in place. Having seen the look on Damien's face when Mike had broken the connection forcibly, Mike was pretty sure he did not want to experience that first hand. It might be more than uncomfortable, given his recently weakened condition.

"I'm sorry, Anne," Mike said quickly. "I didn't know that would happen. I was just tapping it to let you know what to expect, and then when the wall fell..." Mike trailed off, not sure what to say to explain. He wasn't sure how to tell her that he had seen the party where she had been hurt again.

"It's ok," Anne said, the warmth of her voice the only thing to go on to judge her mood. She had the wall firmly in place at this point. "You knew what happened." Mike could tell she was on the verge of tears again, but inside he swore to ask Damien about that night. Mike was silently glad that she couldn't see or hear his thoughts. It had become apparent during their talk that she lacked any real strength in that area. She had to be in close contact, if not physically touching her target, to be able to do anything. This made it easy to keep her in the dark that Mike knew someone who might know where her attacker was. *"And that I'm going to hunt him down."*

"Well, I should let you go," Mike started, after the awkward silence had gone on another minute. "I'm still pretty worn out and I have to go to work tomorrow. Maybe all of us can get together this weekend? Or some night this week if there is time."

"That would be great," she said. "Thank you for helping me, and for understanding Mike. I think you and Laurie would be great together, if you decide to not worry about your going home. Later." Then she hung up, before Mike could say anything. The only thing Mike knew for sure was that with that little tangle avoided, he could begin to think about what the rest of the summer might hold.

***

Damien finally cornered his old friend late Sunday evening. As he approached, he could feel the rage rolling towards him. Derek was maintaining a good front, however, and showed no outward sign of his murderous intent. "Derek, why have you made me chase you down like this?" Damien asked, poised to act but projecting calm.

"I have no intention of living under the thumb of the Council any longer. This is our time, Damien. Yours, and mine, and Cliff's. Although we will just have to keep Cliff around because he is the next head of the Council. But you and I will pull the strings on his puppet reign. Why can't you see that it is our time?" Derek said, some of his anger leaking into his voice. "We need to stop messing around with these loose families and either bring them in or eliminate them. It is time for us to take over."

"Derek, you're a fool," Damien began, "You realize what you are saying, right? You are again talking about going above your station and power. Take over the Council? That's nonsense and even your father would tell you so. He knows what can happen when someone goes against the wishes of their betters."

"Don't give me that crap, Damien," Derek spat out. "My father would support me in a bid to take over, but he doesn't have the influence to get special consideration like you do. It is time for the old guard to go. I will eliminate or turn this Keller and then the Council will have to listen to me."

"You know what they said," Damien continued, speaking calmly, "I am supposed to try and win him over and I am making progress. He has talents the Council hasn't had access to in generations. He could be a powerful ally if you will just let me handle this my way."

"Forget it, Damien," Derek snapped, "I'm going to do this my way, and you will never know when I'm going to strike. There are others who feel like I do, but I had hoped you would be by my side, instead of an enemy."

"I am not your enemy," Damien said to the empty air as Derek vanished again. "but I will be if you don't stop." Damien ended to the blankness around him. He then turned and went home. He would have to wait until the next time Mike left the Johnson property to talk to him, but at least Anne had been able to confirm that he was alive. *I'm going to have to keep an eye out for Derek too. He's completely lost it,* Damien thought to himself.

Chapter 18

The next morning Mike felt back to his usual self, all traces of pain and tiredness gone from his limbs. As he ate breakfast, he thought about the past few days and what he needed to ask Damien the next time he saw his new friend. Something must have shown on Mike's face because he hastily checked and confirmed that the mental wall was firmly in place when Uncle Jim spoke up. "Is everything alright with you, Mike? I know it is just cereal but you look to be chewing something awfully hard." He said fairly calmly, lifting his coffee mug to take a sip.

"Oh, yeah," Mike said, somewhat surprised and forcing himself to swallow a mouthful before speaking. "It's just that I am trying to figure out what to do about what happened this weekend. I can't pretend that things haven't changed, Uncle. It's only a matter of time before someone else comes along. What if they want something from me and I'm not willing to give it? Did you ever have to fight?"

Uncle Jim set his mug down and stared at his nephew a moment. Mike could see a trace of weariness around the edges of his Uncle's eyes. "Yes. Once I had to fight," he said after a moment. "I almost lost your aunt then. That was when I had to tell her about our family, and I thought I would lose her a second time when I did." Aunt Jenny, who had been moving about the kitchen, but quiet up until now, came over and put a hand on his shoulder, smiling at him. He reached up and took her hand. "Thankfully she loved me too much by then to be scared off. We've been careful since to avoid any trouble. Are you worried that this Derek or even Damien will attack you sooner rather than later?"

"Actually, Uncle," Mike said, pausing to take a drink of juice, apple this morning, "It isn't Damien, but I plan to take the fight to Derek. Last night when I talked to Anne, she asked me to teach her about the mental shield that I used. Well, I was tapping on it when she got it in place. She let it drop because she got excited that she actually did it. She could feel me trying to access her thoughts. When she did, I saw what happened to her again, and who did it. It wasn't Damien, but he was at the party where it happened. The attacker was actually Derek. He used his gifts to manipulate her. It was some sort of joke to him." Aunt Jenny gasped slightly, and Mike could tell she had tightened her hold on her husband's shoulder.

"I can see why you would be upset, Mike," his uncle started, "but don't get ahead of yourself. If this guy did what you think he did, it could be dangerous to face him before you are ready. While you have made great strides in only a couple days, he apparently doesn't suffer from a lack of experience. Hell, that was a few years ago and he apparently had a command of some powers even then. Who knows what this guy is capable of now."

"Uncle," Mike said, cutting him off, and surprised at himself for doing so. "I cannot sit back and let this slide. He doesn't know I know, and he doesn't suspect that I would do anything to him anyway. But I cannot let this slide. You were the one that told me our family righted wrongs and stood up for those who couldn't help themselves. I may not have even known Anne existed back then, but I feel obligated to act since she told me about it. I have to use the fact that this guy may not know that I know to my advantage before anything else happens."

"I know, Mike," he replied resignedly, but with a hint of a smile at his nephew's vehemence. "Just be careful. Your mother would kill me if something happened to you. While I applaud your stance, I cannot help but caution you against trying to take on the world right now. There is a lot out there that even I do not know because I stayed out of anything not immediately nearby. Your grandfather was more of the hero than I ever hoped to be. Let's try to get through this summer, shall we?"

"What would mom say if I ended up staying in the fall?" Mike asked quietly, but it was something that had crossed his mind after yesterday. "If it could be managed, why not stay around? I only have one year of school left, and technically I could be graduated retroactively because I have more than enough credits for graduation. My senior year will just be taking some college credit courses anyway. What if something happened this summer to keep me around?"

"What do you mean, Mike?" Aunt Jenny spoke up for the first time. "If something kept you here when fall came around?"

"Just a thought I had, Aunt Jenny," Mike replied, smiling. "It had to be something you entertained, or you wouldn't have tried to match me up with the daughter of one of your oldest friends. And I don't think Uncle Jim would have allowed you to if he hadn't already had that talk with my mom and she had approved of the possibility. I would suspect that she has all the important papers and such packed up and ready to overnight here if I should decide to stay at the last minute. And you've been pretty transparent, Aunt Jenny. Even without hearing any thoughts, you said plenty." The shocked looks fading to smiles on their faces said Mike had hit the nail on the head. Yes indeed, this summer certainly was going to be interesting.

"Well, if that is what you decide, the arrangements would be easy to make," Uncle Jim said after a moment, still smiling. "We should get going to work, if you feel up to it." Everyone cleared away breakfast from the table and the two males headed to the truck.

The drive in stayed fairly quiet, both of the men lost in their own thoughts. Mike wasn't sure what Uncle Jim was brooding over, but Mike knew that, for himself, he was quietly reviewing everything he could recall from that brief flash inside Anne's head, cataloging all the things he had witnessed. He spent most of the day and the rest of the week, when he had a spare moment, devoted to thinking of any way to approach Damien about it. *"What if they still are friends and Damien doesn't want to give the guy up?"* Mike wondered to himself. Fortunately, or unfortunately, Damien didn't show up at all that week and Mike did not try to contact him. Mike worked and came home, spent free time practicing his gifts, studying the family book, or talking to Laurie. That weekend a group of them were to go bowling and then to the under twenty-one club.

***

Damien had waited patiently all week, keeping tabs on those around Mike to make sure he was ok, but most of his attention had been on trying to track down Derek. He seemed to have gone to ground somewhere and was plotting his next emergence. Damien didn't dare bring his father or the Council into this, for he was sure they would see it as a sign of weakness. As the week drew to a close and Damien knew of the planned outing, he decided that would be when he would approach Mike and try to talk to him again. It was just too risky to try and approach him at work with his uncle nearby all the time.

***

When Damien showed up at the bowling alley Saturday night, Mike knew it was time to talk to his new friend. Mike caught Damien's eye and motioned him over towards the snack bar. Before heading over, Mike gave Laurie a quick hug, "You want anything? I think I am going to get something to munch on." She shook her head no and after a quick round of negatives from the rest of the group, Mike headed towards the line waiting for pizzas, fries and sodas. Damien grinned as he came up and clapped Mike on the shoulder.

"Looking good, man," Damien said, leaning in conspiratorially. "I see things are going well with the lovely Miss Laurie. You sly dog, you."

"I have something serious to ask you, Damien," Mike said as they waited in line. A cheer from his little group revealed Chad had just gotten another strike. It was going to take all of Mike's meager skills to not get shown up too badly when he got to his next frame. At least the tension between Laurie and Anne was gone. Even Liz seemed to be enjoying herself this time instead of waiting for something to blow up.

"Shoot, man," Damien said calmly. Inside, his thoughts were in a maelstrom. Between almost thinking that Mike had killed himself, to Mike not reaching out once this past week, Damien wasn't sure what was going on. If only he had been able to keep a tracer on Mike's thoughts.

"I need to ask you about a party a few years ago," Mike said. When the person at the counter asked his order, he quickly ordered some nachos and dropped a few bucks on the counter. "Anne, the dark haired one in the pink top, she was there. I saw her memory of the party and you were there too. Something happened to her at that party and I am hoping you can tell me where the guy is that did it so I can have a talk with him. He hasn't shown up around me since that one night, but it was Derek, the one you tried to drag out of my car the night we met."

Stunned, Damien stood there speechless for a moment. He had not been really expecting this to be what Mike wanted to talk to him about, but it was certainly easier than what he feared. Damien took a long look at Anne as if he was trying to place her in his memory, even though he knew full well what happened. After a moment he spoke, "I think I remember her. If it was what I think happened, then he was dealt with rather severely already." Damien wasn't sure if that would put Mike off his course or not, as obvious as it was.

"That is fine that someone else dealt with him then, but I am going to have words with him now. Consider it someone checking up on him, like a parole officer. Besides, he has already approached me once and made it clear he intended to again. I half expected him to show up here tonight instead of you," Mike stated. "I don't have to check up on it to know there were never any formal charges or anything. Someone had seen to it she wouldn't report it. That is unacceptable." Mike had a feeling that the lack of report had something to do with the Council. They were not above the law as far as he was concerned and Mike intended to make that clear from the beginning.

"Mike, I get it, she is pretty and you feel bad for her," Damien began. "But you do not want to go off half-assed and bite off more than you can chew. Just trust me when I say he is being watched and you won't do anything but stir up a lot of trouble by going after him now." Damien didn't have to read his new friend's thoughts to know where this was going. He himself had thought Derek deserved more than the slap on the wrist he got, but one didn't question the Council's decisions unless you were prepared for the consequences.

Mike paused a moment to pocket his change and pick up his tray full of nachos and cheese. "I understand if he was or is a friend of yours, Damien. But this is a matter of principle for me. What is the point of being in the position I am without being able to right this wrong and help her get some closure? I will find out where he is another way, but I was hoping that as my friend you might help me out with this one. Maybe I was wrong about you. Maybe you just use your gifts for selfish reasons after all."

Seeing his plan begin to fall apart, Damien made a snap decision. It was helped that he agreed with Mike's stance, and felt bad that he had never spoken up before himself. "I do know where to find him, or at least I used to. He is on the run now. His family and mine have been friends for generations. That's why I was pushing you to drop this. His family has some influence in our world. That is why they covered this up and quietly moved him off to another town. He is no slacker when it comes to his own abilities. If you go after him, you will be painting a target on your back. And maybe mine for giving him up."

"Damien," Mike began, now that he knew what the problem was, "You, and Derek, said it yourselves. Guys of our caliber are answerable only to ourselves. This is something that I have to do. If he has the same skills as you and I, no one is going to be able to police us but ourselves." Mike could tell Damien was torn between old family ties and their new-found friendship. He hoped that he wouldn't make an enemy out of Damien, but Mike had no intention of dropping this subject so easily.

"Alright," Damien relented. His father might not be pleased, but he had to see this through his way, and making an enemy with Mike over something so trivial would not score him any points with the Council. "His full name is Derek Gohr. If I see him, I will try to get word to you, but as I said, he is on the run, ranting about all kinds of nonsense. He is convinced that you are a threat to him rising to power within our society."

Clapping Damien on the shoulder with his free hand, Mike said warmly, "Glad that you are on my side about this, Damien. We will have to talk about this society and the Council. Yes, I know a little about it as I researched what I could when you said that you were associated with them in some way. Now, if you aren't busy, you should come hang with us for a bit. More the merrier. I will just tell everyone we ran into each other at the bookstore and then I saw you here and invited you to chill with us." Damien nodded and followed Mike over towards the rest of the group.

Everyone was waiting on Mike to bowl his frame and were surprised by the addition to their group. Mike and Damien both noticed that it was actually Liz that was sizing Damien up, where Mike thought for sure it would be Anne. Laurie wrapped herself around Mike and stole a nacho from his tray before darting off to sit next to Deb while Mike put the plate down. "So, where did you and Mike run into each other, Damien?" Laurie asked while Mike wiped his hands on a napkin and grabbed his ball.

"We were looking at the same author at the bookstore in the mall," Damien replied coolly, spouting the lie Mike concocted as if it were the truth. "Turns out we both have an addiction to Sci-Fi. Isn't that right Mike?"

"Yeah, when I saw him over by the counter, I told him he should join us if he wasn't doing anything," Mike replied, lining up to start his frame. "Now be quiet and let me focus." Laurie and Deb were both making faces at Mike to mess up his game.

"You look familiar," Anne said suddenly. Mike nearly slipped onto the lane and his toss was less than perfect. He managed to clear the left side of the pins, but it was going to be an ugly spare to pickup.

"I get that all the time," Damien said, rubbing his jaw for a moment and making a show of looking Anne over. "I have one of those faces or something. I am sure I would have remembered you, though." Damien flashed a prize winning smile and was surprised himself when he encountered resistance to his attempt to influence Anne to let it go. He backed off quickly and hoped she didn't notice. He could be very subtle when he wanted to be. Anne just shrugged and got ready to bowl; she was up after Mike, who was struggling to line up for his spare attempt. When he didn't pick it up, he parked himself next to Laurie, who began rubbing his shoulders in mock sympathy. She took his poor frame as her and Deb having distracted him and was enjoying their little flirtations.

"So where do you go to school?" Liz asked into the brief silence while Anne bowled. "I don't think I have seen you around." Normally the quiet one, for Liz to not only speak up, but to be obviously probing like this was rare. It was a measure of that first look that Liz and Damien shared. Mike gave him a questioning look which Damien just shrugged off.

"I don't like to talk about it," Damien began, "My father is a rather wealthy businessman, so I have always been homeschooled with private tutors. I find it dreadfully embarrassing to talk about." Damien grinned at Liz, appreciating the attention from someone outside the small close knit families he was used to. Until recently, he didn't associate with anyone who wasn't gifted on a regular basis, and he had had moments of jealousy over the somewhat normal life Mike had been able to live until now. "I guess you could say I am in that phase where I shun my father's way of life and do whatever I want. Believe me, he hasn't been very happy with me lately." Damien laughed slightly. Liz laughed with him and slid over a little closer to him until it was her turn to bowl.

As the night progressed, it became clear that Liz and Damien were attracted to each other. The only hiccup seemed to be later that evening at the club when Anne pulled Mike aside. "Mike," Anne began, "I cannot shake this feeling that I have met Damien before. I don't think it was anything bad, just like we passed in a hall sometime you know?"

"Anne," Mike said, having to lean close to be heard over the music in the club "So what if you did? As long as you know that it wasn't anything bad, then why worry about it? You two probably passed in the mall or something one day." Anne just nodded and everything went back to normal from there. At the end of the night, Deb and Chad left together first, while the remaining members of the group said final goodbyes. Liz and Damien exchanged numbers and Mike overheard Damien telling Liz he would call her this week for sure. Anne, while seeming withdrawn at first, seemed quite pleased with herself as she needled Liz after Damien left. Mike and Laurie left together for the drive back to Laurie's house

"Damien seems nice," Laurie said once they were alone. "That's good that he and Liz hit it off. She is always so shy around guys." Laurie was leaning towards Mike in her seat. The evening had gone very well considering the unexpected addition and Mike was hoping that he could keep Laurie safe if he did confront this guy from her and Anne's past.

"I'm glad," Mike replied. "I don't know him all that well, we have only talked a few times, but he seems to be alright." Mike shifted his hand that was holding Laurie's as they drove. Laurie beamed and Mike could hear her thoughts clearly, knowing that she was pleased with the recent turn of events. The more he listened the more he was sure he was going to stay at the end of summer. "So, tell me about the high school? What clubs do they have? And what are the teachers like?"

Laurie, seeming to catch something in his tone of voice squealed in delight, and launched into a rambling story that took up the rest of the drive to her house. When they got there, Mike just let her keep rambling for another few minutes after he put the car in park and turned in his seat to watch her expression. At this point she was telling a funny story from her World History class the previous spring semester. The teacher had dressed up as Napoleon and talked with an exaggerated accent for the entire day, even when they saw him in the halls between classes. When she wound down, Mike leaned over and kissed her softly on the lips. Mike wasn't prepared for the jolt of electricity that left both of them breathless. Glancing at the clock on the console, the two teens jumped at how late it was getting. Mike quickly unlatched his seatbelt and climbed out of the car. He headed around to the other side of the car and opened Laurie's door.

She slid gracefully out and immediately into his arms, this time they shared a slightly longer kiss. The current intensified between them and, breathless, Mike took her hand and they headed for her front door. There was only a small porch light left on and under its meager glow the two began kissing again. Laurie clung to Mike and he could feel her heart beating rapidly. When they came up again for air, Mike just gazed into her eyes when suddenly a light inside flashed on. They separated with a jerk. The door never opened but Mike felt the eyes of Laurie's dad on them from behind the thin curtain.

"Tonight was wonderful, Laurie," Mike stammered. "I'm glad things have worked out the way they have. Will I get a chance to talk to you tomorrow? Or will you be too busy with the choir?" During the course of the night, Laurie had said there was a Choir special the next day and that she was singing a solo. It was the first of three weeks in a row that she would be singing solo. She had invited Mike, as well as his aunt and uncle. Mike wouldn't miss it for the world, especially after tonight.

"I will see you after the service for sure. Depending on how early you guys get there, I might see you before," Laurie replied, trying to catch her breath. Her face was flushed and Mike thought she looked beautiful. They shared a chaste kiss and hug then said their goodbyes. Mike headed back to the car and couldn't help the grin that split his face. Things were definitely looking up.

***

"Daddy," Laurie said, when she turned around after watching Mike back out and drive away. She blushed furiously, knowing that her father had probably seen her kissing Mike. Though still seventeen for a few more months, her father had always been protective when it came to boys and wasn't taking her impending adulthood very well.

"Did you two have a nice evening?" Mr. Sterling said softly, unable to hide the smile from his voice though he kept it off his face at first. He approved of the Johnson boy, as he had come to call Mike. He had recognized something inherently good about the boy when he had been at the house for the first date. He wasn't about to let his daughter know he had gone soft though. He was still worried about his girl getting hurt. There had been talk with Mike's uncle that the boy might be going back east in the fall.

"We had a wonderful time, Daddy," Laurie beamed, catching the smile in his voice. She went over and hugged her father. "I really like him and it looks like he feels the same way. He even hinted that he might stay after summer is over. Isn't that great?"

"That's wonderful, sweetheart," He replied, letting his smile touch his face. "Now, run along to bed, you have an important day tomorrow. Don't let some boy distract you from using your gifted voice." He was very proud of his daughter's singing talent and needling her about Mike brought a grin to his face when she pouted at him in mock indignation. "Good night, honey."

"Night, Daddy," Laurie said as she started up the stairs toward her room. Her dreams that night were filled with many wonderful dates with Mike, each ending with them kissing on her front porch.

Chapter 19

Mike drove home in a euphoric cloud thinking about Laurie. Each thought brought him closer to affirming to himself that he really was going to stay in Washington with his aunt and uncle. A measure of sadness came over him when he thought of his mom and sister being left behind. But if they weren't happy, maybe they could move out here as well. Then everyone would be together. Suddenly Mike's swirling thoughts were broken by a chuckle from the backseat. Mike glanced back and saw Derek, he nearly pulled over there on the highway, but the new arrival spoke first and Mike decided to play this out a little to see what he could learn. His anger was spiking though and Mike saw the red begin to tint his vision. He shook his head and focused on Derek's words while watching the limited traffic around him.

"So, I hear you have been looking for me," Derek said once he was sure he had Mike's attention. "I have been waiting for a chance for us to talk again, but Damien has been making it difficult for me. Hopefully my distraction will give us a chance to talk without his interference this time." The teen dissolved into mist and reappeared in the passenger seat, just as he had the first time he appeared in Mike's car. He again ran his fingers along the arm rest and then brought them to his nose. "You know, I met your precious Laurie a few times. She was quite taken with me, prior to my setting my sights on Anne."

Furious, but not sure what to do while they drove down the road, Mike settled on listening and trying to figure out if Derek was there physically or just a projection, as his Uncle had suggested. Perhaps he would be able to work out how Derek was doing it, like he had with the things Damien had shown him. "So what do I owe the pleasure of this visit?" Mike asked through gritted teeth. The rage was trying to explode and if it did he wasn't sure he would be able to control the car.

"I just thought we should have a chat when it was less likely you would try to attack me. So I figured a car ride would suffice as a distraction," Derek continued, smirking. "She would have been a nice trophy on my wall, but that Anne, she was something else." Derek was intentionally goading Mike, trying to see if he could push him over the edge. He was so intent on the rage rolling off Mike, he never noticed that Mike had figured out the string of power linking this projection to the host and where Derek was hiding at that moment.

Filing away the location of Derek's hiding place, at least currently, Mike replied, trying to sound casual, "You will leave them both alone. They are finally healing the hurt you caused with your little stunt. And about that, what did they give you? A slap on the wrist? It couldn't have been much given that you are still breathing. You better be thankful that it wasn't my choice in your punishment, you scumbag." Mike could give as well as he was taking and Derek's fuse was obviously shorter. *"How did he know that I knew about Anne?"* Mike wondered briefly.

"Listen here, you punk," Derek began ranting, his form shimmering and he didn't even notice, "I am going to rule the Council, openly or via proxy, and no one is going to stop me. Not you, not Damien. You mark my words, James Michael Keller, you will wish you had never crossed me."

"You listen, Derek," Mike began, having latched onto the thread of power holding the projection. It became obvious Derek noticed this as he began to panic, thrashing in the seat in a fit and knowing that he could not escape. "To quote an old movie, There is a new sheriff in town. You will answer to me." With that Mike envisioned snipping the cord of power with a pair of scissors and with a shocked look fading into pain, Derek vanished. Smiling to himself, Mike continued his drive home. He was secure in the knowledge that he had figured out Derek's trick, and at least wounded his adversary.

In moments, Damien appeared in the seat so recently vacated. He had been looking for Derek and caught up with him just in time to see what Mike had done. It was impossible, but from what Damien could see, Mike had just severed Derek's astral projection. The consequences could mean that Derek had been permanently weakened or even lost that ability. No one on the Council spoke of such an ability because it was long thought impossible. Inside, Damien paled at the power that Mike had no idea he was wielding. "Mike, that was incredible," he said to the expression on his new friend's face.

"I hope that taught him a lesson," Mike said. While surprised at Damien's sudden arrival, he was glad to see his new friend. "I am not sure what I even did, but he did teach me a new trick in the process. Watch this." Mike pulled over to the side of the two lane road just a mile from his uncle's property line and then, concentrating, projected himself into the back seat. It was disconcerting at first to be seeing from two perspectives but he found by focusing he could separate the two lines of sight as if he was working with two computer monitors. After a minute he let go of the projection and looked at Damien, who was sitting there still in shock.

"Mike," Damien began, "That was very good for your first attempt. And you picked that up by watching him do it?" When Mike nodded, Damien continued, "Incredible. You are a marvel, my friend. I have known people who grew up with the power who can barely do half what you do. I think you may have wounded Derek more than you think, though. What was that last bit you did? I couldn't see what happened, just felt the explosion of power and pain as his projection wasn't pushed back, but destroyed entirely."

"Destroyed?" Mike mused a moment, thinking over what Damien said. "I could see his power stretching back to where he really was. That was how I figured he wasn't really here and that I couldn't get him right now if I even wanted to. That was also why when he started ranting he didn't try to grab the wheel or touch me; he couldn't really interact with me. He was just like a hologram."

"You say you saw his power?" Damien questioned. His father had mentioned knowing a man when he was younger who said he could see the tendrils of power that encompassed all those with the gift. It was how he could tell someone's strength or even their talents. He had died when Damien was too young to have remembered meeting him but his father spoke highly of the man's skills. *"Did this mean that Mike could do something similar?"* Damien wondered to himself. The prospects were daunting.

"Yeah, so since it was like a cord or string, I just cut it," Mike said, getting caught up in Damien's enthusiasm. It was obvious this wasn't something that even Damien encountered every day. "I also think I could track him anytime I wanted to now. I caught a glimpse of a very nice room somewhere, so that must be where he was holding up. I am sure he will be long gone before I could find it or him, though. Next time, I won't wait so long to act. I just wanted to figure out what he was doing or wanted."

"I know a little about that. He and I have been friends since we were children, so we have always recognized each other's handiwork," Damien remarked, caught up in awe of what Mike was grasping without any formal training. A natural talent like this could be very powerful, or they could self-destruct. "Look, I have to get going, I am still trying to clean up a mess he left for me to keep me from intervening when he arrived. It looks like I need not have worried since you have it handled. I will see you around, Mike. Call if you need anything or just want to talk."

Damien disappeared and Mike was struck by the difference in his departure than Derek's. It occurred to him that Damien had been there

234

in the flesh. Mike reached out towards the traces of power left in Damien's departure. His hand passed through something that felt vaguely like a cobweb, but he could tell it was made of the same stuff he had felt when he cut Derek's projection. *"Maybe if I figure this out, I can track Derek down."* Concentrating on the feel of the air, Mike felt he could, given more opportunities. Mike put the car in gear and finished the short drive to his uncle's house.

***

Gasping for breath while his heart threatened to explode, Derek quickly began gathering up his belongings. This safe house wasn't going to be safe for long if Damien caught wind of his trail. When he tried to shift himself to another location, he was shocked to find himself on his knees doubled up in pain. Whatever Mike had done had wounded his powers considerably. Standing slowly, he quickly shouldered his bag and ran from the apartment. He headed down the stairs to the ground floor and merely waved off the odd look from the doorman who was sure the teen looked to be in some sort of trouble.

Derek began walking down the street as he pulled out his cell phone, not trusting to try and communicate with his father telepathically. "Father," he said the moment his elder picked up the line. "Something is wrong." He proceeded to relate his latest visit with Mike and what had happened. When there was no response, Derek began to panic, "Father, what is going on with me? What did he do to me?"

"Son," Samuel Gohr began, "I think he cut off that talent. I have only heard rumors of it ever even being possible, but what you describe sounds like that. He could have just wounded you somehow, but it could be more serious than that. I would lay low and not go near him. The Council is already starting to suspect that I have been in contact with you and want me to have you brought in for questioning. Be careful, whatever it is you decide. I have to go."

Derek stopped in the street, looking at the phone in his hand. His father had no instructions or wisdom to offer and he was now on his own. Knowing he had to gather a few allies, he started calling some of the other friends of his from families lower in the Council's eyes than his own. Some of them were little more than thugs, but their help could be useful until he regained his strength. A plan formed in his mind, a wicked grin splitting Derek's face.

***

As Mike pulled into the drive, Uncle Jim was standing on the front porch, his arms folded across his chest. "I was wondering if the car had broken down from the improved defenses you had built," he said, coming down the steps to meet his nephew by the car. "I could tell you were coming, but what on earth made you stop where you did? What did you do to cause that ripple?"

"Derek paid me a visit on my ride home, compliments of his projected self," Mike said, watching for a reaction. Uncle Jim's face was stone all of a sudden. "He isn't going to be too happy with me for some time, I think. I also think that it is a good thing I reinforced the defenses, because I am sure he will be coming for me sooner rather than later." Uncle Jim merely nodded. He thought he had felt something several times over the last week. Like someone was testing the defenses.

Suddenly, there was a big crash and it felt like a hole might be battered in the dome. Then it rebounded and held firmly. "I also think you might have to tell me the details of how you won the fight where you almost lost Aunt Jenny. How did you get them to leave you alone like they have these past years?"

Uncle Jim stared a moment, then nodded. "Events seem to progress ahead of anything I could have expected or hoped for, but I guess you have a right to know. Come into the house and we'll talk." He turned and headed back up the porch steps. Mike followed him in and they took seats at the dining room table again like they had many times to discuss their shared legacy.

After a moment Uncle Jim began, "It was after the car accident that took your father and grandfather. I was approached by someone claiming to represent some sort of Council. I had recognized the name from the book, but I didn't recall many details. They wanted my allegiance, saying that my father, your grandfather, had been punished for refusing to join them. They threatened to take your aunt from me, and I had no doubt that he would be able to. You were far too young to have shown any presence of the gift or not, so they apparently had disregarded you. I was still fairly young and my inability to have children was not really known outside the family. It seemed safe to assume that I would be the one to continue the family line. Our line, turned to serve their ends, was what they had been after when they approached your grandfather. I am sorry that his refusal also took your father from you. He was a good man, good for your mother." Mike merely nodded. He was old enough to remember his father a little, unlike his sister Connie. Mike had dealt with that pain already and didn't care to relive it tonight.

Uncle Jim paused briefly, and went to get a glass of water. When he motioned with the glass towards his nephew, Mike waved him off, eager to hear more of his tale. He sat back down, draining half the glass of cool tap water before continuing. "I asked for time, to consider, and I poured through the family book, looking for a way out of this without losing your aunt or my own life. It was then I found the small note in one of the margins regarding oaths sworn on the gifts bound one to their very soul."

"That was how I started to put together a little of what was going on," Mike interrupted, then shut his mouth quickly. When Uncle Jim paused, Mike continued. "I realized it when I examined the defenses after I had recovered. You said you had never seen anything like it, and I realized why. Yours were purely defensive and warning. There was nothing harmful or offensive at all to them. I had inadvertently planted all sorts of countermeasures within them to lash at those that would come after us. Then I started to think about how little you do with your gifts and realized you must have made some sort of promise in order to protect Aunt Jenny and yourself. I must say, Uncle, I don't think they were held back at all by the dome you had before."

He nodded when Mike's narrative was done. "That's exactly right. I promised to stop being the crusader, stop trying to right wrongs, so that your aunt and I would be left alone to lead our lives. If I was no help or hindrance to their schemes, then I was not worth bothering. They seemed content to wait and see what would happen with the next generation, or perhaps they went on to some other project. That left me room to shield the property, and set warnings, but not to be able to counter attack, as that would be seen as a sign of aggression that I was not allowed within my oath. It has allowed us these years of peace. When it became clear that you would carry on the family line instead of me, I hoped that by shielding you it would keep you safe from them as well. I distanced myself from you and your sister so I wouldn't draw attention to you. They would surely come after you like they did me. That is why your mom was alright with letting you stay here in the fall if you wanted. You were safer here, within my wards and protections. I guess you have surpassed them and wouldn't quite need my protection anymore." He trailed off, brushing again mentally against the dome around the property.

"I think I may have severed Derek's ability to astral project. Damien seemed to think so," Mike continued, relating what happened in the car in more detail. "Somehow I snipped his connection to the projection he had made into the car on my way home. I don't know if it did what I hoped, but if it did, it gives me an edge on him that he won't have on me."

"And what do you hope you accomplished, nephew?" Uncle Jim asked, plainly interested in what Mike had figured out. His self-imposed limitations didn't stop him from being curious. Their discussions of late included many what-ifs and possibilities as Mike was preparing his future with these talents. That future probably meant an encounter with the Council, and specifically Derek, in the near future.

"I hope it means that he has to come after me in the flesh, while I can still strike at him from relative safety through a proxy," Mike said grimly, noting the approval of the tactic flashing in his uncle's eyes. "I have played too many war games and read too many books to not know that if I can take away one of his weapons and make it my own, then I have already turned the tide that his experience gives him over me." Mike then projected a copy of himself to the chair opposite so that his uncle was forced to split his attentions between the two images of his nephew. Mike again felt that split and concentrated in turning the two perspectives into two separate images in his mind, like two computer monitors again. He found he was able to actively control both the projected self and his physical self simultaneously. It was difficult with two sets of perceptions warring in his mind, but it became infinitely easier to close his real eyes and only see out of his projected self. Mike saw his uncle reach out and place a hand on the projected copy of his nephew. At first his hand started to pass through the arm, but by focusing Mike was able to give himself solidity.

"That is amazing, Mike," he said, when his hand rested on the arm of projected copy. "It is incredible. You learned this by watching him?" Mike's copy nodded, wavering slightly before firming back. It was harder to maintain than he thought, and Mike didn't trust enough yet to talk through the copy. After another minute he let it drop, opening his real eyes, the sudden shift from one side of the table to the other slightly disorienting.

"It will take some practice but I think I can manage it," Mike said softly. "I also think I can track him. At least, if he tries anything that I catch, I believe I can trace it back to his physical self. I'm going to have to practice teleporting. Working with the car and Anne with me was more, in the moment than concentrated effort. Then I'll be ready to strike him as soon as he or anyone else makes a move. I don't hold any illusions that the war is not on. I just hope my makeshift weapons and on the fly tactics will see me through this without drawing me down Uncle." *"I don't want to have to resurrect my Darkness if I get in over my head. Though it's confidence would be useful,"* Mike worried to himself.

"I am sure you will do just fine," Jim said, standing from the table. "Now I think I am going to go to bed, if I can get any sleep with that constant hammering." Mike nodded and headed to bed myself, trying to ignore the hammering against the protective dome around the property that had started up just after Mike got home. It seemed that someone was rather upset and determined to strike at Mike tonight if he could get through the defenses. Mike wasn't sure who it was, but it didn't feel like Derek. The power being exerted had a different feel to it. Mike also wasn't sure if the attacker was using all his force or not, but if he was, then Mike could already see how to thwart him. As Mike slipped himself into a deep sleep, a trick he had picked up while learning more about dream walking, Mike directed a thought of laughter towards the source of the attacks. They paused for a moment, then they redoubled in fury. It seemed the attacker had not been using all of his strength, but he was easily taunted. That could prove useful knowledge as well. An enemy who lacks patience and guile is easily tripped onto his face.

240

Chapter 20

Sometime during the night, whoever it was had given up attacking the dome in a flurry of blows, hoping to batter it down. He was still attempting to probe it, looking for a hole or crack. At random times as Mike showered and got dressed for the day he would slap away the probes, as one slaps the hand of a child away from the cookie jar. A resounding boom against the dome generally followed as the assailant lashed out in fury. As Mike walked into the kitchen and dining area, his uncle looked up from the Sunday paper.

"I think I understand why you are doing it, but do you think you could stop taunting him for an hour so we can have a peaceful meal?" he asked. Mike could see lines under his eyes. Apparently he hadn't been able to get as much sleep with the constant attacks all night.

"I am sorry, Uncle," Mike said, grabbing a banana from the fruit basket and proceeding to cut it into pieces to add to his corn flakes. "If he knew how much about himself he was teaching me I think he would stop, or at least try something else. However, I don't think it's Derek." Mike slapped another gentle probe, again sending laughter towards him. Mike had been focusing more and more on the direction and thought he could pinpoint the assailant within a few hundred yards, unless he moved suddenly. Mike was rewarded from his taunt with another crashing blow against the dome. He was prepared for it this time and set a cushion against the mental vibrations of the dome. A pillow behind his head all night had made him think of trying it at some point this morning. Mike had wanted to try and track his assailant first before he let him slip away. It dulled the attack that unless Mike was trying to feel it, he didn't even notice it. Mike extended the cushion to cover the dome, so as to protect his uncle from the game he was playing with whoever it was.

"Whatever you are doing nephew, thank you," Uncle Jim said from behind his paper. "I think I am going to take a nap this afternoon sometime. I didn't sleep so well."

"Good morning you two," Aunt Jenny said, stepping into the room from the hallway that led to their bedroom. She was dressed a little fancier than Sundays had been around the house for the last month. She took in Mike's casual jeans and t-shirt, a disapproving frown crossing her face. It was then Mike noticed that Uncle Jim was wearing a dress shirt with a tie.

"Did I miss a memo or something?" Mike asked, after finishing the mouthful of cereal he had started while Uncle Jim was talking.

"Apparently young men don't listen any better with gifts then they do without them, or one generation removed," she continued, passing her glare to her husband for a moment. "Laurie said that she had talked to you about her choir performance this morning and that you were on board about going."

Mike thought back over the last two weeks of phone calls and texts with Laurie, remembering her mentioning it again last night. The events of their first real kiss and his encounter with Derek had momentarily pushed it from his mind. Mike now distinctly remembered agreeing to whatever she had asked me that had stopped our brief round of kissing before she got out of the car. Mike could tell from the grin on his aunt's face that even without the ability to read minds, Mike's face told her all she needed to know. He didn't bother putting words to the situation but quickly finished breakfast and went to change clothes into something more presentable for church attendance. His aunt's laughter followed down the hallway. Mike was glad she found it so amusing.

***

Derek assembled his small band of troublemakers Sunday morning as soon as he was alerted to Mike having left the protection of the wards. He looked over the few fellow gifted he was able to amass and thought it would look better if he had been able to win over Damien, or at least been able to find Cliff. Cliff may be nearly a 'normal' but at least his siding with him would have been something to instill some courage in the lackeys he had gathered. Clifford had not been home when he went calling last night however. Derek suspected Damien had something to do with that.

"Look here, guys," Derek began, pacing in the small classroom in a distant wing of the church where they had gathered. "Keller is going to be here with his family. I am going to stage a little scene that will force him to reveal himself or let his precious Laurie get hurt. I care nothing for the girl, but I need him to run. I need him to feel forced to hide from public, then we can step in and extract a promise and force him to our bidding. He cannot hope to hold out against all of us in the wake of the public finding him. He will need our resources, once we present him trussed up to the Council, in order to come out of hiding."

The few guys weren't sure what Derek was talking about, but they were on board with anything that got them access to his kind of money and power. Most of them, while not poor or even middle class, were not in his league financially. Greed is a powerful motivator. Two of them knew about phase two of Derek's plan, and were even more eager for that.

"Phase two will involve just a few of us paying a visit to an old conquest of mine," Derek continued. "Turns out I missed that she has some talents of her own and we are going to use them to our benefit. As well as use her to our enjoyment." He began laughing madly and the rest joined in. "I will meet up with you three at her house after I have finished here. Don't get too far into the party without me." He then waved them off and began giving orders to the others.

Unknown to him, Clifford was hidden in a closet nearby. He had known that Derek was looking for him and decided he would wait and see what his friend was up to. What he heard appalled him. Never a brave soul, Clifford was frozen in place, scared to even breathe fully until the group left the room. He then went in search of Damien.

***

The large church building had a full parking lot and it took some time to find a place for Uncle Jim to park his truck. Soon the trio filed into the chapel and looked for seats. Mike noticed Laurie already sitting up in the choir loft behind the pulpit and smiled at her. She smiled and gave a little wave before turning to a slightly older woman next to her. Aunt Jenny solved the seating problem as she led them over to Laurie's parents, who had saved room on the pew next to them. Mike shook hands with her father but was able to sit himself on the aisle seat, his uncle beside him. Mike was looking around at the stained glass windows behind the balcony seats when he heard Uncle Jim talking to him.

"Your aunt and I were married in this very chapel. We normally try to attend once or twice a month, but hadn't gotten around to it this summer," he was saying, having seated himself next to his nephew, with Aunt Jenny on his other side. She was chatting with Laurie's mother, the topic of conversation probably Laurie and Mike as glances were cast in his direction or up to the loft where Laurie sat patiently. Laurie smiled brightly again when her eyes met Mike's.

"It's very pretty, Uncle Jim," Mike said in response, again turning his attention to the stained glass scenes right out of biblical text. The second floor behind the balcony pews seemed to be nearly all window from one side to the other, wrapping around the classic large pipes of the organ that framed the choir loft. A motion in one of the balcony pews caught his eye, but when Mike looked closer there didn't seem to be anyone in that particular section yet. Mike chalked it up to a trick of the light reflecting through the stained glass windows.

The service started with general announcements and an opening prayer, then the preacher launched into his sermon for the morning on the temptation of Christ and how we must all overcome our own temptations into evil during our lives. Mike was never much of one for religion, and this one hit a little too close to home. He let his mind wander a bit and kept glancing at Laurie in the choir loft. She apparently wasn't paying much attention to the sermon either as she kept blushing when their eyes met. Mike caught a flicker of movement again in an otherwise empty section of the balcony but didn't see anyone up there when he looked again. Uncle Jim must have noticed his nephew's distraction because he took a moment while everyone was standing to sing a hymn at the end of the sermon to whisper quickly, "Is everything alright?"

"Just something weird about that empty section of balcony," Mike replied quickly, flipping to the page listed in the program for the hymn they were all supposed to sing. After that Mike got lost in the music and strained to pick out Laurie's voice from the harmony of the choir. He found it not as difficult as he might have thought given his abilities and let her voice wash over him, as if she was singing just to him in an empty room. That was when it happened, a sudden and determined jab at his personal mental shield. It felt like a sword as sharp and fine as a needle striking against his mind and Mike nearly dropped the hymnal when he closed his eyes and pressed fingers to his temples. Uncle Jim grabbed the hymnal before it could fall, but a couple of people close by saw Mike clutch his head and leaned forward to try to whisper to Uncle Jim. He waved them off, but the concern on his face was evident when they sat back down and Mike turned to look at him. Mike whispered quickly to him when he leaned close, "Either I have a new enemy or

Derek has realized we are not at home. I fear things are going to get interesting in the next few minutes."

"Just be careful, you don't want the attention that could bring," he replied. "I doubt he does either." Mike nodded and tried to focus on what was happening around him. It was time for the choir performance and Laurie had stepped forward where she was to stand while she sang her solo. Mike found it hard to keep focused on her as the attacks resumed upon his mental shield, coming from multiple locations around the church. Instead of tensing to counter every blow, Mike reached out trying to trace their sources, and was surprised when one directed back to the empty balcony that he had been looking at all morning. This time, Derek was lounging arrogantly with one foot put up on the pew ahead of him.

Mike tensed, readying to do anything he could think of to destroy him for interrupting this morning, when there was a faint whisper in his mind, *"Now, don't be hasty friend,"* the last word dripping with sarcasm. *"We don't want a scene with all these people watching. It would lead to many unpleasant questions."* There was a pause, if Derek was merely making his presence known, then Mike would wait for now. Relaxing, Mike tried to turn back to listening to Laurie, not wanting to let Derek ruin the enjoyment of her singing, when his adversary spoke again, *"Her voice is something else, isn't it? Almost like an angel made flesh. It's a pity that I will have to hurt her and Anne both for your refusal to serve me."*

"You want a repeat of last night, Derek?" Mike thought back, laughing inwardly. Putting a smile on his face, Mike was enjoying the sight of Laurie in her element, singing from her heart.

"Ah, but you fail to realize something, friend," Derek continued, his voice dropping even more until Mike could barely hear him. *"I have friends with years of experience over you. What you did was a minor*

wound, easily healed. You didn't think you had really beaten me, did you? Now, what should I do about Miss Singing Angel."

Panic formed in Mike's gut, sure it was a bluff, until he glanced around and noticed a couple figures hiding in the shadows under some of the columns that supported the balcony. Mike thought for a moment it showed on his face as he heard something from the pew ahead. Soon people were gasping as one of the large metal organ pipes snapped loose from the wall and began to fall. Mike followed it down and saw it was aimed at Laurie's head. She didn't realize what was happening yet, continuing with the song she was singing. Quickly Mike thought to move it aside like he had all the logs that first night. There was some resistance at first, and he knew Derek or one of his friends had to be guiding it towards her. Mike fought him with all the strength he could muster. He was able to shift it slightly so it fell next to her, smashing part of the wooden banister that ran across the front of the choir loft.

The next few moments were chaos incarnate as several more of the larger pipes began taking aim at her. Most of the rest of the choir were diving out the little doors in the back that exited the choir loft. Laurie, however, was frozen staring up at the mess that was falling swiftly towards her. Realizing that she wasn't going to move, Mike jumped up from his seat and headed towards the front of the church, jostling a few other people who had moved into the aisle. Mike started calling out her name as he continued to shove the pipes away from her. By now the front pews were pushing back towards those behind them and Mike was being slowed down a little. Fear started to set in his heart that he wouldn't reach her before Derek succeeded in hitting Laurie with one of the metal tubes. As Mike reached the second row of pews he came against a solid mass of people trying to push the opposite way and despair took over. Giving a push against someone ahead Mike focused and teleported himself just on the other side of the crowd of people, nearly falling forward at the step where petitioners knelt for prayer.

Taking a moment to orient himself he noticed that Derek's guidance of the remaining pipes seemed to have subsided and several bounced well off course to crash into the far reaches of the choir loft before Mike could adjust for the lack of resistance. He leapt up the couple steps where the pulpit was and reached up to take hold of Laurie's arm, pulling her down through the opening in the banister behind the pulpit and shielding her with his own body as the rest of the pipes crashed down above them. The pulpit and what was left of the banister served to form a rather nice barrier to deflect the pipes that Mike augmented discreetly with a shield of air. Mike could feel Laurie trembling beneath him and relaxed the fierce grip he had on her arm.

Once the dust settled and the pipes stopped shifting, Mike stood up, covered slightly in plaster or splinters of wood, and pulled Laurie to her feet. She just clung to him as other people started towards the two teens, the danger obviously passed. Mike pushed some of the fallen organ pipes aside with a foot and tried to make his way down the couple of steps to the waiting congregation. Laurie had a death grip on his arm as she was guided towards her waiting parents, who had been given room to get to the front. The rest of the choir had circled around and were approaching from the side doors of the church. Mike glanced briefly up towards the balcony but didn't see Derek up there any longer. None of the shadows seemed to be hiding another person so Mike started to relax a little that the danger was passed. He didn't have long to contemplate where Derek had gone as he was quickly being thanked and clapped on the back by anyone who could get close enough. Soon Mike found himself face to face with Laurie's parents. Laurie had given her mother and father brief hugs then wrapped her arms around Mike, pressing her face into his chest, her panic and fear pouring from her eyes and onto his shirt.

"Thank you for what you did there, son," Mr. Sterling said softly. Mike could tell there were the beginnings of tears in the corners of the older man's eyes. His wife was weeping openly as she murmured her thanks as well. "I don't know what I would do if something had happened to Laurie," he continued, then stopped. He laid a hand on Mike's shoulder and made way through the crowd towards the front pew where Laurie and Mike were sat down, her still clinging to his side as close as she could without sitting on his lap. Mike tried to console her a little and managed to get an arm around her to stroke her hair as she cried into his chest. With her parents, along with Uncle Jim and Aunt Jenny standing guard over the two, most of the congregation started to head towards the exits. The reverend called out to everyone to give the families some space and that he would make some phone calls during the week.

Mike looked up at Uncle Jim, his face stony and unreadable. Mike mentally reached out to him, feeling the slight resistance from the medallion he wore. *"It was Derek,"* Mike whispered softly to his uncle's mind, similar to how Derek had done. Uncle Jim nodded grimly, though his eyes shone at yet another trick his nephew was controlling. Mike turned his attention back to comforting Laurie. After a few more minutes, it was just the six of them in the chapel. They were joined by the reverend who spoke with the adults, then left to make some phone calls regarding the cleanup. "No one would probably be open today, but messages should be left," he said as he departed the room.

After about ten minutes Laurie finally lifted her face away from Mike's chest, her eyes red and puffy. She looked around, flinching when her eyes passed over the jumbled mess of organ pipes filling the choir loft and spilling down the front portion of the church. Then she looked at Mike, who tried to smile reassuringly. She threw her arms around his neck this time and pulled his ear down, whispering fervently, "Thank you so much. I couldn't move. I didn't know what to do. You saved my life. You are my hero, Mike." Mike held her and looked up at the adults. Aunt Jenny and Mrs. Sterling beamed approval, echoed by a reserved Mr. Sterling as well. Uncle Jim gave another grim nod, as if he could read that this wasn't going to be the end of it.

It took nearly another half hour of talking before Laurie was convinced to let Mike go and leave with her mother to hang up her choir robe in the closet set aside for them. During that time the reverend reappeared to express his sincerest apologies again over the unfortunate accident. The adults assured him that they held no feelings of blame against the church. How was he supposed to know that the bindings would let loose on the organ pipes? He paused briefly to say how brave he thought that Mike's actions were: that it was a miracle Mike was able to get there and save Laurie in time. Mike just shook his hand and accepted the accolades much as had been done with the rest, numb inside from the absence of the adrenaline that had taken over during the confrontation with Derek. Soon Laurie and her mother returned from the choir room. Laurie had splashed water on her face in an attempt to recover her sense of calm.

Mike moved to her right away and put an arm around her, leaning close to whisper, "You going to be alright?" She put an arm around him as well and gave a fierce hug, nodding her head against him. Mike let her go to her parents at that time, where she stayed between them as they all started to leave the church. As everyone headed for their cars, Mike asked, "Mr. Sterling, would it be alright if I called later tonight, to check on Laurie?" It seemed the right thing to ask him, as Laurie was already ducking into the back seat of their car. It was his wife that responded first though.

"The young man that saved my daughter's life isn't getting off that easy," she said in a hurry. "I expect you over by five for dinner. Your aunt and uncle are welcome as well, of course." Then she ducked into her seat in the car, immediately turning around to talk to Laurie. Mike nodded to Mr. Sterling and said that they would certainly be there before heading back towards his uncle's truck.

Once they were in the car and heading towards home, Mike could feel the tension in the car building. "What on earth happened in there, Mike?" Aunt Jenny asked when it was clear neither of the other two were about to volunteer anything. Uncle Jim made a sound as if he had wished his wife hadn't asked.

"I'm sorry, Aunt Jenny," Mike started, finally letting himself feel the fear and panic that had been suppressed in the rush to save Laurie. "It was Derek. I thought that I had wounded him last night and we would have some peace, but apparently his friends helped him out. Which means…" Mike trailed off, realizing what that meant. He quickly pulled his cellphone from a pocket and dialed Anne's number. It rang several times then went to voicemail, Mike didn't bother leaving a message. It was faster to reach out towards Anne mentally since he knew how he could find her. That was another little trick he had taught myself while he had been trying to learn how to find Derek and deal with him. What Mike met was a blank wall, not like she was shielding herself, but like she wasn't there at all. Mike looked back up at his aunt, and he thought she could read his face.

"I am sure she is alright, Mike. You yourself taught her the trick of shielding herself," she said softly, as if she was trying to convince herself. "Besides, there is nothing you can do at this point anyway since we are clear across town."

"That's not entirely true, Aunt Jenny," Mike said, reaching out again, trying to find Derek this time. Mike knew that even if he had shielded Anne while he did whatever he planned to her, he would leave Mike able to find him, just so he could gloat. Mike found him readily enough, his joy in whatever he was doing apparent the moment Mike touched his mind. Mike heard his laughter in his head as clearly as Derek's voice had been in the church.

Derek sent an image of what Mike had feared was happening, Anne cringing in a corner as several figures in hoods and ski masks were edging closer. Mike could see the fear and panic in her eyes, her clothes already ripped in several places where she had apparently tried to fight them off. While Mike sat there in the truck, Derek showed him how Anne was about to be tormented with her worst nightmare. One of the guys reached down and grabbed her arm and when she tried to swing at him, caught and pulled her to him. Suddenly Mike was there, standing behind the group.

Mike looked around; Derek was nowhere to be seen. The three attempted rapists were oblivious to Mike's presence at the moment and he looked around again, this time for a weapon. He saw a baseball bat, recalling that Anne said she had played softball for a time on a community league. Mike grabbed it and laid into the back of the nearest one of the three guys with all the force he could physically and mentally muster. There was a sickening crack as the guy yelled and collapsed on the floor. The force of Mike's swing carried him off balance and the second one was missed with the roundhouse swing. Not that it would have mattered much as the bat was cracked nearly through. The one holding Anne's arm, apparently the leader, pointed towards Mike and his remaining accomplice pulled a gun from a pocket. The guy, who looked to be about the same size as Mike, turned and took aim at Mike.

Things seemed to slow down to a crawl. The one on the ground twitched feebly, Mike was sure the guy had a broken back with the reinforced swing he had taken. The one with the gun was shouting something at Mike, as was the leader, but he could hear nothing. Wrapped in the utter silence Mike lashed out, flinging a mental blow at both of them simultaneously. That was when it seemed a mask fell and Mike could see that the one holding Anne's arm was, in reality, Derek. He had been disguising himself. Anne, who had been looking from her attackers to Mike when he appeared suddenly, saw Derek's face as well. Recognition dawned, then rage. Mike started forward and swung what was left of the bat at the gun, hoping that he would be fast enough. Anne jerked towards her desk, scrambling to grab something that was laying on it. That was all the time Mike had to see what she was doing as then he was in a pitched battle with the one with the gun.

The gun toting thug was forced to drop it as his arm went numb, Mike's swing snapping the bones in his forearm with an audible pop. He went to club Mike with his other arm but Mike ducked, looking up to see that Anne was standing over Derek's body. She was plunging a little letter opener fashioned like a sword with a fairy on the hilt over and over into his chest. The one who's arm Mike had just broken swung again and this time caught Mike against the side of the head with his undamaged forearm. Mike felt his feet lift off the ground just before he slammed into the wall and fell to the floor. Apparently either this guy could augment his strength as well, or Derek had done it for him. As he turned back towards Anne, Mike gathered myself and leaped towards the guy's back, bringing both of his fists down against the other guy's shoulders as hard as he could muster. The guy collapsed in a heap and Mike looked down at Anne.

"I... couldn't stop them," she said, looking up at Mike from where she was knelt over Derek's body, the now bloody letter opener in her hand. It fell from her fingers as she fell backwards into the corner, trembling. It stained the carpet where it bounced before settling, the little fairy face looking up at everyone.

"It's ok, Anne," Mike said, reaching towards her. At first she flinched away, but then started to relax and took the offered hand. "Where are your parents? We've got to figure out what to do about this." She looked up from the body in front of her to Mike, her eyes going wide at the mention of her parents. She turned and took off into the rest of the house, looking into every door in the hallway. At the end of the hall she found them in the master bedroom and paused with the door half open. Anne's parents were laid out on the bed, appearing as if asleep. Mike went over close enough to see that they were in fact breathing, then turned around. Anne was standing behind him, carrying what was left of the bat that he had lost during the brief fight. She relaxed when Mike nodded and smiled, pointing towards her parents. They retreated into the hallway before speaking.

"Mike, I don't know how you got here, but thank you," she said softly, still shaken by what had nearly happened to her. It was apparent that the intent had been for all three to have turns with her. "How did you get here? What did I do for him to come back?" Clearly she was indicating Derek with the "him".

Mike took her arm and led her back towards her room, away from her sleeping parents. He felt pretty sure that they would wake up and not know that anything had happened. Once they were nearly to her room, Mike replied, "I fear that he came here in order to strike at me through you. I thought I had wounded him, but it didn't work." Mike proceeded to explain quickly about how he had encountered Derek before and how he recognized Derek as the one that had raped her originally. She smiled and hugged Mike when he told her about planning to make Derek pay for his crime since it had been covered up. Mike also told her about the morning incident at the church. "But it would appear you've ended Derek's threat with that little letter opener of yours." Mike turned and pushed the door to her room open the rest of the way, thinking she had partially closed it when she had come out with him to look for her parents. The room was empty except for the bloody letter opener lying on the floor where it had been left.

"Where did they go?" she said when she could see past into the room. "I swear they were here when we went to look for my parents." She walked over and picked up the letter opener, still stained red with blood from when she had stabbed Derek.

"You didn't think I would actually risk myself in such an undertaking did you?" Derek asked, standing casually near Anne's bed, halfway between her and Mike. "They were dupes, expendable. Some fools will do anything for a little bit of power and the promise of doing some harm to another. No matter though. I congratulate you, Mike, on winning this round. But can you keep saving them over and over? I must say though, Anne dear, wonderful performance with the letter opener. I almost felt the jabs myself there when you thought it was me."

"Leave them out of this, Derek," Mike replied through gritted teeth, imagining all the things he wanted to do to the asshole. Mike wanted to tear him apart limb from limb, his rage feeding on itself until Mike nearly rushed him right then. "If you want a confrontation, then pick a place and time and I will be glad to oblige you. Just leave innocents out of this. Or so help me, I will find you and seeing yourself stabbed by a letter opener will be the least of the nightmares I will inflict upon you."

"Tsk, Tsk, Mike," he said, waving a finger admonishingly. "Is that any way for the Champion of Good to talk? All that anger at a little prank. Are you sure you don't wish to reconsider and join the Council that your grandfather and uncle spurned? You would be of standing more than they ever could have aspired to. Together, we could take control of it ourselves and rule as we saw fit. Course, you would have to swear allegiance to me."

"You really don't understand," Mike said, struggling to find calmness within. If he lashed at him right now, Mike was not sure he would stop short of actually killing him. Mike couldn't stoop to his level or he would be no better than Derek was. "I can't join with someone who would treat their fellow humans the way you do. As objects purely for amusement until one is bored, then cast away in favor of another."

"Fellow humans?" Derek demanded vehemently. "Those without the power to stop me are beneath notice. You are the one who doesn't understand. We are not like your so called fellow humans. We are meant to rule, like Alexander the Great or Genghis Khan. We are as gods to these people. They should be taught to see us as so."

"And that is the difference between the two of us," Mike said, finding his calm the longer there was to contemplate the situation. Mike could tell now that Derek was here in the flesh this time. Either it was his arrogance or Mike had actually hurt Derek's ability to project, regardless of his statement at the church. Nothing else seemed to make sense as to why he would risk being face to face with Mike right now. "I see people as people, whether they have these powers we do or not, Derek. This Council may have thought they won something by taking my grandfather and father, as well as forcing my uncle to give up most of his power. I am not going to go easily or quietly, and I will take you and them down before you can stop me." Mike took a step towards Derek, raising hands to grab hold of him as Derek backed further against the wall.

"Don't you threaten me, Mike," Derek said, his self-assuredness slipping from his voice for a moment. "I can take your precious Laurie, or Anne, or even your aunt and uncle from you anytime I wish. I will make you regret ever standing against me." He started to shimmer and fade out.

Mike reached over and grabbed hold of Derek's arm before he totally dissolved and felt himself shifting. Anne's bedroom faded and Mike found himself in a dark room lined with bookshelves. It flickered and became Anne's bedroom again, her staring in shock from across the room. Derek looked at Mike, the panic and stark fear in his eyes as he tried to jerk his arm away from Mike's grasp. He swung with his other arm and hit his captor on the side of the head, causing Mike to lose what grip he had on his peer. Derek vanished and Mike nearly fell forward into the wall the teen had been leaning against.

"Please tell me he can't come into my room anytime he wishes," Anne said, fear causing her voice to tremble slightly. She had picked up the letter opener, holding it like a dagger to strike against anyone who came near her.

Seething over Derek's escape, Mike barely kept the heat in his voice in check as he replied, "Not for much longer." Mike closed his eyes and started copying the dome from his uncle's property but on a much smaller and deadlier scale. His anger fed into the power and Mike felt the pendant start to go cold against his chest. Mike was prepared for it this time and pulled back, keeping his eyes closed to test the shield. Satisfied that it would hold, Mike opened his eyes to see Anne standing right in front of him, looking up into his eyes. "That should hold against him while you are home. I am sorry I don't know how to help you when you aren't here." She just threw her arms around Mike and hugged tightly.

"Thank you, Mike," she said, sniffling, as she stepped back away. "Thank you for everything. How did you know to come here, though?" From the look in her eyes this was going to be something else she would want Mike to try to teach her. So far they had discarded almost every type of ability except for her minor compulsion and reading thoughts, and those were limited to close distances or touch.

"I teleported, like the night in the car," Mike started. "When I found out that you were gifted like me. I did it twice today. Once when I had to get to Laurie before she was crushed by the organ pipes, and now to get here before they could hurt you. I hope I can use it to get home."

"I can give you a ride to your aunt and uncle's house," Anne said grabbing her keys off of the nightstand next to her bed. "My parents, if they even wake up before I'm back, won't think anything of me not being home. Might even be easier that way, since I need some air to clear my head anyway. Wait, what happened to Laurie?"

"Derek tried to crush her with organ pipes while she was singing. I stopped it. Probably did a better job than I did here though," Mike shrugged. They went outside to get in her car for the ride to his uncle's home.

When they reached the car, Anne realized she was still holding the letter opener and her face paled. Dropping it and the keys, she collapsed to her knees on the front lawn. Mike raced to her side. "I..." Anne whispered, "I killed him. That guy, I stabbed him, he was dead." She began sobbing into Mike's shoulder.

"Anne," Mike spoke consolingly, "it was you or him, self-defense. I know right now that may not make it easier, but it will eventually. You just gotta hold yourself together until it gets easier." Mike picked up the keys from the ground beside her, not touching the little letter opener. "Come on, I'll drive, it will give you time to get your bearings and then you can drive home ok?" Anne nodded and let him help her to the passenger door of her car. The little fairy face staring at them from where it was forgotten in the yard. Mike realized that he and Anne had now both killed someone, and that fact made him feel closer to her than before. His self-defense rationale just didn't seem to fit with his own situation though.

Roughly a half hour later, Mike felt the familiar trickle of cold over his skin as they crossed the wards around his uncle's property. They seemed secure but subconsciously Mike checked them over as he had started doing frequently. When they pulled into the drive Mike reached out to find his uncle and whisper to him that he was home. Before Mike could get out of the car, Uncle Jim and Aunt Jenny were both coming onto the front porch. Mike thanked Anne and she headed away, leaving him standing in the driveway facing his relatives. When Mike stepped onto the porch, Aunt Jenny grabbed him by the shoulders.

"Don't you ever do that to me again, Mike," she said in a rush. "I was talking to you, then you vanished right from the truck. What happened? I was so worried."

About then the strain of the shield he had put around Anne's house caught up with Mike and he stumbled, Jenny catching her nephew before he could fall. "I am sorry Aunt Jenny. Derek had shown me what he was about to do to Anne. He had three guys in her house, they had her pinned in her room. I teleported again to get to her in time. I can't keep doing that though, so I put a shield around her house like we have here. I think it took a bit out of me." Aunt Jenny held onto Mike as his knees gave way and the house swam in front of his eyes.

"I think we are going to have to call and cancel our dinner with the Sterlings, Jim," she said as he came over to help his nephew into the house. They brought Mike into the living room and got him seated before Aunt Jenny went off into the kitchen. Uncle Jim stood over Mike, watching his nephew until Jenny returned with a cool rag and a glass of water. The rag she placed on Mike's forehead.

"We can't cancel," Mike mumbled when he was able to find his voice again. Keeping his eyes closed seemed to help with the room spinning around. "I have to find a way to protect Laurie as well. Or at least ward her house. I can't let anything happen to her. She's important." Mike discovered trying to rise was the wrong idea when a sharp pain in his forehead caused him to collapse against the cushions.

"You aren't going anywhere in the condition you're in," Uncle Jim said, placing a hand on Mike's shoulder to hold him from trying to rise again. "You couldn't stop a fly right now. Were you paying attention to the pendant? You could have killed yourself. You know this."

"Yes, Uncle," Mike said, taking a drink from the glass of water that Aunt Jenny was trying to hand over. "I stopped when it turned cold, but with all the activity today, I think I pushed as far as I had that first night, maybe farther. And I still have more to do later." Mike stood up slowly, testing to see if he would be able to support his own weight again before continuing. "I am going to take a nap. I think that will help me. Please don't cancel the dinner tonight, and make sure I'm awake in time to go. Please?" Mike looked to his aunt and uncle, who nodded slowly, as if wondering if they should push for a cancellation tonight or not. Mike didn't give them any more time to argue than it took for him to half stumble down the hall and collapse in bed, kicking his shoes off onto the floor.

Chapter 21

"Son," Samuel Gohr said when his offspring entered and bowed for a sufficient amount of silence to let his anger be felt. "Three useful apprentices sacrificed for your little game, and you are nowhere closer to accomplishing anything. One may be salvageable, but two are dead. Explain yourself," he commanded.

"He knows rage, and has experienced killing someone," Derek replied almost gleefully. Seeing Mike react so violently against the pathetic pawns he had brought in had made him nearly giddy. "I underestimated his ability to learn and copy what he has seen. His raw power and talents are what we feared, Father. It will not happen again. However, it is only a matter of time before he gives into his rage and then he will be ours. He will not sacrifice his gifts like his uncle did. He will either give in to his dark side, or he will be powerless. Either way, the Council will have no interference for another generation."

"That was not what the Council wanted," the older man continued. "They wanted him in the fold. You are dangerously close to treason as it is. There are calls for my resignation if I do not find and rein you in. So far I do not think anyone suspects our real intentions of taking over the Council."

"Meddlers!" the young man said incredulously. "Can't they see what is inside him? He will turn. He will have nowhere to go. His own family will shun him once they are conveniently made aware of the monster lurking within him. I only have to nudge him a little further and he will tumble like a house of cards. Damien's attempt to soften him to us through kind words and friendship are a waste of time. He will be a weapon for us to unleash, not an equal."

"Move quickly, son," the elder Gohr said wearily. "I am stalling as much as I can, but if the Council votes and decides to bring you in, I will not be able to save you from the punishment they deem fit." He watched as his son left without another word.

***

"Damien," Clifford called as soon as he was in the room. He had been trying to locate his friend who had been moving about rapidly seeking Derek all day. Damien had only learned of what had happened with Laurie and Anne when he arrived home to find his father waiting for him. Apparently a big Council meeting was coming soon and something was going to be officially done about Derek, and possibly his father for letting it go to this level.

"Cliff, I'm really busy right now," Damien brushed off his friend at first, but something in Clifford's eyes made him stop. "Wait, what happened?"

"It's Derek," Clifford said breathlessly. "He has lost it. You were right, I should have said or done something sooner instead of letting him walk all over me. He is talking treason. This Mike that you are supposed to be working on, he is going to bind him or kill him."

"As serious as those charges are, Cliff," Damien began, "I highly doubt Derek has the ability. Mike Keller far outstrips anything any of us have power wise, and he is untrained. He runs on pure emotion and instinct. Going against him directly is suicide."

The awe in Clifford's eyes brought Damien up short. They had all wondered what would happen if someone was able to stand up against the Council. Would their world come to an end like it had been foretold it would when the promised one arrived? Those supposed 'fairy tales' from their youth came rushing back to both young men as they stood in Damien's study. "You know we are going to have to testify to the Council, right?" Clifford said meekly. He didn't relish the thought of standing before his father and relating how he stood by and did nothing while Derek moved against the Council's wishes.

"Perhaps not," Damien said thoughtfully, a plan forming in his head. He just hoped he had won Mike over enough to get him to go along with it. Damien wasn't sure how Mike would react to the Council. "If I can convince Mike it is in all of our best interests to neutralize Derek's threat ourselves, then the three of us present a united front to the Council, then maybe they will stop meddling in his life and his family. He is a good guy who just wants to be left alone, if I have read him right."

"You really don't think like our fathers do, do you, Damien?" Clifford asked, recognizing his friend's reluctance to be as cutthroat as his father is.

"No, Cliff," Damien replied, grinning at the insight. "I think the time for all the meddling has gone on long enough. The world may not be perfect, but are we really making it any better with our manipulations? Why can't we turn our attentions to helping the world, instead of helping only ourselves?" Clifford merely nodded, and Damien continued, "Perhaps with Derek out of the way, our generation can do some things differently. Come on, we will have to speak with Mike before the Council decides anything themselves." The two friends departed in search of Mike Keller.

***

Jenny Johnson woke her nephew gently, and the couple hours of sleep seemed to do wonders for his health. Mike felt as good as he ever had the last couple weeks. The complete lack of attacks against the dome worried him however. Mike hoped he wasn't too late to protect Laurie. As he got dressed, Mike resolved to end it once and for all tonight with Derek. Mike wasn't sure he knew how to contact him but was sure his rival would come looking for him as soon as he left the protected property. Mike had also officially made another decision.

"Aunt Jenny, Uncle Jim," Mike said calmly as the trio loaded into the truck to head to the Sterling's for dinner. They both looked at him expectantly. "I want to stay. I cannot go back to my old life. I really like Laurie and today made me see just how much I have come to care about her these last couple weeks. I have real friends here in a month, closer than most back home. And even with the... extras... this summer has brought, I am accepted and liked." Aunt Jenny hugged him, and Uncle Jim merely nodded, saying that they could call his mother that night when they got home. Mike wasn't looking forward to having to tell his mom that he wasn't coming home, but it was the right decision. After a moment, they settled in for the drive to dinner with the Sterlings.

Laurie answered the door, still wearing her church dress and immediately flung her arms around Mike when she saw who it was. Mike held her close and regardless of her parents, or his aunt and uncle standing there, he kissed Laurie gently, staring into her eyes. "I am so glad you're alright, Laurie," Mike said, never taking his eyes off hers.

"Thanks to you, my hero," she responded softly. After a moment the two teens realized they had an audience and separated quickly, both blushing fiercely. Mike glanced at Laurie's father, expecting disapproval, but finding none. Mr. Sterling even seemed to be grinning slightly at his daughter's embarrassment. The six of them went into the dining room for dinner and conversation remained light. Mrs. Sterling, who was adamant about putting Mike between herself and Laurie, repeatedly patted the young man's arm or shoulder and thanked him again for saving her only child.

After dinner, the adults paired off into their respective genders to discuss topics of interest to them, leaving Laurie and Mike pretty much alone. While Uncle Jim and Mr. Sterling discussed changing some of the trees he had planted in his yard into something with better shading, Mrs. Sterling and Aunt Jenny reminisced about something from their girlhood days. Laurie and Mike strolled through the garden in the backyard and took a seat on one of the benches, within eyesight but not hearing of her father and his uncle. As soon as they were seated Laurie buried her face in Mike's chest again like she had at the church, the events of the day still weighed heavily on her mind. Mike just wrapped his arms around her and let her calm herself.

"I don't know why I can't stop crying," she said when she finally lifted her head up to look Mike in the eyes, little tears staining her cheeks.

"You had a near death experience," he said, trying to remain calm as he wiped away her tears with a finger. "I don't know how I would react if I had been the one nearly crushed by organ pipes." Mike smiled a little, trying to get her to do the same. "I think you are handling it better than I would."

"You were so brave, though," she said through her laughter at the compliment. "I just froze. I couldn't even move to get out of the way. And then, there you were, pulling me out of harm's way and shielding me with your own body. You didn't get hurt, did you?" Sudden concern for a mysterious and unspoken injury seized her.

"No, Laurie," Mike said, brushing a stray strand of her blonde hair back from her face; inside he winced at the memory of doing that to another blonde just a couple months ago. "I am just fine. You were all I was worried about. Instinct or impulse took over and I had to get to you." She smiled and hugged him close for a minute. "There is something I have to tell you, though," Mike said after a moment, placing hands on her arms and pushing her back a little to look deeply into her eyes. Mike could see worry flit across her features as what it was he might have to tell her. Taking a deep breath, Mike continued, "I've decided I'm going to stay here in Washington with my aunt and uncle when school starts in the fall. And, I want to make us, official. If that's what you want." Mike paused, waiting for what she would say. Her answer was going to decide how he proceeded tonight with handling Derek and any other threats that came along.

"Oh, Mike, that's wonderful," she exclaimed, drawing the attention of her father and his uncle as she practically jumped into his lap and kissed Mike firmly. Sensing the watching eyes of the two older men caused Mike to pause only a second before he got caught up in Laurie's enthusiasm. After about a minute, his uncle broke up their moment as he raised his voice to be heard clearly when he was talking about removing one of the trees behind the bench and replacing it with something that would weather the colder winters better. Laurie, turning red, slid back onto the bench and Mike reluctantly let her go. Thinking quickly towards his uncle, *"Thanks,"* Mike grinned in his direction. Uncle Jim clapped Laurie's father on the shoulder. Mike could clearly hear him explain about Mike's decision to stay in town, which is what must have gotten Laurie excited. Mr. Sterling certainly didn't seem to disapprove as he smiled broadly and waved at the two teens before turning and dragging Jim over towards another part of the garden to discuss other improvements to his landscaping. Uncle Jim's amateur landscaping skills would be put to the test with Mr. Sterling's plans.

When they turned away, Mike quickly slipped the pendant over his head and put it around Laurie's neck. She looked at him curiously and lifted it up to look at it. "This is something left to me by my grandfather. I want you to wear it for me until I can come up with something more fitting. Please?" Mike asked softly as she looked from him to it a couple of times. Mike closed her hand over it and kissed her fingertips, holding her a moment while he concentrated to put wards around her through the pendant. Mike saw his uncle turn and look, but he just smiled. Laurie and Mike sat on the bench not really talking for almost an hour, before it became clear it was time to go.

As they walked back into the house, Mike saw his aunt and uncle's eyes shift from the pendant clearly displayed around Laurie's neck, to Mike, seeking some sort of clarification. Given that Uncle Jim always kept his tucked in his shirt, it was unlikely that the Sterling's would know that there was another one in existence. Mike just nodded to them both to indicate that he knew what he was doing and hoped they would remain quiet until they got into the car. Mrs. Sterling, who had apparently been clued into Mike's decision to stay, just hugged the young man and said she had hoped he might stay. With a brief hug from Laurie, and a firm handshake from her father, Mike climbed back into the truck with his aunt and uncle. Once they were out of sight of the Sterling house, the questions began.

"What are you thinking giving her the pendant?" Uncle Jim demanded, the same time his Aunt asked, "Are you sure you know what you are doing?"

Mike waited for them both to stop before responding, "Please trust me. I know Derek is watching and looking for any opportunity to attack. I warded Anne's house but I wouldn't have been able to do that at Laurie's and still be functional for what I have to do next. I know you don't approve of going on the offensive, Uncle, but I don't have a choice. I warded the pendant so that Laurie and her family will be protected while I take care of Derek tonight. I told her it was just until I found something more fitting from me to her."

"And just how do you think you will manage to do that without getting yourself killed?" Uncle Jim asked, his eyes not leaving the road in front of him. Mike could feel the nervous tension from them both like a tidal wave.

"I am going to bait him with what he wants most," Mike replied, wrapping himself in calm like he had in silence the night he had crept out to the clearing and surprised Uncle Jim.

"What is that?" Aunt Jenny asked, but from the look on her face she clearly knew the answer already. Mike heard Uncle Jim sigh with realization.

"Me, Aunt Jenny. He wants me," Mike said. "I have to stop him from ever hurting anyone else again. Even if it means doing some of the exact same things he has done." Mike thought again about the tortures and control Derek had wielded over people in the memories he had been able to tap into. Mike thought he had worked out how to do a binding on Derek's powers using some examples in the family book, but would his will be stronger than Derek's?

Uncle Jim reached into his shirt and withdrew his own pendant holding it silently out towards his nephew. Aunt Jenny's eyes widened as she looked from it to her husband. Mike reached out and took hold of it slowly just as the wards around the property washed over him. Uncle Jim felt it too, and when he patted Aunt Jenny on the knee and pointed ahead to their cabin, she visibly relaxed. She hadn't noticed that they were there, safe within the confines of their property. Mike slipped the pendant over his head and tucked it into his shirt so that he could feel the cool metal against his skin. As they pulled into the driveway, Mike looked at them both while Uncle Jim put the truck in park. "It's time," Mike said as he slipped out of the truck and started to walk back down the road towards the boundary. Mike's confidence in the plan continued to grow with each determined step he made himself take.

***

Probing at the mysterious new wards around both girls' homes, Derek was clearly frustrated with the lack of progress he was making. He knew that his fate could be decided any minute, any pleas and protests cast aside. Pouring through an old family book, he muttered to himself, "There has to be a way to turn him into my servant in time." Then he felt it, the call from his quarry. It was muted at first, barely perceptible, then stronger, more insistent. In a flash he was gone, simply shifting himself closer to the object of his ire.

***

Mike waited patiently just within the protection of the wards while he reached out to his enemy. Mike knew that Derek would hear eventually, and hopefully Damien would to. It would be good to have his new friend by his side for this as Mike was about to step into a world he barely understood. Mike knew that Derek would waste no time in getting to their confrontation. Mike casually checked over the wards from Anne and Laurie, seeing that they were intact and in no immediate threat, then he leaned against a tree to await Derek's arrival. There wasn't long to wait. Derek appeared just on the outside of the boundary in the blink of an eye, blue jeans and a dark t-shirt, his eyes full of rage as he sought Mike out. Then Derek spied his opponent leaning against the tree, Mike spoke, "I am glad you answered my call so quickly, Derek. We have business to settle." Mike stood straight and stepped almost to within reaching distance of the boundary edge. The hairs on his arms and back of his neck were just starting to tingle. Mike thought he could almost see a bluish shimmer where the edge of the protective barrier was.

"Then why don't you come out here so we can talk, Mike," Derek replied, trying to keep his voice casual, but Mike could sense the rage still within him. It wasn't unlike his own when Mike thought about the harm Derek has caused others. That similarity was something Mike was counting on. It would give him an edge in their battle of wills. Mike knew Derek was trying to make him angry, but Mike accepted the anger at what Derek and his Council had done to Mike's family and who knew how many others. Derek was easily goaded into a response, his attacks had proven that he was far too impatient. Mike was no chess prodigy, but he had learned something from the game, patience can and often does overcome brutal assaults. Mike was hinging a lot on that this evening. "Or is the great hypocrite of Good too scared to face me?"

"I think I like the view from here much better, Derek," Mike replied, resting on his heels. He almost thought he caught a flicker of light around Derek, but then it was gone. "It keeps us both honest because I cannot reach you without bringing down the shield, while you cannot reach me through it." Understanding registered on Derek's face, or at least he seemed to think he was reading Mike's intentions. Mike noticed Damien and another boy appear behind and off to the side of the road where Derek couldn't see them. For his part, Derek was so focused on Mike he didn't notice the arrival of his former friend. Mike gave them a brief glance and enough of his plan telepathically to Damien to assure that there would be no interference. The relief and acceptance Mike received in return surprised him, he had not been totally convinced that he had read Damien's feelings right. Mike had feared he was being played a fool by the more experienced peer.

"So you have called me here to ask for a truce?" Derek said, one hand gesturing towards the shield while he put his other in his pocket, appearing to stand casually. "I guess the rush of taking someone's life and holding it in your hands was too delicious to give up. There can be no truce. One of us must submit to the other."

"I don't think we are as different as you think," Mike replied, building into his pronouncement slowly. Mike knew he had to string Derek into it or there wouldn't be any way to catch him unawares. Mike nearly faltered as he realized what Derek had said. 'Could he know about Kevin?' Mike wondered briefly. The fight in Anne's room flashed through his mind and Mike thought about the thug he had hit with Anne's bat.

As Mike started again, he began to pace, just a few feet back and forth across the roadway, but inching closer to the boundary each time.

That flicker of light around Derek, almost like he was glowing slightly, spiked when Mike started moving, but then vanished again. Mike wasn't sure what it was, so he put it out of his mind for now. It reminded Mike of when he had seen his uncle repairing the wards, or had severed Derek's astral projection. Mike had to concentrate on his plan. "We are merely two sides of the same coin. While I respect the wishes of others to live as they see fit, without interference from my powers, you deem it your right and privilege to control and manipulate them. Am I right?"

Mike continued without waiting for a reply, knowing Derek was listening intently as Mike walked and gestured, not noticing when a hand nearly stuck out to his side of the boundary. "Of course I am right. You're smart enough to see that, otherwise you wouldn't have tried to reach me on that level. You wouldn't have tried to turn me against my uncle for neglecting to tell me about the other families and this Council. You also then wouldn't have tried to attack me through Anne and Laurie. You should have realized that would only provoke me to act against you. I can only assume you were attempting to lure me into some sort of trap through my ignorance and control me as well." At this point Mike did let a hand and part of his arm breach the barrier, just for a moment, to see if Derek would notice. He apparently didn't.

"What I have come to realize, Derek, is that since we are so opposite, this ends tonight." Mike turned to face Derek, fully on the outside of the barrier. With his final words Mike threw every ounce of will he could into shattering the mental shield he knew Derek maintained around himself just as Mike did. The attack came quick enough to catch Derek off guard, and as his wall shattered, he grabbed his head in pain. Knowing he had but a moment before Derek would recover, Mike quickly formed a new wall to replace the one he had destroyed in the sudden attack. If this worked, Derek would be powerless, if it didn't, then Mike was about to be in serious trouble.

Damien and Cliff, watching from the side of the road, had shared in what Mike's vision had shown them of the plan. From what they saw, Mike intended to bind Derek's powers behind a sealed wall. While the concept was rudimentary and reflected Mike's newness with his powers, the idea was sound and should hold for as long as it would take to get Derek before the Council for judgment. They watched as the plan unfolded much as Mike intended, at least at first.

When Derek felt Mike's initial assault, he was staggered. His anger rose up red hot when he realized that Mike had tricked him. He felt his mental protections begin to fail and fell to his knees in pain from the backlash. Then he felt his power slipping away from him and panicked. He lashed violently with everything he could grasp and threw it at Mike, it manifesting as a ball of energy that slammed into Mike's chest, knocking him from his feet. Slowly Derek climbed to his feet, feeling his power return as Mike's concentration was broken.

Feeling the force of Derek's counter attack hit him in the chest like a punch, Mike landed on his back and found himself staring at the star filled sky. In that last moment he had seen a glow flare around Derek as the shield Mike had been building failed. As he rolled to his side and tried to pull himself to his feet, he caught a glimpse of Derek also getting to his feet, only a little wobbly. The glow that Mike had seen flare up was solid again, reminding Mike of the way he had seen his uncle using the gift to repair and inspect the shield around the property. Before he could contemplate it further, Mike had to dodge to the side as Derek decided a physical assault was better than a mental. Several solid masses of air were speeding towards Mike like cannon balls. The shimmer in the air around the missile would have been near impossible to see in the moonlight if it were not for the glow that Mike noticed around it. He managed to dodge the first two and deflect the third harmlessly into the sky with a gathered air mass of his own. Mike's own anger was burning red hot. Mike was now waging two battles, one against Derek, and one against his fear of resurrecting his own Darkness within. Battling it for control of his own actions again would spell doom.

Breathing hard from his exertion, Derek stood and tried to stare his opponent down. Even he had had trouble seeing his balls of air he had launched in the near total darkness, so how was Mike blocking and dodging so effortlessly? Shaking his fist in frustration, Derek began gathering himself again, this time intending to send a wave over his foe.

Seeing Derek tense up, Mike saw the glow around his assailant begin to intensify. It was clear Derek was building something and Mike wasn't sure he would be able to stop whatever it was since he was acting blindly. When Mike saw the wall sailing towards him he instinctively wrapped himself in a bubble similar to the car accident and the shield around the property. A roaring filled Mike's ears as Derek's strike crashed around him, but failed to penetrate his defenses.

Mike decided two could play this game and began throwing balls of air like he was throwing baseballs towards Derek. Though not necessary, in his inexperience Mike actually swung his arm as if he was pitching. Derek countered his projectiles easily, laughing at the exaggerated motions Mike was making. "You really have no idea how to do anything, do you Keller? How pathetic," taunted Derek, as he began launching his assault again.

Mike found himself hard pressed to keep up his attack and maintain his shield against Derek's projectiles. As easy as that first morning had been for Mike to maintain multiple projects at once, he found this form of combat to be much more demanding. He had also strained himself multiple times recently and was starting to waver. It became harder to maintain his shield and Mike was forced to go all defensive, a position he knew was not the one he wanted to be in against his more experienced foe. Mike quickly reached out to Damien, telling him to stay out of it and that distraction cost him as one of Derek's missiles slipped through Mike's defenses and knocked him from his feet.

Mike quickly rolled to the side and put everything he had into a shield against Derek's attack. As his shield was struck multiple times in rapid succession, Mike watched the flashes of light around Derek and tried to formulate a plan to turn things back in his favor. Suddenly there was a thunder like crack and Mike's shield shattered, causing him to fall to his knees. He looked up to see Derek was only a few feet away, laughing and about to move in for the kill. Mike panicked and clasped a hand to the pendant through his shirt, hoping for some guidance from his grandfather like he had received before. Mike's burning red anger suddenly turned white. Power surged through his limbs.

In the next few moments, the glow around Derek seemed to almost solidify. A wild idea came to Mike. Instead of reaching out to shield Derek's power from him like before, Mike simply grabbed hold of it and tried to wrest it away. The moment he grabbed hold of the glow around Derek, Mike felt the sensation of something or someone trying to pull back. The two became locked in a fierce game of tug of war. Derek let out a scream of anguish as the glow around him ripped away and came fluttering over to Mike's fist. Without even realizing it, Mike pulled the glow into himself, and it sank into his skin, leaving a faint glow. It faded away seconds later. Stunned, Mike stood there staring at his hands.

Derek felt like his soul had been ripped in half. It hurt to breathe and it hurt to open his eyes. He knew instantly what had happened to him. He had done this himself, once, to an apprentice of his father's. The pain had nearly stopped the boy's heart and his father was none too pleased. Taking someone's power like that was reserved as the highest form of punishment the Council alone was allowed to deal out. It had not been done in nearly two centuries. Derek had suspected from his father's reaction it was because no one had been strong enough to successfully and reliably do so in that time. The apprentice was quietly disposed of as a training accident and no one had been told that Derek could perform the feat. The Gohr family had hoped one day to use it to their advantage as part of their violent takeover of the Council. Enraged, he struggled to his feet and rushed Mike in an effort to physically take back what had been stolen from him.

Mike tried to understand what happened. His strange rage and strength, normally blinding, had turned into something more when he reached out to the talisman around his neck. Not paying attention, Mike was cleanly taken off his feet when Derek plowed into him running full speed. Colliding with the ground for the second time in minutes, Mike felt the air rush from his lungs and saw spots dance before his eyes. When Derek reached back to punch, Mike flinched and waited for the blow to land, forgetting the power he could wield against the physical assault. When the blow didn't come, Mike turned his head to see Derek frozen above him. Damien and Clifford were entering into Mike's field of vision. Mike could clearly see the strands of power stretching from the two to wrap up Derek. Sliding out from under his assailant, Mike turned to the other two who were coming towards him. Clifford, as Mike had learned his name from Damien, wore an expression of mixed awe and shock. Damien looked thoughtful.

"Thanks for stepping in there, guys," Mike said, looking down at Derek. Derek was frozen in place, but the hate and rage in his eyes was evident.

"Well, it looked like you had forgotten that you are far more powerful than he is," Damien replied, laughing at the look on Mike's face. "Did you finally get him shielded then?"

It was then that Clifford spoke up. He may have always been less powerful than his peers, but a talent he had hidden successfully was the ability to see the auras around those with the gift. It was the one thing Cliff thought kept him in his father's good graces. "He didn't shield him, Damien. Mike stripped Derek of his power. Completely. And if I understood what I saw as well as I think I did, Mike absorbed it, adding Derek's strength to his own."

Damien paled as realization hit him and he began actively checking his captive childhood friend. There was no trace of ability within Derek at all. "I didn't think that was really possible. I know the Council always held it over people's heads to make them toe the line, but I didn't think it was really possible to take away someone's gift. I couldn't see anything going on, but I felt Derek's power wink out. I thought he was shielded. How did you do that, Mike? And how did you know, Cliff?" Damien turned from one to the other.

"I'm not sure how he did it, but I would assume Mike can do what I can do," Cliff said in start to his explanation. "I can see auras, Damien. I always have been able to, but my father told me to keep it a secret. It was useful to know when someone was drawing in power or whether they were talented at all. That was why I was sitting through all those boring Council meetings. My father had me watching for anything suspicious and I was to signal him in a number of different ways, depending on what I saw."

"Is that what I have been seeing?" Mike asked, not waiting for a response. "I noticed strands of power coming from my uncle once. It was how I knew what to look for when I was around you, Damien, or the times I had seen Derek. But what do you mean, I took his power? I was just trying to stop whatever it was he was planning to hit me with next." As Mike realized what the glow had meant and what he had done, he took in the awestruck expression on Cliff's face in a new light. Looking down at Derek, Mike took over the bindings, feeling the increase in power that must be from Derek's gift. Mike freed Derek's ability to talk, knowing that his foe had heard everything. "So what should we do with you now, Derek?"

"Bastards!" Derek screamed, in anger and anguish. He knew his life was pretty much over. Without his abilities his father would disown him, if there was any inheritance to be had anyway once the Council got done with his family. If his father's treasonous acts were brought to light there might not be anything left. The best Derek could hope for was pity that he would be allowed to live out his life working for one of the other families.

Knowing instantly the thoughts that poured from Derek about his father's plotting, Damien and Mike both looked at each other. A side effect of Mike having stripped Derek's power was that Derek was even more of an open book than he used to be. Nodding to each other, Mike spoke first, after he had rebound Derek's mouth, "We are going to take him to this Council of yours. If they aren't gathered together, then they will come because I call. Or else." Mike felt some of his anger rising, but it was not a blinding rage, just a smoldering fire.

Damien nodded, "My father had told me there was a meeting tonight to decide what to do about Derek's actions today at the church and at Anne's home. Two of those he took to her house did not recover. The other is going to be in pain for some time. I wouldn't have thought she had it in her, but Anne is tougher than she looks. I think you might like her, Cliff."

Cliff wasn't really paying attention, he had a far off look in his eyes, when he focused back on his present surroundings, he found both Damien and Mike staring at him. "What? My father is summoning me to the Council chambers; they are about to begin. I didn't tell them what happened here, that is for you two. I think we should go right away, though."

Taking hold of Derek's upraised arm, Mike looked to Damien and Clifford, "Lead the way. I want to get this over with as quickly as possible. My aunt and uncle are going to be worried sick, but this isn't done until the Council learns to leave us alone."

Grinning, Damien knew he would have an ally when he made his own break with the Council tonight. He nodded to Mike and the three of them shifted to the Council chambers directly, dragging the bound Derek with them.

Chapter 22

Damien, Mike, and Clifford arrived in the center of a torch lit room with a crescent shaped table stretched across in front of them. Mike pushed Derek to the ground in front of him, releasing all of his bindings except the one over his mouth. "I will not let anyone kill you, so just shut up," Mike said to Derek. The fear that had appeared in Derek's eyes had swayed Mike. There was no more threat that Derek could really pose, so that was punishment enough at this time for Mike.

"So, you finally have come to us, Michael," the man at the center of the row of old men said. Several of the others shifted uncomfortably, and more than one eye turned toward a member of their group to the right of the man who spoke. That one seemed to be staring at Derek and shrinking into his chair. Mike guessed he must be Derek's father.

When he turned to the one who spoke, Mike was instantly struck by the resemblance to Clifford and assumed it was his father. It would make sense. Recalling the name from Damien's mental introduction, he replied, "Yes, Mr. Van Doornick. I have come to speak to the Council to discuss the terms of leaving my family alone from here on out. I have dealt with Derek as firmly as can be. He is completely powerless, and according to your own son, his power is now added to mine. I can assume by the looks on many of your faces this is unheard of in your time, and that you rightly fear I may do the same to all of you. No doubt some of you are wondering if I can stand against all of you if you acted at once. Let me put those musings to rest. I did not come here to fight, or argue with any of you. I merely came to make it clear that this all stops tonight. No one will act against my family or friends now or ever again. If it is within my lifetime, I will see to it that each and every one of you pays for the acts of the one who breaks this truce." The words had come to Mike's mind similar to the times he taunted Kevin, but this time they seemed to flow from somewhere other than the blinding rage of the Darkness he had felt before.

Silence filled the hall at the end of Mike's speech. Many of the members looked to each other as if asking if this was all real. Mike noted the ones who brightened briefly as if they were about to use some talent. Clifford shrunk back behind Damien, clearly uncomfortable facing his formidable father. Suddenly, with a yell, the man that Mike suspected was Derek's father leapt to his feet, his aura glowing more intensely than Derek's had during the fight. "That is my son, you little bastard," Samuel Gohr yelled, pointing a finger at Mike.

Several of the lookers on stepped forward, grabbing other members of the inner circle and holding them. A few moved towards the center of the ring and the four young men there. Chaos began to break out as Mike felt Damien tense next to him. Mike reached inward and drew up all the strength he could muster as several of the standing people in the chamber began to attack. Mike was quick to notice that not all of the attacks were directed at him as several of the Council members were struck and fell limply from their chairs. Mike could feel Damien and Cliff both acting to shield and deflect attacks as well.

It became evident that Derek's father was leading some sort of coup against the current leaders. As the young men fought desperately to defend themselves, they quickly settled back to back, so they could face the whole room. Instinctively Mike reached out to the other two and joined his personal shield with theirs. This allowed the three of them to begin returning fire. Their assailants began to turn from an all out offensive to more defensive countermeasures as several were struck down in the first few minutes. Mike and his new brothers in battle quickly turned the tide, knocking out those that were attacking them one by one until they stood breathing heavily in a circle of unconscious bodies. That was when Derek's father stood up from behind the long table and pointed his finger at Mike, rage shining in his eyes.

Mike saw the older man's aura glowing and felt the inward draw of power. He reacted with more assuredness than he had with Derek. The elder Gohr reacted much differently to having his power stripped and absorbed by the young man who glared at him defiantly. Instead of screaming in rage and attacking Mike physically, Samuel paled and slumped over the table, falling to the floor in front of them. One of the people standing in the back, a servant by their looks, ran forward and rolled the old man over. It was soon determined that Mr. Gohr was still breathing but was clearly out cold. Mike's rage threatened to turn red. He struggled to push back the encroaching tint to his vision that signaled the Darkness. He spat out through gritted teeth, "Anyone else want to test me tonight?"

The remaining members of the Council and all the bystanders who had a shred of power pulled back as far as they dared without seeming too obvious. More than a few shook their heads or expressed their wish not to test the young man any further. Several minutes passed before Mike was able to unclench his fist. Upon seeing the young man's temper cool, the elder Van Doornick spoke again, "I think you have proven yourself, Michael. I wanted no conflict with you in the first place. I thank you, however, for your assistance in turning this uprising away. I think we all have a lot to think about in the future. I also think it best if you and Councilman Mauston speak regarding the terms of your truce. It is his family that has been most closely associated with trying to recruit your line. It would appear his son already stands by your side. As does my own son."

Mike turned to Damien before looking at the man to Mr. Van Doornick's left, obviously a powerful member of the Council based on his position. Stepping forward a step, Mike stared down the man he believed responsible for the death of his father and grandfather. "So you are the one that owes me a debt as well. For my grandfather and my father." The rage swirled red and white. Mike could see Leonard Mauston's aura clearly, it would take no more than a thought for him to snatch it away as he had done twice already. Before Mike could move further, he felt a hand on his arm. He turned to see Damien's face, his aura blazing as well.

"Mike, wait," Damien said, verbally and mentally. "There are things you do not know that I have to tell you. If after that you wish to punish someone, I will take the punishment for my father." He paused and waited for Mike to nod for him to go on. "The act that took your father and grandfather was committed by another member of the Council. It was during the time that my family was tasked with watching your family. To see what would happen with the bloodline. It is no secret that your family has been at odds with the Council over the centuries, but has always remained strong. So the Council decided to wait for an opportunity to neutralize the threat your family posed. That was, if they could not bring you into the fold at some point. My father did broker a deal with your uncle after he went into a rage after the accident. At that time, it was believed that your uncle would father the next generation. Just in case, you were kept under observation as well, since your mother is the only other closely related member of the line alive." Damien paused to gauge Mike's reaction. Mike's fists clenched as he spoke, "So, you are telling me, Damien, that your friendship was merely to get inside my head and see if I could be turned like you?" Mike's rage became more red, he felt the Darkness regaining strength. It was reaching for control as his mind spun. He shook, dangerously close to stripping them all of their powers one by one. These old men thought to manipulate the lives of anyone they felt like it, and they were raising their children the same way.

"No, Mike," Damien hastily replied, sensing his friend tense up. "At least, not after I really got to know you. Once I knew how strong your convictions were, I knew that you would be a true friend and that I would have an ally when I made my own break with tradition. I do not want any part of the Council anymore." He turned to his father briefly, "I am sorry, Father, but there is a better way than the way we treat others." Turning back to Mike, "When Derek found out that I was the one who was supposed to see what your convictions and limits were, he was angry. He thought I meant for you and I to rise to take over the Council, and he wanted a piece. A bigger piece than he ever would have gotten on his own. It would appear you took care of his and his father's transgressions for the Council. By taking their power they are automatically exiled. Tradition dictates that they will be allowed to live out their days as long as they do not cause any further trouble. They will be given an allowance and employed in a company that a member of the Council owns. This is one of our rules. We are not all heartless and power hungry." Damien ran his gaze across the table of old men, as if daring one of them to countermand the tradition. Some who had been attacked during the failed uprising were slowly getting back into their seats, attendants bringing them something to drink or offering a towel to wipe away blood. Mike noticed a couple of empty seats other than the one that Derek's father had occupied. Apparently the insurgents were more than minor players in this world.

Damien's words gave Mike pause. His hand went to the pendant around his neck. A white light in the depths of his mind shattered the reforming Darkness. Mike felt his grandfather's presence once again.

"Perhaps they are salvageable," the voice of Mike's grandfather broke through his rage.

"They killed you, Grandpa. And Dad. I should wipe them out," Mike thought back.

"Look into their eyes, grandson. They know the old way is dead."

Mike eyed each remaining member of the Council in turn. He saw them flinch when their eyes met. Mike pondered the situation. *"Damien's values do seem to run closer to my own. It is a humane way the Gohrs will be handled."* Mike turned back to the elder Mauston, "The deal with my uncle is over. As a show of good faith, I will dismantle the shield around the property and we will all try to coexist. The first time I catch a whiff of uninvited guests, there will be repercussions. Do we have a deal?"

Surprised by the turn of events, Leonard Mauston did the only thing he could do. He nodded and replied, "Your terms are acceptable to me. I see now that we have grown into bitter old men, clinging to traditions and values like old men tend to do. You are right, son," he continued, turning to Damien. "You have made me proud this day. We may not always agree, but I am proud of your strength and willingness to stand up for what you believe in. I know you want nothing to do with the Council, but it is clear to me that it is time for me to step aside and let you take my place." He bowed his head to the two young men in front of him. "I release your uncle from the oath he took with me those years ago. I wish your family all the success that you desire. With your permission, I will depart." After a nod from Mike, Leonard Mauston's aura pulsed and he was gone.

Mike turned to Damien, speaking mentally, *"So I guess you should take your father's place or is there some rule that says you cannot?"* The grin on Mike's face was disarming, and Damien was at a loss as to how to respond when his new friend continued. *"This is the best way to accomplish your goals, Damien. Rather than leave, you can fix things from the inside. You can do all the good you talked about doing with your gifts, and now the resources of the Council will be behind you instead of arrayed against you."*

Damien smiled and responded in kind, *"I suppose you are right, but what about your goals? What about your promises?"*

"You are my insurance, Damien. If any action is planned that would break this truce, I would ask that you tell me, as my friend," Mike replied telepathically, making sure that no one, not even Cliff who was standing close, would be able to pick up on the exchange. Damien nodded and flashed to the chair his father had abdicated. Mike turned to the rest of the Council, meeting the eyes of each one in turn. Most stared stoically back, afraid to make any move. Some nodded encouragingly at the younger man who they had witnessed strip the power from one of their own. These were the ones who had some way to sense or see the act occur and had been busily explaining it to their neighbors during Damien and Mike's brief exchange. Finally, Mike met the eyes of Clifford's father, the head of the Council.

"Michael Keller," Mr. Van Doornick intoned in his formal voice, "I hereby grant you all rights and privileges once possessed by the Gohr family, including their spot upon the Council," he paused and in a softer tone added, "whether you like it or not." He stopped and grinned at the young man before him. "As my old friend Leonard said before he departed, it is obvious we have grown into bitter old men. Oh! How the dreams and plans we had when we were younger have fallen by the wayside as we grow older! I hope we can work together for a better future, Mr. Keller."

The elder Clifford Van Doornick sat down and motioned to a few lower ranked attendees. He must have commanded them mentally because Mike only saw a brief flicker of power and then several people came forward, grabbing Derek and his father and taking them to another room. Others began gathering up the other fallen members of the faction that had tried to take over. Some of those were starting to wake and Mike noticed that all were immediately shielded by those that came forward to help them from the room. The younger Doornick moved around the table and stood behind his father. Glancing at Damien and grinning, Mike spoke directly to the head of the Council, "If that is all the excitement for now, I have some things to take care of at home. My aunt and uncle will be worried about me and I want to let them know this is all over."

"Go in peace, young man," the older man said before turning to speak to his son. Several other Council members turned to talk to their apprentices or assistants; clearly they were moving onto other matters. Mike quickly transported himself to his aunt and uncle's, bypassing the shield as if it was nothing, realizing now that he could do just about anything he wanted. His only limitations would be those he put on himself.

Chapter 23

Mike walked from his bedroom to the kitchen where he could hear excited voices.

"I can't believe it," Uncle Jim said. "I've struggled to move more than a couple coffee mugs ever since I made that deal. Now look at me."

Mike watched from the doorway as his uncle juggled half a dozen mugs without touching them. "Impressive, uncle," Mike said, catching the mugs when his startled relative almost dropped them.

Aunt Jenny reached him first, hugging him tight. "I was so worried about you. Are you alright? They didn't hurt you did they?"

"I'm fine, Aunt Jenny. Everything's going to be fine now. They released Uncle Jim from his oath. I'd hoped to get home before he realized it, though."

"Tell us everything," Uncle Jim said. "I'll pour some sodas." He busied himself in the kitchen while Mike pulled up a chair. Aunt Jenny sat next him. When Uncle Jim floated a trio of glasses onto the table, Mike couldn't keep the grin from his face. His uncle's wide smile made him look like a kid in a toy store.

Mike sat at the dining room table and sipped from a glass of cola until well after the tumultuous Council meeting broke up. He wrapped up the majority of his tale to an incredulous Uncle Jim and Aunt Jenny with, "So, they awarded me Derek's family estate and spot on this Council of theirs. It looks like a bunch of old businessmen. Like something out of a mob movie or something."

"You wouldn't be far off, I suspect," Uncle Jim replied thoughtfully. "I would use caution in whatever it is they ask of you. Favors from people like that always come with strings attached." Jim Johnson looked lost in thought a moment before continuing, "So, you really took away the gifts of two separate people? And they say you absorbed the power into yourself? That's incredible. Must have scared the pants off of those bastards."

Laughing, Mike said, "I think it did. I'm not entirely sure how I did it the first time, but it appears my own gifts have increased. I didn't feel the slightest strain getting here, or taking down the massive shield we had."

"I wish that hadn't been part of the deal," Aunt Jenny spoke up for the first time since just after her nephew returned. "I always felt safer knowing that something stood between them and our home. Now I will just have to trust my two men here to protect me." She giggled lightly, but it sounded forced.

"Aunt Jenny," Mike began, "We have nothing to worry about now. They are all aware of my feelings and what would happen if anything comes after us for my actions. With Damien taking his father's place, I have an ally who can watch my back for me. Damien's father releasing Uncle Jim from his oath should make you feel safer as well. Things can finally settle down." Mike had been able to detect a marked increase in his Uncle's strength now that the oath was cancelled.

"What are you going to do now?" Aunt Jenny asked, and true to form, getting right to the girl talk as usual. "What about Laurie? I don't want to see my goddaughter get hurt."

"I," Mike stopped, searching for the words to continue, "I don't really know, Aunt Jenny. What I feel for Laurie is a different matter altogether. Will Laurie accept this part of me? Maybe she would be better off without me." Mike looked glum. He knew that he had to tell Laurie. He felt drawn to Laurie like he had never felt before. He didn't want to lose her.

Patting her nephew's hand, Jenny said consolingly, "I think you should sleep on it. A lot has happened to you today but tomorrow I think you will need to make some decisions." She glanced at the clock and yawned. "I am going to bed. I suggest you two get yourselves to bed as well. Tomorrow is going to be here soon." She stood up, and after kissing the top of Mike's head and her husband's cheek, headed down the hall towards her bedroom.

Yawning himself, Uncle Jim called after her, "Be there in a minute, honey." He then turned and looked at his nephew a moment. "Mike, I want you to take a day or two off and decide what you want to do. You have a lot of responsibility on your shoulders now and a lot of decisions to make. If you are up in the morning, I will see you then." He laid a hand on Mike's shoulder and gave it a squeeze before heading towards the hall to join his wife.

"Thanks, Uncle Jim," Mike said, still pondering the future ahead of him. "Good night." Mike then got up and went to his own room, where he expected to lay in bed for hours with his mind in turmoil. However, as soon as his head hit the pillow, sleep overcame him.

***

"Son," Leonard Mauston said after knocking on the door that led to his son's study. He was curious to know what happened after he left the Council meeting and had just seen the Nicholson's off to the Van Doornick residence. David, always a loyal worker, seemed torn about his decision to stay, and his daughter looked terrified. "May I come in a moment?" The father had always tried to respect his son's space. One never knew if the other was practicing something with the gift that interrupting could cause complications.

"Sure thing, Father," Damien said. He had just arrived home himself and knew that things were going to be different now that he had taken over his father's Council seat. He still couldn't believe what Mike had done and was in shock.

"Damien," Leonard began once he was through the door, "I have just seen the Nicholson's off to the Van Doornick's. It appears that they will be sticking around a while. How do you think Keller will take the revelations about his childhood friend?"

"I have no idea how he will handle it. Is she really as gifted as Mike? I heard Mr. Van Doornick say that to her father. If she is, keeping it a secret from him and her both might be harder than anyone is considering."

Nodding slightly, Leonard replied, "It is possible. She had amazing strength from birth, but it was wild and erratic. Rather than risk her harming herself or her family, it was best to bind her gifts until she was older and could exert control over them. The binding was kept longer because of her close association with the Keller's. No one wanted to disrupt the connection we had to the family. It is unfortunate that events turned out like they did, not the way I would have preferred for everyone to be told. Is there anything else of note? I know I abdicated to you, Damien, but I hope that if you need advice, I am here and still your father."

"Thank you, Father," Damien began, "Nothing much happened from there. I'll be interested to see what the Council does now. Mike being awarded the Gohr estate means he is a rather important member in his own right now. I doubt anyone would challenge him if he tried to take over, but he wants nothing to do with it. We're becoming friends, and I don't want to let him down. Things are going to be different from here on out."

After a moment of uneasy silence, Leonard said goodnight to his son and left for his own chambers. Now that he was officially retired, he thought he would spend some time catching up on his reading. His son would have to take over the family businesses in the morning. A few minutes later, he was pouring himself a glass of wine and preparing for bed when there was a knock on his door. The complete lack of any trace of life beyond the door told him who his visitor was. Sighing, he called to the door, "Come in, Lord Salencious. Would you like something to drink?"

"No, thank you," Marcus said as he entered the room in a flourish of his dark long-coat. "I hope I am not intruding but I wanted to call as soon as I heard there had been some developments with young Michael Keller. I hear rumblings that he bested the entire Council at once and sent you all packing, powerless to boot. I am glad to see that you escaped that fate."

"You should get better spies," Leonard replied after swallowing a large gulp of his wine. He did not want to get into a confrontation with the Blood, but he also didn't want them going after Michael and breaking the truce inadvertently. "Michael Keller stripped and absorbed the power of two members of our kind. Ones who sought to overthrow the Council and bind him to their will, anyway. No loss in my opinion, even if the family was once one of my biggest supporters and friends. They will not be missed. However, Mr. Keller has issued his own edict that his family and friends be left alone. He has promised vengeance on all if anyone breaks this truce. I fear that he may not be ready for any more surprises. His temper is wild and unpredictable."

"I see," Marcus replied thoughtfully, "I suppose then the Blood will wait and let him adjust before we make ourselves known. One of his strength and power is someone I would like to meet. Hopefully we can do business together in the future. Good evening, Mr. Mauston." With another flourish of his long-coat, Lord Salencious was gone. Unnerved again by the vampire's presence in his home, Leonard topped off his glass of wine and retired to his bedroom, draining half of it before he was through the door.

***

The next morning, Mike awoke to the sounds in the kitchen of his aunt and uncle having breakfast. He looked down at himself, and noticed he had slept in his clothes again. A look at the alarm clock and he bolted into action, until he remembered his uncle telling him to stay home a few days and sort out the changes from last night. Thoughts of the Council meeting came crashing on him and he sat on the edge of his bed, reliving the events of the night before. Suddenly, it came to him, he knew how he was going to handle the situation with Laurie. Deciding he would run it past his aunt and uncle first, he headed to the kitchen where Uncle Jim was just about to leave for the office. When he saw Mike coming down the hallway, he paused.

"Morning, Mike," he said, noting the serious look on his nephew's face. "How are you feeling this morning?" He went back to packing up the items that his wife had set out for him to take for lunch.

"Very good, Uncle," Mike began, "I have a question to ask both of you, and it determines how I handle Laurie, and the Council's impact on my life." He paused to gauge the expressions of his relatives, and to take a seat at the table. He grabbed a banana and started peeling it before continuing, "I am going to tell Laurie about my gifts and let her decide if she wants to see me anymore or not. If she decides she doesn't, then I know there was no future between us. I don't know what the future holds, but I have to know where Laurie stands first. Do you think she would be home today?"

"I think that's a very intelligent decision," Aunt Jenny said, coming over to lay a hand on her nephew's shoulder. "I am sure that she is home, unless she had to work today. Why don't you give her a call once you have had some breakfast. You might want to take a shower and change too." She giggled as she walked back over by the counter to pick up a large envelope. She held it while Uncle Jim echoed her opinion and headed off to work. Finally she brought it over and laid it in front of Mike. "You will also have to handle this. Your uncle looked at it and said it looks like the estate and holdings that those Council people are turning over to you. Your uncle wanted nothing to do with it, that's why he left so quickly."

"Thanks, Aunt Jenny," Mike said, holding the packet of papers. He wasn't sure he wanted it either, but was curious at the same time. Having never been very wealthy, he wondered what might be his, and what strings came with it. Deciding it could wait, he left the papers sitting on the table as he went to shower and get changed. He heard Aunt Jenny puttering around in the kitchen, apparently working on something already this morning. Mike wondered what she was planning to bake as he went into the bathroom.

Twenty minutes later he was slipping on his shoes when his cell phone rang. Pulling it to himself without touching it, he pressed the button. "Hey Laurie," Mike said cheerfully, "Your ears must have been burning because I was just thinking about calling you."

"Good morning to you, too, my hero," Laurie said, her mood brightening considerably at the sound of his voice. Mike could feel she was still shaken up a little by the events at church the day before. "Are you at work? I don't want to get you in trouble but I needed to hear your voice and thank you again for saving me yesterday." She fingered the pendant he had given her while she waited for his response.

"Well, I was hoping you might be free for lunch? I need to take care of some things today so Uncle Jim gave me the day off," Mike replied. He focused his mind on her and could see her, sitting in her room on the phone, holding the pendant he had given her. He smiled, enjoying the sight of her smiling, even though there was still a little puffiness and redness in her eyes. Withdrawing, he turned his attention to what she was saying.

"That sounds wonderful," she was elated, "When will you be here so I can be ready?" She was already planning what she was going to wear. She really wanted to see Mike.

"Give me a couple hours? I need to run an errand or two, then I'll be over," Mike replied. He couldn't wait to see Laurie, and talking to her confirmed his feelings for her. Mike prayed that she would accept him, gifts and all. "I gotta get going but see you soon, ok?"

"Sure, Mike," Laurie replied. "Can't wait." She hung up and began getting ready.

Meanwhile, Mike headed into the dining room and picked up the envelope of papers. He figured he would have to at least begin looking over what was involved with the events at the Council meeting last night. Aunt Jenny put a ham and cheese omelet and a glass of orange juice next to him as he started flipping through a list of assets and holdings. Notable was a property listing for a mansion and land about an hour away, as well as a condo in the panhandle of Florida with an expanse of private beach. The business and investment holdings confused him so he put those aside. In the bottom of the envelope were two bank cards with major credit card logos on them. Going back to the account papers, Mike found that both accounts had multiple deposits of several thousand dollars a week, with available balances in the high six figures. He was rich. His good mood was quickly deflated as he wondered what strings were attached to this wealth. He put the two cards in his wallet and finished his breakfast.

Taking the dishes to the sink and quickly washing them up, he went in search of his Aunt. She was in the living room, folding a load of laundry. "Aunt Jenny," Mike began, "I am going to go out for a few hours and take Laurie to lunch. That way I can tell her about what's going on. I'll have my cell, but do you need me to get anything while I am out?"

"No thanks, dear," She said, not really looking up from her laundry piled in the basket. "My car keys should be on the counter if you can't find yours. I shouldn't need the car today but keep your phone handy and good luck."

"Thanks Aunt Jenny, but I don't think I will need to borrow your car," Mike explained, "Apparently I have several in a garage outside the house that came with this deal from last night. I am going to check it out and see what this whole deal is before I turn anything down. Maybe this will be a good thing for our family." He thought about the money just sitting in the accounts and what he could do with it. *"I hope this is on the up and up,"* he wondered to himself.

"Just be careful, Mike," Aunt Jenny said before he transported himself to the address on the holdings sheet.

***

Raymond Burke paced impatiently in the study where he and his now former employer, Samuel Gohr, conducted their usual meetings. He knew that the packet of information he had had to put together last night had been delivered before the sun was up to his new employer, a young man named Michael Keller. Raymond wasn't told the specifics of what happened, but then, his employer was always pretty tight lipped. Raymond was paid very well for his talent and his silence, with which he was fiercely loyal. If the Council decreed that his new boss was some wet-nosed eighteen year old, then that was what it was. The checks always showed up in his bank account and for years not much had changed as the Gohr family had been content to sit on their fortune. Raymond knew they were plotting something, but it must not have gone as they planned since they were ousted last night. He poured himself a drink and had just taken a sip of the aged whiskey when there was a knock on the study door. One of the maids stuck her head in.

"Mr. Keller has arrived, Mr. Burke," the young lady said. The staff had been briefed this morning that there was a new owner and that no one would be seeing the Gohrs. No one seemed that upset that their employer was changing, although they were all curious to meet the new boss. With a nod from Raymond, the maid ducked out of the room and ushered Mike into the study.

"Good morning, Mr. Keller," Raymond began, crossing the room and shaking his new boss's hand enthusiastically. "It is a pleasure to meet you. My name is Raymond Burke and I am your accountant and finance manager. I handle the mundane aspects of your affairs, with direction from you, so that you are free to do whatever it is you wish to do."

Mike had been surprised to find that he was expected and a full staff bustling around the mansion when he arrived. While not a several hundred room Hollywood affair, this was still an impressive home. After shaking hands with his account manager, Mike took in the richly appointed room he was standing in. Real leather chairs in a sitting area, shelves of books built into the wall, and an opulent desk complete with its own leather chair backed by large bay windows let in a lot of natural light. Realizing that Mr. Burke was waiting on a response, Mike said, "It is nice to meet you as well, Mr. Burke. I guess I just had to see this all for myself. I didn't believe the papers left at my aunt and uncle's this morning."

"Please, call me Ray. Mr. Gohr," Raymond stopped quickly, covering his mouth a moment, "I mean, my previous employer did. I would like to think that we will become friends as well. If you wish to keep me on, that is. I am here to facilitate the transition, but ultimately all decisions are yours and I will abide by them. All the necessary paperwork has already been taken care of with the various banks and institutions mentioned in the paperwork I left for you. Given the amount of business that you are involved in, the banks were more than happy to open up last night and take care of everything swiftly."

"Oh, ok, Ray," Mike said, taken back. Banks opening in the middle of a Sunday night merely to handle a transfer of property and bank accounts meant serious money. He would have to go over those documents a lot closer, preferably with his uncle's help. Uncle Jim ran his company, so he must be able to understand the lingo. "I think we will just keep everything the same for now, if that's alright with you, Ray. I'm a little lost as to where to begin right now and it's going to take me some time to familiarize myself with what goes on here. Can you give me a brief rundown of what you need from me? I have some other things to do today."

"Certainly, Mike. Can I call you Mike?" Raymond asked, and at a nod continued, "Well, unless there is some major change you want to make in your holdings, there is nothing for you to do except enjoy the wealth. The dividends and profits will deposit into your accounts as they have for months. You have the home here and the property in Florida, there are several cars in the garage and two BMW's at the other home. The staff here will maintain the home whether you live here or not, as is the agreements previously. There is a cleaning crew on standby that will prep the condo in Florida if you decide you wish to visit. I only would need as much notice as your flight there, unless you were going to use other means, then I only ask give me a few hours to have it ready for you. Besides that, you have holdings in several businesses and investments in stocks and bonds totaling well over several million dollars, should you ever feel the need to liquidate those assets. Here is my card with my direct line on it. I can be reached any time of day or night. You are my only client." With that Raymond handed over a crisp business card with his name and phone number on it. "Do you have any questions or anything I can assist you with right away?"

"No, I don't think so," Mike replied a little overwhelmed by the facts Raymond was just so casually rattling off. "I...Thank you, Ray. I want you to continue in your current role and tell everyone here no one is losing their job, but I don't think I will be staying here anytime soon. I'm going to stay at my aunt and uncle's and can be reached there. Should I give you my cell number, in case there are any emergencies or something I need to sign?"

"That would be excellent, sir," Raymond replied, producing a pen and another card so that Mike was able to jot down his number. "I will inform the staff that they can go to a lighter rotation since the home will not be lived in presently. Is there anything else?"

"Could you show me how to get to the garage?" Mike replied. "I want to take one of the cars so I'm not borrowing from my aunt all the time."

"Certainly, just follow me," Raymond replied placing a hand on Mike's shoulder to turn him towards the door. "It is just through here and down at the end of the hall. There are several vehicles, but if none are to your liking, just let me know and I can arrange for whatever you would like." He led his overwhelmed client through the large house and into an underground garage. Ray showed Mike where the box was that held all the keys, and turned over the master keys to the house as well. When it became clear that Mike could handle himself from there, he took his leave. "I will depart then now, sir. Call me if you need anything."

"Thank you again, Ray," Mike said, "And you can drop the sir, please. My name is Mike." Ray just waved as he got into his own BMW and headed towards the exit doors. This left Mike to survey the bounty in front of him. There were several choices, including: a large Cadillac SUV, all black with a gray interior, a red Camaro convertible, a BMW two door coupe, and a four door model. Mike, talking to himself as he walked around the garage, "Well, I think I am going to take the SUV, I always thought those would be fun to drive. Maybe Uncle Jim or Aunt

Jenny would like a new car. I wonder what Mom would do if I sent her that Camaro." He laughed to himself, "Oh, I need to call her soon." He made a mental note to call his mother as he grabbed the keys for the big SUV and started towards it. Suddenly, Damien appeared at his side, Cliff a moment later.

"Hey Mike," Damien said cheerfully, "Settling in? When I heard you weren't at work I thought I would stop over and see how you were adjusting. Cliff was at my house so we thought we could see what you were up to today and if you wanted to hang out."

"Hey guys," Mike replied, grinning, "I would, but I have a date with Laurie for lunch. I need to tell her about my gifts and gauge her reaction. I need to know if she is ok with what I can do before I know if there is any future there. I owe it to Laurie to see where she stands."

"Good idea, man," Damien spoke up encouragingly.

"Wait, how did you know I wasn't at work?" Mike asked he tensed up at the thought of them spying on him. "How did you know I was here?"

Cliff spoke first, "Don't be upset, Mike. We were worried about you after last night. So we had someone watching your uncle's office. When you didn't show up, we thought we'd check here. We had to initiate all the transfers last night after you left. Mr. Burke is a good accountant. He called me as soon as he left to let us know you were keeping him on for now."

"He said I was his only client," Mike retorted. "Why is he reporting to you?"

Damien tried to explain, "He knows too much about the Council from his years of working with the Gohrs. If you wanted him replaced then someone had to modify his memory."

"Makes sense," Mike replies, mollified by their explanation. "No more spying. Just call me. Or text. Something other than spying."

"How about this?" Damien's voice rang in Mike's head.

"I'd prefer a text first," Mike said before laughing. "Rain check on the hanging out?"

"Oh, right," Damien said. "You don't want to keep Laurie waiting. Give us a call later if you want to do something, ok?"

Mike nodded and climbed into the driver's seat of the big vehicle. His new friends waved before vanishing. Mike saw their auras and noted that Cliff's seemed muted in some way, like a bulb that was on a dimmer switch. Shrugging, he started the engine and pulled away.

Chapter 24

Laurie was pacing in the living room when the big black SUV pulled up in front of her house. The windows were tinted and she had never seen it before so she wasn't sure who it was. Her mother came from the other room when she heard the car, "Is that Mike, dear?" she asked.

"I don't know, Mom," Laurie replied. "I've never seen that car before." They both watched as Mike climbed out of the driver's seat and started towards the front door. "That's him, but where did he get that car? I thought his aunt and uncle just had the car and pickup truck." Laurie was beside herself in anticipation. She hadn't seen Mike since he left the evening before after giving her the necklace that she had even worn to sleep last night.

"Well, at least let him get in the door, dear," Mrs. Sterling said, patting her daughter's arm affectionately. "I will be in the kitchen if you two want to eat lunch here. Just let me know when you leave. And have fun."

Laurie waited by the door and pulled it open as soon as Mike was on the porch. Against her mother's admonition, Laurie flew out the door and wrapped herself around Mike, kissing him firmly. "I missed you. Where did you get that car? Where are we going for lunch? Can you stay all day?"

Catching his breath from her initial assault, Mike started from the beginning, "I missed you too, Laurie. I'll explain about the car and everything else in a moment. I'm yours for the day. Are either of your folks home? We should tell them we're leaving."

"Yeah, mom's in the kitchen. I think she was hoping we would have lunch here so she could thank you again for yesterday," Laurie said, still wrapped around Mike's arm. "Let's go get that out of the way so we can go." She practically dragged him into the house and to the kitchen, calling for her mom. "Mom! We're leaving. See. He's in the house." She giggled when her mother turned around and smiled at the young couple.

"I just wanted to thank you again, Mike," Mrs. Sterling said, as she continued smiling at the couple and gave Mike a hug. "The way she was pacing I didn't think she would let you get out of the car, much less in the house. You two have fun today and just give a call if you'll be late."

"No problem, Mrs. Sterling," Mike replied. "Shall we?" he extended his arm to Laurie and led her out of the house to his newly acquired transportation. After helping her up into the seat and shutting her door, Mike braced himself for what he had to tell her as he climbed behind the wheel.

Taking a deep breath, he began, "Laurie, I have to explain some things to you, about this car, about me, and about my future." Mike could see the fearful look come into her eyes and panicked, "But it's good. Well, I think it is, at least. I hope you will too." At her nod he continued, "I'm different than most people."

"Of course you are. Most people wouldn't have ran towards those big organ pipes to save me."

"Maybe. But what I'm saying is, I can do things that other people can't."

"What do you mean?" Laurie asked, more confused than frightened now. When he mentioned self and future, she thought maybe she had misread him and that he didn't care for her, but here he was in this new car and claimed it's all good things. "What do you mean you can do things others can't?"

"I want you to stay calm and let me finish before you say anything, but it might be easier to show you," Mike stated, reaching into his pocket to grab some coins. These he laid on the dash and then concentrated to cause them to move. He set them to spinning like tops, then lifted them into the air. Laurie was staring back and forth from the coins to Mike, then she reached out and tried to see if he had them on strings or something. Mike grinned, "There is no trick. I am moving them through force of will. That isn't everything I can do. When those pipes started to fall, I was pushing them away from you like this, while I was trying to run through the crowd to you."

"This is crazy," Laurie said, leaning as far away from Mike as she could in the car. "You're telling me you're psychic or something? So what happened yesterday at church was what?"

"Someone who was jealous of what I can do; and tried to hurt me by hurting you," Mike stated plainly, seeing Laurie cringe away from him.

"Someone was trying to hurt me? It wasn't an accident?" Laurie questioned, her heart thudded in her chest.

"I have dealt with him and he cannot harm us again. In fact, that brings me to the next part. That is how I got this car, was because I beat him. Sort of a, to the victor go the spoils."

"Beat him? Who?"

"Yes, and you actually know the person. His name is Derek Gohr. I hear he went to school with you and Anne. He was the one that attacked her," Mike said and could see the wheels turning in Laurie's head. He refrained from trying to listen to her thoughts. "For some reason he saw me, and these gifts that I have, as a threat to his own abilities and power. And when I found out what he had done, I couldn't let it stand. After he tried to crush you with those organ pipes, he took some friends of his and attacked Anne at her house. One of them is going to be in the hospital for awhile. The other two didn't make it." Suddenly Laurie was across the car and wrapping her arms around his neck hugging him fiercely. Mike just held her and could tell she was crying, but wasn't sure why. "Laurie, are you ok?"

Straightening up and wiping her eyes, she smiled weakly, "I just cannot believe all this. So you're telling me you are some sort of wizard or something? And you punished Derek for what he did to Anne? He was like this too? He could do what you did? What else did he do? What else can you do? And how did you beat him to win a car?"

She was babbling and Mike let her wind down before responding, "I don't know if I would call it wizard or something, that sounds so medieval, but it is probably close to accurate. I guess. He could do a lot of those things that you only read about in fiction books, as can I. And, to beat him, I took away his abilities. Entirely. He couldn't so much as lift a penny unless he physically touched it. He won't be ordering anyone around either. As for winning the car, this isn't all I inherited. There is a whole estate. Money, cars, a condo in Florida," Mike stopped suddenly because Laurie had an odd look on her face. "What?"

"What are you trying to tell me, Mike?" Laurie asked, concerned that this 'inheritance', as he called it, was going to come between them. "Are you breaking up with me now?"

"What? No," Mike replied emphatically. "I care about you, Laurie, I'm worried you won't want to be with me once you find out what I am and what I can do. That was why I wanted to talk to you today. To tell you what I'm just discovering about myself and make sure you are alright with being with me."

"You still saved my life, Mike," Laurie said, tearing up again, but she was smiling this time and Mike couldn't help but feel the pure joy rolling off her. "That tells me all I need to know about you. The rest is just wrapping and ribbon, as my mother would say. Are you sure you want to be with me? I can't do the things you can, is that going to be a problem? Is someone else going to come after me?" She got nervous and frightened again thinking of a repeat of what happened at the church. The last couple days had been a wild rollercoaster and her head was spinning a bit.

"I want to be with you. I care about you, Laurie," Mike repeated. Then the two hugged and shared a brief kiss. Just then, Mike's stomach rumbled and they burst out laughing. "Guess we should go find something for lunch, shall we?" Still laughing, Mike started the vehicle and they drove off. Mike was relieved things went as well as they did. He had been worried knowing that Derek had been behind the church accident would scare Laurie off.

Chapter 25

"Hi, Mom," Mike said as soon as she answered the phone. He had just dropped Laurie off, and after fending off the gentle insistence of Mrs. Sterling that he stay for dinner, he managed to get home. His afternoon with Laurie had gone very well. She was on board with his gifts and all that his life brought. They had spent the afternoon just hanging out like a couple of normal teenagers, albeit she made him repeat the coin trick a half dozen times. Mike had offered to take her to buy her something pretty in place of the heavier pendant he had given her, but Laurie declined. She liked the idea of having something that was unique to Mike.

"Honey, how are you? How was your day?" his mother asked, putting the bag of groceries on the counter. She had called her brother at work and found out that he had given Mike the day off to spend with Laurie. While happy that her son was happy again, she wasn't sure she liked him skipping work. Her brother had assured her there was a good reason and that Mike promised to call after he had taken care of some things today.

"It was good. Just dropped Laurie off," Mike replied. "You would like her. I can't wait for you to meet her. Listen, Mom. Some things happened this weekend and it changes a lot."

"I suspected that you wouldn't be coming home in the fall," Sally said sadly. "I have everything together and I even talked to the school here. They will forward your transcripts to wherever you will be going to out there. You still need to finish school."

"I intend to Mom, but, there is more," Mike began. "There was, a confrontation of sorts, with others like me and Uncle Jim. Well, I won, and part of the deal is that I take over the estate of the family that I beat." Mike quickly explained about Derek and the council meeting where he was awarded their seat and estate. It still took him most of the drive to his mansion to relate all the details. As he pulled into the garage, he finished the tale. "So, I am going to bring you a present and visit with you and Connie tonight. We are going out, my treat." He pulled the SUV into its place in the garage and put it in park.

"How on earth are you going to visit tonight? It is a plane ride both ways," Sally said, putting the milk and eggs she bought into the fridge.

"Don't worry about that, Mom," Mike replied, grinning as he sat behind the wheel of the convertible. He started the engine and while keeping the cell phone to his ear, he shifted himself and the car to his driveway at home. "Look outside." Through the phone he heard his mother start down the hall to the front door.

"What on earth?" Sally exclaimed when she saw her son climbing out of the driver's seat of a beautiful Camaro parked in her driveway. She stood on the front step stunned as he walked over, grinning like the Cheshire cat.

He took the phone from her hand and hung it up, sticking it in his jeans pocket opposite his cell phone. He then placed the keys in her hand. "For the world's greatest Mom. It's all yours."

"Honey, You can't afford this, I can't afford this," She stammered, staring at the keychain in her hand. She was a girl that loved cars growing up, but never had the means for anything this nice.

"It is all paid for, and yes, I can afford this," he said, smiling at the expression on her face. He had just explained on the phone to her that he had inherited a large income, but hearing it and seeing it are two different things. "Is Connie home? I am starving and we should get going if we are going to get dinner."

"She's upstairs in her room," Sally whispered as she walked towards the car. She was still in shock a little. She barely noticed when Mike climbed the steps into the house and went in search of his sister.

Entering his childhood home, Mike almost regretted his decision to stay in Washington. With a flick of his wrist he tossed the cordless that he had taken from his mother down the hall towards the charger in the kitchen. He knew it would find its home. All the practice with Laurie today had really helped. He would have to remember that. He then bounded up the stairs, taking some two at a time. He crept down the hall, using his talent to keep himself silent. He could tell Connie was listening to music and it was turned up rather loud. She probably wouldn't have heard him if he had been shouting. He paused in front of her door, then pushed it open loudly and yelled, "BOO!"

Connie shrieked and grabbed the pillow off her bed and launched it at the doorway before she saw it was her brother. "Mike," she said, trying to catch her breath. "You scared the crap out of me! What are you doing home?" She ran over and gave her brother a hug. "Mom didn't tell me you were coming to visit. When did you get here?"

"Just now," Mike replied, hugging his sister back. "I just got here. Mom is downstairs checking out the present I brought her. I have more gifts for you both. I also have to tell you something." By the serious expression on his face, Connie knew something was up and so she backed up and sat down on her bed. She nodded at him to continue.

"When I was in that accident, I could tell that you didn't quite buy Darrell's story," Mike began, "not completely. Well," he paused, searching for how to tell his sister, "I have these abilities. I can make objects move, and I can even get from here to Washington in a matter of a second." He saw the wheels in his sister's head turning, so he decided to demonstrate them. He looked at the pillow on the floor he had blocked when she threw it. He used his power to lift it and send it over towards the bed.

Connie had a small moment of panic when she saw the pillow moving on its own and jumped up to move over by her desk. "What is going on?" she asked tremulously. Her knuckles turned white from the grip she had on her desk chair.

"It's just me, Connie," Mike said, walking over towards his sister. "You knew something wasn't right with Darrell's story, all those things at school... that was part of this. I saw a short glimpse into the future and was able to change those little things. Uncle Jim can do some of the same things and Mom has known about him all along. I wanted to be the one to tell you though." He reached out to his sister and she stepped close enough for him to hug her.

"So, you got all these magic powers now, huh?" She said after they separated. "What does that mean for Mom and me?"

"It means that I am going to be able to take care of you guys," Mike said, having thought about the fact that his mother had only worked as much as she wanted as they grew up. Uncle Jim must have been helping with what resources he had. Now that Mike's were considerably larger, things were going to be different. "Come on. Mom might leave for dinner without us. It's my treat." He led his sister downstairs and out the front door. Their mother was sitting in the driver's seat of the car Mike had brought.

"Whoa..." Connie said incredulously. "Where did the car come from? That rocks." She ran over to run her hand across the hood. "How did you afford this? Did you rob a bank or something?" She turned back to her brother. He walked over to join the rest of them.

"I already explained to Mom, but I will retell it all and answer all your questions over dinner," Mike said, ushering his sister into the passenger seat next to their mom. He casually leapt the side of the car and slid into the smaller compartment behind his family. It was only a little cramped, given his stature. "Pick any place you want, Mom. Nothing is too fancy for you two." With a look of disbelief at her son in the back seat, she put the car in reverse and backed up to the end of the drive. As she headed into town, Mike mentally communicated with his uncle that he was at home with his mom and sister, to not worry and he would be back later. The feeling of relief he received back from his uncle was reassuring. Mike wondered briefly if he would have been able to do that at this distance before his confrontation with the Gohrs, but decided it didn't matter.

***

Jenny had watched the far off look appear in her husband's eyes. He had come home early and they were talking at the table. He had taken another look at the papers dropped off for Mike and had seen that his nephew was in a much more secure financial position than he thought. When he focused back on her, he smiled. "I will have to get used to this talent of his." When he saw the blank look from his wife, he grinned wider. "Mike, he went to visit his mom and sister tonight after he dropped Laurie off. He says he will be home later tonight."

"And you got that when your eyes glazed over and you were looking at me without seeing me?" Jenny asked. Her husband nodded. "Why did we give that boy a phone if he is going to communicate like that?" Then she started laughing, remembering what they had learned about Mike's finances. "I suppose he will be moving up to that big mansion of his and leave us here. Do you think we can borrow his condo in Florida for a few weeks in the winter?"

"I think he is enjoying the idea of the freedom he has, but he is a grounded young man," Jim replied. "When he gets back we can have a sit down about the living arrangements."

***

As his mom and sister finished the last bites of the delicious dessert they had ordered with their meal, Mike pulled the two small boxes from his pocket where he had been keeping them. While he and Laurie had been out, he had stopped into a mall jewelry store and bought two pendants that had swirl patterns similar to his necklace. These were speckled with a couple diamonds and looked more feminine than the solid silver piece he still wore that his uncle had given him. He had forgotten to return it and would have to ask about that when he got home. He had placed wards on both of these so that he could keep watch over his mother and sister while he was away from them. He pushed a box at each of the women.

Mother and daughter looked from Mike to the boxes and back. Connie had not really understood everything when Mike explained how he had come into this wealth, but she did understand the college fund he proposed, and that she would have her pick of any car she wanted when she got her license, "As long as your grades stay up." Mike had said laughing. The two women opened the boxes and both nearly squealed simultaneously. Before he could react they both were trying to hug him.

"It is beautiful, Mike," his mother said, returning to her seat. This was a fancy restaurant and their outburst had not gone unnoticed by neighboring tables. "What is it for? You already gave me the car, and you tell me we won't have to worry about money, but this is a lot." Connie was staring into the gems, almost mesmerized by the light.

"I wanted to give you both something to remind you of me while I am in Washington," Mike said, smiling. He had already made it clear to his sister that he wouldn't be back so she wouldn't have to be at school with her big brother as a senior. She had joked that she was glad of that, but it was clear the siblings would miss each other. "Not that I cannot pop back anytime and see you, and of course I have the cell phone Uncle Jim and Aunt Jenny got me. But I wanted you two to have something special. Mom, because you have sacrificed so much that it is about time you received some good things from this family legacy. Connie, because even for a lame little sister, you are *my* sister. No matter what happens, I love you both. Without you two, I wouldn't be who I am."

His mom was crying and wiped her eyes with her napkin. "Mike, honey, you are spoiling your mother and going to make a scene in this nice restaurant." She was smiling through her tears. When the waiter came with their check, he paused when he saw the state of the women at the table. Mike quickly handed him one of the bank cards and he rushed off, noticing that the young man did not even look at the total of the bill. He smiled to himself, customers like that were usually big tippers. When he returned, Mike quickly added a generous tip and signed the copy for the restaurant. He then walked his mother and sister out to the car.

"Well, I should get back to Uncle Jim and Aunt Jenny. I have work tomorrow," Mike said. His mother smiled. "You two drive safe getting home and I will check in with you in the next day or two. Love you two." He hugged them both and after they were both seated in the car, he simply vanished and reappeared in the garage, next to the SUV. Pleased with how things were turning out, he climbed into the driver seat and headed towards his aunt and uncle's house.

Thank you for reading my story. I hope you enjoyed it as much as I have enjoyed writing it. If you are so inclined, please leave a review on Amazon, Goodreads, or wherever else you frequent. Reviews let authors know in a very tangible way that what we do is appreciated. I hope you'll connect with me via one of my social media links below.

Facebook:
http://www.facebook.com/andrewmferrell

Twitter:
@AndrewMFerrell

Instagram:
AndrewMFerrell